RIVER'S END

RIVER'S END SERIES, BOOK ONE

LEANNE DAVIS

LEANNE
DAVIS

This is a work of fiction. Names, characters, places, and incidents are either the product of the author's imagination or are used fictitiously, and any resemblance to actual events, locales, or persons, living or dead, is entirely coincidental.

River's End

COPYRIGHT © 2014 by Leanne Davis

Contact Information: dvsleanne@aol.com

Publishing History First Edition, 2014 Digital

Digital ISBN: 9781941522127

River's End Series, Book One

Edited by Teri at The Editing Fairy (editingfairy@yahoo.com)

Copyediting: Sophie@sharperediting.com

For the Property
The place that owns all the summers of my youth and to the friends and family who have shared it over the years.

Acknowledgments: As always I must compliment my editor Teri who so thoroughly goes through my books with her red ink. Thank you for always doing it so well, and cutting my work in half.

CHAPTER 1

$\mathcal{E}$rin Poletti cursed when the pavement ended. She slowed her car; cringing as her low-riding Honda sedan hit the ripples and valleys of the barely maintained dirt road. Her car struggled over the jarring series of bumps that left her feeling like she'd been put into a margarita shaker. There was no rail or turn-out to separate her car from the drop-off that followed the river, a good twenty feet below her. As she drove further, the drop-off turned into thirty, forty, and eventually, fifty feet as the road continued up the mountain. She gripped the wheel tightly and hugged the side of the road, blinking her eyes to banish the gritty feel of sleep deprivation. She was almost there. She had to keep driving. Now wasn't the moment to get lazy driving.

Rounding the corner, she stopped her car in the center of the road. There wasn't a soul around her in a five-mile radius and no reason to pull off to the side. She stared out before her. There it was. The small town of River's End spread at the base of the valley and nestled along the white water Rydell River that spilled over the valley floor.

It was as odd a landscape to her as a drive across the

moon. She had never traversed the Cascade Mountain range, which dissected the state of Washington into two halves: the western and eastern sides. Seattle born and raised, she rarely drove thirty miles beyond the radius of the city.

But now, hours from Seattle, after having crossed an entire mountain range to escape the mess of her life there, she hoped to find a new one here with her brother, in River's End.

At least she assumed the small streak of houses that were across the river was the destination she had in mind. River's End was smaller than a neighborhood. A white church steeple was the only indication it could be a town.

Her hands tightened over the steering wheel and her stomach heaved. How could her life become so dependent on her brother? It wasn't like that was a good thing. It was a place she never thought she'd go, asking her brother for help. Or seeking an escape. Help he didn't know he would be giving her, and certainly, never willingly offer to her.

She pressed her foot on the gas and started down the rough road again. It was another half mile before the large timber sign with the words "Rydell River Ranch" came into view. The driveway curved right, then left, like following a woman's hips, ever so gently, as she drove her car over the land. When the road turned abruptly, her view of the valley changed. She gasped. She never expected this kind of spread. She assumed she was heading to a godforsaken ranch with sagebrush and dust as the only relief.

Instead, before her lay a scene straight out of a picturesque calendar. Grazing horses raised their heads when her car passed, dozens of them peppering the gently rolling land. It sloped downwards gently toward the river in front of her. The tall mountains encircled the entire idyll in a bowl-like effect. Pine trees and cottonwoods dotted the land-scape. There were white-washed wood fences hugging the road, which all took off in various directions to make up separate fields and pastures. She rounded another turn before the ranch came into her sight. Her stomach recoiled with nerves. It wasn't some dive she could easily blend into. It was exquisite, and she felt as if she had discovered a secret yuppie mountain retreat.

There was a large, two-story, rambling, log house perched on a small mound that elevated it gracefully from the land surrounding it. It had a green roof to offset the natural colored wood and the big river rock chimney. A covered porch encircled the whole homestead with an elaborate front that dramatically enhanced the house to appear like a resort.

The driveway approached the housing site, and widened into an ample swath of parking, outbuildings, and further off, a grid of roads that all went in different directions. She nearly groaned in dismay. The few e-mails to her mother, which Chance rarely sent, made the Rydell River Ranch sound like it was a hapless, dirty, poor enterprise, and certainly not this sprawling complex that had barns and fields as far as the eye could see. *Shit.* This would not work out. She couldn't crash here. She couldn't even imagine getting out of her car here.

She slowed to a stop, and sat there with the bright March sunlight glinting through her windshield, and highlighting the film of dust. Where was Chance? How could he, her loser, ne'er-do-well brother, end up working at an outfit like this? They appeared to be a real working ranch, why would they risk that on a man like her feckless, opportunistic brother? It didn't make any sense. And it stole away any prospects for her to count on.

Leaning her head against the steering wheel, she realized she had nowhere left to go. And nowhere to stay. She had come here to stay with her brother, no matter how much she loathed the idea. In the few bits of correspondence, he had with her mother over the last few months, Chance made it sound like he was kicking back and lazing around an old, rundown dude ranch. The only feature that drew her here was because the owners gave her brother his own place to stay in on their land. A place she prayed he'd let her stay too.

But people who kept spreads like this had to have high standards. Why then, would they allow her nefarious brother to live there?

Sensing movement through her windshield, she spotted a man coming through the wide doors of the barn. He stopped when he noticed her car and raised a hand to shade his eyes from the merciless glare of the late morning sun. Was it her imagination, or did the sun shine harsher here than it did in Seattle?

She took a deep breath and fumbled around for her car door handle. She had to get out and face the man now staring at her after emerging from the barn, and heading towards her, no doubt, wanting to know what she, the stranger, wanted. It wasn't like a place as far out as this one regularly received passing idle traffic or lost travelers. One had to work to get there.

She opened her car door, which wasn't in good shape. The once bright white color had faded long ago and now sported dings and rust along the wheel wells. She'd had the same car for five years and considered it a blessing she managed to hold onto it for that long. Standing in the opening of her car door, she watched the man saunter forward with a relaxed, almost cocky gait. At least, he wasn't carrying a shotgun to scare her off. It definitely seemed like the kind of place that didn't like or encourage strangers. The kind of place where the residents kept their guns proudly displayed in the backs of their pickups. To the right of the house she saw a lineup of half a dozen pickup trucks in varying sizes, models, and shapes.

The man started to smile as he got within a car distance from her and she could only smile back. His smile was that contagious. His eyes ran over her, and he made it clear he was checking out whatever he could see of her, smiling even wider when he finished.

"Well, hello there," he said, his eyes bright with interest.

"Hi," she said, as she stepped away from her car and shut the door. She steeled her nerves, having no other choice. Running her eyes over the man, she immediately noticed he was breathtaking. He looked like a cowboy that should have been modeling a pair of jeans on the cover of a popular horse and rider magazine. Probably in his mid-twenties, he had blonde hair, brown eyes, and a smile that put chills on her arms. She was a couple of inches over five feet and figured he was only a few inches taller.

"You lost?

"No. No, I'm not. I meant to find the Rydell River Ranch."

His grin widened. "Yeah, well you found it. I'm Joey Rydell; why were you looking for us?"

She took the hand he offered as he stepped closer, and felt an undeniable zing as their fingers touched and his eyes finished his visual assessment of her.

"Hi Joey. My name is Erin. Erin Poletti."

His eyes rounded. "Poletti? As in Chance Poletti?"

She cringed at his obvious surprise, and regretted that she indeed was related to Chance Poletti. "Yes."

Joey's mouth dropped open and his eyes lost their initial sparkle of interest. "I had no idea he was married."

She shuddered. "No. I'm not his wife. I'm his sister. I was, I mean, I am hoping to visit him."

"Sister, huh?" Joey said, his eyes rekindling interest and the smile appearing once more. "He never mentioned you."

"I haven't seen him in a while." *As in a year*. But this man didn't need to know that. Or that she was desperate to see her brother and stay on their land indefinitely.

"Joey? Where the hell are you? Augusta isn't going to wait all day."

The shout came from inside the shadows of the barn. Erin turned towards the voice, slightly dismayed to realize there were more men to deal with. She hoped the other Mr. Rydell would be kind enough to take pity on her and let her "visit" her brother.

Joey turned his body and yelled, "We got a visitor."

A man appeared in the dusty darkness of the barn doorway. He stood staring at her car before looking at her. The cowboy hat on his head kept his eyes shaded from the sun and hidden from her. Erin had never been to a place where men really wore cowboy hats. This man looked tall, lean and strong; and his hat seemed more like an appendage than any kind of fashion statement. Like Joey, the man wore blue jeans tucked into brown, worn cowboy boots and a brown jacket made of a tough-looking material. The only thing she could tell for sure was that he was scowling at her.

"Your father looks mad."

Joey laughed and slapped a hand to his leg. "He'd hate to hear you say that. He always looks mad. And he isn't my father. That's my older brother, Jack."

Jack. Jack Rydell. Jack Rydell was the one she was here to see. Chance claimed Jack was the owner of the ranch and an ass who acted like he was master and commander of the pissant spread. Jack might have been an ass, but it was no pissant ranch that he lorded over.

He started towards them in a long, slow stride, and his carriage seemed almost predatory. He made no secret of his gaze skimming over her. He grimaced in dismay as his eyes ran over her starting from her strappy shoes, up her bare legs

6

and flouncy skirt, to the thin, long-sleeved sweater that covered her green t-shirt. She was freezing. She never expected the temperatures to feel so sharply cold here. Spots of snow dotted the mountains around them. The air was nippy and stark on her bare legs. If she had any hairs on her legs, they'd be standing at full attention and shivering.

She pulled her eyes away from Jack. How could he already show such disapproval of her? He didn't even know about her connection to Chance yet.

"Who are you?"

Jack's voice was low, deep, and commanding. He sounded the way she thought any general would have. There was no welcoming, flirtatious smile like Joey offered her. Neither was there any appreciation of her looks, like Joey displayed. This man completely dismissed her. Why? What was it? Her car? Her age? Her skirt? What could have possibly already turned Jack Rydell against her? With one look at her, he clearly decided she was of no interest to him; and therefore, not even worthy of common courtesy.

Not a particularly intelligent person, Erin didn't even finish high school. She had no real talent or hobby or job. But despite having done nothing, in some ways, she'd done everything. She worked as a waitress, grocery clerk, coffee barista, bartender, and janitor, just to name a few. Her limited intelligence was reflected in every boyfriend she ever chose, one loser after the next; although each time she met one of them, she thought he would be the answer to her love life. She already knew all of this about herself; but in one glance, one scathingly rude glance, Jack Rydell also determined his own negative truth about her. She stepped back in surprise, unprepared for how much his scorn surprised her.

The single, remotely positive personality quirk she did possess was her magnetism: most people liked her. She had an easy smile and could be charming enough when she needed to be. Joey was indeed charmed as he stared at her legs. The problem was, Jack was about to order her to leave.

"I'm Erin Poletti."

Jack's face shifted from neutral to distaste in his scowl, and her heart plummeted to her knees. He must hate Chance, made obvious by his physical reaction to hearing her last name. The same reaction she felt. She detested being put on the same level as her brother by sharing the name Poletti. But what else could she do?

"Great. So there is more than one of you Polettis. What are you? His wife?"

"No. I'm his sister."

Jack rolled his eyes and she dropped hers. If Jack detested her brother so much, why did her brother work for him? Jack turned on his heel and walked away. That apparently was that. She was dismissed. Not even worth his time. Much less another glance.

Joey snorted and shook his head, and when she looked at him, he smiled at her. "Hey, don't sweat Jack. He doesn't care much for your brother."

"I gathered that. Why does Chance work here then?"

"I let Chance work here. Jack isn't the boss. It belongs to all of us."

"All of us? How many are there?"

Joey grinned. "Four. Four brothers. We all have an equal stake in this place."

She had two more Jack Rydells to get through? What if the others were just like Jack? She could only hope they were like Joey and easily distracted by a flash of leg and a glimpse of breast. She smiled, focusing her full attention now on Joey. She was nearly blinded by the perfection of his face: deep, penny-colored eyes and dimpling smile.

"So any idea where I could find Chance? Or am I interrupting you too?"

Joey shrugged and waved a hand off towards the barn. "Nah, Jack and I were just working with one of the horses. He can handle it. Chance is supposed to be down near the river, working on a busted sprinkler pipe."

Erin didn't miss the "supposed to be." Obviously, Chance rarely did what he was supposed to be doing.

"You want me to take you to him? Does he know you're coming?"

"No. Has he ever mentioned me?" She could have earned an acting role for how easily she smiled and charmed Joey.

"No. Sorry. He's never mentioned you."

"I came to visit him for a couple of weeks, bringing bad news from our family. I thought I could stay with him and take a break from school while I'm here."

"You're a student?"

Why did Joey sound so surprised to know she was a student? Although she was most definitely not in college, how could Joey know that?

"Yes. Wazzu." Washington State University was her school, she decided, because she heard most kids east of the Cascades went there. It was located in Pullman, on the border of Idaho. She bit her lip and pulled on her sweater so the front dipped just above her bra line. Joey's eyes followed the subtle adjustment. "I'll just get a room somewhere close by. He can come visit me there."

Joey's eyes rose from her chest to her eyes. "There's no need of that. No big deal, really. Chance stays in that trailer over there. It's his business who he lets stay with him. We sure as hell don't care."

Turning, she followed Joey's finger and repressed the groan of dismay. Chance made it sound like he had his own apartment over the Rydells' barn, when instead, it was no more than a travel trailer. It was parked five hundred feet from the main house with three other trailers lined up beside it. Maybe it was the place that their ranch hands stayed.

She turned to Joey with a smile. "Are you sure? I don't want to impose. Maybe you'd better check with Mr. Rydell."

She played on a nerve. Whatever big brother, Jack, was to Joey, Joey didn't want to do as Jack bade. "I don't have to ask permission. I can give it to you, same as Jack. Sure. You're staying. In fact, now I insist on it."

She sagged with relief and her breath nearly hitched. She wasn't homeless. At least, for now. She pilfered some time to figure out what to do next and where to go. Now, all she had to do was make sure Chance didn't tell the Rydells he wanted nothing to do with her, and would never have invited her to come there and see him.

CHAPTER 2

*J*ack watched the entire episode from the shadows of the barn and nearly groaned with chagrin.

Erin Poletti. Chance's sister. That could not bode well for any of them. If she were anything like Chance, only bad things could come out of her arrival. Could his brother really be such an idiot as to fall for the act this woman was so obviously playing on him? How could Joe not see it? The pretty smiles, the subtle flash of bra and legs? *Shit. Poletti.* Just what he needed. Another pointless, worthless Poletti on his land. And this one might just be worse still, judging by how her smile seemed to put Joey into a trance.

Joey was the one who insisted that Chance work there. And look how well that turned out. Chance Poletti was lazy, shiftless and could only do a crap job at any task he was assigned. Jack always ended up fixing most of Chance's work. Chance cost him extra money and increased his workload. But he let Chance stay because Joey needed that. Joey thought he owed Chance, and was constantly trying to prove to Jack that he was his own man. Jack wanted to inform his little brother that his judgment in people sucked, but the more he tried to tell Joey anything, the more Joey rebelled. So for now, he had to let Chance stay if only so that Joey could learn this lesson. Joe trusted people at face value. He was naive to people like Chance, whom he saw as a friend he owed a debt to.

Chance was a polished manipulator and used Joey's youthful innocence and belief in goodness to get what he wanted. What Chance wanted was something that Jack hadn't nailed down yet. But he knew it was something. And to date, he just let it go, hoping Joey would wise up before Chance's real reasons for befriending Joey became known. Joey had to toughen up if he intended to work on and run the ranch, so it seemed better to do it now rather than later.

Jack just never considered having the female version of Chance suddenly show up and screw Joe over.

Erin Poletti. Funny how she showed up out of nowhere and unannounced. She was so inappropriately dressed to be on a ranch, he wondered why Joey couldn't see exactly what she could be doing.

And Joey would be a prime target to whatever trap Ms. Poletti and Chance were plotting.

He glanced over at where she stood, still mooning up to Joey. She was slim and small, with shapely legs that she showed off with a skirt that flounced around her thighs, offering a peek-a-boo effect. She had narrow shoulders and a small frame with small breasts, which she did her best to highlight with the strip of hot pink bra she allowed to show over the top of her shirt.

If a guy could manage to look past all that, ignoring her clothing, which seemed to wink at him, her face could have stopped a plane dead in the air. She was that pretty. Her big green eyes, which even from a distance, Jack could see she knew exactly how to use, by making them even bigger and wider eyed, so she looked more vulnerable. It was a guise for idiots like his brother who wanted to slay whatever pretend dragons someone like Erin Poletti feared. Her hair was pushed off her forehead by a black headband, and hung around her shoulders in twisting black curls. She had a mass of ringlets that must almost reach her waist.

The car, however, gave Ms. Poletti away. It sorely revealed a need for money. Money, no doubt, she and her scoundrel brother were planning to coax out of Joey. Did Chance bring Erin in on his ongoing scam?

What the hell was she doing here?

Jack smashed the shovel into the horse manure he was cleaning from Augusta's stall. Hauling back a full load, he dumped it into the large trailer behind him, which he had to drag out to the larger pile of even more manure, beyond the barns.

Augusta, grazing in the pasture now, was the Rydells' most prized horse. His horse. Augusta was a full-blooded Nokota ranch horse. More importantly, she was Jack's heart; although, of course, he didn't tell anyone that. It was just between him and his horse. Augusta read Jack as if she were Jack's own arm. When they were together, they were that synchronized and in tune. Jack had never experienced anything like it in all the years he trained and bred horses.

His brother was supposed to be helping him clean the enormous barn that housed many of their horses. Some were boarded here, some were there for training or care; and a few dozen belonged to the Rydells. Jack glanced over his shoulder. Joey was leaning into Erin Poletti's car and dragging out a duffel bag. His jaw clenched. *Damn it, Joey, what are you doing? Unloading another untrustworthy Poletti to live with them?* Couldn't Joey ever see past his own nose?

Jack threw the shovel down and kicked at the stall. He didn't have time for that. Not to watch Joey get his ass handed to him by a pair of scheming siblings. He didn't have time to protect Joey from whatever blunder Chance Poletti was setting him up for. He had enough on his plate just making sure Chance didn't actually cause any real damage to the ranch, or the Rydell reputation.

He had the ranch to run, two sons to raise, and dozens of horses to care for, as well as many to train. Not to mention the endless hours of work outside of the horses that still had to be done. He really didn't have any time for this crap.

Meanwhile, Joey opened Chance's trailer and took Erin inside.

ERIN HELD HER BREATH, then let it out of her mouth before taking another breath back in. The trailer stunk. It was putrid. It had garbage overflowing the trash can and littered all over the counter. Dirty clothes and shoes were everywhere. This was the trailer in which she was to live? It wasn't very big and had a door near the back, which turned into a small kitchen, with a half-sized fridge, sink, stove and countertop. With one step, she was in the living area, a small square of couch with a two-seater table across from it. A small hallway with a sink on one side and a door on the other lay beyond that. The toilet? Well, it looked about as big as a two-foot closet. At one end was a bed that took up the front of the trailer. It was wedged between the walls with barely six inches of room to walk around.

She gulped audibly. She had never imagined her brother would be living really nice, but this? No, she wasn't prepared at all for this. He was so dirty. It wasn't just the trailer, which, in comparison, wasn't so bad. It was the gross state her brother left it in. Noticing small black bits on the counter, she shivered in revulsion; they were mice droppings.

"He doesn't exactly clean the place." Joey looked around with a frown. She turned and smiled to cover up her growing disgust.

"Oh no. It's fine."

Joey's eyes twitched, and he found it gross. "Oh. Okay. Then I guess I'll leave this here."

Erin turned and stepped outside. She had to get out of there. She couldn't stand the rancid smell. Inhaling a deep breath of fresh, cold air, she sighed at the clean scents of dirt and pines. When she lifted her eyes and looked past the trailer, she could see behind it was a sloping meadow that trailed off towards the river. The water flashed and sparkled under the stark sun. Further beyond laid an orchard that rose above the river and disappeared into the brown mountains beyond. It was like nothing she'd ever seen before.

Goose bumps had long ago broken out over her skin. Her feet were so cold, it hurt to wiggle her toes. Stepping off the metal stair that led with little fanfare into the trailer, she dropped onto the packed dirt below it. Her small heel sunk into it and she pulled it loose before moving towards the grass nearby. Not five feet from her brother's trailer was the next trailer, which blocked the view towards the driveway. It would be like living in a parking lot.

Only the views that surrounded her reminded her that she was far from anything familiar.

The faint rumbling of an engine was approaching. She walked along the trailer until she could peek around it towards the rest of the ranch. Beyond the house, a road led towards a group of barns, shops, and outbuildings that were lined up along the road in neat parallel rows, like a parking lot of buildings instead of cars. Jack was driving a tractor, going down the dirt road with its front end held up high, and full of something brown. He disappeared around the furthest barn.

Jack Rydell. He didn't like her. From one glance, he knew she wasn't whatever she said she was. There was no fooling Jack. She saw that in his single glance. The thing she didn't get was why he let her stay. Or why Chance was there. It was so unlike the kind of place she had pictured Chance living in. She didn't know what to do. Who cared if she lied to the kinds of people Chance regularly associated with? They were usually creepier and more dishonest than Chance.

Jack could intimidate anyone. Even Chance. He was lean and tall. His body, shoulders, and demeanor suggested that he was in complete control at all times. And that he had all the answers. All the power. And no one bullshitted him.

He wasn't hot like Joey was. Joey looked like he was the star in a western film that was being shot today. Jack looked like a real old-time cowboy: rough, tough, and worn. His white skin seemed like aged leather. He was older than Joey. She simply had to avoid Jack at all costs and maximize her attention on Joey. That was her only chance for remaining there.

Joey came up beside her, his gaze following hers as the tractor came back into sight.

"Jack's going to ream my ass. I'd best get back to work."

"Sure. Of course. I shouldn't have shown up like this and disturbed you. I didn't think it out. To be honest, I've never been on a ranch before."

"No? Where you from?"

"Where did Chance say we were from?"

Joey thought, then frowned. "Don't know that he ever said. I got the impression he was from lots of places."

She nodded. *Sure he was.* Chance had a warrant for his arrest in Seattle after skipping out on his bail for a series of shoplifting charges. He'd been in eastern Washington ever since. Yakima. Ellensburg. Spokane. Now at River's End. He deliberately made a huge detour from all the small towns and was now out in the middle of nowhere.

"We're from Seattle. I haven't seen Chance in over a year or so."

She hoped she could get Chance alone before everyone figured out he had no idea she was coming, and would never have asked her to visit him. The tractor rumbled to a stop near the side of the biggest barn. Jack stood up, then turned and jumped down with the grace of a cougar. He stared across at them and finally, he walked towards them.

Her breath hitched. *Shit.* He was like a cop catching her stealing. He seemed to know she was everything but what she claimed to be.

"Chance will be up in a minute."

She twitched in surprise. Jack found Chance for her? Why? And what was Chance's reaction? Jack's dour face gave no indication. Was he setting her up? Did he figure out by Chance's lack of reception towards her that she wasn't all she claimed to be?

"Did he... did he say anything?"

Eyes as blue as the sky behind Jack stared at her. "Say anything? Like what?"

"I don't know. Just asking."

Jack nodded his head to the trailer. "You're staying here." It wasn't a question.

Joey stepped forward. "I said it was okay. We don't own Chance. Or whoever wants to visit him."

Jack's gaze landed on Joey and his lips twisted into an ironic smirk. "Of course, you gave her permission."

"It's my ranch too."

Erin tensed up at what she sensed in the undertones between these two men. *What was it?* Jack eventually nodded, and smiling at Joey, said, "It is, Joe. You're right."

That was it? Erin almost swooned with relief. She

thought for sure Jack was about to make her leave. He was staring only at Joey, who smiled and nodded. What did Joey think he'd done? Proven his independence and leadership abilities to his brother? He hadn't. Jack had all the power here. It was so Jack's ranch. She almost turned and explained that to Joey. Whatever… Jack seemed to be offering Joey a few crumbs here today. Crumbs like letting her stay. She felt nothing but relief. And gratitude. And she couldn't spoil Joey's little bit of control by explaining that to him.

"It is you. I thought Jack was mistaken. What are you doing here?"

Erin whipped around on her heel in surprise. Chance was walking up from the behind the trailer, his lips curled cruelly in disgust. He came up through the field that was hidden by the trailer. Her heart picked up. This was it. She'd be discovered. Chance would refuse to help her and the Rydells would kick her off their land. And then what would she do? Sleep in her car along the river somewhere?

She meant to ease Chance into all of this; and intended to talk to him alone and lay out a convincing case about why she came and why he had to let her stay with him.

Instead, she licked her lips and glanced at her side. Joey was staring with displeasure at Chance and curious to know her motives. Jack smirked, no doubt ready to point out to Joey he was right about her before he told her to get off his land.

She had no recourse and looked down and then back up at her brother. She only hoped it mattered to Chance what she had to say. "Mom's dead."

CHAPTER 3

*J*ack stepped back. He never expected her to say that. Shocked, he stared down at Erin's profile. Her face was to the ground now, studying the toes showing through the black straps of her idiotic shoes. Jack looked up at Chance, who shuffled his feet in surprise. Then his face went blank. He scowled down at Erin as Jack had previously. He was a cold son of a bitch. Jack always felt a weird chill go through him whenever he was in Chance's presence. He couldn't quite explain why. There was just something off with Chance, almost a kind of evil inside him.

"So? What do you want me to do about it?"

She flinched. "I just thought you'd want to know."

"Okay, I know now."

Erin bit her lip and stared up at her brother. Chance suddenly straightened. "She leave any money?"

"No. No, there's no money. There's nothing."

"You're not lying, are you? I'll find out if you are, you know. Lawyers will know."

She shook her head. "I'm not lying. I thought, maybe, I could stay with you for a few days, to figure this out."

"Stay with me? Here? Are you craping me?"

Joey's head bobbed between them. "Are you for real? You think she's stealing from you? Why would she come here if that were the case?"

Then the strange demeanor that Chance only ever used with Joey suddenly overcame him. Chance purposely tried to tone down who he really was, so Joey didn't see it. Judging by the expression on Joey's face, he really didn't like how Chance was treating his sister.

Neither did Jack. What was wrong with this man? Just because Jack didn't want Erin there, near his brother, didn't mean he needed to listen to how awful Chance spoke to his own sister.

Chance suddenly smiled. "I'm sorry. You surprised me. Joey's right, of course. Let's go inside and talk, huh? You can tell me everything."

Erin stepped back. Perhaps she was surprised by Chance's suddenly affable tone. She nodded and glanced up at Joey before following her brother.

The Polettis disappeared inside the trailer. His trailer. On his land. What was that all about? A pathetic act for his benefit? Or did the woman's mother just die and she came here to tell her brother? He supposed it would be a good reason to need a break from college. Or did that just coincide with her story about the break from college? Yeah, he was that gullible. Joey believed every word. Jack didn't. He wasn't so sure the Polettis hadn't just put on a very fine show for Joe and him.

~

CHANCE CROSSED the trailer and shoved a heap of clothes off the couch. He sat, sprawled with his legs open and arms folded as he glared at her.

"Mom really dead?"

"Yes. She died a few weeks ago."

He didn't express any trace of sorrow. Or ask how she died. He didn't care. He never did. About her. Or their shared mother.

"Why did you come here?"

Erin glanced down and tapped her toe. "Brian was eager for me to join him in ways I would never. When I refused you can imagine his reaction. I didn't dare risk trying to get inside the apartment. I left half my stuff and took off."

"Apple didn't fall far, did it?"

"Like you didn't either?"

He smiled and goose bumps broke out over her arms. She hated him. So much so, it suffocated her to think of them being anything alike. *They were not.* They could never be alike. But she needed his help; and therefore, had to rein in her disdain of him and keep it in check. She vowed if she ever got over this, she would never subject herself to the mercy of her brother again. Someday, she would not have to rely on the kindness of others ever again.

Chance looked her over. "Real fuckable woman now, aren't you?"

She looked away as the chills spread over her. Who said things like that to his own sister? He laughed.

"Guys forget they have brains around a woman like you, huh? Joey looked like you could ask for the keys to his truck and he'd happily hand them over. Must come in handy."

"Not like you'd think."

"Except Jack. No. Old man Rydell could see right through you, couldn't he? Don't sweat it, he don't like me none either. Hate the tight-laced prick, but he ain't dumb."

"How is it you work here then?"

Chance smiled and scratched his crotch. Erin looked

away. She opened the mini-blind behind her. Sunlight reflected the particles of dust floating in the air.

"Joey hired me. He owes me."

"What could Joey possibly owe you for?"

"I saved his dumb ass life."

Hearing that Chance had done anything decent in his life actually surprised Erin. "How?"

"Awhile back, he rolled his truck off one of the roads. I got him out."

Chance had not only done something decent, but courageous too? "That's amazing. You just happened along on him?"

"Nah, we'd been out drinking."

"So you knew Joey before that?"

He smiled. "Drifting around gets tiresome. Finding places to stay, new people to work over, always having to look ahead. Well, I heard in town that the Rydells were the people to know around here. They're like royalty to the assholes here. They been here for a hundred years or more. Own more land than most cities. So I figured I'd get on here. Only Jack refused me. So I made it my business to know Joey. We hung out some. Lucky break he drove off the cliff. Kid thanked me with the job. Free rent. Free use of their truck. Only gotta buy my food and entertainment. Not so bad a setup."

"And that's why Jack lets you stay?"

"Yup," Chance said, lowering his feet to the ground before he stood up and gave her a long body scan. It grossed her out to see how he looked at her. Chance was her damn brother. "I wasn't too happy to hear you'd shown up here. Jack looked pissed about it. But you know what? Maybe I like it. Piss Jack off some. Yeah, maybe I'll find a use for you yet."

She shivered. She would never do whatever sick thing

Chance had in mind for her. Still, she had to stay there. "So I can stay?"

"Guess. I don't have no fancy sheets or nothing. Just my couch."

She nodded and gulped. The couch was too piled high and covered from disuse for her brother to have any clue what it was like. "I have a sleeping bag. Can I clean up in here?"

He glanced around as if shocked by her request. "Just don't start nagging me about anything. And try to stay out of my way."

She almost promised him she would never willingly be near him.

ERIN SPENT HOURS CLEANING. She took out trash bags of rubbish and clutter. She threw aside armloads of Chance's laundry. What did she care if Chance stunk? She scrubbed until her hands were red. There was no vacuum. After debating fruitlessly with herself, she finally decided she would have to ask one of the Rydells for a vacuum. She couldn't stand to sleep there without trying to pick up most of the mouse droppings. She asked Chance, who merely shrugged and agreed there sure did seem to be some mice around. She cringed. Didn't that bother him in the least? First thing she intended to get was a package of mousetraps.

She glanced down and saw her feet had deep tracks in them from the straps of her sandals. She was dressed stupidly. She didn't have a lot of clothes and left Seattle without most of her things, thanks to Brian. Tomorrow, she planned to find a store to buy some respectable things to wear. She refused, however, to slip her shoes off and come into any actual contact with the filthy, mauve-colored carpet.

She opened the trailer door as the evening began setting in, and dusky light filled the interior of the trailer. Chance left her alone hours ago; and apparently used one of the ranch trucks at will. Thanks to Joey. She hoped he wouldn't come back anytime soon. She stepped out of the trailer, and started across the road, heading toward the main house. She stopped and stared. What would it be like to have a place like this to call one's home? She'd never lived in anything more than one-room apartments where she usually bunked down on a fold-out couch.

The house loomed before her, with light shining from the first floor and shadows flickering around the windows. Beyond the solid wood structure rose the black line of mountains, and the orange-colored sky that lingered as sunset deepened. It was so ethereal, almost eerie in peach and white light. She turned and looked out over the valley that swayed and dipped up and down until it met the silver flash of river. River's End was directly across the river from the ranch, but only added a small dot to distract from the mountains that encircled the valley. The river shimmered, long and black, in the twilight. A breeze picked up, lifting her hair. It was cold. So cold, her skin felt blue. She really needed some warmer clothes.

Turning back to the house, she started up the stairs that led to the porch. She stared hard at the front door, her hands suddenly sweaty with nerves.

She raised her hand to knock when a voice behind her nearly made her scream in fright.

"Need something, Ms. Poletti?"

She whipped her hand back and turned. There sat Jack. He was near where the porch wrapped around the house and at the opposite side from where she walked up. He sat in a deep Adirondack chair, his legs stretched out before him, resting on the railing. A beer sat between his legs. He'd been staring at her entire trek across the yard.

"You startled me."

His gaze went from her ankles up to her chin. He tipped his beer bottle towards her top. "Bit cold out here, isn't it?"

"I don't have a jacket," she muttered through clenched teeth.

His eyebrows rose. It sounded so contrived. Who had a car but not a jacket? Anyone who lived in the Seattle area usually had multiple jackets. Unless they were so careless, they let everything they owned get taken from them. Like she'd done. She hunched her shoulders forward and crossed her arms tighter over her chest. He couldn't see through her shirt, but she felt exposed to his disdain and didn't like it.

"How do you not have a jacket?"

Warmth spread over her skin, it was so embarrassing. But she refused to tell this man, who already thought so little of her, that she was kicked out of her own mother's apartment. "There was a fire. I lost a lot of my things. It's why I asked Chance to let me stay with him."

He raised the beer to his lips and drank before lowering the bottle with his fingers holding the long neck as he stared at her. "Mom died. Fire. Lost your things. Life isn't going too well for you, is it?"

He didn't believe her. "No. Lately, things aren't."

"So what was it you wanted? Looking for Joey?"

"Joey? No. I'm sorry to ask this…"

His mouth tightened as he waited for her request. What did he think she was going to ask for?

"But could I borrow your vacuum?"

His eyes narrowed. "Vacuum?"

"Yes. Chance doesn't have one and he's never once vacuumed the trailer."

Jack leaned forward and set his beer on the railing before standing to his full height. He stepped closer to her. He was a foot taller than Erin and she had to lean her head back to see past his chest. Up close, he smelled like fresh air and something more… something earthy. Hay? Horses? She didn't know. She supposed horses could smell good. She'd never been close enough to one to really know. He grabbed the hat on his head and swiped it off.

He had red hair.

That realization struck her as he stared down at her without a smile or trace of kindness in his rugged face. Now hatless, his thick, straight hair swept haphazardly over his forehead. His blue eyes were staring at hers. She forgot to breathe, he was staring so intently at her.

"So can I?"

He startled. "Can you what?"

"Borrow a vacuum?"

His mouth twitched. "A vacuum? Sure."

He walked around her, heading to the door and inside. She stared after him. She looked right, then left, and wondered what she was supposed to do? Follow him? Was he really that rude?

She walked to the half open door and stepped inside before stopping dead. So did everyone in the room. It was filled with all men.

Inside, the door opened into a large room, offering her a glimpse of the kitchen on the right and the living room on the left, as well as the second floor, all the way up to the roof. A giant, river rock fireplace separated the room, and halfway through the large, open space sat a table big enough to seat twelve. Right then, however, it seated five.

Joey sat next to a teenager and a young boy. Across from them sat two more men. A woman was in the kitchen. They'd been eating dinner and now they were staring at her.

Joey jumped up. "Erin. Hey." He came around the table towards her. "I figured you left with Chance."

She smiled. As if Chance would do anything with her. He left hours before without a single word. "No."

Joey frowned and seemed puzzled by her brother's treatment at her. Could Joey really not see what her brother was?

"Who's this, Joe?"

The voice came from a man who was starting to rise from the table. He was a big man, almost as tall as Jack, but beefier, with thick arms, a big chest, and a shock of jet-black hair that was too long and straggly, which skimmed over his neck and shoulders. His short-sleeved shirt revealed tattoos on his magnificent biceps. He didn't look anything like a man who worked on a ranch, but more like a biker.

"Erin Poletti. Chance's little sister. She's visiting him. Erin, this is my brother, Shane."

Shane smiled. He had a smile like Joey that could reach inside a woman and steal her heart. White teeth flashed at her and his charm nearly knocked her for a loop.

"Hard to believe someone as pretty as you is related to that cowpoke."

She smiled. Shane's voice was amused, and his tone kidding. She didn't take any malice from it, like she would have if Jack had said it.

Joey nodded towards the other man in the room. "That's Ian."

Ian stood up then and nodded solemnly at her, but his eyes lacked the heated resentment Jack's gaze held. Ian had a hard time meeting her eyes. He was as shy as his brother, Shane, was a big, loud flirt, who didn't mean anything he said. Ian was tall and skinny, with dark red hair and pale blue eyes.

Erin almost stepped back in dismay. They were all gorgeous. Every one of the Rydell brothers was like a different version of a catalogue model. There was the lanky, shy one; the muscle-bound, cocky one; the movie star-pretty Joey; and of course, the rugged, reserved Jack. It was disconcerting to her.

She turned then and looked at the pretty woman in the kitchen who shut the oven door and wiped her hands on a dishtowel. The woman averted her eyes, almost acting as if Erin wasn't there.

Erin's eyes lifted when she heard a sound beyond the group. Jack was standing there. He'd been watching, listening, and judging her. He came forward and handed her a vacuum. She was so surprised he got it for her, she forgot to reach out to take it.

"Your wife doesn't mind?" She assumed that's who the woman was.

One of his eyebrows lifted. "My wife is dead."

Her mouth opened and she looked towards the brothers and the kids. The tension in the room was thick and unpleasant. She shook her head. "I'm sorry. Chance didn't mention that." Chance mentioned nothing to her because she never communicated with him.

Jack turned from her. He ambled over to an oversized chair and sprawled out in it.

Joey put a hand on her arm. "These are Jack's boys."

At this, the boys jumped up. The older one came over with a silly grin on his face. Erin groaned inwardly. She'd recognize that look anywhere. The young teen couldn't get past ogling her.

"This is Ben."

Ben came forward and shook her hand with a polite "Hello." She glanced at their father in shock. He sat in the chair, his legs sprawled before him, hands locked behind his head as he stared at her with smirk on his face.

He could have learned something from his son's polite behavior.

"And that's Charlie." Charlie looked about eight or nine. He was ducking his head and staring at the table. Erin sighed. He seemed like the spitting image of his father in both his demeanor and looks. She wouldn't have pegged Jack as having kids. Or that his wife was dead. Erin turned to include the young woman behind her, and the obvious question: who was she?

"Oh Erin, this is Kailynn Hayes. She does everything around here. Lynnie, this is Chance's sister, Erin."

Kailynn glanced at Erin and said with a dismissive shrug, "Hi."

"Hello."

Joey glanced at the vacuum. "Cleaning up after Chance?"

She smiled back. "Yes."

"Need anything else?"

She looked up with hopeful eyes. "Mousetraps? I think the trailer has some."

Joey frowned. "I told Chance to set some. He doesn't care?"

"No. But I do."

"No kidding. I'll come over in a few minutes and set them."

Erin relaxed her shoulders. Help. Kindness. How long since anyone had offered her that? She smiled with genuine warmth at Joey. He was so nice. So refreshingly trusting and nice. "Thanks. I would really appreciate that," she said as she looked back towards the Rydell men who were now all watching her. She felt like a cat caught in a pack of coyotes. It was so odd. Kailynn, who seemed reluctant to talk, was what? The housekeeper? Wasn't there a mother? Another wife? A girlfriend?

"Nice to meet you all."

They all responded with smiles and waves. Except Jack. He didn't respond to her at all, but his eyes tracked her as she walked out the front door.

CHAPTER 4

*T*here was a stupid amount of pride invested in what she'd done to the trailer. It was kind of pretty underneath her brother's neglect and scum. By morning, she had it clean, sanitized, and sprayed to get rid of the fouler scents. With a half dozen mousetraps set up, she was able to sleep without thinking an errant critter might scurry over her.

Chance returned late and was stinking like sex and beer. He slept in his clothes. He only left in the morning to go to work because someone banged hard on the trailer door. She sat up, confused and terrified by the sound, only to realize that someone was waking her brother. Jack, most likely.

She scrounged around the trailer, but found nothing to eat. Her stomach rumbled in protest. She hadn't eaten more than a couple of candy bars from a gas station. She was starving. And her brother didn't have any food. Neither did she. She leaned her head into the cabinet. Someday… Someday, she would have all she wanted to eat. Healthy things, like expensive fruits and fattening pastries. She'd wake up each morning and never think about how to fill the kitchen with groceries. She straightened up. In the meantime, she had to survive. As she always did. As she intended to do today.

She dressed in another t-shirt and her lightweight sweater. She put on another skirt and wore the same sandals. She had two thousand dollars stuffed into her duffel bag, but it was all she had left in the world. It was all she had to start over with. She could buy new clothes, but she didn't dare spend too much from the last of her money.

Brian Peterson married her mother only four years ago. He was a miserable, flaky bastard who bled her mother and Erin completely dry of money, emotions and love. She blamed him for why her mother killed herself. Brian had fed her already weak, ill mother more pills and booze than she ever had taken before. The problem was, when her mom died, Brian got everything her mother left.

Although she didn't have much, she certainly had more than Erin did. Brian allowed her to stay for a little while, but it soon became a complicated dance of avoidance and never being there in order to not get cornered by him. He continually leered at her, enough that she worried he'd eventually make a move on her. Finally, he nearly succeeded in trapping her against their threadbare living room sofa and trying to have sex with her. When she managed to get away, he told her to never come back again. She left with only what was on her back and hidden inside her car trunk.

Brian came into their life after she started working for the fast food joint he managed. She had inadvertently introduced him to her mother. When her mother died, and she refused his advances, it was well understood that there went her menial, but desperately needed job. And now here she was. So broke, she had few clothes, little money, no food, no job and now, no home. She only had her car. She literally knelt in prayer that she had the car keys with her, so Brian couldn't take those from her too.

Erin opened the door to her trailer and sighed at the sights around her. Sunlight was gliding over the land, making the air smell alive. New shades of green covered the mountains and fields in a soft, luxuriant blush. She breathed the cold crisp air and tried to ignore the chill that settled over her legs and toes.

Grazing horses could be viewed in all directions that she looked, separated from her only by the labyrinth of fences. How could one figure out how to navigate that setup without getting trapped in the series of gates and corrals? She had never even touched a horse in her life. This was, in fact, the closest she'd ever been to them. She stared at the half dozen she spotted grazing beyond her trailer. A tawny-colored horse raised its head and looked at her. Its brown eyes shone like beautiful, round pennies. She felt like the horse was looking deeply into her soul. She shook it off. They were strictly animals. Farm animals, and not ghoulish mind readers.

She went to her car and dug around in the back, looking for some instant coffee.

"Need any help?"

With a startled jump, she hit her head on the partially opened trunk when the voice came up behind her. Cursing, she rubbed at her head and smiled when she realized who was there.

"Oh. Hey, Ben. You startled me. Sure. If you want, you can grab that other duffel bag. I think I'll take it in with me."

Jack's son was red-haired with blue eyes and a dusting of freckles. He smiled at her. He'd be a heartbreaker someday soon. He gallantly took her duffel bag and followed her into the trailer. She told him to put it on the couch.

He looked around, then at her, then away. She smiled at him. He was so sweet, shy and unsure of himself. She ached for the days when she was sweet and shy and unsure. In contrast to what she was now: calculating, cold, and willing to use her sexuality just as much as Chance said she should. It made her feel sick and hollow when she realized how much she changed from the teen she once was.

"Don't you have school?"

"Not today. Teachers are working, but no classes."

"What grade are you in?"

He puffed up his chest. "Freshman. I'm fifteen. I'll be driving next fall."

"That's cool."

"Dad and I are fixing up my truck. We got it out in the shop."

She sighed. Jack fixed a truck with his son? It seemed so sweet for the stern, rude man she met. Ben, however, was everything but that. Did Jack get the credit? Or the mother who was now dead?

"That sounds nice."

There was a loud yell from outside and she couldn't make out what it was. Ben looked at his feet with a sigh. "Guess I can't now. That's my dad. I'm supposed to be working."

"You help with the ranch?"

He rolled his eyes. "Yeah, got chores. Dad's a stickler for work first, play later."

She almost advised Ben to adhere to that, and revel in it, enjoying that your father wants to teach you things like responsibility and cares that you learn it. Instead, she said, "Well, thank you for the help."

He looked up with a smile as he hunched his shoulders over. He was tall and so thin, his jeans hung low on his hips. She followed him to the door and outside again. Jack stood on the porch of the house, and even from the distance, his frown was obvious.

Ben turned and waved at her and she smiled and waved back. Then she headed inside. It was too cold. She wanted to look around, but would have to wait until the afternoon when maybe she could stand the temperature. She'd have to stand the hunger until then, when she could run into town for a lunch/dinner combination.

JACK WATCHED his son walking up to him. Ben was only inches below him in height nowadays, a fact that made Jack's heart swell. Where had the time gone? When did his son get so old, he could look him in the eye? What happened to the scabby-kneed youth who followed him everywhere with wonder in his eyes and mischief in his smile? Now Ben merely scowled at him with his shoulders hunched, and his jeans hanging too low. He hated how sloppy Ben kept himself. But that wasn't a battle worth waging. He was having enough trouble keeping Ben out of trouble.

"What were you doing?"

Ben shrugged. "Nothing."

Jack waited. Ben didn't say anything further. *Fine. Okay. Shrugs.* That was the extent of his son's interactions with him. Damn adolescence. Jack put a hand to his neck and pressed.

"She's too old for you," he finally said.

Ben's face came up, his eyes furious, as a blush crept over his skin. "I was only helping her in with her duffel bag."

"Look, I don't like Chance. I don't know about his sister; other than she has nothing to do with us."

He shrugged. "She's a nice lady, Dad. I gotta work."

Ben turned and headed out to the barn.

Jack watched him leave with apprehension in his gut. First Joey, then Shane, now Ben? He glanced at the trailer, infested with Polettis. She was trouble. Nothing, but unending trouble. He was sure of it, right down to the pointed toes on his cowboy boots.

He saw her last night, when she stopped before the house, eyeing it up. Doing what? Deciding how much it would be worth to her? What did she want? To rob them? Marry into them? What the hell did she intend to do?

And if he were distracted by the bra and legs, what was his poor, young, hormone-pumping son supposed to do? Or his trusting younger brother? Jack kneaded at the thick knot in his neck. Finishing his coffee, he set it on the porch and stepped off to head towards the pasture. He'd already been out there for three hours. Break time was over; he had to get back to working the young mare he was training for the local vet.

ERIN CARRIED the vacuum with her up the porch and knocked on the door. It wasn't long before Kailynn opened it. She looked her up and down with a frown.

"I wanted to return the vacuum," Erin said when Kailynn didn't speak.

Kailynn opened the door wider, and Erin stepped through it. She had to nearly crane her neck back to meet Kailynn's gaze. She was tall for a woman and slumped her shoulders too far forward, as if to lessen her height. If she stood straighter, with her shoulders back, she would have been a beautiful girl. She had long, brown hair, and a pretty, fresh, wholesome face, that was quite extraordinary with a wide mouth and spray of freckles over her nose and cheeks. They must have been about the same age. However, there seemed no hope of a friendly acquaintance if Kailynn's frown of disapproval at her was any indication.

Erin stretched out her hand with the vacuum dangling off it and Kailynn took it.

Erin glanced about. They were alone in the house. The morning dishes sat around the table, along with a general air of chaos left in the wake of Rydell men.

"So do you live here?"

Kailynn looked hard at her. Would she refuse to answer on the general grounds that she found Erin so distasteful? Finally, she said, "I don't live here. I work here. I'm a neighbor and I work here whenever I'm not working at the diner in River's End. I do the housework, prepare the meals, and sometimes look after Charlie."

"Oh. They didn't mention that to me."

"Why would they? You aren't *their* guest, after all."

"Right." Erin nodded. Ouch. She had definitely pissed Kailynn off, but for no reason she knew. "Not a fan of my brother's, huh?"

Kailynn's eyes widened in surprise. She had an unusual grayish, almost violet-hued eye color. "Why would you say that?"

"Seemed the most likely reason for disliking me on sight. It seems to be Jack's as well."

Kailynn had the grace to hang her head. "I can't speak for Jack. I don't know you. I have no opinion."

Erin grinned. "I'd respect you more if you were just honest about it. Like Jack. Then I at least know who to look out for. Is it Joey? Because I flirt with him?"

She stiffened. "Joey? No. I'm the housekeeper here, not a factor in any of the relationships."

"So not Joey?"

Kailynn shook her head, her expression confused. Erin shrugged. "All right, Kailynn. I thought it might be nice to know another woman around here. Maybe not."

She turned and walked out. She felt judged enough by Jack Rydell, and didn't need it from the housekeeper too.

~

"He's the horse whisperer."

Erin turned when Joey came up beside her. It was three o'clock before she'd finally driven across the river and up the valley several miles. That was where she found a small, country store and spent fifty bucks on some boxed food and milk. She'd also eaten some mac'n'cheese and felt like a new person. Happily fed, and finally not so bone-numbingly cold, she stepped out of the trailer. She was leaning on a wood fence that separated her from the round pen where Jack was working with a small, white-speckled horse. She had no idea what Jack was doing, but observed that he'd been patiently at it for some time.

"What?"

"Jack. He's like that movie Robert Redford made years back. It's like he talks to them. I can train the horses, but not like him. He's the best I've ever seen."

She glanced up at Joey. He was staring out at his brother. The look in his eyes was almost sad or wistful. It contained both resentment and longing. Whatever their relationship, Joey and Jack had a complicated one.

"So how does this work then? What do you do?"

"The ranch has been in our family for a hundred and twenty years. It used to be just for cattle. But in the seventies, my dad turned to horses. And since then, Jack has turned it into a training facility. There didn't used to be a lot of cash. Jack has turned this place upside-down."

"Is that why the river is named after your family?"

Joey smiled and hung his head. "Yeah. More than a century ago."

"What happened to your dad?"

Joey shrugged. "He died when I was five. Jack and his wife, Lily, raised me."

Ah… so she got it now. Jack was his brother and father; and it wasn't an easy transference, she supposed.

"What happened to your mom?"

He looked away. "They were killed together in a car crash."

"Oh. I'm sorry."

He smiled at her and she blinked. He was so perfect, she wanted to merely stare at him in the sunlight. "So your mom died recently?"

She nodded. "Yes. It's only been a few weeks…" A few weeks. But her mom had checked out on her years ago. She had a complicated relationship with the woman who raised her. She had needed her mother, but resented that need and the neglect her mother raised her in.

"It never gets okay. Losing your parents."

"No, it doesn't."

He smiled, and she smiled back, nearly blinded by Joey's flash of white teeth and dimples. He really should have left the ranch long ago to become a movie star.

"Has Chance shown you around?"

"Not at all."

Joey glanced her way and she stared harder towards Jack. He gently laid a whip-like-looking device over the back of the skittish horse. What was he doing?

"Let me," Joey said as he glanced down. "You have any shoes that won't break your ankles? There isn't any pavement. Not that those aren't great shoes. They are. But…"

"But ridiculous to wear here. I lost most of my stuff in a fire recently. It's part of why I showed up here."

He frowned. "That's terrible. You've been through it of late. Can I do anything?"

A knot of regret squeezed her heart. Joey looked so earnest, and appeared to feel actual sympathy for her. How long since anyone felt that towards her? Look at how Jack reacted to her. With unconcealed, total scorn. Joey's first instinct was, *what could he do to help her?* No one had offered to help her in so long. She turned her full attention to Joey and smiled, suddenly appreciating Joey for much more than just his pretty smile.

"Could I borrow a coat?"

"A coat? Are you serious? You don't have a coat? Or decent shoes? Of course, you can borrow a coat. But why doesn't Chance help you?"

She glanced away. "He and I have never been all that close. He's not like you."

"Why don't I take you shopping? We can get a few things."

She was tempted. So tempted, she almost said yes. But she thought of the way Chance looked at her, and the way he expected her to deal with the Rydells. The way she dealt with Joey. However, she looked into Joey's face and knew she didn't have to use him. Or hurt him.

She shook her head. "No, I'll get some things. But I would take a coat to borrow until I can."

Joey looked across at her. He took her hand and pulled her with him towards the house. "Okay a coat. Then I'll show you around the place."

The inside of the house was even better in the daylight. The furniture was big and comfortable, big enough to hold the massive men that lived here. There wasn't a candlestick or dainty piece of furniture anywhere. It was all big and heavy, with square corners and solid legs. The walls were wood, with big windows that dappled the wood floor in squares of sunlight. The only bow to modern comforts was a ridiculously large TV that hung on the wall, which all the seating faced.

Joey came back from a hall closet with a brown coat. It was thick corduroy material. "There is no hurry to give this back. It doesn't fit me anymore. In fact, just plan on keeping it, okay?"

She took it and slipped it on with a sigh as the heavy warmth surrounded her. She hadn't felt warm in days. She smiled up at him. "Thank you, Joey. You can't imagine how I appreciate it."

"Come on; I'll show you around."

Joey took her hand and she followed him outside, breathing in the crisp, clean air, and feeling the sunlight's warmth falling over the valley before her. The view from the porch was breathtaking. How could one wake up to this every day and not be glad just to be alive?

She followed Joey down a road that led past the outbuildings, and bordered a long meadow. He told her they grew alfalfa there all spring and summer. The road they walked on was dirty and dusty, with big bumpy rocks scattered along it. She tried to keep from slipping on them and twisting an ankle in her strappy, heeled shoes. Once past the buildings, the road dipped down towards the river. They came to a flat, camp-like setup. Pine trees were scattered all around with leafless, skeletal cottonwood trees, fat and thick, filling the riverbanks. The river was louder here, and the rushing gurgle echoed back towards them. The water flashed silver through the trees.

The road ended there. Two trails took off: one down along the mountain, and the other going off diagonally from them towards the woods. Joey took her along the mountain. It was a narrow, snaking trail that soon opened up as the river came into view before her.

She paused. She didn't know why. But a feeling came over her. A strange feeling. Of what? *Coming home.* The view before her made her feel like she'd come to the spot she'd been searching for her entire, pathetic, brief life.

Erin walked closer as her feet sunk into the cold, deep sand. She picked over twigs and sticks of driftwood. Then she stood at the edge of the Rydell River. It was a beautiful place. She couldn't explain why. It was special. Different. Better than any place she'd ever been. Before the Rydells' beach was a deep section of calm water, green and clear as it flowed past. It looked so perfect, it urged Erin to put her feet into it, despite the chilly air and icy river temperature. She bent down and ran her hand in it. It was cold. Snow cold. To her left, she saw a jutting of rocks that rose into a formation that stood like a lookout point over the river.

"This is our swim beach."

Erin glanced at Joey. Swim beach? That sounded like a trite description of this place. It was glorious; moving swiftly in the middle, but deep and placid along the shoreline. Across the river, mountains formed a deep V, cupping in the entire view. It was private and perfect.

"That is Rydell Rock. Anyone around here knows it. It's one of the most popular spots on the river. Kids like to jump off it all summer."

"You too?"

Joey shook head and laughed. "Sure."

Erin looked up at him. "This place is amazing." Like no place she'd ever been to in her short, city-filled life.

"Yeah, when the summer hits, and the hundred-degree days come, there is no better place to be."

"Do you guys use it a lot?"

He shrugged. "Sure."

She tried to picture Jack here and couldn't do it. She couldn't see him lounging on a beach towel or floating aimlessly down the river. She couldn't even imagine him taking off his worn cowboy boots to go barefoot in the sand.

"Want to walk by the river?"

"Yes." She barely glanced at Joey, she was so entranced with the surroundings. The soft gurgling of the water as it dipped and tripped over the round river rock that filled the bottom was soothing. The water was so clear, it was like invisible ink streaming next to her.

She could sit and stare at it, entranced, all day. There was something about this place that touched her like no place ever could. She wished she could stop, and just sit, to be alone and figure out why she felt so different there.

The shore was rocky as they walked along it until they came to a set of scary-looking, white water rapids. Suddenly, the banks of the river rose ten feet off the water. She glanced up to the top and oriented herself. The edge of the ranch was there, just behind the barns.

"How much land do you own?"

"Almost a thousand acres. No one has land like this around here except us. We held onto it through all these years."

"That's incredible. I've never heard of anything like this place. You must love it here."

Joey shrugged, his eyes looking across the river at the steep bank. "It's all I've ever looked at my entire life. How do I know what else there is? There's like three neighbors along the road here. You haven't been up in the hills behind us yet. There is nothing up there for miles and miles. It's pretty rough around here. There are places without electricity even. So yeah, this place is special to me, but then it's also my chain and anchor."

"Do your brothers feel the same way?"

Joey shook his head and pitched a rock overhand into the rapids. "I never asked them, so how would I know? Shane doesn't stay around much. He takes off a lot on his Harley. Ian works with the horses and farming the feed for the horses. Who knows what Jack likes. This place is all him. You can't even understand what he is to this place. Or how many hours he works here. I can't do it. I can't work like that. It's a problem that is growing between us."

Among other things. "So you all work here? You don't have to be anywhere?"

Erin couldn't imagine having control over your own schedule and hours, and the tasks one does and when. She'd been at the beck and call of one low-level manager or another ever since she was sixteen.

"Yeah, we all work here if we want. Shane's a mechanic. He has one of the shops turned into a workshop. He takes in work from the outside and can fix anything. He keeps the ranch supplied in trucks and machinery."

"And this is what you want? To work here?"

Joey shrugged, his gaze pinned on the river, but his mind obviously somewhere else. "I don't know what I want to do, or where I want to be. Sometimes I think I should just leave. I don't know where I'd go... but maybe, I should just go somewhere. You know what I mean? Maybe join the military or something. Go see something besides horses and farmlands."

"I know about wanting more than what is right before you. So yes, I know what you mean." Erin looked out at the river too, feeling a kinship with Joey. She knew exactly what that felt like. She had never belonged anywhere and never knew what she wanted to do. Then again, she didn't have the luxury of wondering what she wanted or where she wanted to be. She was usually too busy trying to survive whichever particular day she was caught in.

Joey glanced at her. "You wanna come down here with us tonight?"

"Us? Where?

"Some people from around. We'll have a fire at the beach,

some food, drinks; it would be a good time to meet the people around here. We do that sometimes. No one's going to bother us down at our beach. And we bother no one either."

Joey's eyes gleamed as he stared at her. Shivers of anticipation slithered through her body. What else did she have to do?

"Yes, thanks. Maybe I'd best find some clothes to wear in the meantime. Where do I shop around here?"

He grinned. "Finally got a large discount chain close. Takes about an hour to get to."

"Are you serious?"

"Welcome to the country."

CHAPTER 5

*T*he flames flickered and crackled over the beach and surrounding mountains. It was beautiful and almost haunting the way the shadows danced and shifted from the fire that was burning at the center of the sandy beach. Large driftwood branches were fed into it by any one of the dozens of people on the beach. At times, the flames leaped higher than ten feet. Erin had to step back when the heat scorched her face. The river was behind her, inky and strange feeling. It seemed creepy to her now that it was night; the way it flowed and splashed in the dark, yet she could hardly see it.

Feeling the lovely pull of tequila that warmed her blood, and settled in her gut, Erin found everything looked better, fuzzier, and warmer. She took another sip of the drink Joey had handed her and munched on the handful of chips someone had set up on a rock. Music blared out of a stereo. She met so many people, she doubted she'd remember any of their names. Most of them were young, and all of them knew Joey Rydell.

Her brother, Chance, had his hand up a poor girl's shirt.

Even from a distance across the fire, Erin could see their tongues twisting together. Erin rolled her eyes in disgust as Chance managed to pull the poor blonde away from the fire into the darker shadows beyond. *Yuck.*

Erin looked down until she felt a hand on her own. When she glanced up, Joey was standing close, his face illuminated by the strange light of the fire. Her breath caught, he was that handsome.

Her stomach jumped when she saw his gaze upon her.

"You managed to find some clothes, I see."

She had to spend a hundred dollars she didn't want to spend. But now she had some jeans, shirts, and finally, a decent pair of tennis shoes. At least, she wouldn't be such a disgrace around the ranch. As it was now, she needed to stay there awhile before she could figure out what to do next. The questions, the indecision, and trapped feelings of her life sent a rush of acid into her gut. She hated knowing she had nowhere else to go. Nothing else. She now had nineteen hundred dollars between herself and nothing at all. The thought made her want to throw up.

"Hey. I didn't mean to make you upset. You'd look good in a burlap sack. The jeans look great."

"It did take an hour to get there." The trip took her up the valley, opposite the way she came from the west side of the state. It was as beautiful a drive as the mountain pass. After driving out to the main road, there was again pavement and a two-lane road. Turning within two miles, the twisting highway brought her through the small scattering of buildings that made up River's End. It was directly across from the Rydells. If the river hadn't been there, it would have been within feet of the edge of their land. The town was raised above the ranch, which spread over the valley floor, and butted up to the sway and pull of the river. The town had a diner, a church, a post office, a bar, a small convenience store, and a closed gas station. About thirty houses comprised the rest of it, and that was all. She had to drive nearly an hour to find a store that was more than a small grocery outlet or convenience store.

Joey smiled at her. She smiled back and felt the warmth of his hand over hers. It was so good and comforting. Almost like she wasn't adrift without a soul in the world to care about her. The din of music, light conversation, and the warmth of alcohol made it seem like Joey's presence could keep the dark unknown of the future, and her instability at bay. She shifted, and stared into Joey's eyes.

"You okay, Erin?"

He asked. He cared. He was so sweet and kind to her. She nodded.

He nodded back, taking the drink from her hand and setting it into the sand. Then he took her hand and led her away from the fire. When he stopped, they were a good distance from the crowd. The fire was only a dot of orange. The stars overhead shimmered down brightly and vividly. She swore she could reach up and touch them, they were so clear and visible here. It was as if she stepped into a different world: a world of nature and beauty, of clean air and pristine land.

A place she almost wondered if she could be clean in.

Joey had a coat on and glanced at her before dropping the objects he snagged in his other arm: blankets and sleeping bags. He spread a big, flannel blanket over the sand and glanced back at her and smiled. It was a shy smile. A sweet smile. A smile that said, *Hey, I hope this is okay*. She dropped down to her knees and he did the same next to her. His hand came out to pull her closer to him. His mouth found hers and the kiss inflamed the warmth already burning in her gut. They fell back to the downy warmth of the blanket, over the rumpled, soft sand. His weight covered her, as his mouth trailed down her neck, and into the loose opening of her top. Staring up over him and at the stars farther off, she felt his heat and the wetness of his tongue as well as the grip of his hands over her. It was all so pleasant, she thought, in a haze of alcohol. Why not do this? It was far more pleasant than usual. It was outside, in the clean air, totally private and Joey was so nice to her. Why not do this?

She opened her legs and shifted so he could settle against her as his hands found the top of her new, cheap jeans. "This okay?"

"It's fine. It's fine, Joey."

And it was. It was fine. It was nice. Joey was sweet and much gentler than some men. He was far more solicitous of her than most men too. They kissed and felt each other and used protection. So yes, it was fine. They were safe. They were kind. It made her feel not so alone in a world in which she seemed less than a pinprick of a star.

A VOICE WOKE HER UP. Erin felt the hammer-like pounding against her temple as she started to awaken. She opened her eyes to the strangest sky. She blinked several times to place herself, and stared at a sky so white, so sluggish and soft, the world had yet to illuminate. *Shit. She was on a beach. Outside. Freezing.* And it was probably dawn. Her stomach heaved in protest. She partied way too hard. She sat up straight as it all came rushing back into her brain.

Jerking to attention, she saw shoes on the edge of the blanket, and glanced up with a sickening thud in her gut.

Jack. Jack Rydell was staring down at her. Why? What did he want? How could she have fallen asleep out here? Goose bumps broke out all over her skin. She clutched the stack of blankets up around her chest. She was naked, wrapped in the blankets and next to a naked Joey.

Jack's face didn't show a trace of recogniztion or a hint of feeling. He stared into her eyes. Then up at her hair. She raised a hand to it and flinched. It felt like a rat's nest, except gritty with sand.

Jack's eyes left her and she sat there, burning up in shame. She'd never felt so exposed or so humiliated as she did in this moment. At the expression of disgust in Jack's face. At being on the beach, with a killer hangover and ice nearly crusting on the ground.

"What the hell were you doing?"

Glancing up when Jack's calm, mean, cold tone demanded an answer, she followed his line of sight to Joey next to her. Jack took a booted toe and nudged Joey, a lump of limbs under the blankets. Joey groaned and mumbled. Finally, he opened his eyes. He looked at her, then up past her, no doubt, realizing his brother was standing over them.

"What the hell do you want?" Joey asked, suddenly blinking awake in astonishment.

Jack bent over and grabbed something, which he threw at Joey. Joey took the shirt and put it over his chest, while Erin clutched the blanket in horror.

"What the hell am I doing? Looking for my fifteen-year-old son, you stupid, little shit." Jack stood over them with his hands on his hips. He didn't spare her a look. All of his wrath was directed at his brother. Erin tried to sink into a ball and curled her shoulders to hide herself.

"Ben? What about him?" Joey asked as he stood up, half naked, and pulled jeans over himself.

"Yeah, Ben, over there, puking his guts out. What did you think? That it was funny to let him come here?"

"I didn't," Joey said as he pulled on his jacket. Erin sat

there, naked, looking up at the two men towering over her, now arguing. She wished she could sink into the sand.

"Yeah, while you were over here, Ben got drunk and nearly succeeded in having sex. You never think. You never think that what you're doing has consequences. Did you imagine Ben even carries a condom? Or did you offer one up to him?"

Erin opened her mouth to protest, but seeing Jack's eyes when he glanced at her kept her from speaking. She couldn't remember ever seeing someone look at her with so much disgust in his face. Jack pushed the cowboy hat on his head back.

Joey shook his head. "He wasn't there last night. At least, not while I was down there. He must have snuck up later, after I left."

Left to have sex with her. Erin heard the statement in Jack's accusatory gaze at her.

Jack crossed his arms over his chest. "Get up to the house."

"I'm not fifteen. I didn't do anything wrong. Maybe you need to keep a better eye on your son."

Jack glanced at Erin and threw a jacket at her. "It's forty degrees out here. Yeah, I'm the one who needs to be smarter."

Jack turned and left and Joey's gaze followed his brother's rigid back. He sighed and sat down next to her.

"Asshole. He still thinks I'm Ben to him. Like I answer to him. Or still his responsibility. So the kid snuck down and got into the booze. What teen hasn't?"

Joey finally looked at Erin. "You seem cold."

Cold? That was such an understatement, she nearly slapped him. She was cold to the point of feeling numb. She was naked, exposed, and hungover. She pushed away the hand he put out towards her, grabbing her clothes scattered around them and getting dressed hastily. She shoved her foot into her new tennis shoe and made her way over the brittle ground, back towards the ranch. Her head throbbed. Her muscles ached from sleeping outside at a stupid time of the year, and her humiliation was so complete, she wanted to sink into the river.

She slammed the door on the trailer shut. It was cold in there and the heat wasn't on. She walked over to the thermostat and spun it to eighty degrees while waiting for the propane to kick in. Her teeth were chattering. She looked up then and stopped at the sight of her reflection. She touched her face. Black rings outlined her eyes with day-old mascara. Her hair was a tousled, ratty mess of black. She had a hickey on her neck.

So she had a good time last night. She'd done it before. So why did it feel so different this time? So much worse?

Sinking down onto the couch, she crawled into her sleeping bag to ease the shivering chill that was on her skin and seemed to have settled over her soul. What was she doing?

That's all she could think about lately. What was she doing with her life? Nothing. The simple answer she always gave herself. She was doing nothing. And everything. There was no one who gave a crap about her. Oh sure, now there was Joey, for a few weeks... maybe. But he didn't love her. He just wanted to sleep with her. He wouldn't think about her much once it was over. She knew that. And yet, as always, that was fine with her. It was all she expected.

She shook her head and closed her eyes to the bile climbing up her throat and the images in her head. The ones that sent her life reeling into a chaos she couldn't seem to rebound from. Her mother. Her mother being dead. Her mother sitting dead in *her* car. A car her mother left purposely running in the enclosed garage stall that they rented. The car Erin found her mother dead in. And her mother's excuse? A sad, insignificant, *I'm sorry, Erin*. That was it. All the explanation of why her mother decided to kill herself. And in Erin's car, in the only way she was sure that Erin would be the one to find her.

Erin opened her eyes at the image. The feeling of her mother's cold hands. And the sight of her lifeless eyes. She tried to close her heart from falling into the deep pit of her stomach that wondered why she wasn't enough of a reason for her mother to stay alive?

Of course, it was so much more complicated than that. It involved the mental illness, pain and heartache that her mom tried to live with in. But... the child in her, couldn't stop the irrational feeling that her mother had left her.

She blinked at the tears and shook her head. *No.* She wouldn't. She refused to cry anymore. She stood up to shower. That was enough for now. She had to realize that. It was all she had. Today. Today she had a place to live and food to eat. Who cares what tomorrow would bring?

JACK STARED out the kitchen window. It was a view that any resort would put on the front of its brochures. He looked towards the sunlight, now filling the valley that spread in a gentle slope towards the river flashing below. Horses dotted the scenic green pastures starting to appear over the land. Mountains brought the sky closer to the earth. All was as it had been Jack's entire life; except for Erin Poletti's trailer, which marred the lower corner of an otherwise perfect view. Jack drank from the coffee cup in his hand.

He felt old. As he stared down at his hands, gripping a white coffee cup, a sense of weariness filled him that almost made him sit down.

He was now the chaperone. Out at his brother's party,

collecting his underage son. His son who snuck out at night, to drink alcohol and make out with Marcy Fielding who lived up the river. At least, she turned him down to have sex. The thought made Jack's stomach churn. In a handful of years, he could be Grandpa Jack if Ben did anything stupid. Which was what Ben seemed hell-bent on doing.

It made his joints ache to think of sleeping all night on a cold, hard, ground as his stupid, little brother had just done. Didn't they notice the bitter chill of the morning? Any of them? Ben? Joey? Erin?

There was quite a crowd down at the beach, strewn over it in different spots. He found Chance as naked as his sister, his white ass hanging out, with some woman Jack didn't know next to him. He found his son curled up beside Marcy, near what was once the fire. By then, it was no more than a small circle of charred wood and glowing coals. Most people had already gone home. But a few couples still littered his land and he didn't like it. He really didn't like his son being down there and a part of it. Joey was one thing. Joe did stuff like that still. But Ben was too young to start already. Fatigue overcame him; how could he fight the teenage rebel his son seemed determined on becoming?

He overreacted to Joey. He knew it even as he gazed down at his coffee. His brother had the right to do what he wanted, where he wanted, and with whom he wanted. He had no right to speak like that to Joey. Didn't he have the sense to realize Erin Poletti had set her eyes on him the moment she stepped foot on their land? Perhaps she intended to use him to end up with a chunk of Jack's ranch. Jack slammed the cup down. He'd be damned if that little parasite would get any part of his land, his house, or his brother.

If that was her plan, of course.

The trailer door opened and Chance came out and

started puking in the grass. Jack turned away. One way or another, it was high time the Polettis got the hell off his land.

"Jack?"

Joey came into the kitchen and sat down at the table. He rested his head in his hands. He looked up at Jack.

"I didn't know Ben came down there last night."

"I guess you probably didn't. I overreacted when I saw Ben there."

"When Erin and I left the fire, he wasn't there. You know that. I wouldn't let Ben stay there. Or drink."

"He was with Marcy Fielding."

Joey grimaced. "Did they…"

"Not yet. My guess is she said no. This time." Jack stepped away from the counter, and started pacing. He couldn't handle this. His son having sex? It was too soon. Too much. What the hell was he supposed to do with a teen? A teen who was rapidly growing up and wanting to listen less and less to authority. Jack felt a fist in his stomach and pressure in his neck.

"Fifteen? You don't think he's trying to…"

"Of course, he's trying to. Weren't you? I was. I just hope he's smart."

Joey pressed his lips together. "I'll be more careful."

"I shouldn't have yelled at you. Sometimes I just get in the habit, you know? Years of practice."

Joey nodded. "I know. I know you did this for me too. Don't be so hard on yourself. I didn't turn out too bad, did I?"

Jack looked toward his little brother. No. Joey hadn't turned out too bad. But he was naive. He didn't see through the manipulations of Chance Poletti. And Joe wasn't nearly as grown up yet as he thought he was.

"You careful with her?"

"Who? Erin? Of course. Always. I'm not careless."

"I don't think you are. But don't underestimate her."

He laughed and grabbed a banana from the bowl in the middle of the table. "You're way over thinking it. We had fun together. We're not even, well... much beyond that. It was just sex."

Jack turned away. He didn't want to know, and didn't want details. He simply wanted Erin and Chance Poletti to leave the ranch and never come back.

"The fence along the main road has a section that needs to be repaired. Meet me out there in an hour."

Joey nodded. "Sure. See you then."

Jack walked out of his house. He paused before continuing across the dirt to the barn to begin cleaning the stalls and feeding the horses. Morning routines didn't change. No matter the day or the season, Jack did all the chores. His brothers helped. Whatever ranch hand they currently employed also helped, but usually, no matter what, it was still Jack's job. He liked it. He could check on his horses. He let the rhythm of the work flow through him, relaxing him, and letting some of the tension out of his neck, stemming from the rest of his ordered life.

For their personal horses he put more work into their feed routine. He started mixing the morning rations of food for their horses that consisted of soaking alfalfa pellets in warm water, and adding sea salt. Evening chores included feeding each of the horses a pound of barley. Part of their care was intended so if they ever got lost on one of their remote mountain rides, the horse would come home, looking for its evening meal. Most of the training he did for his horses was in relation to trail riding. Jack didn't mind the extra care. Ever. And today, he was particularly glad for the distraction of his horses.

His head kept going back to the beach. He never intended, of course, to stumble across his naked brother. Or Erin. It shouldn't have surprised him to realize it happened.

He's witnessed their flirting. He thought perhaps it might be a few more days. But then again, it was hard to fault Joe. She was that beautiful. It was as exactly as Jack knew it would be; and why he didn't want her there so much. Jack suspected it in his gut, Erin Poletti was going to be like a stone being thrown into the still waters that usually characterized Rydell River Ranch.

And so what if he'd stolen a glance at her? Sound asleep, she looked almost ethereal in her dark-haired ringlets and snow-white skin. So what if his gaze followed the lines of her body below the blanket that was precariously covering her? She'd been the one naked outside on *his* ranch. He sighed as the tension reclaimed the same spot in his neck again.

CHAPTER 6

*E*rin loved the ranch. She didn't know how else to describe how much she liked waking up each morning. She'd never felt that way before and was never particularly happy about anything. But she couldn't wait to open her trailer door each morning and view the valley all around her and the horses. She loved the clear sky and endless tracts of land encircling her. She loved how free it made her feel, but also sure of where her feet stood. She had no right to love the ranch as she would be leaving it soon, but she did love it. It intrigued her like nothing else ever could. Perhaps that was half of the draw she felt toward Joey. He told her about the ranch, as well as the work they did.

She let him into the trailer most evenings. Chance was usually gone on one of his nightly jaunts. She didn't ask and they rarely spoke. She did her best to pretend Chance didn't even exist.

Her favorite place soon became the river and she went to the beach each day. She gazed at the river before closing her eyes. The deep, undisturbed quiet of the land seemed to speak to her. A silence she'd never heard before filled her ears. Bugs. Birds. River. Breezes. They all filled her ears and her head. It did something to her, something that was new and better. Something she guessed maybe church might have tried to give her.

She avoided the main house at all costs and stayed in the trailer or at the beach, sometimes walking the endless dirt roads that ran in all directions from the ranch. She did everything she could to stay out of the others' way, especially Jack's. She didn't miss his scowl after the morning he found her with Joey.

He believed she were just like Chance and using Joey. He wanted to kick her off the ranch. She hoped if she avoided him, and kept to herself and out of their way, perhaps he would ignore her presence there for a while.

Just long enough until she could figure out what next to do with herself.

She couldn't stop Ben, who came over frequently to talk to her although she shooed him along. She nearly hibernated in the trailer without any TV or radio to entertain her. There were no books to distract her from her dire thoughts. What good would they do her?

So she had a lot of quiet time. The more quiet she became, the more thoughts went through her brain. And she felt even worse about what she saw and who she was.

Late one afternoon she left the beach and started back along the narrow path to the trailer. She hummed while feeling the warm rays of the sun on her skin. It was nearly April and spring was exploding with color all over the valley.

She was almost to the trailer when she heard a sound. Glancing down towards the trailer steps, she screamed. Then she screamed again before jumping back and running. *There was a snake!* And no way past it. She stared at the despicable spot with chills breaking out all over her skin.

Chance came running at her screams from across a field.

"What the hell are you screaming about?" he asked once he spotted her.

"That!" She pointed at the snake.

"That?" Chance repeated, walking forward with his voice full of disgust. "The snake? Spring's here so they'll all be coming out now. Didn't you know that? Gotta be careful around the rattlers." Chance reached down and grabbed the snake from behind its head. She stepped back further and Chance saw her. His chilling gaze focused on her.

"You afraid of this harmless snake, sis?"

He used to enjoy tormenting her for no reason and did terrible things to her as a young girl. He often took her stuff and hid it. Then he would smear it with feces or something equally repulsive. Once, he ejaculated all over her favorite Barbie. She was ten years old. He was sadistic and liked to be. For no apparent reason.

She stepped back again. Her gaze was riveted on the writhing snake as it undulated against Chance's grip.

"Put it down! Damn it, Chance. Just let it go."

He grinned. Most grins didn't cause the flesh on one's arm to bristle with disgust. Chance's, however, did. "No. I think my little sister is afraid of the snake. Gotta get over that to be here. This area is infested with them. Come on, touch it, it'll help get you over it."

"No." This time she turned to run from him, never doubting he'd do just that. And maybe it was a harmless snake, but it had her heart sinking in actual fear. All snakes terrified her.

Chance caught her wrist and she yanked it back as hard as she could. He had an iron grip on her arm. She yanked harder and didn't turn, but kept straining as far away from Chance as was possible. Tears filled her eyelids.

"Let me go. *Damn it, Chance!* This isn't funny."

"Come on. It's just a little snake. Touch it. Come on, you like to touch things, don't you, Erin?"

She refused to look back at him and expected to have bruises from the intense strength of his grip on her. She fell into the dirt, trying to pull free in a crazy, manic rush of energy just as she realized what Chance intended to do.

The snake touched her and he rubbed it over her arm. She squeezed her eyes shut, all the while screaming. She knew it was unreasonable, and just a snake. But the fear of it touching her ignited inside her and left her crying, and nearly hysterical.

"I think you need to get over your fears, little sis."

"Stop it!" She was screaming irrationally. "Let me go!"

"You're not particular, never were. Come on; open your hand for it."

Then it was gone.

Erin opened her eyes. *Jack.* He was on Chance after yanking her wrist away from her merciless brother. He pushed Chance down before Chance could react. Jack grabbed the snake from her brother as if it were nothing more than a piece of rope. He obviously didn't fear the snake, but neither did he think it was something to torture her with.

"What the hell is going on here?"

Jack glared down at her brother, then glanced at her. She was on her ass in the dirt. She wiped at her tears and jumped to her feet, stepping back from where Jack stood with the squirming snake.

Chance laughed as he started to lumber onto his feet. "Ahh shit, Rydell, I was just messing around with my little sister. Haven't you ever messed with your brothers? All siblings do it."

Jack stared at her brother. "She was screaming." His acidic tone suggested the statement said it all. She hesitated. She was about to start apologizing to Jack for the commotion she inadvertently made, but he wasn't looking at her. He was scowling at her brother and his tone was quiet, almost lethal. *Huh.* Maybe he disapproved of Chance doing that to her.

"She was overreacting. It was no big deal."

Jack one-handedly pushed Chance backwards. "Get out of here, Poletti. Get out of my fucking sight *right now.*"

Chance stepped back and Jack stepped forward. Her cowardly brother suddenly turned and fled towards the south field. Jack watched him go, then turned and walked out past the house before he squatted down and gently released the snake.

Maybe he'd simply go back to work. No. No such luck. He walked back to where she stood, still rubbing the dirt off her butt and legs.

"What was that?"

She glanced up into his face. He was tall, and seemed high above her. She licked her lips in humiliation. She had overreacted. Her screams drew not only her brother, but also Jack from his work. He probably thought something was really wrong.

She shrugged and looked at her feet. "I'm sorry. I overreacted to the snake. I didn't expect it. I mean, I never knew they were here."

"Overreacted to the snake?" he repeated as he frowned at her. He pushed the tip of his cowboy hat back and shook his head. "That's not what I meant. What was Chance doing to you?"

"Oh. He…" Erin didn't know quite how to word what Chance was doing to her. He was being mean to her. No, malicious, even sadistic to her, but he never quite did anything so physical or obvious as abusing her. Sometimes, his incessant humiliation felt worse. How could she explain that? Then again, she couldn't. Jack couldn't know that. Jack was barely letting her stay there as it was.

Jack's gaze was on her and when he finally spoke, his tone was quiet. "He do things like that to you often?"

She dropped her head. She could not look up at him for the humiliation swimming in her gut. "He thinks it's funny."

Jack was staring at her and she could feel his eyes boring into her scalp. "That wasn't funny. Not funny at all."

She looked up after hearing the quiet tone. She expected him to be mad at her, and not, well, so kind. Jack's hand came out and he took her arm. She jerked back at his touch and looked down to see what he was doing. His touch wasn't like Chance's, however. There was no pressure. No pain.

He pushed the long sleeves of Joey's coat up her arm. Her wrist was bright red where Chance held her while she twisted like a maniac to get free.

"Chance often leave bruises on you, Ms. Poletti?" he asked quietly and gently. His gaze brushed over her and she stared at her red wrists.

She shrugged. "I haven't lived with him in years."

She hadn't answered his question, and he, of course, realized that. "Why would you come to him now? Here?"

She looked up.

"You might as well be honest with me, Ms. Poletti. I'm not quite as blind as Joey is. I see exactly what your relationship is with Chance; and if it's possible, I think you must detest him even more than I do. Explain that to me. Explain to me what the hell you're doing here."

Erin dropped her shoulders as she stared at Jack's boots. She swallowed before she finally looked up at him. "I didn't come here just to be here. I came here because I had nowhere else to go."

"You're not a college student." He said it as a fact. He always knew she was lying.

She shook her head.

"And there was no fire, was there?"

"No."

"Then why did you come here without any clothes?"

She dropped her head down. "My stepfather never liked me. Or maybe it was he liked too much. But I detested him. After my mom died, he inherited what little she had and kicked me out after trying to… take advantage of me. I fled with what was on my back and whatever was stashed in my car. My mom had met him through me. He was my boss. So I lost my job and apartment in the same moment." It was the same car her mother killed herself in. But Erin failed to add that pathetic, albeit gruesome, fact.

"And Chance was your best option?"

She shook her head and raised her eyes to the horizon. "No. Chance was my *only* option."

She couldn't meet Jack Rydell's eyes. She couldn't take the shame of having Jack see what a loser she was.

He was silent for a long, drawn-out moment and she squirmed under his intense, sharp gaze and muteness. He cleared his throat, finally, and simply stepped back. "Spring brings the snakes out. They're pretty lethargic though this time of year. Just give them some space and they won't bother you."

She glanced up. "That's it? You're not forcing me to leave?"

His gaze seemed flat. "I have to insist that Chance leave at some point. He's a terrible worker. I don't know how much more I can take of him, even for Joey."

She nodded, feeling puzzled. Meaning what? She could stay until Chance got evicted? She had no time and had to come up with a plan soon.

Jack stepped around her and started back towards the barn. She watched him leave and rubbed her wrist before turning to head for the trailer. She had to think of something fast. She could no longer hang out here. Chance wasn't going to like what happened today. She'd gone from just being a nuisance to a major problem.

JACK POUNDED nails into the loose boards of a horse's stall. Sweat beaded on his face. He finally stopped and swiped at his head with his shirt. When he looked over, he saw Ian standing in the doorway.

Ian was seven years younger than he, while Shane was ten, and Joey had a full fifteen years difference. Since their father died, Jack became the only father figure to all of them. It was a responsibility he accepted right down to his bones since the age of only twenty years old. The ranch. His brothers. The house. His wife. His two sons. All had been thrust upon him, and around him, and in need of him since he was just barely done being a teenager.

Ian was the quiet one. So quiet, he rarely spoke unless he had something important to say. He usually just said it and that was over. Jack couldn't have handled the ranch, his kids, and his brothers in the ensuing months after his parents, and then his wife's death, if not for Ian.

"You working through dinner?"

Jack sighed. "I could and still not make a dent in the work that needs to be done around here."

Ian nodded. "It all gets done eventually."

Jack smacked at the board. "We should hire some decent hands."

"Joe still set on Chance?"

"Yeah, well, we're having a talk tonight about that."

"'Cause of her?"

"Her? Erin? Yeah."

"Joey likes her. You gonna throw her out? Joey won't like that."

Jack rubbed his neck. "I thought about it. But no. Besides, that's not what I meant. Today, I heard her screaming. Like terrified screaming, not kidding around screaming. When I got to the yard, that creep, Chance, had his own sister pinned to the ground, and was rubbing a snake all over her. She was terrified of the snake. It was just a blue racer, but she didn't know that. She was really afraid. He bruised up her wrist. Never seen anything like that in my life."

Ian sat back on a sawhorse, and crossed his arms over his chest. He was quiet a long while. Finally, he said, "I don't think she's like him."

"She also told me she isn't a college student visiting her brother that she first claimed to be."

"Well, sure, considering who Chance is. We suspected that."

"Then what is she?" Ian stared at him through the gloom of the barn, and Jack shifted his feet. "What? Spit it out."

"Right now, she's Joe's girlfriend, whether you like it or not."

"I don't care who Joey's with."

"You do. You've cared ever since you laid eyes on her."

Jack paused and looked up at Ian with the hammer he'd been swinging raised in his hand. "What the hell are you talking about?"

Ian shrugged. "Just saying you seem to care a lot that Joe is with her. But you don't have any cause to ruin it for him. Now, taking care of her brother, yeah, we have the right to do something about that."

"Why is Joey so hell-bent that he stay here? Doesn't he see it? What a shit Chance is?"

"He's just trying to prove himself to you."

"How did you get that from this situation?"

"He's looking to prove himself around the ranch. He's more like your son than your brother, yet his stake in the ranch is the same as yours, and he knows he can't pull the weight you do. No one can. He's looking to make decisions, and throw his weight around. I'm not saying he's right; I'm just saying he's putting himself behind decisions that aren't so good so he doesn't look wrong."

Jack had a feeling Ian was right. "But will the ranch survive while Joey figures all this out before we get rid of Chance?"

Ian shook his head. "It'll last. It'll last as long as any of us are alive."

Jack took comfort in his brother's quiet words.

"Leave Erin out of it. She's not Chance, and she's Joey's business right now. If you want to make more of it than it is, then keep criticizing Erin. If you want Joey to bore quickly of her and move on, as he always does, then let it go."

Jack nodded. "Okay. You have a point. I just don't trust her. It's hard to when she's related to Chance Poletti. It seems suspect she started seeing Joey and Joey is who Chance befriended."

Ian grinned. "Might be. But it might just be that Joey's charm worked on her. Joey has that happen from just smiling at a woman. Joe's that pretty. It's not his fault, it just is."

Jack grinned back. "He is pretty."

Ian picked up a board and started hammering it in. They worked together for the next couple of hours. Jack always appreciated Ian's silence, along with his presence and steadiness. Especially, when compared to the drama evoked by their handsome, flaky, little brother who brought trouble onto the ranch in his childish need to declare his independence from Jack. Jack again felt the tension in his neck. He was getting sick and tired of rebellious teenagers.

CHAPTER 7

*E*rin didn't see Chance that night. Glad to escape him, she went outside to greet another brilliant day. She could easily get used to all this sunlight and aridity. Seattle rained so much, she sometimes felt like moss could sprout from her toes. Who knew that driving four hours could bring her to a place that seemed as far removed from Seattle as if she'd traveled to Arizona?

She breathed in the soft morning air. The sun was warm on her face, and the quiet so intense, she nearly sighed at the sheer pleasure of it. The air was cool and the land was still, other than the occasional sounds of horses and insects.

She glanced towards the barn. Of course, Jack was already out there. The barn stood a couple hundred feet from the house. From there, a long, rectangular, covered arena, filled with sand and lined with more stalls was the place where Jack spent most of his life. If not working somewhere on the ranch, or in the barn, Jack could always be found in the arena. She could view it from the couch side of her trailer. Watching Jack work with different horses, nearly daily, she observed him doing strange things with them, and in return, they did strange, un-horse-like things for him. For example, right now, he had a horse circling him one way, then going the opposite direction by the mere flick of his wrist on the whip-like wand he held. He never touched the horse with it. Then the horse suddenly stopped, and sank down to the sand, before it rose back up. Erin almost applauded.

She avoided going close to the barn, where she knew she wasn't welcome. She learned to spend most of her time down towards the river. She was, however, still an outsider like she'd never been in her life before. The air was so fresh and invigorating, she felt different being there. Healthier and more aware of her surroundings.

But the horses intrigued her. She watched Jack with them all afternoon. Chance came in at one point, but didn't speak to her. She sighed.

Putting her tennis shoes on, she went out to report to Jack that her brother was back. She assumed Jack wanted to know when he came back in order to fire him. She dreaded leaving the ranch. She had no idea where she'd go next; but knew she had no choice. Jack was leading a horse around in a circle. She walked closer and paused along the fence. He stopped and glanced at her.

"Need something?"

"Chance is back. I thought you'd want to know."

He nodded and looked her over. "I don't think Joey's ready to fire him yet."

"And you're willing to let that be?"

Jack shrugged. "Not my call right now."

She looked down at her shoes. *Why now?* When she wanted to write Jack off as an unfeeling asshole, why was he then so not like that? Giving his little brother so much leeway, on a ranch that was clearly Jack's, surprised her. Most older brothers would not put their egos aside.

Erin looked up when Jack started moving again and watched for several moments. Finally, she couldn't take it anymore. "What are you doing?"

He didn't look up at her as he turned the horse. "This filly is only two years old. She hasn't worn a saddle very much, so I'm introducing it to her. Each day a little more, and a little longer, until eventually, she'll be riding me around."

"The training takes infinite patience, doesn't it?"

"Sometimes," he said, stopping the horse. He walked closer to where she stood. "Surprised you haven't gotten Joe to take you on a ride."

She stepped back. "I can't ride. I've never even touched a horse before."

He jerked his head with a startled expression. "How can that be?"

She grinned. "I didn't have one stored in the local parking garage. This is as close as I've ever been to one."

He regarded her. "Go into the barn."

"The barn? I thought I wasn't allowed in there."

He frowned. "Who told you that?"

"No one. I just thought, since, well… I just thought I shouldn't."

"Let me put this filly away. Then I'll show you a horse."

After walking the horse through a gate, he turned and headed into the barn. She went in through the front door. Her stride was unsure. It felt strange to be stepping into a place she'd spent so much time watching strictly from the outside. It was cooler in there, and it smelled, but not unpleasantly. It smelled earthy. Several horses peered at her over their stall doors. The stomping of hooves and thrashing of the beasts filled the silence. Jack came from the other end of the barn and shut the door behind him. He put the leather strips in his hand onto pegs nailed into the barn's walls.

Finally, he looked at her and she shuffled her feet, feeling awkward.

"Are you afraid of them?"

"Not afraid... exactly. Maybe just intimidated," she said with a small smile of self-deprecation. "They're huge."

"They are. Being aware of their size is always something you should remember. Know where your body is when compared to theirs. They startle easily, and their first natural reaction is to run. So they can be jumpy, and having a nearly half-ton animal getting startled near you is something to respect. I always respect that and I've worked with them continuously since I was boy."

"Have you ever been hurt?"

He turned and tugged his gloves off before walking over to a workbench and tossing them down. "Probably more than I should admit. But not from touching them. From doing things I know better than to do with them."

She eyed him. "Like how hurt?"

He grinned and she stepped back. *He was so different looking when he smiled.* His eyes changed, and his whole face lost that usually sour, grumpy exterior. His smile took years off his age. "Like a few broken bones, some sprains and bruises."

She gulped. "Broken bones?"

He shook his head and chuckled when he noticed her reaction. "Don't worry; nothing like that will happen to you. Come here."

She stepped towards where he indicated. The stalls lined both walls of the barn and each had a door with wood on the lower halves and metal bars on top. That allowed the horses to stick their noses through the openings. Their breaths filled the barn with warm humidity. She was short, standing next to Jack, and came only to below his shoulders. Her throat constricted at being so close to him. He wore blue jeans, as all the men on the ranch did, with his brown, worn cowboy boots, and a button-up, flannel shirt. Looking up, she noticed the faint shadow of red hair along his chin. He couldn't grow a thick beard. His black cowboy hat covered his red hair. She felt like she had just stepped into a western historical novel. Who knew men like Jack Rydell existed nowadays? It was so odd. Yet, he looked so right there, in the barn, and in command of all the horses around them.

Standing next to a stall, he reached in to pet a black horse whose head had streaks of gray running through it. "This here is Georgie. She's as sweet as they come."

He handed her a carrot and she gently took it from his hands. They were big, tan hands with calluses on his fingertips.

"Open your hand flat out and let the horse take it from you. She won't bite you, so don't jerk your hand away."

She looked up at him before eyeing the long nose of the horse. And the teeth that were as big as quarters up close. She swallowed, but opened her hand, feeling too embarrassed not to do as Jack said.

She closed her eyes in trepidation until she felt the carrot lifting out of her hand. She opened one eye, then the other as she watched the horse munching through the carrot, almost transfixed by the grinding of the horse's jaws. She glanced up at Jack.

"Can I pet her?"

"Sure. Put your hand out."

The horse nudged her hand, and Erin assumed she was looking for more carrots. She gently touched the top of the horse's nose. The skin felt soft and warm. She smiled at the horse, and was surprised when the horse let her touch her. The horse nudged her and urged her to rub harder.

"Hi Georgie," she said finally. The horse seemed to look at her, and even right into her. She felt like she had to talk to it.

"You want more carrots, huh? Maybe we can talk Mr. Rydell into one more for you."

Jack was intently observing her. She could feel him looking down at her as she stared, utterly transfixed, at the horse. He probably thought she was crazy talking to the horse like that. But it was impossible not to. Like looking at a baby and talking baby talk; it simply had to be done. He didn't comment, but turned and came back with another carrot, which he handed to her. She smiled up at him in appreciation and fed it to Georgie as Jack taught her. She reached her other hand out when Georgie took it to eat.

"How many horses do you have here?"

Jack looked from the horse into her eyes. "It depends on how many we are training or boarding at any given time. Right now, we have close to seventy. But we board more than half of those and I'm training twenty or so, and so is Ian. We are pretty well known for being selective. We get people from all along the west coast asking us to train their horses for them."

Her head spun just trying to figure out the logistics of such an operation. Like how much each horse must eat a day. She kept petting Georgie and the horse turned her head when Erin reached up and scratched her ears. Georgie seemed to really like it. She forgot her hesitation and scratched with more vigor. The horse almost fell over, pushing her head into Erin's hand, which made her smile.

Jack stepped back and crossed his arms over his chest.

"Why do you keep some in the stalls and others outside, running relatively free on the pastures?"

"It depends what they are with us for. Some are merely boarded here. So they are free to roam the pastures, and receive less daily care from us. Others are here specifically for training. While being trained, we have to keep them in stalls to limit contact with the other horses. That way, when I or Ian start working with them, they are eager for the attention and thus more eager to please us."

"I had no idea they were so sensitive. I always thought one horse could be substituted for another."

"No. Not unless you don't give shit who they are. People like that shouldn't own them. Or breed them. Or train them."

"Do you train some of them every day?"

He shook his head and leaned on top of the stall. "No. It depends on lots of factors when and how much I train them. Often, I give them several days break in between training sessions. It's why I can train so many horses at one time… I'm not doing each and every one, every day."

"Are they all different breeds?" she asked, grinning at the way Georgie turned her head into her hand.

"All horses are different, regardless of their breeds. Work with them enough and you'll see how different each one can be. But no, they are not all the same breeds. The ones we own are a breed of mustang known as Nokotas. They are pretty rare with only a thousand or so left that are pure-blooded like ours. We are one of maybe only a hundred owners that still breed them. The rest of the horses are here for training or boarding. We do some breeding and redistributing of Nokotas, however."

"Redistributing? You make it sound like they are just a product."

"It's a business."

She glanced at him and shook her head. Despite his cold, frowning face, she didn't for a second buy that comment. "It's a business for Joey, Shane, and maybe Ian. But not for you. I've seen you working with them. They aren't just a business to you. You respect them all. You'd keep them all if you could, I bet."

His eyebrows wrinkled at her as he frowned. "When have you seen me with the horses?"

"Chance's trailer overlooks the arena."

"And you watch me?"

"I watch the horses. I watch you working with the horses. I'm not sure what you do, but Joey's right when he called you the horse whisperer."

"Joey called me that?"

"Yes. The first day I was here. He thinks you're amazing with the horses, you know. I think he resents it too, though. I don't know; whatever you two have going on is pretty complicated."

"What would you know of Joe and me?" Jack's face went stony. She knew she had said too much, and rambled too much. She shouldn't have. It was none of her business. Especially with Jack. Joey was barely her business, and only a degree more than this man here, who was so suspicious of her.

She dropped her hand from Georgie. "I don't know. I just noticed the tension. I mean…"

"Dad!"

Jack turned at the shout coming from outside the barn. There was a strange rumbling sound. Jack stepped around her and outside. *Damn it.* How could she manage to alienate Jack even more than she already had to date? She didn't intend to. Especially after feeling how stunned she was to find him willing to show her the horses. Or let her inside the barn, something she considered *his* domain.

Dad. She forgot for a moment that Jack was a dad. Jack was the authority here. Jack could easily have her thrown off his land. She let out a long breath.

Turning, she went out of the barn and found Ben, Joey, and Chance on four-wheelers. The rumble of the three ATVs filled the air. All wore helmets and goggles that blocked out their faces.

"We're heading out," Ben yelled to his dad.

"Don't break anything," Jack called back. Then the three of them gunned their vehicles and took off with a cloud of dust trailing behind them. Jack watched them leave and Erin looked up at him.

"You let Chance use your vehicles?"

She almost clapped a hand over her mouth. Why did she persist in pointing out to Jack what a problem her brother was? Was she just trying to get herself kicked off the land sooner, rather than later by continually demonstrating to Jack what an oaf her brother was? The problem was, although she might not have liked Jack, she still respected the place he ran, and hated to think of what her brother might do to it.

Jack looked up from the road to her. "There again: not my decision. It's Joe's. He thinks Chance is fun, which, I'm sure, he is."

Fun? She was surprised Jack cared if anyone had fun. He seemed the type who did nothing but work.

"Why don't you go?"

She looked up sharply. "Go where?"

"With Joey on the four wheelers? They're pretty fun to ride."

He never asked her, she thought before dismissing it. Joey was no more into her than she was into him. They had decent sex together, but that was the extent of their connection. He no more wanted to hang out with her than she did with him.

"Like the horses. I've never been on one. I didn't even know you had them."

"The boys like their toys."

"What? Your boys? Or your brothers?"

"Both. Anyway, try them sometime; they're easy enough."

She eyed Jack, feeling puzzled, no shocked that he was

being so nice to her. Why was he suggesting anything for her to do?

He turned to head back to the barn.

"Mr. Rydell?"

Jack stopped and looked back at her.

"Thanks. For showing me the horses, I mean. And again, for the stupid snake incident with my wretched brother."

Jack turned fully towards her. "What was that, Ms. Poletti? Does your brother often leave bruises on you?"

She dropped her gaze to her feet. "No. Chance usually likes to embarrass me, or torment me with teasing and pranks."

"So that was his idea of a prank?"

"Not so funny, huh?"

"No. Not so funny." Jack's gaze felt heavy on her. She could feel him staring and she looked off towards the river.

"I don't want any shit like that again on my land."

"Oh. Okay. I'll—"

"I didn't mean you," Jack interrupted her. "I meant Chance. No one should treat you like that, but somehow it's worse that it's your own brother. You let me know if he does anything like that again."

She jerked her eyes to Jack's face. It was cold as a stone as his eyes studied hers. She didn't get Jack, and couldn't read him. His obvious distrust of her was evident, but then, these periodic flashes where he noticed her, and cared for her, were stronger than anything Joey ever offered her.

"Okay. Thank you, Mr. Rydell."

He waved her off and disappeared into the barn. She just stood there, staring off at him. Why did he bother to show her the horses when he so obviously wanted nothing to do with her?

~

WHAT THE HELL was wrong with his brother? Jack didn't know what to make of Joey as he began brushing the horse he was about to ride. He told his brother what Chance did to Erin, and Joey responded by taking Chance out for a four wheeler ride? Leaving Erin behind without even a hello? Who taught Joey to treat his girlfriends like that? Certainly, not he.

He might distrust Erin and treated her as such, but Joey didn't. Or at least he trusted her enough to be sleeping with her. The fact that Joey was so blasé in Chance's abusive treatment of his own sister didn't sit right with Jack. Sympathy for Erin percolated for the first time.

He lifted the saddle over the blanket and began tightening the cinch. Erin wasn't exactly like he first thought. Not that he trusted her any more. She just wasn't as manipulative as he originally guessed. She was almost cute about the horses. He was a little surprised to learn not only had she never been near horses, but after weeks on a horse ranch, no one had ever showed them to her. Not *her* brother; nor *his* own brother. Although he didn't prefer her company, he knew it was the only decent thing to do, to *show her the damn horses.*

She was new to everything, from the horses to the snakes to the off-road vehicles. Her big eyes widened at seeing it all. What he first saw as her interest in wanting to get her hands on the ranch, now he was starting to think she was merely big-eyed with surprise. His world was really that far removed from hers.

The guys returned from their ride, and had dinner, but Erin did not reappear to him. He didn't get his brother's lack of interest in her outside of the bedroom. For that, Joey's interest hadn't waned. But why didn't he make any kind of effort to go out with her? Do things with her? Date her? There wasn't a woman in five hundred miles as beautiful as Erin Poletti. Why wasn't Joey making a real play for her?

Jack mounted his horse and decided he wasn't training tonight. He was riding... for himself... and his horse. He spurred Augusta forward and she reacted by shaking her head and rearing onto her back legs. Augusta was half-wild, and half untrained. No one else could ride her. Tonight, however, Jack welcomed the intense concentration, the fire, and the aching muscles as he rode the hell out of the horse by galloping in circles around the arena. He stopped abruptly. Then he started again. He made the horse go in and out of the obstacle course he had set up. He used Augusta to help him pound out his frustration.

She was in his house.

The knowledge kept echoing through his head. Erin was right now in his house, and in his brother's room. Jack glanced at the clock in the arena and saw it was nearly midnight. He'd already put Charlie in bed and Ben was watching a movie. He only came out there to avoid the rest of them. Erin came in while it was still daylight. He heard her voice when he was up with Charlie. He even stayed longer than usual in his younger son's room, just to avoid her. Finally, her voice was quiet and she was in his brother's room.

Winded now, Jack dismounted his horse. Augusta was breathing in long, deep snorts. Her stomach went in and out under the sweat-slicked fur. He took the saddle and bridle off before rubbing the horse down with a towel and patting Augusta's head. After he led his mount into her stable for the night, he replaced the saddle, blanket and bridle where they belonged before locking up the barn office for the night. He crossed the yard and noticed the stars were out tonight. It was still quite cold at night and his breath looked smoky in the chilly air. He pressed his hands deeper into his jacket as he stepped onto the porch, and entered the house. It was dark and everyone was in bed. He grabbed a beer from the fridge, popped the top off, and threw the cap towards the sink. Heading towards his brown leather recliner, he sank his whole body into it.

Erin and Joey were none of his business. Ian was right and their conversation kept replaying in his head. Didn't he make an effort with Erin today? Try to be nice to her? Actually, he was more than a little surprised that he didn't totally hate her company. She asked intelligent questions and seemed genuinely interested in their operation. She almost sweet in the way she handled the horse. And how she conscientiously did as he said. And how she didn't think she was allowed to enter the barn? Why wouldn't Joey fix that?

Of course, it could all be an act. She knew he was suspicious of her.

Jack sat forward when he heard a noise, and glanced toward the stairs when one of the treads squeaked. Erin stopped dead in her tracks and her hand came to her mouth.

"Mr. Rydell," she said, sounding so stunned, it was obvious he startled her. "I didn't think anyone was up."

He took a drink of his beer as his gaze went over her. At least, she was dressed. Her hair was crazy curly like always. She kept it off her face with a headband and a rubber band at the nape of her neck.

"I was just going ho…" Her voice faded as he waited to find out where she was going.

"To our trailer, you mean?"

She nodded and took the steps to reach the bottom of the stairs. "I just thought I should leave. You know, Charlie and all. I didn't think I should be here when he woke up."

Jack considered her. Was she for real? He never gave it that much thought. He wondered sometimes what other things he and his brother missed about raising kids. His kids needed a mother. A grandmother. An aunt. A woman from somewhere to teach them the softer side of life. But his gut twisted knowing what he really wanted for them was *their* own mother. He didn't know how to make up for that.

"We've shared more than one meal with a woman. Four men live here."

"Oh. Still, it didn't seem right."

Jack took another drink of beer and stared at the last embers of the fire that glowed as the only light in the dark room before looking through the dark windows. Then he let out a big sigh as he got up. "Where's Joey?"

She looked away. "Asleep."

His brother was too tired to walk her home? And why was that okay with Erin? Why did he waste time with women who required a modicum of effort on his part just to have sex? Things like buying dinner. Or, at the very least, he would expect to walk the woman he just slept with, home. Apparently, not so for Erin and Joey.

"Right. So you're walking across the yard alone? Do you have a flashlight?"

She shook her head. "I planned to run."

"And twist an ankle in the process? There isn't a paved path across the yard." It wasn't grass or gravel either, but dust and loose rocks. He sighed and set his beer down, then walked towards the door, grabbing the coat he just hung on a chair. He went into utility room off the kitchen and grabbed a flashlight.

"What are you doing?" She came closer to him.

"Cleaning up my brother's mess, as usual."

"I'm not his mess to clean up."

"No. You're not. But you are down here. And he's not. Do you at least have a coat?"

Glancing down, she shook her head sheepishly. He handed his to her. She stared at it as if it would lift its sleeve and bark at her. "I'm okay. It's just across your yard."

"That's debatable," he muttered, now shoving the coat at

her. "You should think about demanding a bit more from your boyfriends, Ms. Poletti."

Then he opened the front door and stepped out. She finally came through while putting an arm in his coat. He clicked the flashlight on and scanned it over the ground, picking up movement.

"Was that a *snake?*" Her voice sounded close to a shriek.

"Yeah. Still want to run across alone?"

She didn't answer, but hovered closer to him. Too close. Her long hair brushed his hand.

He chuckled. "You really don't like snakes, do you?"

Her body shuddered with revulsion. "No. I really don't. They don't bother you?"

"No. Snakes don't bother me."

"I didn't realize there'd be so many here."

"We can go weeks without one, then find several in a row. Seems to be the way of it."

"Is there anything else I should worry about around here?"

"Black widow spiders. The females are poisonous. They are shiny black with a crimson mark of an hourglass on their bellies. They're pretty hard to mistake."

She was quiet after hearing that, but finally sighed. "It's a good thing you told me. I usually pick up spiders with my bare hands and take them outside."

Jack stopped. "You pick up spiders? But you run from snakes?"

She shrugged. "They don't bother me. I know they eat bugs so I don't see the point in killing them. I pick them up and throw them out. Guess that would be a mistake with a black widow."

"I assumed your unreasonable fear of snakes expanded to all critters."

"No. Just a freakish fear of snakes."

Once at the trailer, she turned towards him and slipped the coat off. She handed it back to him. "I was wondering if it's all right if I sometimes went into the barn just to visit the horses."

Jack stepped back, needing space from her face looking up at him.

She wanted to pet his horses? Well, she wasn't exactly turning out to be whom he thought she was. She was polite and respectful; while her brother would prefer to spit on him and his horses then ask permission for anything.

"Yeah, it's fine. Just don't mess with any of the stalls."

"I would never. Thank you, Mr. Rydell."

He waited a moment and then asked, "You like the horses?"

"I do," she said with a smile that set off a dimple on her chin, and made his heart start racing. *Damn it.* Why did he react to her like that?

She opened the door and went inside the trailer as he turned and headed back to his house. Now he had a feeling Erin wasn't what he thought; and that might mean she was going to be a disruption to the status quo that extended far beyond what he first estimated.

CHAPTER 8

*E*rin spent all of her free time in the barn. Jack wasn't sure what to make of her. He found her there first thing in the morning in her now familiar outfit of jeans, sneakers and his brother's coat. She looked up at him as her hand stroked Georgie and quickly exited when he started to work. She also seemed hell-bent on staying out of his way, which was good, because he wanted her out of his way. It was bad enough he had to experience her presence with Joey. He didn't need her in his space too.

But every moment he wasn't in the barn, she was there. He wasn't quite sure what to do with her. Each day she asked new questions: about the horses, their care, and the specific personalities of the different horses. She watched him too. He could feel her eyes on him as he worked through their training. She would stand at the fence and watch him quietly. If he felt even remotely friendly towards her, he would have been flattered over her interest in his job and the horses. But since he didn't want her to be here, and didn't want her to like being on the ranch, he didn't encouraged her to talk to him.

After school, Ben always made a huge effort to find Erin and hang out with her. Jack would see them at the fences or in the barn, talking and laughing. It irritated the hell out of him. The last thing Ben needed was a crush on the woman his uncle was sleeping with. Jack felt his muscles pinching in his neck at the thought of that. She was nothing, but one more headache to a ranch that was, at best, a migraine of worry to him.

Glancing past Erin and Ben, towards the pasture beyond, Jack saw Chance walking towards him. The screw-off was supposed to be loading up one of the flatbeds to pick up some extra hay bales he had ordered from another farmer down the road. Jack could so easily fire him. He'd had enough, no matter what Joey thought. Why then did he still hesitate? Why wouldn't he just fire him?

Erin. He simply didn't fire him because of her. Because she was Joey's business right now, so he couldn't just kick her off his land along with her ne'er-do-well brother.

Jack pressed a hand on the aching in his neck. He glanced at the numbers before him. Not only did the physical demands of the horses never cease, neither did the book-keeping, or the staggering amount of money it took to keep the horses fed and well cared for.

He glanced up when Chance finally spoke. "Need money for the hay."

"Where's the flatbed?"

Chance shrugged. "I'll get it. But I need some petty cash." Chance nodded towards the metal box beside Jack's elbow. He kept a small amount of money for employees to run errands for him. The box was kept locked inside his office.

By then, Erin and Ben had already entered the barn and were getting carrots and feeding some of the mares. Jack's attention strayed for a moment, becoming distracted by

Erin's laugh as the horse nosed her hand. Chance looked at him, then at his sister.

"Too late, boss, didn't your little bro already beat you in fucking her?"

Jack eyed Chance and his fist tightened. He'd never had the urge to smash his fist into another man as often as he did with Chance Poletti. "I was looking at my son. And has it ever occurred to you that she's *your* sister? Why don't you have even a trace of decency towards her?"

"Question is, boss man, why do you?" Chance smirked as he stared into Jack's eyes.

Jack stood up. "Forget the hay run. I'll do it."

"So I'm done here?"

Jack would happily have paid Chance to get out of his face forever. "Yeah, you're done. Give me the keys."

Chance tossed them at him. He should never have trusted Chance with his truck anyway. He snagged them before watching Chance stride out and give his sister an excessively hard shove.

"Ben, come here," Jack yelled out.

Ben glanced back at Jack with a glare, but finally came towards Jack and stared at him, his stance obviously belligerent as he crossed his arms over his scrawny chest. "What?"

Jack tossed the keys at his son. "Get the flatbed hooked up to my truck."

Ben's eyes bulged, and for a moment, the too cool, too bored teenaged look was gone. "By myself?"

"Yeah. You can handle it."

Ben nodded as he grinned and backed up. "I can. Sure."

Jack stood up and started clearing his desk off. He ignored the knot of worry in his stomach. He could not afford for Ben to mess up his truck or the trailer; but he knew if he didn't start trusting Ben more, he'd lose him in rebellion. Almost like he was losing Joey.

"Mr. Rydell?"

He turned and found Erin in the entrance of his office. "What?"

"Uh, well, it's probably not for me to say but..."

"What is it?"

"I noticed Chance staring at that. I just didn't like the look in his eye. You should maybe think about keeping it in your house." Jack turned to see what Erin was talking about and found she was pointing at the petty cash box.

He hesitated. "You think he'll try to steal it?"

"I think he will try. I think he's getting ready to bolt. That's what he does. He up and leaves a place and disappears for weeks at a time. My mom used to get a phone call or an e-mail with his new address, his new job, and his latest lies about how well he is doing."

Jack didn't get her. "Why would you warn me? You know how badly I want to fire him. Why give me the ammunition?"

She glanced away. "I don't want him to steal from the ranch."

From Joey? Jack figured that's what she meant and why she'd put her position there in such jeopardy.

"What happens to you if he does?"

"I'll go stay with friends."

"Why didn't you to start? Why subject yourself to him? He's a terrible brother."

She smiled. "He really is a terrible brother. I wanted to get out of Seattle. I wanted to start a new life. I thought it might be a good jumping-off point."

"So if Chance leaves, you'll go back to Seattle?"

She nodded and looked him in the eye. "I really do know my place here, Mr. Rydell. You've given me a lot of latitude here as it is. I get that."

"I didn't. Joey did. You're here at my brother's insistence."

"I'm here because you let me. I know whose ranch this is, even if Joey doesn't."

He regarded her. She was observant. And right. Was she playing him? And why put herself in immediate jeopardy to warn him? Was there more to her scheming then he could see? Was gaining his trust the goal here? Were Chance and she playing something like good cop/bad cop, and really planning a heist together? He hadn't ruled that out yet.

Jack crossed his office, taking the metal box off his desk. When he stepped out, Erin followed him. As he locked his office up again, he said, "Next year, the ranch will be Joey's ranch too. I'm trying to let him have a bigger role in it. As do all my brothers. It's not just my ranch. Ian runs the horses with me, as well as getting the alfalfa and hay grown each year. Joey and Ben have always helped with the horse care and other miscellaneous issues that come up, anything from fence repairs to sprinkler additions. "

"What's next year for Joey?"

"Joe turns twenty-one. My parent's will was written so when each brother hit the age of twenty-one, he gets his share of the ranch."

She made an odd, strangling-like sound. He glanced over his shoulder at her.

"When Joey turns twenty-one? Meaning he's only twenty now?"

Jack turned fully to her now. She had his attention. "Yeah? You didn't know that? How old did you think he was?"

"I don't know. Mid-twenties. He looks older than twenty."

"He's so pretty, it distracts women. You're not the first," Jack quipped. She seemed genuinely shocked and bothered by Joey's age. Tilting his head he inquired, "How old are you? I guess I thought you were about the same age as Joey."

"I'm twenty-six years old. I didn't know he was that young."

Jack shrugged. "It's not that far apart. Why does it bother you so much? It's not like he's Ben's age. Now that I'd take up issue on."

"Ben's age? He's a little boy. Why would you even make that comparison?"

"Why? Because my son stares at you all the time."

Her jaw dropped open and her eyes bugged. "Ben doesn't look at me. Not like that. I mean…"

Jack crossed his arms over his chest. Did she expect him to really believe her? That she didn't know what kind of effect she had on the exclusively male-dominated ranch?

"You mean what, Ms. Poletti? You think he runs over to you every afternoon, volunteering to help you with anything out of some kind of little brother vibe?"

She shook her head. "I swear to you, I never encouraged Ben, not like that. And I didn't know Joey was so young."

Jack regarded her. Why did she seem so shaken? "Why does Joey's age bother you so much? It didn't before."

"Because it's young. It's not adult. It's not old enough to do… this."

"This?" He saw her hesitate to answer him. Oh, he knew exactly what she was getting at.

"When someone is twenty, barely out of their teens, they take things differently than an adult does."

"You mean casual sex isn't quite so casual to them?"

She winced and turned away from him.

"Next time, ask the guy's age. For that matter, a few other questions might be advisable."

She turned back to him. "The girl who came here the other day. Who was she? She kept glaring at me. I thought she was giving me that look because she had a crush on Ben.

89

You know, she was jealous because I was here. But it wasn't Ben, was it?"

Jack was surprised at hearing that. "Who? Jocelyn?"

"I guess. The girl with blonde hair, who looked about seventeen."

He nodded. "She is. She's one of our neighbor's daughters. She comes over sometimes, and hangs out with Ben or Joey. There are several teenagers that come by and ride the horses for me. The horses get exercise and the teens get to work on riding."

Erin closed her eyes. "I would not have stolen some teenager's... crush. I didn't know. I really didn't know. And I'll tell Ben to go home from now on."

Jack stared at her. She seemed to mean it. She seemed really disturbed by it all. He tilted his head as he considered her. "When I told you I raised Joe, how old exactly did you think that made me?"

She finally looked up at him and scowled as she swallowed. After a long pause, her lips started to tip into a smile. "I thought you were forty-ish."

"Thirty-five. You're not real good at determining ages, are you?"

"You have a fifteen-year-old son," she pointed out quite reasonably.

"Yeah. I do. My wife and I were young."

"Oh, I see."

"Not like you think. We got married when we graduated high school. We meant to have Ben."

She glanced up and studied his face. He pushed his hat lower over his forehead. For some reason her, scrutiny made him feel exposed. "What happened to her? Your wife?"

Through the barn door, Jack saw that Ben had pulled his truck and trailer around and it was idling in the driveway. "I gotta go now. Look, as long as you're not encouraging Ben, it's fine if he hangs out with you."

JACK JUMPED INTO HIS TRUCK, which was a beast of a vehicle like all the men there drove. They had varying styles and colors, but all were pickup trucks. Jack's seemed to be the biggest: a black, crew cab beast with a long bed and dual wheels. The loud diesel roar of the massive engine gunned as he put it into gear and pulled out of the driveway.

She wandered to the river after he disappeared, and couldn't believe their last conversation. It changed everything for her there. And what was even more surprising, was how much Jack voluntarily revealed.

Once at the river, she sat on a rock along its banks. The water went by in a beautiful, sweeping current. She stared into it, lost to the soothing gurgle and hypnotic flow. Joey was twenty years old. She closed her eyes. She would never have slept with him to begin with if she'd had any clue. He didn't look that young, probably because of his blinding smile. She didn't like it for some reason. He was way too young, and should have been with someone like Jocelyn. Not her.

He was immature, simply because he was. *What must Jack think of her?*

Jack? Who cared what Jack thought of her? She frowned; where did that thought come from? She didn't care what he thought. No way. Why would she? He hated her. He distrusted her.

There were times, especially when they were near the horses, he was cordial. Informative. Almost nice. She snorted. He was far nicer than her own brother was to her.

What if she'd had a man like Jack for her brother?

Imagine how different her life might have been with someone like Jack looking out for her; instead of the brother who made it his life's goal to humiliate her.

Or, imagine if she could just look out for herself.

When Jack mentioned she should expect more from her boyfriends, he didn't realize his statement made her nearly lose her footing. It was so simple, so logical, so what most women expected. But no one had ever said something like that before to her. No one. Not one person had ever said, *Hey, maybe you should respect yourself a little more, and expect a little more out of men.*

Her mother was worse than she was; and her brother? Well, he'd just as soon spit on her, hit her, trip her, or mock her, as he would glance at her. And as for a father? There never was a father. Only stepfathers. And multiple boyfriends for Mom.

She leaned back on the cool, lumpy river rocks as anxiety filled her chest. She hated her life and who she was. She irrationally hated her mother for sending her adrift in a world she could not navigate.

She had to leave the ranch. There was no place for her there. And it wouldn't be long before Chance did just as she warned Jack. Perhaps she shouldn't have warned him, but she clearly saw Chance eyeing up the metal box. She'd seen that look before: when Chance stole from their mother and ran off. The only difference was their mother never had a lot of money, but the Rydells did.

She was hastening her own exile, but she couldn't stand by without at least warning Jack.

Jack was suddenly very different to her than what she'd first thought of him. When she first arrived, he seemed so fierce, she avoided even looking at him. But now? Now she couldn't take her eyes off him. As she watched him move and work around the ranch, it was like watching someone do what he was meant to do. Every muscle and movement was in sync. His face grew more handsome the more she knew of him, watched him, and talked to him. He became younger, and when he smiled, she felt a punch in her stomach. It stunned her. She didn't know what it was or why. She didn't know what to make of Jack being only nine years older than she. It changed everything somehow. He wasn't quite so much her dad's age, as she originally thought.

Maybe she preferred he be closer to her father's age, because she was starting to find his personality utterly compelling, far more so than any of the other brothers. Even Joey. And now she knew why. Joey was a kid. Joey was already bored with her. He never wanted to talk much to her. Or, as Jack noted, even do minimal niceties for her.

She needed to get a job. Her money was dwindling with every trip to the market she made to survive there. She was living about as cheaply as one could, but she still needed to get a job. She bit her lip and tears filled her eyelids. How could she get a job without her mother?

Who would fill out all her paperwork? Who could she ask to help her read and write out an employment application? Chance? If she had to ask her brother, she'd have to deal with his taunts, jeers, and name-calling. He loved to point out how stupid she was, *for even he could read*. Even the debauched asshole, Chance Poletti, could read a damn restaurant menu.

Unlike her.

She had tried to learn. With earnest. Both when she was young and later on. She'd finally embraced the obvious truth, she just wasn't that intelligent.

She needed a job in order to survive once her brother took off. And she needed someone to help her get it. She sat up on the rocks. She couldn't ask Jack. She couldn't face the humiliation of asking him. This man, who ran the ranch and raised two kids and his brothers, would never understand how stupid and helpless she felt in the world he nearly totally dominated. She could ask Joey, but she sensed Joey wouldn't care enough to take the time to help her. Who then? Who could help her? Who would want to help her?

She sighed. *Ben.* Ben could read and write and he could help her. He might even have a crush on her, which just might make him want to help her more.

CHAPTER 9

*B*en was crossing the yard toward Shane's shop when Erin caught up with him.

"Ben? Can I talk to you?"

Ben turned at her approach with a smile and his eyes ran over her. She hugged Joey's jacket around herself. She hoped Jack's suggestion Ben had a crush on her wasn't true. "Sure. What's up?"

"I need your help."

"My help? With what?"

He was fifteen and probably wouldn't understand an adult being illiterate. She couldn't trust him with the knowledge; nor should she burden him to keep it a secret. Yet, she needed a job, and she needed money. She had to ask Ben to do this favor for her.

"I need to get a job."

"Okay. There might be something in town. Or you could ask my dad. There's always work around the ranch."

The ranch? She'd never given that a thought. She might be able to work without filling out any forms. She could learn to do whatever Jack wanted, couldn't she?

"Does he hire women?"

"Of course. If they can the do the job. He isn't like a chauvinist or anything."

"I don't ride."

"Oh. Well, in that case, town might be a better place."

Erin licked her lips, closing her eyes before slowly opening them. "I can't fill out the employment applications."

"Why not?"

"I can't—I can't read, Ben."

His eyes rounded. "Are you for real? Why not?"

She shrugged and glanced up towards the tops of the mountains. "We moved a lot and I got lost in so many schools, somehow, I never managed to catch up. Even additional reading supports didn't work. Eventually, I gave up. I finally got a job. I'm a hard worker. I just can't read."

"What do you want me to do?"

"I need someone to help me fill out the forms."

"Why me?"

"Because my brother will mock me, and everyone else wants me to leave here. I thought maybe you would help me and not think I'm totally stupid."

Ben's face changed towards her. She wasn't sure why. "I'll help you."

"You will?"

"I will. And I won't tell anyone. I promise."

Impulsively, she got on her tiptoes and hugged Ben's tall, lanky body. He awkwardly patted her back. She almost smiled at how uncomfortable and young Ben seemed. His entire neck and face turned red.

"I'll go to town first thing tomorrow and see what I can find."

"All right, just let me know."

Erin turned to walk away, but first, she smiled at him.

"Thank you, Ben, you have no idea how much this means to me."

~

ERIN SPENT all day in Pattinson, which was a far larger town than River's End and even sported its own McDonalds. She was looking for employment and returned to the ranch mid-afternoon, carrying several application packets. Now all she had to do was figure out which job she could do while remaining an illiterate idiot. She was a good waitress. Everyone thought she was brilliant when she managed to remember all the orders and drinks without ever writing anything down. Little did anyone know it was purely survival; she simply couldn't write it down under pressure or quick enough, so she had to remember it all. It was her best chance at work around there, or so it seemed.

That afternoon, and the following three, Ben ventured out to the trailer and helped her painstakingly make her way through four applications. She could write letters decently enough, but her spelling was almost indecipherable. That would need complete reworking.

When they finally finished, she sighed and closed her eyes in relief. The task exhausted her. She could never thank Ben enough for his help. He was kind and straightforward, with no comments about her stupidity or slowness. The next day, she couldn't wait to turn them all in, hoping she got a call back. She had to use the Rydells' phone number as her contact, along with the ranch as her place of residence. Ben promised to try and field the calls while not mentioning to his dad that she used the ranch address as her home.

Needing to relax, Erin changed from her skirt and sandals into her jeans and tennis shoes. She started to head out towards the barn when she heard her name being called.

Joey was jogging towards her. She hadn't seen him since discovering his young age. An uncomfortable warmth filled her and she felt more awkward with Joey now than before they slept together.

"Jack mentioned you'd never been around the horses. He kind of reamed my ass for not noticing that, but anyway... you want to come for a ride with me?"

Erin gulped back her fear. *Get on a horse?* Sure, she loved to reach into the horses' stalls and pet their silky noses and necks. But stand right next to a horse? Or get up on one?

"I don't know how to ride."

"I know. It's not hard. I'll teach you."

"Really?"

She felt a spark of interest. When would she ever get such a chance again? Perhaps she could learn to ride a horse? She licked her lips and straightened her shoulders. "Okay. I'll try."

He grinned and she blinked, still just as surprised by his blonde good looks and killer smile as before. No wonder she failed to notice how young his eyes were.

Joey led her into the barn and spent the next twenty minutes saddling his mount. Then he pulled Georgie out of the stall and saddled her. Erin watched with utter fascination. Staring up at Georgie, the horse she was supposed to ride, sent beads of sweat trickling down her back.

"Are you sure I can do this?"

"Sure. We've had lots of novice riders here. Georgie's a stop and go horse. She doesn't do much except follow my mount, or try and eat along the trail. All of our horses are trained the same. I'll show you the commands, but with Georgie, you pretty much only need to hold on and keep your balance. Come here; I'll help you up."

Joey lifted one of Erin's legs to help her mount Georgie before placing them into the stirrups, which he adjusted. He handed her the reins, showing her how to hold them and said to barely move her fingers when indicating which way she wanted to turn, or stop. She was amazed at the barely-there pressure she needed to exert on the reins before the horse responded. It was amazing how sensitive the horses were.

"Worst case, pull one rein as hard as you can, so the horse's nose is facing towards its butt. They can't run if they're going in a circle."

She listened closely as Joey explained how to squeeze her knees, using firm, but gentle pressure against the horse's stomach to match her steering commands. Her butt already hurt and her body was taut with nerves, so Joey told her to relax, as the horse could sense her anxiety. She tried to breathe as Joey advised, and focused far out in front of her, instead of on the horse's ears, which felt more natural. Joey explained that watching their ears caused the horse to look straight down. However, if she looked ahead to where she was going, apparently, so did the horse. She had no idea horses were so sensitive, or that their massive heights and great muscles took so little to control. She felt sure she had to use more strength in holding back a dog than she did in prompting Georgie through the few commands Joey tested her on out in the corral. Finally, after fifteen minutes, Joey mounted his horse, which was named Commander, and started up the driveway with a click of his tongue. Georgie followed right behind Commander, and suddenly, she was riding a horse.

She gulped back the fear, and clutched onto the saddle horn with every ounce of her being. She told herself to breathe in and out, as if she were in yoga class. She ordered her stomach to cease cramping and churning with nerves. She was terrified. The horse was so high off the ground. Although Georgie plodded along as slowly and calmly as a golf cart, she could feel the awesome power beneath her. If the horse chose to take off, or turn, or abruptly stop, Erin would be at her mercy.

She was very aware of the four heavy hooves that stomped down, and how easily they could trample her if she fell. She barely registered her eyes on the trail Joey followed. So busy remembering all the instructions on how to ride, there was no way she could enjoy the beautiful landscapes they were traversing. Until they began to climb. Looking around, she saw they'd taken off from the dirt road and were now... nowhere. Not on any trail or road. They were crossing over sagebrush and fresh, untrodden grasses. There were pine trees all around them and nothing else. They climbed up one hill, then another. However, Erin nearly closed her eyes through it all. She held the reins tightly around the saddle horn and her breathing increased. She thought she was going to faint if she looked down.

They were climbing up a freaking mountain!

Being directly over the ranch now, she looked below, and saw the most incredible view of her life. The ranch, in all its glory, spread out over the valley and the river was now only a small, shiny line, stretching this way and that across the valley floor. She was on what felt like the top of the world. The sky seemed much closer, and the world below oh so tinier.

If her horse misstepped, even by six inches, she would surely plummet to her death down the mountain, which dropped precipitously below her. Having come up the mountain from one side, the one which was a gentle rise of hills, now they were nearly at the top of the mountain. It dropped a good two hundred feet to the road, straight below them.

She wanted to turn around. But there was no way she could. She was stuck. The only escape from this stretch of trail was to continue forward. Her throat felt so swollen with the anxiety lodged there, she couldn't even yell at Joey. Her breathing grew more rapid as her head felt lighter; she was getting dizzy. She was going to die. That's all she could think of as she stared straight down. Then she saw the small, dirt footpath her massive horse was supposed to follow. It was no more than a deer trail, if that.

She knew she was going to faint. She could feel her chest tightening, and her breathing grew more difficult. Something was wrong.

"Joey," she finally managed to croak out through her ever-tightening throat. "Joey… help me!"

Joey turned in his saddle. He hadn't so much as glanced at her once while they rode. His eyes widened and his mouth dropped when he finally saw her. He stopped his horse, dropping the reins and jumping down. The horse didn't move a single step. Joey ran to her.

"What's the matter?"

"Can't breathe," she said, starting to really panic now.

"You're white as a sheet. Okay, okay, Erin, calm down, and take some deep breaths. Are you scared?"

She nodded, but wanted to scream. *Was she scared?* She was terrified. She was about to die from plunging down a steep mountain. After being thrown from a monstrously large animal. And Joey wanted to know if she was scared?

He looked genuinely surprised by her reaction. "Okay, let's get you down. It's okay. Really, you're fine."

He helped her down off her horse and pulled her uphill from the horses by a few feet before setting her down on the grass. They sat fifty feet from the top of the mountain, and when she looked down, she saw they were crossing a narrow, flat section before the land completely became a steep rock that dropped straight down. There wasn't a hint of humanity, and only the strange, far-off sound of wind moving over the grasses. It was almost eerie in its silence.

"I think you're having a panic attack."

A panic attack? She put her head in between her knees. No way. It had to be more than that. She had to be dying, judging by the pain in her chest, and the dizziness of her head. Joey kept encouraging her to breathe. Then to slow down her breathing and just think calming thoughts. She did that until she opened her eyes and saw the view: she was indeed *on top of a mountain* with two horses grazing not twenty feet from her. There was no way down. She was petrified. It felt like concrete had been poured around her.

After another ten minutes, Joey quit talking. Finally, he asked, "Are you okay?"

She shook her head no. Joey looked around, utterly lost. "Maybe I should go get Jack."

Erin lifted her eyes. She didn't want Jack to know, but her head was swimming and she couldn't speak. Joey looked into her eyes. "Yeah, I'd better go get him. I'm not sure what else to do. You have to get on the horse, or walk down; you can't stay here."

She shook her head adamantly in fear. She wasn't moving.

Joey stood up over her, running his hands through his hair. "I'm going to get Jack. It won't be long. I promise. Okay?"

No! So not okay. He intended to leave her on top of this mountain all alone? She thought she'd pass out from the dizzying fear of that suggestion. She couldn't look down. She had to turn her head towards the upside of the hill. Joey finally patted her shoulder with more banal words of comfort. Then he left her there, all alone, dragging Georgie by a lead rope behind him. Erin pulled her legs up to her chest, and curled up into a ball as tears flooded over her eyes and she tried to remember to breathe in and out.

⤳

JACK WAS FINISHING up some invoices in the office when he heard the stomp of horse hooves and loud yelling. He stood up and ran out of the office, through the barn and into the yard to find Joey riding hell-bent down the driveway towards him with Georgie right behind him, saddled and riderless. *What the hell?*

Joey stopped his horse. In a rush, he yelled, "Erin's up on the mountain. She had some kind of freak-out and nearly fainted. I don't know what the hell is wrong with her, but she refuses to move. She's really freaked out right now and I don't know what else to do."

Jack grabbed Joey's mount and held Commander's head still. "You left Erin up on the mountain?"

"She refused to come down."

Jack glanced at the saddled horse. "You took her up The Horn? On Georgie? What the hell were you thinking? She's never even been in a corral with a horse before."

Jack swore as Joey swung his leg and dismounted. "Maybe I could get the four-wheeler up there."

"It's too steep. Trail's too small."

Joey looked stumped. "I didn't know what else to do."

Jack swung his leg up and over Joey's horse. "I'll be back."

He left without another word to his little brother to clean up yet another mess. What the hell was Joey thinking? Jack ran his horse up the mountain at a swift canter, leading Georgie behind. He slowed when he hit the trail across the rim of the mountain called The Horn.

Jack spotted Erin about a third of the way across the mountain, in the worse spot of the trail, from her point of view. He glanced down. The trail was skinnier there, merely old game trails that stretched across the sloping pasture and ended with the rocky drop-offs that plunged towards the valley below. It was one of Jack's favorite spots. He and Lily used to ride up there a lot. First as kids, then as teens, and finally, young and married. They came there to get away, and be alone, or make love, talk, and share their lives. Jack sighed as the memories revisited him.

Now, however, he saw Erin Poletti curled up into a small ball off on the side of the trail. She looked miserable. Her head was down and her eyes were scrunched tightly shut like a small child who imagines the monsters in her closet.

He slowed his horse and Commander reacted to the slightest pressure. He dismounted and dropped the reins. All of his horses were trained to stay when their reins were dropped. It was essential to trail-riding that he trust his horses to stay put if he had to get off to cut a tree limb, or adjust his gear. Or, as in this case, to save a woman.

He stood over Erin and she turned towards him, opening her eyes finally. Tears streaked her cheeks and she was ghastly white. He put his hands on his hips as he tried to figure out what to do and glanced off towards the horizon.

He eventually walked towards her and sat down. He was pretty sure rushing her wasn't going to help her predicament.

Sitting down, he stretched his long legs out before him and leaned back on an elbow. Then he picked up a strand of grass and ran his fingers over it. He was quiet as he waited for her to get past her panic attack long enough to talk to him. Lately, it seemed like all he'd been doing was fixing Joey's mistakes. What was Joey thinking by bringing Erin up there? He told Joey she'd never even touched a horse before now. Why would he drag her up there across the mountain? Despite his distrust of her, he was pretty sure she wasn't faking it. But he was not so sure how he could get her down.

CHAPTER 10

*T*he snorting and stomping of horses alerted Erin that Jack was coming for her. He appeared around the corner with his horse going way too fast over the too narrow trail. She closed her eyes at the pitch of her stomach and pictured him simply falling off to the side and tumbling to his death. He stopped his horse and jumped down. She was mortified at being caught up there, but even more afraid to look up at him. She couldn't stand to look out towards the horizon. She stared at her feet, anticipating his derogatory words to her for being such a wimp.

But… he didn't speak. He came closer to her, and sat down, stretching his long, muscled legs out beside her as he leaned back on his elbow. After several long moments without a word to her, she finally peeked at him from the corner of her eye. His hat was pulled down low, and he was chewing on a blade of grass while looking out towards the valley. He seemed as relaxed as one might be sitting on the couch watching a favorite movie. She concentrated on his dark blue–jean-clad legs that stretched a foot past her own, and the boots that he wore so often, she wondered if he took showers with them on. They seemed as much a part of him as other men might wear a watch.

She swallowed the lump in her throat. "I can't get on that horse again."

"Okay."

"I can't walk either."

He nodded and his gaze finally shifted to her. His startlingly bright blue eyes stood out against his red hair. His eyebrows that now arched up over his eyes were a darker auburn to his red hair. He had a few freckles that seemed almost lost in the tan he managed to hold onto throughout the winter. He grabbed the blade of grass from his mouth and tossed it. "So what do you have in mind?"

To cry. That's why she was almost physically ill. She didn't have anything in mind and didn't know how to get down. She sucked on her lower lip while trying to hold back her tears. She could not spill them in front of Jack. It would only emphasize what a pointless, worthless, inept woman she was.

He continued to look at her and she dropped her gaze to her knees, now tucked up to her chest.

"Are you only afraid of heights and snakes?"

"I didn't know that I was. I've never experienced something like this."

"Why didn't you tell Joey to stop?"

"I did as soon as I realized where we were."

"As soon as you realized?" He repeated her words, but his tone conveyed he had no clue what she was talking about.

"Yes. My eyes were closed. When I reopened them, we were here."

His gaze settled on her face. She turned completely away. She didn't want to see the smirking, or his anger directed at her. But... suddenly, Jack was *laughing*. He was laughing out loud at her. She looked up with a frown. Why would he laugh at her? He was shaking his head as he pushed off his elbow and sat up.

"So you were holding onto the horse with your eyes closed?"

"Yes."

"My brother's such an idiot. He didn't notice that?"

She shrugged with surprise. He thought Joey was the idiot? She thought for sure he'd say she was the idiot. She dared to peek up at him.

"He should have noticed and stopped. He should have never brought you off the trail and certainly not across here."

"Oh. He said he'd ridden with lots of novice riders."

Jack grunted. "There're novice riders, and then there's you. You didn't even know how to touch a horse through a stall door."

"I didn't want to look like a jerk. I thought I could do it. But the horse seemed much taller once I was on it, and all I could think of was how easily it could bolt. Then I thought if I closed my eyes, maybe I could make the ride, and then… we were up here. And I all I could picture was one of the horses losing its footing and hurling both of us to our deaths. The trail is skinnier then one I'd ever walk on. How can a horse with four legs stay on it if I can't with two legs?"

Jack was fully grinning at her and she blinked in surprise. Jack never grinned at anything she said. But now he was, and she couldn't figure out why. Or why he didn't seem all that mad at her. She felt sure that once Joey told him where she was, Jack would have been furious at her and ordered her down without even getting off his horse.

"Horses are more sure-footed than any human. They won't fall off the trail. They've all been across here dozens of times. But you couldn't have known that. You should have started off by riding the horse in the fenced arena. Maybe someday, I can show you properly; that is, if this experience doesn't scare you forever from riding horses."

"More like, if I make it off here alive."

He shook his head, still smiling. His smile made his eyes sparkle, and his face appeared almost boyish. Almost fun. She didn't expect this out of the stern-faced Jack. She liked it. She liked seeing him for once not looking at her with total disdain and distrust.

"I'll get you down." The confidence in his words was almost reassuring. And she almost felt like she could trust him.

His gaze settled on the valley and he nodded towards it. "Sure is a pretty spot, huh?"

Pretty spot? It might be the last place she ever saw, and Jack thought it was a pretty spot? If she were actually interested in the view, she couldn't have called it pretty. It was a breathtaking, soul-stirring, coming-to-God kind of beautiful. They were on top of the world, which spread out before them and even the largest trees appeared small from where they sat atop the mountain. The ranch below them had an aerial view usually only made possible from airplanes. The river meandered in a twisting ribbon near spotted squares of farmland, orchards, and cleared housing sites that looked minuscule below them.

"It would be the most beautiful spot I've ever seen, if I were looking at it from a flat, scenic, turnout on a highway."

"Probably why Joey brought you up here."

"Why would he bring me on this impossible trail?"

He shook his head. "Because we've been riding it since we were kids. All of us have, my boys too. He probably didn't think a thing about it."

She jerked her head back in reproach. "You don't let Charlie up here."

Jack laughed again. "Yeah, I let Charlie up here."

She shuddered. Were they crazy? She thought Jack was a better, more reliable and vigilant father than that.

Jack pushed his hat back and scratched his hair before sliding the hat off and flipping it next to him. He shook his head and his red hair fell into place. She looked away, wondering why she suddenly found his movements so compelling to watch, so interesting, so... almost sexy.

The thought riled her. Jack was sexy? No. Jack was scary, intimidating, and kind of mean even. But not sexy. He was too stern, too old, too critical of her for him to be sexy.

But then, he had a body of a lean, muscled cowboy. He had hair that caught sun and light like it was on fire around him. He had a smile, though rare, that set her pulse skittering in a weird sensation.

She stared down again at her feet; not the best place for her thoughts. She slept with his brother. There was no getting around that.

Although, what if they could ever turn into friends?

But no. Chance's legacy most likely made that reality impossible.

"This was Lily's favorite spot on the ranch."

She turned her eyes up to his profile. Jack rarely revealed personal information to her, or in front of her.

"Lily was your wife?" She knew that Lily Rydell was Jack's wife, but thought to say it if only to keep Jack talking to her.

He nodded. "Yeah."

"When did she die?"

Jack glanced at her. She blushed and dropped her head, staring harder at the grass clumps surrounding her feet. Maybe that was asking too much.

"More than five years ago now."

"Charlie was young."

"Charlie was way too young then." Jack's voice changed, and became huskier.

"You were all too young. I'm sorry. It must have been terrible for you, and for the boys. Does Charlie remember her?"

"Not much. But Ben does."

She wanted to ask more, and know more, to know everything. But it wasn't her right or her place, and she feared it would piss Jack off at her. This was about the friendliest he'd ever been with her, and she did not want to ruin the moment.

Jack finally looked at her. "You're looking calmer now. You think we could try to get out of here? Rain's not too far off."

She glanced up at the edge of the sky where he pointed. It did look dark.

He had distracted her long enough to get her panic under control so he could get her out of there.

"How? How do I get out of here?"

"Any chance you'll let me lead you out of here on Georgie? You can close your eyes and hold onto the saddle horn. You don't have to do anything."

The horses stood waiting where Jack left them. Their heads were down as they calmly munched on the grass springing up green and lush around them. They seemed calm and even majestic against the sky and valley beyond them. But to get back on one of them? And ride down the mountain? *No.* She could not do that.

But she didn't have a choice now, did she? What if Jack simply got disgusted and left her there? Her hands immediately became moist with sweat. *No!* She could not be stranded here alone again either.

Her stomach knotted as the dizziness swept over her head and right down into her gut.

Jack jumped to his feet. "By your face, I'm guessing that's not going to happen."

"I want to. I just… I can't. I know you can't understand how I don't just buck up and do it but…"

He stood over her with his hands on his hips, and his elbows out. "I do understand. I don't think you're faking it. If I did, I would have long ago gotten you down."

"Oh," she said with a hesitant glance his way. "Then what do I do?"

"You ride with me."

Her eyes jerked up to him and he looked huge over her. Ride with him? As in, on his horse? *No. No way.* That required still getting on a horse in the middle of a mountain, and it too, included Jack touching her. She didn't touch Jack. She could not touch Jack. That was way too awkward to contemplate.

"I can't do that."

"It's about all you can do. You know I can handle the horses. You can trust that much, huh?"

She nodded. Yes, she knew he could handle any and all horses. But with her on the same one too?

She stood up slowly and her legs shook while her stomach pitched. She stared at his hair rather than down or across the valley.

"How? There can't be enough room."

"I didn't say it would be comfortable. I'm just saying it'll get you down."

She stared at the saddle. How could they fit? That thought kept her mind engaged rather than contemplating if she would panic once atop the horse and teetering above the valley.

"Where do I sit?"

"With most people, I'd have you hanging onto the back of me. You, however, are too afraid to even do that. So you'll have to sit in front of me."

"But the saddle horn is in the way."

"Just be glad you're a small adult," he said, turning away from her and walking towards his horse. He grabbed the reins and led the horse towards her. She stepped back, almost stumbling in terror.

Jack let go of the reins and moved closer to her. Before she could realize his intentions, he reached out, grabbed her waist, and lifted her up. She exclaimed her surprise and instantly struggled out of sheer annoyance. He was manhandling her! She couldn't believe it. Then, that quickly, he sat her on the horse. She opened her mouth in shock to be up there, then looked down, and almost tumbled off as wave after wave of dizziness overcame her. She groped for the saddle horn and squeezed it with all her strength as she slammed her eyes shut.

She was going to die.

Jack mounted the horse behind her. He swung a leg over the saddle and straddled the horse, perched on each stirrup. He one-handedly scooted her forward. Her crotch banged painfully into the saddle horn and she was forced to open her eyes. She grasped the small knot of the saddle horn as her body strained to get past it, feeling like a damn contortionist. Then the heat of Jack's body was behind her and he sat half in the saddle, half on the back of it. The old westerns made it look romantic to ride in tandem. However, they didn't show how much pain and discomfort it involved, which made it awkward and awful. And it put her way too close to Jack.

His arms came around her and she jerked back in surprise, causing her head to smack into his chin.

"Hold still," he muttered right into her ear, his tone grumpy. His breath was warm over the side of her face and she froze in horror. She didn't mean to do that to him. His head had to be ringing. She just hadn't expected him to be all around her.

"I need the reins. Don't move."

He reached around her again and pulled the reins up. His arms stayed around her and rested just in front of the saddle horn as he inelegantly steered the horse.

"This isn't going to work."

"It'll work. I told you; it's just not going to be comfortable."

"What if the horse bolts? You can barely control it."

He exhaled and she could feel his chest deflating behind her. She was way too close to him. She should *not* be able to feel Jack's body, any of his body, and especially not against her own. "The horse won't bolt on me."

"You don't know that."

He sighed even louder. "I do know that. Just close your eyes and I'll get you off the damn mountain."

She slammed her eyelids shut, gripping onto the horn until her hands cramped. She felt the horse starting forward at Jack's soft clicking sound. Thankfully, the horses reacted to the slightest signals and pressure that Jack gave them. Then they were moving. The horse's sway and gait made them bump and grind together as it moved. She tried to ignore it, and tried not to think about what the trail looked like, or the drop-off beside her.

Jack's arms encircled her. That's what finally overcame her panic. Jack's arms were all around her, and nearly holding her. She could feel his muscles flex and sway as he guided the horse down the mountain, and his thighs cradling her, along with his hard chest, as she jolted against him.

It was strange, and such a different feeling. Every nerve ending hurt from how she was seated while trying to hold her body rigidly away from him. Yet, she was aware of every muscle he had and the way he moved. Then finally, he stopped and she opened her eyes. They were down. Now off the steep section of mountain, they were back on the rolling slope that had brought them there.

She let out a breath of relief. "Oh, thank goodness."

He chuckled behind her and his breath stirred her hair as he laughed. She was surprised he was so understanding about everything. He was being nicer than he ever had been to her.

He stood up in the stirrups, and released the pressure that kept her pushed into the horse's neck. With a swing of his leg, he was off the horse and just below eye level to her. She had to look away and felt suddenly different with him.

He waited patiently as she finally, clumsily, got her foot into the stirrup and was able to stand up, swing her leg over the horse, and dismount. Her legs shook with cramps as the blood started flowing and the adrenaline dissipated.

She glanced up at him, licking her lips with raw nerves. "Thank you, Mr. Rydell."

He nodded, and she stared, caught by the power of his gaze and the deep blue of his eyes.

"You're welcome."

She had to look away, feeling confused by the sudden embarrassment flowing through her. And the sudden rush of heat in her cheeks.

"Now, I walk. I'll see you later."

He grabbed her elbow as she started to turn. He was frowning. "I'm not going to leave you up here."

"Oh. Okay."

He looked at her oddly. "Why does that so surprise you? It's strange country for you. You could get lost, or run into another snake, or who knows what else could happen to you."

Why? Because every person in her entire life would have easily left her up there and taken the easier horse to ride home. Because her brother would have left her in the middle of the mountain and laughed as he returned home alone. And then not checked to see if she ever showed up alive.

She exhaled a lungful of pent-up air from her mouth. She was safe and Jack wouldn't abandon her. "I'm sorry about all of this. I know you hate me staying on your ranch. You hate my brother. And it was really kind of you to come after me, and not leave me up there."

He leaned down and grabbed the horse's reins. Georgie was still loosely connected by a lead rope to the saddle and had followed as easily as Jack promised she would.

"No one could have faked that kind of fear. I don't punish people for not knowing how to ride; and it was Joey's fault for getting you stranded. So we can blame Joey. And really, Ms. Poletti, judging how people treat you shouldn't be compared to the way your brother treats you. Because your brother is shit," he said, his tone becoming fierce. He looked right at her. "But you are not."

Her back straightened with surprise. He didn't think she was like her brother? That was news to her. Jack didn't wait for her response. He started leading his horse down the slope and she fell in step several feet behind Georgie. She followed Jack around the pines and sagebrush, until eventually, they hit the dirt road before finally arriving at the ranch.

Joey came running from the porch with Ben not far behind him. "Erin! What took so long? I was starting think something awful happened."

She looked past Joey, toward Jack's back. He turned his head, met her eyes, and glanced at Joey too. Jack just smirked, shook his head, and kept walking until he disappeared into the barn with the horses behind him. She turned back towards Joey, suddenly furious.

"I could have died up there! What were you thinking by taking me up there? Taking me anywhere, but in the arena to ride? I told you I didn't know how to ride."

Joey stepped back in obvious surprise. She'd never lost her temper with him. She'd never spoken to Joey in anger, but always in flirting and fun. But he put her in a dangerous situation, and with Jack as her only witness, she knew she might be hastening the date when she would get kicked off the ranch, but in that moment, her anger far outweighed her caution.

Joey threw his hands up as if in surrender. "I didn't know you were that bad. You should have said you were scared up there."

"My eyes were closed. If you'd just once glanced back, you'd have known that." She suddenly spun on her heel and stormed off to her trailer before slamming it shut on both of them.

JACK CHUCKLED TO HIMSELF. He couldn't hear Joey's words, but heard loud and clear what Erin said, repeating word for word some of what he told her. He busied himself unsaddling the horses and rubbing them down. Joey should have done it, but he guessed by now, poor Joey was confused by what he'd done to the usually flirtatious, mild-tempered Erin Poletti. Joey really had no idea how scared Erin was.

She was so beautiful. It was hard not to notice when she was nearly pinned in front of him. Her head was just below his chin and her dark curls sprang off her head and flew into his face before sticking to his lips. Her hair smelled good. Like sunshine. And softness. Like anything but horses and the ranch. So he liked her in his arms. So what? He wasn't dead. It meant nothing.

Jack sighed when he saw how woebegone his brother looked when he stared after Erin. But… she honestly thought that once out of danger, he'd leave her up there, all alone in the mountains, in what, to her, was forsaken country. That didn't sit well with him. She really didn't think she deserved much from anyone. Including Joey.

He wasn't sure what to do with the woman Erin Poletti was turning out to be, compared to the woman he pegged her to be initially. Maybe with this Poletti, his gut had failed him completely.

CHAPTER 11

*E*rin hadn't spent much time in the main house other than the few occasions when she'd gone into Joey's room late at night. He didn't invite her to dinner, and she never asked to come. They had sex, and she went back to Jack's trailer. She had little interaction with Jack's brothers or his younger son. She knew Ben because he was friendly to her every afternoon, coming to see if she wanted to hang out with the horses. He was a nice kid. Nicer than anyone else was to her at this point in her life.

One afternoon, she was crossing along the yard when she noticed Charlie sitting on the porch. He was crying. She stopped dead and looked around. There wasn't another man in sight. Charlie held his head down and no one else was close by. She hesitated. She didn't feel right even going up to the front door. That was for guests and she wasn't even the hired help. So... she would what? See what was wrong with Charlie? But... how could she ignore the kid sitting there, heaving his guts out in tears? What if something was seriously wrong? What if he needed medical attention?

She jogged across the yard, went up the steps and sat

down next to Charlie. He scooted away, and deliberately angled his body unnaturally just to stay away from her. He pushed a hand at his eyes and dirt mingled with the wet streaks.

"Are you okay, Charlie?"

He sniffled and turned closer to the porch railing. Where Ben was outgoing and talkative, Charlie seemed shy and reticent with both his emotions and thoughts. He was more like Jack.

"Something happen at school?" He had gotten off the bus just minutes before and his backpack was still behind him.

She waited awhile before stretching out her legs. "I went to fifteen schools in thirteen years. I know all about bad days."

He glanced towards her and she took that as a sign to continue. "My mom moved a lot. She didn't manage to stay in the same school boundaries very long. I even went back to the same school twice."

Charlie looked at his feet. "I don't have a mom."

"I know you don't. I didn't have a dad. It really sucks, huh? At least, you have your uncles too. I had only my mom, and she was often distracted."

"My dad's busy too."

"But not distracted. When he's with you, he isn't distracted, is he?"

Charlie shook his head no and rubbed his eyes again, seeming to size her up. Finally, he sighed and said, "My school has a Tea each year for Mother's Day. If your mom can't come, you're supposed to bring your grandma or aunt or some other person who matters to you. They don't say it needs to be a girl, but eveyone always brings a girl. Almost all of them bring their mom or grandma. I always bring my dad. There's no mom for me to bring. Or any other woman."

Erin paused. The kid was right, there seemed to not be

one woman in his life. As Jack told her that night he walked her home: there was far too little female influence in the Rydell sphere. Her heart blipped thinking of the stern cowboy Jack going to a mother's day tea for his son's school.

"Isn't there a family friend or something?"

Charlie shook his head no again. "There's Lynnie. But everyone knows she's our housekeeper."

Well, crap. It wasn't like she could volunteer to take him. The woman who was having casual, meaningless sex with his uncle wasn't exactly whom she pictured should be invited to a Mother's Day Tea.

"What about that girl, Jocelyn?"

"She's a stupid friend of Ben's."

"Hmm. So that's a no?"

He shook his head, and turned towards her. "Who are you?"

Erin was taken aback. She was barely introduced to Charlie, but really, she'd been on the ranch for more than a month. "I'm Chance's sister."

Charlie rolled his eyes. "I know that. I mean, aren't you Uncle Joe's girlfriend?"

Erin wanted to roll her eyes at that question. And how did Charlie pick up on it? "I'm... yes, I guess I'm Joey's friend." *No. No, she so wasn't.*

"Couldn't you come with me?"

Erin's mouth opened. *No.* Jack would kill her if she consented to that. Not to mention the complete inappropriateness of the situation. She couldn't pretend to be his mother at a school tea party. Or even someone special in his life. She wasn't.

"I don't think that would work."

Charlie stood up and fisted his hands. "Look around, you're the only woman here. Who am I supposed to take? There isn't anyone. It's not like you're doing anything else.

You're always just here, doing nothing. Why couldn't you do this for me?"

Erin stood up. "Charlie, you don't even know me."

"So what? You're a girl."

"It's not appropriate."

"And going alone is? Or to be the only kid there without my mom? Or grandma? The only kid to bring their dad? It makes me feel stupid." Plus how did they still have things like mother day celebrations? How could they not be conscious of what that might cause for the kids who don't have mothers or grandmothers in their lives? Or maybe if they have two dads? But from what she got out of Charlie it seemed that was encouraged but the other kids seemed to bring their moms and Charlie just wanted his own mother.

Erin's heart pinched. He was so young not to know his mom.

"I don't think your father would allow it."

"What won't his father allow?"

Erin whipped around when Jack's voice came from behind her. He was standing at the bottom of the stairs. He raised an eyebrow at her and then at Charlie, and his eyes narrowed when he saw Charlie's tears. He came up the stairs, his boots clattering on the wooden steps with each heavy footfall. Erin moved back to give them more room. Jack leaned down on his knees to his son's height.

"What's the matter, bud?"

Jack's voice was different, gentle and kind. The normal, surly briskness was gone. The glacial edge with which he usually laced his tone around her was softer. She blinked. He sounded so different and so kind. Exactly what a father should be to his child. What no man had ever been to her.

Charlie pushed off his dad's hand on his arm. "Nuthin'."

Jack glanced up at her. "I heard yelling. Did you do something to him? What's wrong?"

121

"She's bothering me!" Charlie suddenly said, pointing a finger at Erin. Tears gathered in his eyes. "She-she wants to live here and she was bothering me about it! She wants to be Uncle Joey's girlfriend, but I don't like her."

Then Charlie turned and fled into the house. Erin's mouth dropped opened in shock. Her compassion towards Charlie froze as soon as the little shit blamed it all on her. He sold her out. Like Jack would ever believe her instead of his own son. She shook her head when she felt Jack's gaze settling on her. He rose to his feet, now looming a foot above her.

"That is not what happened. I was crossing the yard, and I saw him crying up here on the porch. I came up and asked him what the matter was. His school is having a Mother's Day Tea, and he said he had no one to take. He was crying because he didn't want to bring you this year. Then he asked me to take him. I told him it wasn't appropriate, and that's when you walked up. I did not come up here to weasel my way in with him. It had nothing to do with Joey."

Jack's face didn't change during her entire tirade. He didn't believe her.

She kicked the bottom stair in frustration. Wearing her tennis shoes, all it accomplished was to make her toes vibrate in pain. "Why would I use your son? If I'm really plotting to take over the Rydell River Ranch, as you seem so convinced I'm trying to do, why would I approach your younger son? I wouldn't. I would approach your older son. And that's beside the fact that it wouldn't get me anywhere. It's not like I'm after *you*."

His eyebrows lifted and his expression seemed strange. She swallowed and quickly snapped her mouth shut. She really said way too much. She dropped her eyes to her feet.

"I actually hadn't thought you were doing any of that. But it's good to know you're not after me."

She raised her eyes to his. He was smiling. *Jack Rydell was smiling at her.* He was amused by her. How dare he? He obviously suspected she was trying to take his ranch through his brother, and now his son accused her of the same thing. What was she supposed to do? Not react?

"Nor did I think you were trying to use my eight-year-old son."

She nearly screeched as she turned on her heel to stomp down the steps. Then she spun back around. "Well, then maybe you can quit acting like I'm brainwashing your brother to steal your ranch. You can rest easy; he's more than moved on from me. I saw him with a brunette and he was getting into her car last night. So now you can do it. You can fire Chance, and get rid of the trash now ruining the perfection of your stupid horse farm."

She spun around again and stomped away. Passing the trailer, she continued down the road and hit the trail that took her to the river. It was a trail she hiked down with her frequent daily trips there. And now, it would probably be her last trip.

JACK WATCHED ERIN LEAVE. He was surprised flames didn't ignite under her feet from the friction of her stomps. She was furious. He didn't move for a moment as he'd never seen Erin lose her temper. She usually was pretty reticent with him, and all of the guys, actually. She kept a low profile and was excruciatingly polite. Jack frowned. He never realized, until then, just how polite she was. Why didn't he notice how nice she was? How quiet? How respectful? He'd go days sometimes without actually speaking to her. He saw her, but only because any female would stick out on the place like a purple dinosaur. But really, Erin didn't seek out any of them.

Not even Joey. She… well, shit, he had no idea what she did all day. He knew she went to the river a lot. A freakish amount, in fact. He'd seen her from the pasture, although she didn't realize it, of course.

She walked down the road each morning and left every few days in the car, but was back within a few hours. That was the extent of Erin's life, at least, as he saw it. Jack rubbed a hand to his chin.

He had work to do and was in the middle of training a new mare when he heard Charlie. And now there was Charlie to deal with. The stupid Tea. Every year, he and his son sat together with thirty women. You'd think there would be one other situation in Charlie's class that mimicked their own. But no. Charlie was the only kid in the class that didn't have a mom, grandma, aunt or even cousin to take him. It really wasn't advertised as a Mother's Day Tea. It was officially called the May Day Tea, but every called it the Mother's Day Tea.

So he made do as Charlie's special person. He tried to sit on the tiny, child-sized chairs at the butcher paper-covered, small tables that his damn pinky didn't fit under, let alone, his legs. He had to drink out of thimble-sized china cups and eat off flowered plates. He looked as ridiculous as he felt.

But until now, Charlie never minded so much. As long as he was there. Now, Charlie was in third grade, so of course, he cared this year. The pounding started in Jack's temple as he thought there was always something. Something he didn't get done, or do right, or someone he was failing, or not getting to fast enough or thoroughly enough. But it should not have been his son. His younger, quiet son, who rarely asked for much. Charlie wasn't like Ben, who would, one day, run the ranch. Of that, Jack had no doubt. Despite Ben's current teenage rebellion and limit breaking, Ben was a good kid. He was an outgoing, take-charge kind of kid and he

124

worked hard. He would be tall, strong and very similar to Jack in that respect.

But not Charlie. Charlie was small for his age and had red hair and freckles that shamed him. He spent most of his spare time with his nose in books or off by himself. He didn't take much interest in the ranch, the horses, the river, or the mountains; not like Ben did. Or the rest of the Rydell men. Charlie was different. Quiet. Shy. Sensitive.

He needed his mother. Jack lowered his head and rubbed his knuckles into his eyes. He could do many jobs, and work his fingers to the bone to accomplish many tasks, but manufacturing a mother for Charlie was something he couldn't even begin to fake. However, he couldn't pretend that Charlie wasn't upset; so Jack turned around and headed inside to find his son.

Erin heard a noise. Still terrified of snakes, her eyes always instantly scanned the land around her, no matter where she was or what she was doing. *Jack.* It wasn't a snake, but Jack, walking through the pine trees toward her.

She stood up, wiping the sand off her butt and kicking it off her shoes. She licked her lips. She should not have yelled at Jack. She should never have approached Jack's son, and well deserved her eviction tomorrow, which would render her homeless.

Jack came closer to her, but his expression seemed devoid of feeling. She moved her weight from one foot to the other. She didn't like feeling as though a predatory cat was just waiting to pounce on her. She hated being at Jack's mercy.

He glanced around before his intense eyes landed on her. They were turquoise-blue, not like the river behind her, but more the color of the ocean in Hawaii.

She also couldn't wait for him to speak to her. "I shouldn't have upset Charlie. I'm sorry."

He didn't answer her, but came closer. "What is it you do down here?"

She blinked. "What?"

"You're always down here. Why?"

"Why?" she repeated, somewhat stunned. He wanted to know what she did here? Why would he care? He hated her. She was leaving tomorrow. At the thought of her departure, her stomach churned. The unknown invariably left her nearly breathless.

"It's safe." She blurted out the first thing she thought to his question.

His eyebrow lifted. "Safe from what?"

"Not safe from what. It's a safe feeling. It's quiet and protected. And beautiful. Look at this. There isn't another place like it."

He looked past her, towards the river, beyond where the mountains rose, one step at a time, until the top ridge seemed to scrape the sky and fill the entire horizon. Frowning, he seemed as if he'd never seen the place before.

"Don't you ever come here?" she asked finally.

"Sure, when it's a hundred degrees out to swim. But not with quite the appreciation you seem to have."

She processed the image. Jack swimming? Jack relaxing on a beach? Jack without his signature frayed jeans and worn cowboy boots? His concession to warm weather seemed to be a t-shirt. She couldn't imagine him relaxing, or worse, in a pair of shorts.

She finally shrugged. "You grew up here. You probably don't know what a gift this place is."

His gaze narrowed on her and he said quietly, "I know what this place is. I just didn't expect someone like you would."

Someone like her? What was it about her that so set Jack off? Her last name matching Chance Poletti obviously did her few favors.

She turned away and looked at the river. "So why did you come to find me? This is about Chance, right? You fired him. Do you want me to leave tomorrow?"

"No. I talked to Charlie and he told me what happened. What *really* happened. You don't really think I'm so gullible I believed Charlie, do you? Oh wait, judging by your reaction, I think you must have."

"So it's not about tomorrow?" she said, her voice sounding determined and her face stoically placid. She would not look at him. She would not cry. She would not beg him to let her stay there. Or keep her safe. Or let her be there another day.

"I haven't fired Chance yet. So unless you feel like leaving, I have no intention of evicting you."

She let out a breath and looked up at him sharply. "You're not kicking me out?"

"No."

"Not yet," she clarified.

He frowned. "Okay, not yet. I wouldn't word it kicking you out. Just there might be a time when it's time for you to move on."

She nodded. Good. She needed to keep it real. She had to keep the reality in her brain that was quickly going soft whenever she pretended she could stay there. As if her world could ever be that stable or secure.

"Charlie's punishment is apologizing to you. Why don't you come up to the house for dinner tonight?"

She stepped back and almost fell into the sand. Jack Rydell had just invited her to his house? She looked up at him, and her eyes narrowed. He was making his son apologize to *her*. She couldn't believe it.

"Ms. Poletti, did you hear me?"

She nodded. Finally, she found her voice. "Yes. Are you sure?"

"About what? That Charlie can't lie and yell because he feels like it? Yeah, I'm sure."

"I mean about me coming to dinner?"

"Yeah. Why? Is that a problem?"

"No. Not at all. I just didn't expect it. He really doesn't have to apologize. He was upset, and it wasn't about me. I just happened to be there. I get that."

"He'll apologize."

Jack looked at her for a moment, then turned and left the beach. Erin collapsed into the cool sand. She wasn't kicked out. She wasn't yet left with nowhere to go.

And she was going to dinner.

With Jack.

CHAPTER 12

*J*ack looked up when he heard the soft knocking on the door. It was so loud in the living room, with his brothers and Ben watching a movie, that he almost didn't hear the timid, tapping of Erin's knuckles. Getting up to open the door, he felt a strange hitching in his gut, somewhere in the center of his chest.

Erin stood there, nearly as small as Charlie. Her head didn't even hit him mid-chest. Her hair spiraled around her face before it was collected at the back of her neck. Her eyes looked big and deep under the porch light. She wore a skirt. One of those annoying, flouncy skirts that brushed over her legs. He hadn't seen one of those since her first few days here. He thought she wore the ridiculous get-ups to attract his and his brothers' attention.

Now he realized how judgmental he'd been about her based on nothing real. Nothing substantial.

He was staring at her. Jack realized it, but only after a prolonged moment of his eyes studying her from her head to her toes. He stepped aside and let her in. She walked through, sliding her arms out of Joey's jacket as she passed.

129

He stared again. Her shirt's scooped-neck dipped as she took the coat off. She quickly adjusted the neckline so it was higher up, but not before he glimpsed a peek of her magenta-colored lace bra.

Joey hadn't turned from the TV until he heard Jack shutting the door. He stood up. "What are you doing here?" Joey asked her as he glanced up at the wall clock. "It's a little early, isn't it?"

The rest of the brothers turned. Erin looked down as a delicate blush started in her neck and flushed through her cheeks. Jack stopped in the process of hanging up her coat. She was blushing because of what Joey just said. She didn't like Joey's comment. Or that everyone knew what Joey was talking about. Jack frowned when he realized just how much he didn't like it either.

"Jack invited me to dinner."

Joey glanced at Jack. So did Ian, Shane and Ben. Charlie merely scooted deeper into the couch. Jack stood up straighter. "Actually, Charlie did. He has something he'd like to say, don't you, son?"

All the gazes switched to Charlie, who stared at his feet. "Charlie?"

"Maybe we should talk in private," Erin suggested suddenly.

Charlie's head came up and he nodded vigorously. Jack considered that. He supposed Charlie might be embarrassed. Yeah, that wasn't such a bad idea. Jack nodded, and threw Erin her coat. "Charlie, why don't you join us on the porch?"

Charlie got up, but his shoulders slumped. Jack opened the door and let Erin pass, then Charlie. He was glad when she zipped her coat; there were less distractions that way.

Erin leaned against the porch railing and Charlie stared at his feet. Jack nudged his son's shoulder. "Okay, Charlie, you can quit acting like I'm about to spank you. I think everyone gets the idea how traumatized you are with my punishment."

Charlie's face lifted and he finally smiled. Erin's gaze landed on Jack, who caught her eye over Charlie's head. What surprised her? That he had a sense of humor?

"I'm sorry, Ms. Poletti, for shouting at you. And saying that stuff. I was upset and I shouldn't have taken it out on you."

Erin smiled softly and Jack blinked. It had been a long time since there'd been such softness at the ranch, much less, in his life. He missed it. In that moment the surprising shock of how intensely he missed Lily, punched him in the gut.

But Lily was long gone. Dead. And the bitterness he was left with often tainted how he interacted in the world. He'd grown used to it being all men, but sometimes, like this moment it fully showcased what he and his sons had lost. The family they should be. Sighing he tried to put the thoughts away. It wasn't new that Lily was gone from them. Or that he was all alone trying to raise his sons and take care of his brothers.

"It's okay, Charlie, and you can call me Erin."

Charlie glanced at him for permission. "It's fine, since she said you can."

Charlie grinned. "Thanks, *Erin.*"

Jack put a hand on Charlie's bony shoulder. "Next time I catch you lying, Charlie, it won't be a simple apology."

"I know, sir. I won't do it again." Charlie turned and hugged him. "Can I go inside now? We were watching a movie."

Jack nodded and watched Charlie scamper back inside. He turned and found Erin watching them. The sun had set, and the sky behind her was orange, making the trees and barns appear black. The twilight glowed around her. Their eyes met and stared. The silence went on too long and she shifted the weight on her feet.

"You're really good with him."

"Who? Charlie?" he asked, surprised. "He's my son. Why shouldn't I be?"

She shrugged. "I mean you're... just different with him and Ben than you are with the others."

He had no idea what she was talking about and looked at her strangely. She tried again. "You're just kind to them. And supportive without being a jerk about it. I guess I was a little surprised at how much so."

He smirked. "You mean because of how I am towards you?"

She nodded.

"Much of that was the unfortunate fact of Chance's stink and that you shared his last name."

She snorted. "Believe me, I get it. I mean about Chance." They shared a smile and then their gazes lingered for a long pause. It soon became too intense. She glanced away. "Maybe I should go. I don't have to stay for dinner."

Jack looked past her, feeling uncomfortable as to why he kept staring at her. He shrugged. "Ian cooked dinner. So it'll be pretty decent if you want to stay."

"Ian cooks?"

"We all cook. I just suck at it. On the weekends, we each take turns, except for Charlie. We always look forward to Ian's night. He's the only one who's pretty decent at it."

"I don't think Joey wants me here."

Jack crossed his arms over his chest. At the mention of his brother's name, his teeth gnashed. "Aren't you... here often for Joey?"

She looked away and stared at the chairs haplessly arranged over the long porch. "Joey doesn't have me here with you all. Besides, I don't think I should be here anymore... like that, I mean."

Jack stared at her downturned face. "I see."

Her eyes shot up to his. "It's not like I'll break his heart or anything. We were just..."

"I know."

She nodded. "So I should go."

She should. She should go. And he should let her. Except, as she turned to take a step, he asked, "What do you do in that thing?"

She faltered and stopped as she looked up at him. He nodded towards the trailer.

"What? The trailer? I just stay. Chance is never there. He must have a woman in town or something. And a bar, of course. He rarely gets home before two or three."

"There's nothing to do in there. No TV, no internet, nothing. You read a lot?"

"No. I don't read a lot. I go to bed early mostly. Then I can get up earlier to enjoy the sun longer. At home, it's never sunny this many days in a row."

He squinted at her. "What is it you plan on doing? I mean, are you staying on this side of the mountains? Getting a job here? What?"

"Yes, I'd like to stay over here. I like it. And yes, I am looking for a job. I'm not as lazy as you think I am."

"I never said you were lazy."

"You did. You don't know the things you say without actually saying them to me."

He uncrossed his arms. "All right, you got me. Can you blame me? Chance is your brother. Not like that's a good reference. You very well could have turned out just like him."

"So you don't think I am? Like him, I mean?"

Why did her big-eyed look seem so hopeful? For what? His approval? Did his opinion matter so much to her? He shook his head. "No, you don't appear to be a lying, stealing, shiftless piece of shit like your brother is."

She laughed.

"That doesn't offend you?"

"About Chance? No. I understand exactly how you feel about him."

"Then, I ask again, why did you come to him?"

She looked away and crossed her arms to hug her middle. "My mom died. I lost my job. My stepfather wanted me out; and I guess I hoped to find something better than what I had."

"When did your mom die?"

"A few months back."

"I'm sorry. I know how hard it is."

She glanced at him. "I guess you do. Anyway, I should go."

"Erin?" He stepped forward. "Why don't you just come inside?"

She eyed him skeptically. "Are you sure? There is really no need."

"Neither is no reason for you *not* to. So yes, I'm sure."

JACK WATCHED HIS BROTHERS' eyes following her. Ian didn't say much to her, but he didn't say much to anyone. However, his gaze followed her as much as Shane's unconcealed interest. Shane had no problems engaging Erin in small talk. He flirted with her outrageously. If Joey hadn't gotten to her first, Shane would have most definitely put the vibe out there to Erin. At least, Shane wouldn't send her out in the middle of the night alone. Ben, too, had a raging crush on her. Each time she talked to him, he blushed and stammered. He followed her around like a puppy, and seemed just as eager to please her.

She appeared overwhelmed with all of them in one room. Jack noticed it now, when he hadn't before. She was shy, almost timid. And nice. Way nicer than he expected her to be. He could tell she was nervous by the way she waited before speaking or acting, as if to see how those around her did first. She tried to follow what everyone else did.

Dinner was usually a quick meal. They ate, cleared the dishes, cleaned up, and they were done. Tonight, however, was different. They lingered because Erin ate such small, polite bites. She chewed with her mouth closed and her napkin in her lap; and cut her meat and potatoes into small mouthfuls. So they all slowed down, cut their food smaller, and half-closed their mouths while chewing too. After dinner, she jumped up to help, but Jack waved her off.

When he looked up at the sound of soft murmurs, he paused with a dripping plate in his hand. Drops of water slid off his hand to the floor. Erin sat at the table with Charlie next to her and their heads were bent over a notebook. They were talking quietly. Finally, she took the spiral notebook and pencil and started sketching. How long since he last saw a woman sitting so closely with his son? Over five years. Longer than five years since Lily sat at that very table *with Ben*. For Lily had never sat at the table and helped Charlie with his homework. She was dead long before he entered school.

Jack shook himself and turned away, jamming the plate into the dishwasher. He stared out at the now darkened yard.

"Dad, come look at his."

Taking a breath, he turned around. His déjà vu feelings were quickly stowed back inside his heart, which was where they mostly resided now.

"Yeah, Charlie?"

"Look at what Erin did."

He walked closer to the table and she looked uncomfortable at his approach. Charlie slid the spiral notebook towards him. On it was a drawing, which he found kind of offensive: it depicted him, Ian, Shane, and Joey. All of them were drawn in full caricature, with exaggerated representations of their more apparent personality traits. Jack towered, big and tall, over the entire drawing. His cheeks were puffed, and his arms crossed. Ian was smaller and looked solemn; Shane's grin dominated his face with flirtation, and Joey was so pretty, she drew a sparkle at the top of his head. Jack stared at it, totally surprised. It was amazing. It looked like something professional. Yet, she managed to draw it in the few minutes he spent washing dishes. He glanced at her. Her face was close, and just to the left of him. She looked back and her eyes got big, while her pink tongue darted out and licked her lips. His gaze narrowed in on that. She quickly dropped her head.

Grabbing the tablet, she explained, "I was fooling around. Charlie has to draw his family for school, and we were just kidding around."

Now they had attracted the others' attention, who all walked over. They started laughing. The depiction was right on.

"Wow, can you draw. You take classes to do that?"

She shook her head. "Classes? To scribble a cartoon? No. Of course not. It's just a joke. For Charlie."

Ben laughed. "Dad, she's got you down perfect. Instead of lord of the dance, it's lord of the ranch."

Jack started to frown, but he couldn't help smiling. He did tend to think he was lord of it all. "I don't know; Joey's sparkle about sums him up."

Erin grabbed the sketch and her cheeks were fully pink. "It was just a silly joke."

Ian glanced at her. "You shouldn't sell yourself so short.

It's good. And your observations are true. You have a real talent there."

She wrinkled her brow at Ian and shook her head. Why did it come as such a shock to her? Did no one ever compliment her on her artwork before? There was no denying her talent.

"No one's ever said that to you?" Shane finally asked.

She shrugged. "I hardly ever showed my drawings to anyone to elicit any comments about them. Anyway, it's just a doodle."

Jack let her have the notepad back. It seemed that important to her. His brothers wandered off and he stared at her. Who was she? The woman who he first believed was intentionally seducing his brother? Or this, quiet, unsure woman who ate dinner with them tonight?

She closed the notebook and stood up from the table. "I should go."

Joey got up from the couch. "Why don't we talk first?"

"Oh. Okay," Erin said. She glanced at Jack and he wasn't sure why. He didn't comment as she went around the table and followed his brother up the stairs before disappearing into Joey's bedroom. Jack sighed and took his son's hand.

"Time for bed, bud."

ERIN DIDN'T WANT to go anywhere with Joey. She didn't want Jack, Ian and Shane watching her walk upstairs with their little brother. She doubted it was lost on no one that Jack invited her to dinner, not Joey.

She followed Joey into his room and he closed the door.

"What was all that about?"

"All what about?"

"Why did Jack invite you to dinner?"

"Because he wanted to."

Joey crossed his arms. "Jack isn't controllable. He wouldn't just ask you here. You realize that, I hope. If you are running some kind of scheme, he won't fall for it."

She stepped back with her mouth open. "You think I'm using you? Now Jack? Why did you sleep with me then?"

He rolled his eyes. "Because I could. It's not like I would let you get away with anything."

"Jack invited me here only to fulfill a punishment for Charlie; he had to apologize for something to me."

"That's it?"

"Yes, that's it."

"Oh. Sorry."

"Sorry? You seemed to be accusing me of something pretty big. Sorry is supposed to cut it?" He shrugged. "What exactly did you think I was doing here?"

"Chance warned me about you. I thought maybe since you realized I don't yet have my share of the ranch, maybe you were after Jack."

She shook her head. "And you believed him? You know what, Joey? You're not only young and naïve, but you need to watch out before Chance burns you. I'm not the one you need to be careful of. And if you were half as observant as you think you are, you'd know that."

Joey shrugged. "Just calling it like I see it."

She rolled her eyes, thinking she deserved that. She jumped into bed with Joey because it was easy, because she could. Because it never occurred to her not to. Maybe Chance wasn't so off about her.

"I have to go."

"Where, Erin? To my trailer? You're not here because Chance lets you stay; you're here because I've let you. I thought you knew that."

Her mouth opened, then she closed it. She supposed she

did know it. But not like Joey thought. She was here only because Jack let her stay because of Joey.

"You know why you like my brother despite everyone else telling you that you shouldn't? Because Chance plays into your ego. He tells you everything he knows you want to hear, like about being as important and powerful as Jack is. But you're not. You know it, but you let Chance stroke your ego. He's using you, not me. I was…"

"I know what you were doing. You're pretty good at it too."

She nodded. "Really? That's how you're going to act? Well, consider maybe *you* weren't all that good at it. But then again, considering you're barely out of high school, that might explain why."

Joey sneered. "Get off my land. How about that? Is that grown up enough for you?"

She closed her eyes, then opened them and nodded. "You're right, Joey. I shouldn't have stayed so long in the first place."

CHAPTER 13

rin's stomach cramped as soon as she woke up. She slept, but it was fitful and restless. Now the morning daylight seeped between the closed blinds of the small trailer. She took the three steps to the thermostat and turned it up higher. With a glance in the mirror, she cringed. She felt dirty and sordid after her fight with Joey. Worst of all? He was right. She was allowed to stay there only because she'd been sleeping with Joey. And it shamed her to the core to realize maybe she had done it for exactly that reason; just so Jack would let her stay.

She shook her head. No. That hadn't been the case. They'd started out with an easy, friendly flirtation and he'd responded to her just as she had him. There hadn't been an ulterior motive, no matter how he tried to spin it now.

Today, she had nowhere left to go. The pain in her stomach increased. She had nowhere else to go. Literally. There was no friend in Seattle. No job. No family. Very little money and no home. She was homeless. She was illiterate.

She pushed her hair back into a headband and secured it with a rubber band. She brushed her teeth and threw cold

140

water on her face, looking towards the front of the trailer. It was empty. Not unusual. Starting towards her clothes, she abruptly stopped. With a frown, she realized it was gone. Her duffel bag wasn't sitting next to the table. Her heartbeat sped. *Shit. No!* She got to her feet and looked outside the trailer. Her stomach pain nearly knocked her onto her knees. Her breathing stopped, and her hands clenched. *Her car was gone! And her money was gone!* She sank into a chair and closed her eyes as hot tears fell over her cheeks.

Her brother had just stolen her entire life.

Dropping her hands from her face, she couldn't just sit there. She crossed the trailer, jerked the door open, and threw on her sneakers before running across the yard, up onto the porch, and pounding loudly on the front door of the Rydells' house. She tapped her foot until Joey answered.

He rolled his eyes and rubbed a hand over his face. "I meant it. Don't start already."

She pushed past him. They were all there: every big, intimidating man who held her entire life in his hands. Even Ben and Charlie were at the table, eating cereal, and paused to stare at her.

She was still wearing her pajamas, and hadn't even put a coat on. Or a bra, she now realized. Still, it didn't matter. There was no time to waste.

"Erin?" Ian voiced all of their obvious surprise at her early arrival.

"He stole my car! He stole my car and everything in my duffel bag. *He's gone!*"

They didn't move and she frowned. No one acted as if they'd even heard her.

"Didn't you hear me? He stole my car. You have to call the police! We have to go after him. Don't you understand? We have to do something!" Hysteria tinged her words, and tears started to fall down her face. They didn't get it. Her entire life was that little bit of money and her car. Without them, she was destitute.

"Who stole what? Why don't you calm down a little bit and start over? And maybe you want to borrow this."

"Chance! He's gone! He stole my car." She glanced up when Ian came towards her carrying a coat. No one was reacting. At least not like they should be! Her entire future was in her car and duffel bag and it was all gone! Why didn't they see that? If there had been anything to throw nearby her, she would have hurled it at the first head she could find. She grabbed the coat and wrapped it around her.

Turning, she found Jack at the stove. He was pouring coffee when she burst in. "Jack... Jack, please you have to do something. He's gone."

Jack finally seemed to hear her and slammed the coffee pot down before stepping forward. "Are you sure? Maybe he just borrowed it."

"I kept the keys hidden under the couch that I slept on. Not easily found. He took all my money. He didn't borrow it. He's gone."

Jack frowned and glanced at his brothers. "All right. Ian, you and Shane go south; Joe and I will go north. Ben, call the police for me, okay? Tell them where we're looking. Write down the make, model and license plate of your car for Ben. You have any idea where he might go?"

She shook her head. "No. None. He didn't talk about anything to me."

"There's one highway up and down the valley, so it's doubtful he got too far."

"I should come."

Jack hardly spared her a glance. "You should get dressed and wait for us to get back. Ben, get Charlie to school, okay?"

"Sure, Dad."

Jack was putting his hat on. He looked at her one last time

before walking out the door with the keys in his hands, followed by his brothers.

~

ERIN PACED FOR AN HOUR. Then, a squad car pulled in. She ran out and met the officer, describing her car and Chance, along with the theft of her items. He wrote it all down. But she felt like screaming because no one seemed to comprehend how dire the situation was.

The officer left, claiming he would search above the ranch. There were miles of dirt roads that trailed through the back of the mountains. There were dozens of spots to hide and plenty of abandoned buildings for temporary cover.

She finally sat down and put her head into her hands. There was nothing more she could do. She never felt so useless, stupid, or helpless in her life. She jumped when she heard a knock at the trailer door. Standing up, she quickly crossed the small space to open it.

Jack stood there. He had to duck his head to enter the trailer. He took his hat off first and his red hair glistened in the sunlight. His eyes looked around, taking in every detail of the trailer, then he looked at her. He frowned when he saw what she was still wearing.

"Did you find him?"

Jack shook his head. "No. No one's seen your car."

She dropped to the chair and glared angrily at her hands.

"You probably should get dressed. The police intend to come by here."

"They did already. I gave them a statement."

"O-o-o-kay," Jack said as he finally sat across from her. She looked up at him. He was so big, he didn't fit in the trailer chair and had to rest his long legs at the side of the small table. He made the trailer seem like a car. He was quiet for so long, she finally couldn't stand it.

"He took everything I own, Mr. Rydell. All I had left in the world."

"Everything? As in your clothes?"

"Everything. It was all there, in a duffel bag. Other than my toothbrush and a few toiletries that I keep by the sink, it's all gone. Down to my damn underclothes."

"Down to your..." Jack started to say, stunned, before he stopped himself. "Shit. He actually stole your clothes?"

She nodded.

"You really think he did that and isn't coming back?"

Jack's words hit her. It was like concrete being tied to her feet before being sunk into a river. "I really think he did it and isn't coming back," she whispered.

Jack's gaze was on her face. She kept her eyes down. "And your money too, you said earlier?"

"The last of my money. It was hidden in the trunk of my car. I never dreamed he'd steal my car."

"Why wasn't it in the bank? Who does that?"

"I didn't know where I would end up. Look, Mr. Rydell—"

"Erin, I think we're past the Mr. Rydell bullshit. You ticked me off when I first met you and my formalities toward you were simply to keep you at a distance."

She nodded and raised her eyes to finally make eye contact. "*Jack*, I don't have anything. I don't even have a change of clothes."

His gaze stayed on her and she was too ashamed to hold it so she stared at her hands.

"Is there anyone to call? No bullshitting me this time, either; is there any friend in Seattle to call?"

She could not look up at him as she shook her head no.

He was quiet, then stood up. "I figured as much. There

could be no other reason you'd come to Chance for help except if you were desperate."

She looked up. Was he planning to throw her out with only a pair of pajamas and sneakers?

"Wh—What are you going to do with me?"

"First off, we'll find you some clothes."

"And then?"

"Then I guess we'll figure out what to do with you."

JACK WAITED for Erin to come out. His truck idled with a loud gurgle as he looked out the windshield towards the mountains beyond. He tapped a finger to his steering wheel. What kind of brother would steal his own sister's entire belongings? Or leave her stranded without even a dollar or clothing to her name? Jack couldn't comprehend what kind of lowlife did that. Or that she was now completely stranded there. And suddenly his responsibility. He felt the tightening in his neck. Another damn complication to his already complicated life. Didn't he know she'd turn out to be just that from the moment he laid eyes on her?

She closed the trailer and came towards him. Still wearing Joey's coat over her small, light pink tank top, and pink little shorts, she looked miserable, right down to the tennis shoes on her feet. She didn't even have a pair of socks. The rat bastard might as well have left her naked on the side of the road.

She opened the passenger door and climbed up into his truck. Settling into the seat, she snapped her seatbelt on while adjusting Joey's coat to cover her. He pulled the truck into gear and left the driveway.

"Where are we going? I can't go in like this."

He sighed. No, she probably couldn't. "Okay. You tell me what to get and I'll go in."

"You're going to buy me clothes?"

"You have a better idea?"

She shook her head and bit her lip.

"It looks like I'm going to be buying you a lot of things before we figure this thing out, so you might as well get used to it."

Her gaze jerked up to him. He adjusted the heater so it wasn't blowing over him only. He had warm clothes on and wasn't as cold as Erin must have been in her shorts.

"And how, exactly, will I pay you back?"

"Can we first get you properly dressed before we go into that?"

She glanced out her window. "You know, I need a bra. Are you going to pick that out too?"

Didn't he know she needed a bra. "I can probably manage it. Don't they have sizes on them? Can't you just tell me which size and brand to buy?"

She folded her arms over her chest. "You don't have to sound so agreeable to this."

"How would you rather I sound?"

She shrugged and closed her eyes. "I have never been so humiliated in my entire life."

He stared at the road. What else could he say to her? The situation was what it was. There was no other way. She had nothing. He had to help her even if he didn't want to.

She was quiet for a long while before finally saying, "I feared he'd rob you, and never considered he might rob me because I didn't have very much. I never thought this would happen."

"They might find him still. He could easily make a mistake."

"He won't when it comes to saving himself."

Jack swung his truck into the parking lot. She looked faint with embarrassment.

"Do you want to write down exactly what you need?"

She shook her head vehemently. "No. I need pants, a t-shirt, bra, socks, underwear, and maybe a sweatshirt."

He looked at her. "Do you think I have any clue what sizes those would happen to be?"

"I'll tell you."

"And I'll forget. Just write them all down." He handed her a tablet he found on his car door. She stared at it, then up at him. To his surprise, she bit her lip and tears filled her eyes as she shook her head. She pushed the tablet back at him.

"I can't."

"What do you mean, 'you can't'? We already went over this. You'll have to accept some help until we get through this. You can't walk around like that."

She closed her eyes. "I know. I mean, I can't."

He stared at her. "What do you mean?"

"I mean I can't write down anything."

Jack sighed. He had no idea what she was referring to. "All right then. You want to come in like that?"

She bit her lip and stared out the window. Finally, she nodded. He couldn't begin to guess what her mood was, but she seemed determined that he wouldn't know her sizes.

CHAPTER 14

*E*rin's heart thumped in her chest as she waited for Jack Rydell to pay for her new wardrobe. He pulled his wallet out, dug into it and handed the cashier his credit card. She waited off to the side, with Joey's jacket wrapped tightly around her. She could not believe this was happening to her. She could not believe that, in the span of a single night, she had become completely destitute. The only lucky part was that Chance abandoned her in the backyard of decent people. She was so embarrassed, she could barely look Jack in the eye. He waited patiently as she picked out basic clothes and undergarments. She selected as little as she could. But still, it added up. He, blessedly, didn't comment on any of her items on the conveyor belt, including her new bra and underwear. Finally, the garments were bagged and Jack handed them to her. She quickly disappeared into the restroom to put on more than what she slept in last night.

He waited for her. It was nine o'clock in the morning, and already, her life was ruined. What could she do? She owed money now and had no transportation. The ranch was a number of miles from any real civilization, and a good thirty from an actual town. It wasn't like she could take the bus to get around, as she might have done in the city.

Finally, they pulled back onto the ranch. As they were exiting the truck, Shane came up to them. "He stole the petty cash box too."

Erin's heart dropped lower. *No. Not more.* When she glanced up at Jack, she saw his jaw clench and she closed her eyes in mortification.

"How much was in it?" Shane asked.

"A grand or so," Jack said through gritted teeth.

That gave Chance over twenty-five hundred dollars and her car. She shook her head. "I'll never see him again. He won't ever be back."

"Yeah, well, you won't be missing out on much now, will you?" Jack snapped. She stepped back. Of course, Jack was angry. Of course, she was merely an extension of Chance. And now at their mercy.

Shane gazed at Jack and then at Erin. "What about her?"

Jack glanced at her too. "Not so sure yet."

"She really have nothing?"

"Really."

Erin straightened her back. "*She* doesn't need you speaking about her in the third person. If you would drive me to the nearest bus station, I'll go west, back to Seattle. And I promise to send you the money and pay you back for the clothes."

Jack turned away and started walking towards the house. Over his shoulder, he said, "That's a crock of shit and we both know it. There's no one else and nowhere else to go. Come inside, it's time we had a talk."

She stared after him. He didn't even have the decency to look at her as he spoke. She stomped her foot and cursed Chance. Then she cursed Jack. Then Joey. Then Shane, Ian, her mother, her stepfather, and finally, herself. She mostly cursed herself for having nothing else left in life. But she eventually followed Shane and entered the house.

They were all there: all four brothers. All of the big, intimidating brothers. Ian indicated for her to sit down and Jack was pouring coffee. Joey was scowling at her from the living room, and Shane sat across from her at the table. He didn't seem all smiles and charming this morning, however.

Jack leaned his hip into the kitchen counter and folded his arms over his chest after setting his coffee cup beside him. She looked away and stared down at the bare wooden table. She could feel all their eyes on her.

"Now what?" Shane finally asked.

"Now Erin gets to tell us the entire truth. Not half-answers, half-truths, or half-assed stories, but the entire truth, from start to finish."

She raised her head to find Jack staring at her. The easy going ways of the last few days, which she enjoyed so much, were gone. He was right back to distrusting her.

She started to say something when the door opened. Ben stepped through.

Jack straightened up and frowned at his son. "Why aren't you at school?"

Ben glanced at her, and then at his dad. Sometimes, it still threw her to realize Jack was the father to this six-foot plus boy. Ben didn't look nearly as cocky beside his father as he did behind his father's back. "I thought she might need me."

"*She* might need you?" Jack repeated, his surprise evident. Then, turning to her, he asked, "You think Erin needs you? For what, Ben?"

"For, you know, support. She can't help what her brother did, Dad." Jack sighed as he glared at her. Ben's interference was not good for her, and definitely not needed. He was only making a bad situation much worse.

"I know you think you know her, but she really doesn't need you here. Now get to school."

"I do know her. More than anyone else has bothered."

Jack's gaze grew weary, and something mean and unhappy overcame his face as he looked at her. Ben was only making it all worse.

"You have to let her stay here. She has nowhere else to go. She can't go anywhere else. I mean, really, she needs…"

"Ben, stop," she said, standing up quickly. "Do what your dad says."

He looked wounded at her rebuff. Jack didn't like Ben's fierce reaction to defend her.

"Erin?" Ben started to say, but she cut him off.

"Don't, please. I'll handle this."

Jack stepped in between them. "What exactly will you handle? What exactly is it you two spend your afternoons doing?"

She frowned. "Nothing."

He went still. "What did you do with my son?"

She jerked back, completely grossed out. "Nothing! I mean nothing like *that*."

"Like what then? If you so much as touched his hand I'll…"

"Dad! Stop. She's not like that. At all."

"Oh, I don't know about that," Jack said as he started to approach her. She stepped back after seeing the rage directed toward her in Jack's eyes. How easily he could think that of her.

"She can't read! That's what I was doing with her, helping her read."

Jack stopped and his mouth opened. No one said a word. Ben came closer, his tone quieter now that the entire room was staring at him. Erin closed her eyes and dropped her head down toward the table. In her whole life, she'd never felt so humiliated or miserable.

She sat down, now that the entire fight was over.

Ben continued, "I've been helping her fill out job applications. She can't do it alone. She can neither read the questions or spell the words to write down. That's why she doesn't have a job yet. That's also why you can't kick her out of here. Where would she go?"

She felt Jack looking at her. "I see. We'll take care of this. Get back to school now."

"Promise me, you won't let anything happen to her."

"I promise. Now go."

She refused to look up or acknowledge what was happening. She couldn't bear to see the pity and disgust in all of the Rydells' faces.

The silence lasted long after Ben shut the door. Dear, sweet, young Ben who seemed to worry about her even though she didn't deserve it, and who thought staying there could somehow protect her from a world she could barely navigate through to survive.

"Is that true?" Jack spoke. His tone sounded less harsh than before.

She finally nodded as tears rimmed her eyelids. "Yes, it's true."

"You had Ben helping you?"

"Yes."

"You had no right to ask him to keep that a secret."

She closed her eyes and nodded.

"Erin?" She didn't look up and he finally said, "Look at me."

She lifted her eyes to Jack's.

"What exactly is your situation? All of it. How? How can you not read? And how have you ever worked?"

"How? I don't know. I just can't do it. People tried to teach me, but I couldn't do it. I knew I was stupid when I was pretty young. I learned how to compensate for it and hide it most of the time. Most people never guessed. *You* didn't guess."

Jack eyed her. "I didn't say you were stupid. I realize it's a learning problem, not a matter of intelligence. I just… I mean it's hard for me to get how you survived this long without being able to read."

"Not well," she said finally.

"What was Ben doing? Teaching you?"

"Oh no. I can't do it, so there's no point. He helped me read through the employment applications so I could fill them out."

Jack's eyebrows rose. "And how did you work in the past? Have you ever worked in the past? What do you do if you can't read?"

She shrugged. "I've always worked. I waitressed. I worked fast food. I cleaned offices and houses and stores. I've done a lot of different jobs."

"How do you take orders?"

"I remember them?"

"You remember them?"

"Sure."

"Who helped you before? Before Ben?"

"My mom. It's part of why I lived with her. She could read pretty well."

"The mom who died, and was indirectly responsible for bringing you here?"

"How did she die?"

Erin looked up and stared at Jack, then at Shane and finally, Ian. "She started my car in a closed garage and died of carbon monoxide poisoning."

They looked away, since no one could hold her gaze.

They didn't know what to do or say to her now. She almost relished their obvious discomfort.

"She left a note for me that said she was sorry. That's all the note said, 'I'm sorry' not 'I love you,' or anything more substantial. She did everything for me pertaining to reading, spelling and writing. So it's been both a loss of her and how I was able to cope in the world. You know the rest of how I ended up here."

Ian spoke first. "You *really* have nowhere else to go then?"

She scoffed. "No. This is impossible for you to believe, I know. I have no one. There is no money. There are no friendly neighbors or a thousand-acre ranch waiting for me. There is nothing. Except Chance."

"How come someone your age doesn't have friends to go to?"

"Because I spent all my time pushing everyone away. I never let anyone get too close to me because then they'd guess I could not read. My entire existence has been about trying to hide that."

Joey stood up and walked into the kitchen, but glared at her. "Chance was my fault. I know that now. I screwed up. You all tried to tell me and I refused to listen. But she isn't our responsibility. I doubt we can believe all of this."

"She's your girlfriend," Shane said finally.

"Not as of last night. And funny how Chance is gone this morning and look who is stranded here. I don't buy it. Not for a second."

Looking up at Joey, she finally stood up, sliding her chair back slowly. "I had nothing to do with what Chance did. I have never been involved or had anything to do with what Chance does."

"You can't be so different."

"You didn't even see what he was until this very moment.

I told you what he was, and you wouldn't even believe me. If I wanted to play you, why would I have told you that?"

"You also said you'd be gone today. If all this was true, then where were you going to go?"

"Last night, I had a car, clothes and over a thousand dollars. I know it wasn't much, but a lot more than I have today."

"Who doesn't use a bank?" Joey demanded, his face expressing how distasteful he now found her.

"Someone who can't read a deposit slip, or an ATM screen," she said finally, after a long pause.

"How did you ever get a license?"

"I didn't."

"What? You drive around without a legal driver's license?"

"Yes," she said, looking straight into Joey's eyes. He couldn't for a moment guess what her life was like.

"But how about tabs and registration? Insurance?"

"Until my mom died, she took care of all that. So while I paid for everything, it was my car, she had to do all the paperwork on it and put it in name."

"What did you do for work? Steal? Use people? Or is that just us?"

She pulled her head back as if he slapped her.

"Joey! That's enough."

Joey glanced back at Jack. "She played us. Just like you said she would. Don't fall for it now. Get her out of here."

"Yeah? And how do I do that? She can't drive air. I checked the trailer, and there's nothing there."

Erin eyed Jack. She didn't know he checked her story out. He looked back at her, unashamed. He didn't trust her. He had to be convinced she wasn't lying.

"You think she's really stuck here? That she's telling you the truth?"

155

She watched Jack. And so did Joey. Jack finally nodded. "Yeah, she's telling the truth."

"And so what? She's now our problem?"

"Joe, you were the one who…"

"Screwing a woman doesn't mean you have to live with her."

Erin shut her eyes. This was intolerable to listen to her need being argued over.

"I was going to say you were the one who brought Chance here and therefore, the place that Erin found refuge at." Jack snapped.

"It still doesn't mean she is our problem."

Jack finally stood up. "You can be a real little shit."

Joey glanced at her and slammed his fist down, then turned and marched out the door, letting it bang shut loudly behind him.

Erin couldn't look around the room or even look up. She got to her feet and ran out the front door, down the porch steps, and straight into the trailer. She locked the door, shut all the shades, and fell down onto the couch and cried. She wept for the humiliation, for being stuck there, for Joey's unkind words, and worst of all, for having Jack, Ian and Shane witness her desperate need. And the pathetic fact that she could not read. She cried because she had no one left in the world, no place in the world, and her only hope was a family who still didn't trust her, but would help her out of basic decency, which was far more than her own family ever showed toward her.

CHAPTER 15

*J*ack stared at the shut door. Shit, that didn't go very well. And there was far more wrong with Erin than he was prepared to deal with.

"What are we going to do?"

Jack glanced at Ian. "Do? Nothing. We don't need the trailer. She'll stay there. We'll have to get her something to drive though, so she can get around."

Ian's body stiffened. "You're going to just let her stay here? You're sure this isn't some kind of scheme?"

"I told you I checked the trailer. Chance is gone. There's nothing in there. There were only her toiletries and a few boxes of food. She hasn't been eating well. There wasn't anything hidden in there. Short of dropping her in the middle of the street somewhere this place is all she's got."

Ian sighed and Shane groaned. "This is a real shit storm situation. Now Joey's gone from infatuated to hating her. Ben's obviously got a raging crush, and here she sits."

"Do you really think she can't read?"

"I doubt she'd fake that," Jack said dryly. Rolling his eyes.

Ian shifted under Jack's gaze. "Why are you so calm about this? You hated her more than anyone else."

"No. I just didn't trust her before. Now, I know for a fact she isn't lying."

"Her situation is only to add to the tension between you and Joey. This is trouble, pure trouble."

"I knew that the first time I laid eyes on her; now you finally believe me?" Jack said as he got up and headed out to work. There were still chores to be done. Erin Poletti could wait until this evening for him to deal with. It wasn't like she could go anywhere.

THE KNOCK at the door woke Erin from her sleep. She finally cried herself out and fell asleep just to stop the aching burn of her swollen eyes. She was about to roll over and ignore whatever angry man was waiting for her reply when Ian yelled, "Someone's on the phone for you."

Sitting up quickly, Erin wiped her eyes as she pushed the blanket off. She stumbled to the door and opened it. Thanking Ian as she followed him to the house, he walked several paces in front of her, most likely to avoid having to talk to her.

She entered the house and found Charlie at the table, writing, while Ben was lying on the couch, watching TV. She spotted the cordless phone lying next to the kitchen sink. Puzzled, she picked it up.

She was delighted when she heard who was calling. She'd gotten a job! She nearly started doing somersaults before she hung up the phone. Of course, she knew why she'd been hired, and it wasn't for her lame application. She was only glad she was hired. A coffee barista. She'd done it before and could get through it. She could count change and make the coffee. She could also wear the bikini that was required in this particular coffee establishment. So what? It wasn't that big of a deal to her, and the tips would hopefully be good, or at least, decent. Then her heart dropped. She had no vehicle to drive the eleven-mile distance from the ranch to where the stand was located, just off the main highway.

She was hanging the phone up on the cradle when Jack came walking in from the utility room. She stopped short and didn't realize he was inside. He stopped short too.

They stared at each other. What now? She didn't know. She had no idea what to do now, or say, or how to act. His eyes followed her hands hanging up the phone.

"You don't have a phone, do you? I assumed all this time you used a cell phone."

She shook her head no.

He scoffed as he passed around her. "I should have realized that. We keep the landline because our internet signal can be so spotty. But use it when you need."

She didn't answer since she wasn't sure what to say. She rarely made friends in her attempts to conceal her illiteracy. She spent all her time pushing everyone away. That was why, when her mother died and she was stuck with Brian, there was nowhere else for her to go. She'd spent so long hiding her shameful secret that she'd never cultivated the normal friendships and acquaintances that most people did.

He nodded towards the phone. "Is the news good enough to ask if your brother was found?"

"No. I-I got one of the jobs I applied for."

He turned to her and the surprise on his face was so obvious, she felt offended. "Where?"

"Coffee stand."

"Oh. Those seem like a waste of money to me. But I guess they do well, even on this side of the mountain."

"Uh, they... I mean, I can start tomorrow."

"Good."

"That is, if… well, if I can get a ride there."

"Right. Yeah. What time?"

Ben's headed popped up. "I can drive her."

"You don't have your license yet."

"I have my permit. And she's an adult."

"She doesn't have her license so it doesn't count. No. One of us will take you. What time?"

"Early. Four."

He nodded. "Fine."

"That's fine? Leaving here at like three-thirty?"

He shrugged. "I get up early too. Not much else we can do, is there?"

She shut her mouth. Of course, there was nothing else to do. She was stranded there. "I'm sorry. For all this. For earlier. For what this is doing to everyone. For being stuck here. For tomorrow. For how it upsets Joey."

He nodded. "I know."

"Oh. Okay then, I'll just go."

"Go to the trailer to eat some boxed noodles? Sit. You can stay for dinner."

She shook her head. "Thank you. But no. That's not a good idea. Not for any of us. Especially Joey. He doesn't need me here. It's bad enough I have the trailer. Do you need the trailer? For anyone else?"

"It's for temporary workers. We don't need it though; we have other ones. We will, however, be hiring a decent ranch hand, now that shit-face is gone."

"Shit-face being my brother?"

"Yeah. Exactly him."

She stepped back and turned. "Okay, then I'll be ready at three-thirty."

"Someone will be there. Get some rest, you look like shit."

She turned in surprise at his comment. He was grinning

at her. Teasing her. She appreciated seeing the smile that lifted one side of Jack's mouth before she spun around and hid inside her trailer.

SHANE GOT the job of driving her to work and didn't look too thrilled about it. He growled at her when she said good morning and didn't speak the rest of the way to town. She felt bad; but also thought he could be a smidgeon more graceful about her situation. It wasn't like she was disturbing Shane's industrious life. Of all the brothers, he worked the least. He was usually off in his murky shop, rebuilding a machine of one kind or another.

When they pulled into the coffee stand, Shane noticed the sign, *Bikini Babes Barista*, but he merely raised his eyebrows, and gratefully for her, didn't comment. She jumped out of the truck and waved him off, then waited for the manager to show up. After he opened the stand, he would have to provide her with a uniform to wear. She explained that everything she owned burned up in a fire when asked why she lacked a swimming suit. The manager was a guy in his fifties with a protruding belly and a bald head. He looked her over, just as he did when she turned in her application. She knew then, after assessing how much extra in tips her body could bring in, as well as repeat customers, that this stand was her best option for a job.

Luckily, she'd done it before. It didn't take much for her to learn the drinks. She'd just take home the menu and memorize the prices. She'd have to fake it through today and hope no one noticed that she couldn't read one drink from another.

She also had to figure out a way to get there each day. She

couldn't rely on one of the Rydell brothers to cart her there and back to the ranch each day. It was ridiculous.

The job worked out. She faked her way through all the awkward moments, and flirted to increase her tips. She needed any money she could get. If that came from her chest out a little further or wiggling her butt a little wider, so be it.

She had to do something to fix her life.

A week into her strange new career, she came out of her trailer to find Jack parked in the driveway. He waved her over. Despite their proximity, she rarely saw Jack, or Joey either, for that matter. She stuck to her trailer, or the beach, and now work. Shane drove her there and back, but said nothing to her; and that was the extent of her life.

She ran over to Jack and he looked up when she walked around the hood of the nineties model truck. He was sitting half in, half out as he gunned the engine, listening to it.

Then he got out and threw her the keys. "This should get you around."

Her mouth opened. "You're giving me a truck? But why? Where did it come from?"

"It was parked out beyond Shane's shop for a few years. I don't remember where we got it. Anyway, Shane spent a few hours to get it running again."

She didn't know what to say. Thank you, yet again? It wasn't enough. It was never enough. Jack looked at her face, then laughed, "Shane was tired of driving you; that's all."

She nodded and looked away as tears felt close to falling. Everyone was tired of her. She was even tired of her. Yet here she was, desperate to receive their continued charity and pity.

"How are you fixed for food?"

She looked back at Jack. He was leaning his arm along the top of the open truck door. His eyes were fixed on her face. "Fine. I got paid yesterday. I can shop for groceries today."

His gaze ran over her. "Do you have enough to eat?"

"Sure."

"Have you shopped since I was last in there?"

She shrugged, and avoided his eyes.

He nodded. "Just as I thought. Joey's had a week to get over it. We all have. Just come to dinner from now on. It's stupid you're out there all alone with nothing to eat and nothing to do."

She shook her head no, feeling adamant on this one issue. She would not be more of a burden than she already had to be. "I have been thinking... I could do work around here. Or in the house, you know, to offset some of what I owe you."

He shook his head. "Lynnie does the house, and makes most of the meals. She counts on the job, so I can't dismiss her."

"Perhaps I could help in the barn."

His eyebrows rose. "The barn? Like with the horses? You don't even know how to touch them."

"I could learn. I mean, if you'd take just a little time to show me, I could learn. I could learn to do whatever you needed done. Like cleaning the stalls."

"I don't think you could clean the stalls."

She looked up at him. "Please, Jack. I need to do something, anything to help earn my keep here. I can learn to do that. I'm not totally stupid."

"I meant because you're scared of the horses."

"Maybe if you could teach me how to handle them, I wouldn't be so scared. Besides, it does get boring in the trailer; it would give me something to look forward to."

He tapped a finger against the truck door as he frowned at her. "All right. Okay. I can probably find something for you to do. Come out to the barn this afternoon."

She smiled. If he'd been anyone else, she would have

thrown her arms around him in gratitude. But since it was Jack, she settled for just smiling.

He moved away from the truck and she took his place, scooting the seat forward. She nearly sighed in happiness as she shifted it into gear and headed out of the property, alone and with a new sense of complete freedom.

~

JACK GLANCED up when he heard her. Erin was standing against the barn doors, dressed in jeans, a sweatshirt and her once white sneakers, which were now brown from walking around the ranch. He set down the pitchfork he'd been using to pitch fresh straw into one of his mares' stall. She was due to give birth at any time. Erin looked terrified, as usual. Was it him? Or the horses? He was never sure. He only knew the woman Erin became with him was a far cry from the flirting Erin that first attracted Joey.

Jack walked up to her. "You sure about this?"

"I looked forward to it all day."

Her eyes were bright and her cheeks were flushed. Was she telling the truth? Could she really want to work in the barn?

He touched her shoes with the tip of his boot. "Tomorrow, stop in town and buy some boots. You need proper cowboy boots."

"Oh. These are fine."

"No, they're not okay. Get decent boots."

"Okay."

Money. He forgot. She had none. He sometimes didn't fully realize how privileged they were. "I'll lend you some money. Consider it an investment for your work here."

"Are you sure?"

"Yes. You can't do this work without them."

She nodded, her eyes grateful.

"How'd the truck do?"

"It was wonderful."

"It's not pretty, but it should run for you fine."

"It's wonderful."

He nodded. Of course she was grateful for a little bit of control and freedom, and the ability to run to the store or wherever she chose. Being so far from civilization, she had to feel completely isolated and stuck.

He spent the day getting his chores and horse training finished before she got there. He was hers the rest of the day.

"I thought we'd start from the beginning. I'll bring a horse out."

She nodded eagerly. He quickly brought around Jenna, a ten-year-old mare, and tied her to a ring hung high on the barn wall. Erin stood off to the side, watching him intently. Her eyes moved from the horse, to him, and back to the horse.

"First rule, always let the horse know where you are. Gently put your hand along her body, and especially when you pass behind her. If she knows you are there, you won't startle her, and there's less chance you'll get hurt."

She nodded, her eyes intent on the horse's butt as he passed behind it. He walked back and forth a few times.

"You want to try?"

She nodded and came forward, but suddenly seemed so terrified, she couldn't even speak. "Actually, the very first thing, is to breathe. In and out, in and out. Don't pass out."

Her eyes shot up to his and she finally smiled at him. He noticed her chest rise and fall as she took in several deep breaths.

"Where do I start?" she finally asked.

He came nearer and pulled her hand from her side, putting it on the horse just behind the neck. The horse didn't even twitch at the contact. But Erin did. He could feel the tension rising in her. She flinched, as if expecting the horse to buck or rear.

"Forget your terrible ride with Joey. This is how you should have been introduced to the horses. So we'll start slowly, and work from there."

"But what about the stalls?"

"You can't do anything until you feel comfortable handling the horses. I'm going to teach you how to be, and how to ride. I can teach you, if you want to learn."

She glanced at the horse, and then up at him. "I do. But that doesn't get the work done."

He sighed. "No offense, but you're not that strong. Your brother was a shitty asshole, but he had a strong back. I assigned him work he could handle. You're not physically strong enough to do much of the ranch work that needs to be done around here. And you're also not experienced enough to handle the horses on your own. I have several people who come in here weekly and help me ride, train, and care for them. Before you can do that, you have a lot to learn."

She frowned. "So my being here just makes more work for you? That's not doing you any good. I wanted to help. To work off some of what I owe you."

He shrugged. "I don't mind."

"What do you mean, 'you don't mind'?"

"I like doing anything with the horses. I don't care what. So for a while, it's helping you learn to handle them. It's good for the horses too. They have to work however I tell them. Back to the basics is good for them. If you want to learn, that is."

She nodded vigorously. "I do. I just don't want to burden you anymore than I already have."

He shrugged. "It just is what it is. I was there. We all know what happened and why you're here."

She looked at the horse as she asked him, "Why do you accept things so easily?"

"I've had to accept a lot worse than this," he said, looking at her profile, then at the horse, becoming lost in his own memories. "I had to accept terrible things. So your situation is not so tragic for me."

"But you hated me."

"No. I just didn't trust you."

"And you do now?" Her gaze shot up to his face and he finally looked down at her. She was far too pretty for his own good. Her eyes were big, sad and vulnerable. *Save me* kind of eyes. Jack shifted the weight on his feet, uncomfortable with his thoughts about her.

"I think you proved you weren't here for reasons that had anything to do with the Rydells or the ranch. And I really don't think you intended to end up stuck here."

She shook her head no and pressed her lips together. "Thank you, Jack. You could have thrown me out."

"No. Really. I couldn't have. You'd have been walking down a dirt road a good ten miles from the nearest form of help. I, quite literally, couldn't have thrown you out."

She blushed, and glanced at her feet. Then she nodded. "You still went above and beyond what most people would have done, especially considering what my brother did to your family. The fact that he stole from you and you still trust me enough to let me stay, well, it means the world to me."

He reached up and rubbed the horse's flanks. Anything was better than trying to avoid what he wanted to do, which was stare into Erin's eyes.

"So I'm getting bored with how wonderful I am. Do you want to do this or not?"

She nodded vigorously and gently laid her hand back on the horse. She looked up at him, her fear suddenly very real in her eyes as she took a first step, then another, until she eventually circled around the horse, all the while running her hand along the horse's body.

When she got back to where he stood, she let go of the horse and let out a big breath with a huge smile. "I did it!"

He nodded and turned away before his proud smile seemed out of proportion with Erin Poletti's relationship to him.

"So I guess it's time you learned how to groom a horse."

He spent the next while showing her how to rub the curry brush over the horse's body, and brush the entire horse, her mane included. He watched her do the entire process. She was slow and clumsy at first. He soon discovered she did better when he walked away and found something else to do. She didn't perform well under scrutiny. But she liked having him close. Just in case.

She came back each afternoon and worked with him and the horses until dinner. By the end of the first week, she had enough confidence to groom the horse and position the saddle blanket on the horse's back. By the end of the second week, she could put a saddle over the horse's back. It was hard for Jack not to step in and take the saddle from her. She was so short and weak in her arms, the heavy, cumbersome saddle looked like she would fall forward just carrying it. But she managed to wrestle it up over the horse, and beamed at herself as if she accomplished something truly important. He began to think she wasn't just trying to pay her debt at the ranch, but actually enjoyed and looked forward to the work they did with the horses.

Week three: she could saddle the horse, cinch it, and wanted to learn how to lead the horse around. Jack soon had her walking the horse all over the ranch, the road, the pastures, and all the while, made her stop and start, walk fast, then slow, and kept showing her where the horse was to be in relation to her. He cringed whenever the horse's feet got too close to hers. Last thing he needed was for her to break a toe. But eventually, she started to lead the horse, becoming much more aware of where it was, and where she was, and soon possessed a real command instead of the unnatural fear she began with.

Jack spent quite a while showing her several different exercises she could do with the horse as ground work. One was merely standing in front of the horse and gently shaking the horse's lead rope toward the horse indicating for the horse to step back. When Erin managed to get the horse to do as she commanded she almost started dancing around. Who knew she could actually command a horse to do something? Another "horse game," as Jack called them, was to start twirling the end of the horse's lead rope whichever way she wanted the horse to start trotting. She eventually got the horse to circle around her in the desired direction. Jack was able to then make the horse stop and switch directions with barely a flick of the rope. She was just happy to get it doing what she commanded one way.

Finally she was able to get her horse to do all the games and she was able to tie it to the hitching post. All alone. Jack was saddling one of his horses for a ride. He leaned against the doorjamb as he watched her. She'd come a long way from the very first day.

"I think tomorrow, you'll be ready to get on her."

Erin turned around at his voice. "You mean get on the horse?"

He nodded. "I mean get on the horse."

"I don't think…"

"I'm the teacher, right? That's why I do the timeline about this stuff."

She bit her lip and slowly nodded. "Okay."

"It won't be like your ride with Joey. I'll hold the horse, and lead you. I won't let you go, not tomorrow anyway. We'll do it in the enclosed arena. You'll see, as far as you've come, you'll do just great."

"You think I've come far?"

"Sure. You didn't know that?"

She shook her head. "You don't ever say."

He didn't? He watched her. He probably could have been a little more encouraging towards her. He stayed back and kept his distance. "You're doing great. With the horses and overcoming your fear."

Her face lit up and her smile broke through her conscious reserve with him as her eyes flashed. He stepped back. There were reasons for him to keep things distant between them. She was too pretty not to. She was lived on his ranch, was too far into his debt, and had slept with his little brother. There was every reason to keep them separated. The simple fact that he had too much power over her current situation.

"Thank you. I look forward to this all day. I hope it doesn't take too much from your work."

It did. It actually took a lot from his work. He didn't tell her that. Or mention it to anyone else. He quickly did his leftover chores after Charlie was in bed, or cut corners on the others. He was uncomfortable whenever he considered why that was.

"Tomorrow then?"

She grinned, nodded, turned and left the barn. He watched her walk away and stared too long at her small butt in the blue jeans. The way her hips swayed in her heeled cowboy boots. She looked so different from the woman who first stood in his driveway. There seemed to be a bit of confidence starting to build in her.

"Dad?"

Jack glanced up when he heard Charlie calling him. He walked out of the barn and found Charlie. "Yeah?"

Charlie stood there, fidgeting, and hanging his head. "Don't forget the Mother's Day Tea is tomorrow at school."

Damn. He'd forgotten. Charlie looked miserable at the news. He glared down at the dust over their feet. "Okay. I'll be there."

"What about Erin? I'd rather she come."

Things felt different now then when the subject first came up. He rubbed a hand to his chin and then nodded. "Okay. I think that would be fine, if she's willing."

Charlie's head jerked up, and a smile brightened his face. "Do you mean it, Dad? Would she do it?"

"I mean it. Again, only if she says yes." He had the uncomfortable knowledge that she would most likely say yes to anything he asked of her. Due to the whole power imbalance of their situation. That knowledge, however, made him slightly ill at ease. "I'll go talk to her."

Charlie grinned, then hugged him as he ran off with a "Whoop!" Jack crossed the road and knocked on the trailer door.

"Jack?" Her eyes lit up with surprise as she opened the door wider.

He hadn't been over there since the morning Chance left. "Can I come in?"

She looked at him with weariness in her eyes, but allowed him to enter. He walked in and glanced around. The trailer looked a lot better. She moved her stuff to the bedroom, and tidied what there was of the living space. He still couldn't get over how her brother stuck her on the couch, or that this place was all she had in the world.

"Did you want something?" She spoke from behind him and he turned around. The trailer was small and she was way

171

too close. Her long black hair curled over her shoulders, and sprang around her headband.

"Uh, yeah, actually. You remember that Tea Charlie was crying about?"

"Sure."

"Would you be willing to go with him?"

Her eyes rounded and her mouth opened in a giant O, but she finally nodded. "Of course. I'd be glad to."

"He specifically asked if you would go. I think considering how things have changed, it would be appropriate now, if you were comfortable."

"I'd be pleased to. It's the least of what I'd like to pay back for the way you've let me stay here."

"You'll have to miss work because it's at noon."

She shook her head. "I'll be there."

He nodded. "Okay. Good. Thanks. I really appreciate you doing this."

She let out a breathy laugh. "It doesn't even begin to pay back what I owe you."

He stuck his hands in his jean pockets. "Actually, when it comes to my kids, this isn't nothing, it's everything to me. So, yeah, I appreciate it."

She smiled and turned to walk into her small kitchen. She reached over the stove and opened a cabinet, standing on her tiptoes while she rummaged around. He noticed her bare feet and painted pink toenails, and the way her shirt rode up her back an inch whenever she raised her arms. He commanded his eyes to stare only at the sink beyond her until she settled her feet flat on the floor again.

"I wanted to give you this."

He looked down. She had money in her hands. Cash. Of course, no bank for Erin.

"For what?"

"For what? I don't know. Everything. A down payment on what I owe you. Clothes, food, rent, gas. Take your pick."

He pushed the few twenties back towards her. "Save it. I mean it. Pay me when you can actually support yourself."

She kept her hands out. "Please take it. I intend to pay you back for everything, and start to support myself soon. I just wish I could pay you all of it."

He took it, wishing she would just keep it. But he respected the sentiment. He was fully starting to respect her. "You are. Tomorrow at Charlie's school."

She looked up and smiled. "Noon."

He turned and left the small space. Shutting the door behind him, he breathed deeply as he glanced up toward the hills above the ranch. The spot he rescued her from. He liked being in the open space, and the fresh air, after being suddenly unable to breathe right inside the trailer with her. What the hell was that all about?

CHAPTER 16

*E*rin walked into the classroom at noon with her stomach churning in knots. She hadn't been in a classroom in years, but had never liked them. However, she didn't want to do anything to draw attention or shame to Charlie, and by extension, Jack. Jack, who had strangely become the most important person in her life. She would be alone, destitute and in serious trouble if it weren't for Jack's intervention.

He had rescued her from a terrible situation, in every sense of the word, all the while teaching her new and exciting things. The horses and the ranch became something that made her wake up filled with energy and interest towards the coming day, where nothing in her entire life had ever interested her before. Previously, she'd woken up to work, to survive, and to make it through. She never had a hobby, or a passion, or whatever her love for the horses and ranch was to her now.

Charlie beamed when he saw her. She smiled back as she glanced around. The classroom seemed transformed with paper butterflies hanging from the ceiling, and the desks set into squares of four with pink butcher paper and plastic table settings. It was quite elegant and lovely for a third grade classroom. No wonder Jack didn't want anything to do with it. It was all women; mothers and grandmothers encircling their precious students. There wasn't a man in sight.

She walked over to Charlie, having carefully dressed as best she could with her spare wardrobe. Wearing jeans and sandals, she added a dressy, purple top, which she found at a thrift shop this morning in preparation for the Tea. She wasted precious tip money on it, but felt it was important to make a good impression on behalf of the Rydells.

Charlie's smile was so shy, it twisted Erin's heart. He looked relieved that she was there as she sat down at the desk next to him.

"Good afternoon. I'm Allison Gray, Charlie's teacher."

Erin glanced up. Before her stood a pretty woman who, to Erin's surprise, looked to be about her own age. She was of average height with a curvy figure, which she carefully tried to minimize under well-made slacks, and a pretty, ruffled, pale pink blouse. Allison's hair was a bright, glossy red color, and was startling and unusual, owing to the way she wore it slicked back into a tight ponytail at the nape of her neck, which she tried to keep concealed. Erin almost told her to let it loose, so the beautiful, rare color could speak for itself. The red hue made her think of Jack's dark red hair.

Allison smiled at her and Erin couldn't help smiling back. She had a welcoming kind of face, with flawless, white skin and freckles, and beautiful blue eyes that sparkled with genuine interest and life.

"I'm Erin Poletti. Charlie's... well, I'm a friend of the family."

Allison leaned in towards Erin with a smile as she spoke softly so Charlie couldn't hear, "I'm so glad you could make it. Charlie's been upset for nearly a month now. He was adamant he didn't want Jack to come."

Erin kept the real relationship she had with the Rydells to herself. She also wondered how much Allison knew about Jack. She wanted to ask, and wanted to know so much more than she already did, but instead, she merely smiled back at Allison, and primly folded her hands on the desk, hoping to get through the hour without creating any drama or obvious blunders.

Soon, the classroom was overflowing with a crowd of women. Erin hated it. She wasn't sure how to act.

Soon, a card was passed out to each woman from their respective student. Erin looked at the handmade card with a drawing of stick-Charlie, standing in a grassy pasture with a rainbow, and the sun, clouds and trees all around him. Next to him was a hastily added woman figure that Erin suspected was supposed to be her. She assumed Charlie snuck it on sometime this morning.

"All the students wrote a little poem to their mothers, or grandmothers, or special friends, whatever applies. I'd love to hear some of them."

Erin's heart froze as Allison spoke to the group and she stared at the white card. There were words across the front of it, as well as inside it. They were hand printed in crayon with the penmanship of a typical third grader. Allison wouldn't call on her. *She couldn't.* They didn't know her. She'd call on people everyone else knew.

Charlie glanced at her. "Don't you like it, Erin?"

She looked down at Charlie's hopeful face. Caught in her own horror for not being able to read the elementary school card, she never imagined how her reaction would appear to Charlie. She forced a smile onto her face. "Oh, Charlie, I love it. I'll treasure it. No one's ever made me a card before."

"Never?"

"No. Never."

Charlie beamed in appreciation, then happily raised his hand. Erin's smile faded as she realized what Charlie was doing. "Mrs. Gray, we can read ours."

Allison turned at Charlie's waving hand and small voice over the crowd's murmur. The attention of the entire room was fastened on Charlie, and therefore, Erin too, who held the card. She quickly handed it to Charlie. "Go ahead, Charlie."

He nodded. "Oh yeah; you can't read, can you? I'll read it to you."

She felt every eye shifting towards her. Her face was bathed in red as she blushed uncontrollably. She stared at the desk in front of her without lifting her head. Charlie's voice rang out over the classroom as he easily read the poem he composed. It was a lovely little poem, a "roses are red" variation. Allison's gaze was kind toward her as she thanked Charlie for his poem. Finally, the class moved on to the next reader. Erin sunk down into the small chair as low as she could get. She'd had numerous embarrassing situations, when she couldn't hide her stupidity, but nothing that equaled the humiliation of that very moment. She didn't taste the cookies or the tea that was served. She didn't raise her eyes again to look at anyone. She barely mumbled thanks when Allison came around to the tables, chatting to each student and parent again. She accomplished that, at least; Charlie seemed totally clueless that he managed to mortify her in such a way that she vowed to never show her face around the school or valley again.

After the tea and cookies were served and cleaned up, Erin followed and did what the other women around her did, like tearing up the butcher paper and helping to tidy up the classroom.

"Excuse me?" a voice said behind Erin.

She turned to find a tall, pretty brunette in a long skirt and sweater standing there. "You're Erin? Joey's girlfriend? Or are you Jack's? Hard to tell. I'm surprised Jack let you come here with Charlie."

Erin stepped back. The woman was staring at her and her mouth puckered in disdain.

"I'm sorry; who are you?"

"Who am I? I'm Kara Fisher. I was Lily's best friend. You know... Jack's wife. We had our kids together. Charlie and my son, Anthony, are best friends. We were over at the ranch just the other day."

"I didn't know Lily."

"Who are you then? Charlie said you live there now?"

"I don't live there. I'm staying there for now. My brother worked for the Rydells. He caused some trouble for me, and the Rydells are only helping me out."

Kara let out a breath with a nod. "Oh. Okay. I didn't think someone like you would be Jack's type. Joey's maybe, but never Jack's. He and Lily... they were together since we were fifteen, you know. There was never anyone else for either of them. It broke his heart when she died."

"I honestly don't know anything about it."

Kara eyed her up. "Charlie's had a hard run of it, you know. His mother dead. His grandmother dead; and Jack's so busy with everything on the ranch that he's responsible for. I'd hate to see anything else go wrong for them."

Erin got the insinuation. As in *she*. She would be wrong for them. Staring with disdain at the woman before her she wondered if anyone could really be that horrible to another. Right to her face!

Erin was the first guest to leave. She quickly made it out the corridor with her heels clicking rapidly on the vinyl floor. She opened the door to the school and hurried to her borrowed truck, where she leapt inside and peeled out of the school parking lot. When she reached her coffee stand, she let her head fall onto the steering wheel.

After she finally got out, while wiping at her tears, she undressed down to her swimsuit and opened the stand back up. It wasn't long before the first fifty-year-old man, towing a trailer full of cows, came through. His eyes never rose above her collarbone as he ordered and paid for the coffee he didn't seem to care all that much about drinking.

JACK WAITED for Erin to show up that afternoon and got annoyed by how much it bothered him when she didn't show. He kept glancing towards her trailer, waiting for her to pop out. Her truck was parked just in front of the trailer, so he knew she was there. Why, then, didn't she come out? She came out to the barn every day, over the last three weeks. Today, she was due to get on the horse; so why wasn't she there?

"You want me to get her?"

Jack glanced at Ben. He offered to help get Erin on the horse. Ben finally seemed over his crush on Erin. He did, however, seem to genuinely like her as a friend. He liked helping her out a lot. She went to Ben with any reading she had to do. He helped her read through the menu at her coffee stand until she learned it by heart. She would have rather crawled into a hole than let Jack or any of his brothers help her. But with Ben? She found him comfortable to ask for help, now that Jack had given his permission for her to do so.

He thought it was incomprehensible that she made it this far in her life without learning to read. But she remained closed-lipped about it, as she did with most of her life.

She turned out to be a hard worker. Also an avid listener, she tried with all her heart to obey whatever he asked her to

179

do with the horses. She overcame all her own fears and weaknesses. Where Chance was a nothing, Erin turned out to be really something.

Charlie was spinning in circles and getting dizzy until he walked in a drunken shuffle, then giggled happily and started the process all over again. When Ben asked about Erin, Charlie stopped to glance at Jack. "She was okay at school today. I read her my poem and she liked it, even if I had to read it to her. No one else minded though."

Jack glanced at Charlie's spinning red hair. "You didn't mention to anyone else that she couldn't read it, did you?"

Charlie stopped and frowned, but shrugged, looking unconcerned. "I guess I did. Why? Was it a secret?"

Jack ruffled Charlie's hair as he passed by him, and Charlie looked unhappy suddenly. "I hurt her feelings, didn't I?"

"You didn't know, bud, so it's okay. I'll talk to her."

Jack crossed the driveway and passed around her truck to the door. He knocked, but got no response.

"Erin? Open the door."

There was muffled noise and movements. Finally, the door opened, and she frowned at him, then turned and walked towards the couch, where she flopped down. She wore a sweatshirt over a pair of jeans and her hair was messed up, as if she'd been lying on it.

He stepped inside. It always felt like the trailer shrunk to a pop can size when he went inside with Erin. He wasn't sure why, but guessed whatever energy existed between them wasn't meant for small spaces.

He was aware of how attractive he found her. He didn't react to her like most females of the valley. Kailynn came to his house nearly every day, and he never even looked twice at her as she moved around him while working. But with Erin, when she was anywhere near him, every cell in his body seemed to jump to attention and become aware of her.

Leaning back into the kitchen counter, he folded his arms over his chest. "Both boys are waiting for you. They wanted to help you learn to ride today."

She grimaced as she stared down at the carpet. "I forgot. I'm not in the mood today."

"You know, Charlie hasn't quit raving about how much fun he had with you. It was the first time he's ever gone to it with a female. It was huge to him."

She smiled faintly. "Good. At least, I didn't fail him."

"You're really going to skip the horses today?"

She finally looked up at him, with a hesitant gaze. "Can't I skip one day?"

He shrugged. "Yeah. It's your choice. It's not like it's mandatory for you to keep living here."

"What is mandatory for me to keep living here?"

He frowned. "What do you mean?"

"I mean how long before I wear out my welcome? How long do I have left to get out of here?"

"I wasn't aware you hated being here so much. But I guess, it makes sense; the ranch isn't for most people. It's an isolated, tough way of life. I'm sure you must miss the city."

She laughed a hollow, bitter sound. "Miss the city? I don't miss one thing about it. But this isn't my home. How long will you let me stay? I need a timeline. I need to figure out what to do."

He cleared his throat, and answered gently, "Where do you think you're going to go?"

"I noticed a couple of trailer parks in town, and they only wanted five hundred a month."

"Yeah, for the worst ones. You hate the ranch that much? You'd rather live in town?"

She looked up at him and her eyes were fierce. "I love the

181

ranch. I mean I love this area, the river, the mountains, but I can't stay here on your charity and crumbs."

"Has something changed about your situation since yesterday?"

She shook her head.

"Then where is that coming from? I told you could stay here, and I meant it. You don't cause trouble, you don't try to steal from us like your brother, and you're not taking up any space we need. So I don't care how long you stay."

She stood up and started pacing. The living area was only six feet long, so she came close to him as she turned around and paced back.

"What's going on? This about what Charlie did today? He's sorry. He doesn't understand about being discreet. He didn't realize he should have kept it to himself."

Erin stopped with her back to him and her head sunk. "I don't blame him. It's not his fault that I can't read a third grader's poem. Or that I have no money, no skills, no family, no home, no clothes, and no life at all, really. Or that the only reason I'm not homeless right now is because of the charity of his father."

Jack felt his hand twitch and he wanted to reach out, and touch her shoulder. Just to touch her. But he didn't. He wouldn't. He would never. Not only did she live on the ranch, which automatically made it a terrible idea, she'd already slept with his brother, and therefore, was the worst possible candidate he could think of for himself as a date.

"None of which is your fault, nor mine. Again, it just I so. And it's not all that new. What does this have to do with riding a horse today?"

She turned around. "Everything. If I stay here, I'll embarrass you, or your brothers and your boys. People are already talking, and no doubt, wondering why I'm still here. They probably are discussing which one of you I'm fucking. But then, that's why I stayed here to begin with."

Jack's eye twitched. He had no idea what to say or how to even begin to respond to her remark. He dropped his hands to his side.

"Okay, yeah, they talk. There's been gossip about Joey from the night you spent on the beach with him. So they talk. Anything that happens here, even as small as a paper cut, gets gossiped about. But I don't remember the last time I actually paid any attention to it."

She went completely still at his voice and finally glanced at him. "Do you remember the night you walked me across the yard in the dark?"

"Yeah. What about it?" he asked as he shifted his weight and felt uncomfortable with her sudden scrutiny on his face. He shouldn't have said anything to her. At the time, however, he thought she'd only be a temporary visitor and not a fixture on the ranch.

"You asked me why I didn't expect more for myself, from Joey."

"Yeah, I guess I did."

"No one ever said that to me before. Not one person ever told me I should expect more for myself. My mother never once said anything like that to me. I started fully sleeping around when I was sixteen years old, Ben's age, and my mother never once said, 'Don't do that, Erin.' She knew I had the boys over. And she knew I did it because I struggled so hard with school. It was a way to fit in. Forget. I wasn't doing it out of enjoyment or anything healthy. She knew that and still she encouraged it. It never even occurred to me to expect more until you said that to me."

Jack shifted the weight on his feet and didn't know what to say. It seemed so sad to think of her having sex for all the wrong reasons. It seemed to be the key to Erin. Suddenly, her sleeping with Joey seemed somehow tragic when before it seemed annoying.

"I'm not the kind of person you want to have around your kids."

How Jack wished Lily were here. She'd know what to say to Erin. She'd know how to counsel a woman whose entire self-esteem seemed to depend on how he reacted to her right there, right now. Lily would understand why a woman chose to sleep around even when they didn't seem to want to, or even enjoy it. It seemed to be something that caused Erin negative self-esteem. He had zero idea what words to say to ease that.

Instead he settled on, "I decide who gets to be around my kids. I did keep you away. I thought you could be like your brother. You're not. Now, I don't. Take that as you will."

She frowned. Then her eyes rose up to meet his. He really had no idea what to say or think, much less, what Erin thought. "I don't understand you," she finally said quietly.

He nodded. "That's okay, because I don't understand you either. But we both like to ride horses. So? Now do you want to learn to ride a horse today or not?"

"What that simple? Nothing has been solved."

He shrugged. "That simple. As far as I'm concerned nothing has changed. You had a crappy day. I'm sorry about that. But it happens. It doesn't mean there is anything bigger going on here."

"I thought it did."

"You said it did. I never said a word. Other then, thank you for going with Charlie today. I'm sorry you were humiliated. But I still appreciate it. He had no idea you felt bad and had a great time with you. I appreciate that."

"He didn't?"

"No. None."

"Then... I guess, you're welcome." She stared at him

184

before a slow smile started across her face. "Nothing has changed?"

"No. Nothing."

"Then, yes, I'd like to learn to ride a horse."

"Good. Then let's get to it, I have a lot more to do still today."

WITH THAT, Erin began her first horseback riding lesson. Jack told Ben to hold the horse by his bridle and keep him still. Jack talked her through, once again, all the basics he taught her so far about riding a horse. There were a lot of small details, and he made her repeat all the answers to the questions he posed. He taught her so thoroughly, she knew all the fundamental basics inside and out. Now, she just had to execute all of them, starting with climbing into the saddle.

She managed to get up onto the saddle, but was slow to let Ben start walking to lead the horse. It all came very slowly for her. After several hours, she finally did an entire circle with no help from Jack, Ben or Charlie, and with her horse under her control. When she made it all the way around, both father and sons clapped, whistled, and cheered for her. They all stood leaning against the rails to watch her. She brought the horse to a complete stop, and finally looked up when she broke her concentration. She grinned maniacally, and her heart felt like it might explode in her chest. *She'd done it!* She had ridden the horse, and not only that, but she'd done it correctly and while in complete control. She knew she still had a long way to go, but she was at a place she never thought she'd get to. And all because of the patience Jack showed her over the course of a month, using time he didn't have to spend with her, and patience he didn't have to teach her.

They came over, and waited for her to dismount. Jack held the horse as Ben and Charlie both jumped around, smiling as happily for her as she did for herself. When Charlie hugged her waist, she eagerly hugged him back and high-fived Ben. Ben had been bringing a girl in his class home often to hang out with him. His crush on Erin seemed to have faded completely and he now regarded her purely as a friend.

Jack grinned at her over his boys' heads. She smiled back, her heart rate suddenly racing at his visible pleasure with her achievement. Seeing the way his eyes held hers, and seemed to grow warm watching her, she had to turn away. She didn't know exactly why, except that the heat she felt inside confused her, and the excitement he set off in her gut didn't make any sense in her mind. She could barely hold his gaze these days because of the strange new reaction in her chest.

CHAPTER 17

*M*other's Day dawned a beautiful sunny day, with the highs predicted in the eighties. The valley and land were lush with new green leaves and grasses growing tall and full. The pine trees sparkled in the morning dew and the air smelled spicy, of fresh dirt and pines, a scent Erin never had quite grown used to. It felt so invigorating and pure, almost as if she were breathing an exotic perfume, and not simply the country air.

She dreaded today and knew it would be hard. She woke early as usual. Sundays and Mondays were her days off at the coffee stand, but her regular, three-thirty wake-up usually intruded onto her days off all the same. She watched the sunrise change the sky into pearly colors of peach and orange. It shadowed the mountains in dark, inky lines as the day slowly began to bloom from behind them. Stretching slowly, like a cat, the warm morning rays drew minute-by-minute closer to where she sat on the steps of her trailer, watching.

It was about eight o'clock when she spotted movement at the ranch house. She stood up when she saw all of the Rydell brothers walking along the porch, trailed by the kids. They were all dressed up: each wearing slacks, a buttoned shirt, and clean, polished cowboy boots. Jack even wore a tie. She stared from her trailer steps, still clad in sweat pants and a baggy sweatshirt. *Where were they all going?*

Sunday. She supposed they could be going to church, although she didn't know if they ever went. Perhaps today, being Mother's Day, was why they chose to attend. She almost called out, but refrained. It wasn't her place. Besides, if they did happen to invite her, she had nothing appropriate to wear.

She watched them piling into two trucks and pulling out. The dust ballooned around them, and slowly settled back. Dust seemed to be everywhere lately, and Ben informed her that it would last until next October. That soon, Ben predicted, the temperatures would become so hot and uncomfortable, she'd wish for overcast days without the hot, scorching sun. She, however, doubted she would ever wish for that. And if Ben had ever spent the months of September through July in Seattle, she had no doubt he'd agree.

She felt dejected today. Much more so than usual. Although she never felt good about herself, what with squatting on the Rydell land, wearing a bikini for work at a coffee stand, still hopelessly illiterate and the effects that had on her sense of self, while accepting all her material needs as charity; today, she felt much worse than she usually did.

She knew, of course. It was the first Mother's Day that should have technically meant nothing to her. She had no mother and could ignore Mother's Day just as easily as she spent her entire life ignoring Father's Day.

She dropped her head onto her drawn-up knees, feeling too depressed for words. Though her mother certainly wasn't the best, she was still *her* mother. Lorna Poletti was only sixteen when she had Chance, and eighteen when she had Erin. Both children had different fathers. The only reason Lorna didn't proceed to have another half dozen kids or more was because she wisely had her tubes tied.

Erin could remember her mother continuously having boyfriends over, one right after the next. And when one didn't work out, her mother cowered in her room for days, refusing to eat, and sleeping all day, while crying all night. Erin quickly learned to stay out of her mother's way at such times and provide for herself. She couldn't remember a day when she did not have to fend for herself. From the time she started the first grade, she had to get herself to the bus and home again.

Then, inevitably, after her latest break-up, Lorna always decided they should move. Somehow, that managed to fill the void that always seemed to consume her mother when she was mateless.

Erin didn't understand her mother's condition until she was older. She suffered from debilitating depression and manic highs. Erin suspected her mother suffered from some kind of mental disorder. But her mother refused to seek help or treatment. So they continued to live in this strange, unpredictable cycles. Sometimes Lorna was crazy fun and amazing to have for a mother. They did wonderful things together, like taking off in the middle of the night to look for "magic." Erin didn't realize until she was a bit older, that the "magic" was really her mother scoring some street drugs to make her feel better. But when Erin was just a kid, they were enchanted journeys that left her mother smiling, as she pretended all the street signals and streetlights were fairies and angels.

Every time Lorna crashed into depression was usually when they decided to move again. She couldn't hold any job for very long, and they were never well paying. She had nothing then, just as she had nothing now.

When Erin hit third grade and still couldn't seem to grasp the basics of reading and spelling, despite endless tiered reading interventions, her mother always reassured her that it didn't matter. Erin was different than other kids, and special. She alone had "magic." Erin, however, knew she wasn't special. She was just stupid. So she began her campaign to hide it. With each new school, she learned how to compensate for it temporarily. After she was discovered, and her well-meaning teacher called her mother in to discuss what they should do, her mother simply yanked her from school and kept her home until the next school, where it would all start over again.

Lorna never really cared that Erin couldn't read. As Erin grew older, Lorna simply did all of her reading for her. At age sixteen, when Erin totally dropped out of school to work, Lorna filled out all her paperwork. She worked until Lorna killed herself.

She shuddered as the images refilled in her head. Her mother. Dead. Her mother in the car, lifeless. She closed her eyes and re-experienced herself crying, shaking, and screaming at her mother. But Lorna, for once, didn't reply.

It was complicated to love someone and also feel such anger. Not just how it all ended but for how Lorna had raised her.

Tears started to fall down her face. She stood up, and started toward one of the ranch roads. She zig-zagged over the fields and ended up along the river. The river lay thirty feet down the bank with boiling rapids. It was where the Rydells had their private cemetery. Erin had seen it, but never ventured very close. Today, however, she felt bad and morbid enough to wander through the gate. Looking around, she saw a dozen tombstones that were raised up in perfect, perpendicular lines. Many of the dates on the gravestones went back to the mid-eighteen hundreds. Erin glanced towards the opposite end, where the most recent additions lay: the Rydells' parents, and Jack's wife. Erin stared at the headstone. Lily Marie Carter Rydell, Wife, Mother, Beloved. She died over five years ago.

Charlie would have been three, and Ben only ten. Jack would have just been thirty. That seemed so young to be widowed and alone, having to raise two boys, along with Joey, who would have been just fifteen at the time.

Erin sat down on a stone bench near Lily's grave. The river sparkled like a new quarter in the sunlight. The air was soft and comforting, as the sun's rays warmed her face. Erin closed her eyes. It was so quiet, she could hear the insects in the grass, as well as the birds twittering in the trees. It was the most peaceful spot she could think of spending her time today.

Tears tipped over her eyelids again. She never had a moment's peace in her entire childhood. Not while living in the chaotic, transient, volatile world that reflected her mother's emotional turmoil.

Somehow for the first time in her life, this place gave her the peace she'd always sought. The quiet that never matched her heart, emotions or environment. Somehow she'd found it.

Here with Jack.

Her eyes opened. *No.* She was here just to be here. This beautiful spot. She was ensconced in the quiet security and peace that the land provided, and the mountains embraced, and most of all, the kindness of the entire Rydell family.

She shook her head. This was not a good day for her. All the grief from her past felt thick in her lungs. She felt like someone laid her down and piled a ton of river rocks on her chest.

She stood up suddenly when she heard a strange noise. Coming down the road were Jack, Ben and Charlie. She cursed softly. Of course, they would come here today. Mother's Day had to be as bad for them as it was for her.

Jack looked completely different than she'd ever seen him. He wore black dress slacks with a light blue, button-up shirt. He'd taken his tie off, undone the top buttons at his throat, and untucked the ironed shirt. Still, he looked different. She'd only ever seen him in jeans, t-shirts, flannels, and worn boots. His red hair glinted under the sun in deep auburn and blonde highlights. He was rarely without a hat, and she nearly stepped back in shock. He looked younger than usual.

She bit her lip. She should not have come here. Not today. Not while they came to pay their respects to their wife and mother. She only came there because she sought the ambiance of the cemetery for her unfettered grief. Now she just looked weird and morbid.

"Erin."

Erin smiled as Charlie came running up to her. In the few days since the Tea at his school, he decided she was his friend. He always had bright smiles and good cheer when he spotted her. He often joined her while she tended the horses or went to the beach.

"Hey," she said, smiling at Charlie, and casting a weary glance at Jack. He couldn't possibly be glad that she was there.

Ben came towards her, looking like a younger, fresher version of Jack with his own dress-up clothes. He leaned down and put the pink roses he carried on top of his mother's grave. Erin stepped back, which resulted in her stepping into Jack. She instantly pushed herself away from him and jumped to the side.

"I should go."

"Why do you have to?" Charlie asked as he came nearer and slipped his hand into hers. She looked down, feeling as startled as if a bee just stung her. Her heart melted at Charlie's small, clammy, boy hand in hers. He was looking at his mother's grave with an expression of confusion. It must have been hard to grieve for someone you couldn't remember.

Jack's gaze was on her profile, and dropped to where his son held her hand. She finally turned her head to him, fearing the scorn she expected to find on his face.

"Enjoying the vibes?" he asked finally.

She frowned at him. His tone and facial expression were utterly neutral. But she saw the slight tic at the corner of his mouth. He was just kidding. Unbelievably to her, Jack was kidding while she stood near his wife's grave, holding his son's hand.

She shook her head vigorously. "It seemed like the place to go today."

He nodded. "I get that." He stepped forward, dropped to a knee, and lay down the single red rose he held in his hand. His head bent into the gravestone as his lips moved silently. He was praying. Ben, too, held his head down, but Charlie merely stared out towards the river.

Jack straightened up and walked a few feet over, where he laid the other bouquet of wild flowers on top of his parents' grave. She noticed he didn't bend over them with quite the sickening gravity that he did with his wife. *What a burden.* Losing both his parents and his wife. The man literally looked like he had the weight of the world on his shoulders. And how did he respond to his newfound responsibilities? By becoming the most capable, accountable, dependable, caring, stable man she'd ever met. She couldn't even manage taking care of herself with any kind of decent, sustainable consistency. By the time Jack was her age, he'd already been running a ranch, raising three young boys, while supervising his other two brothers. The clashes in their life patterns were staggering, and their choices of how to deal with their lives were just as drastic.

It depressed her to realize what a pathetic, disappointing slacker she was in comparison to someone like Jack.

She glanced at Ben and saw tears streaming over his face. He wiped them with his knuckles, pressing hard into the sockets of his eyes. He obviously didn't want to cry. Erin's heart twisted for him. The poor kid. He remembered what Charlie never knew.

Erin itched to put her hand on Ben's shoulder, but she knew that he was furiously scrubbing his tears so that she didn't see them. The last thing she should do is acknowledge them. Jack seemed to get that too and walked over towards Ben. He raised an arm and wrapped it around his son's shoulders. Ben's head was within inches of Jack, but neither man said anything. Charlie didn't join them, and only held more tightly onto Erin's hand. She squeezed it back.

Finally, Ben hung his head as he nodded to something Jack said to him quietly. Then Ben straightened up, and smiled abashedly at her. His eyes were red-rimmed. She ached to reassure Ben not to be shy or embarrassed. She found him much sweeter, kinder, heart-wrenching, and more impressive for grieving over his mother than if he merely stood there, uncaring, and displaying raw teenage ambivalence.

Ben glanced at Charlie. "Hey. Wanna go pitch some rocks in?"

Charlie nodded eagerly and they started off together through the cemetery, skirting around the fence and down towards the river. Erin watched them leave, glad they were getting space from all this, but also intensely aware she was now all alone with Jack at his family's cemetery. It wasn't just odd, it was wrong.

"I should have realized you'd come here today. I... well, to be honest, I wasn't thinking how hard this day would be on you guys too."

Jack looked down at the grave in front of him. "Today sucks. But we've had a few years to practice. It's pretty fresh for you. It'll get easier next year."

She didn't expect his kind understanding. "You're not mad I came here?"

He glanced at her. "I find it curious you came, but no; why would I be mad?"

"I wish I could visit my mother today."

"Where is she?"

"Cremated. I spread her ashes at one of her favorite beaches along Puget Sound in Seattle."

"Alone?"

"Yes. No one lasted very long in my mother's life. She drove everyone away. Even Chance."

"Except for you."

She smiled. "Yes, well I had to have her in order to navigate my life. So I never had any choice."

"You miss her?"

She glanced off towards the meadow to her right, which disappeared into brown, rolling mountains that rose into the pixie blue sky. "I wish it were that simple. Or that I merely loved her and missed her. I'm angry. She's not supposed to be dead. Intellectually I know it's so much more complicated then that. But in my heart, it feels like she deliberately left me. I'd always hoped we'd someday find a way to have a better relationship and now that chance doesn't exist. How could she just leave her only daughter?"

"I don't know. How do you leave your only son because you don't like where you live?"

She jerked her head towards Jack. "What do you mean?"

He nodded towards his parents' grave. "That isn't my mother. My mother isn't dead. She left me and my father when I was two years old. My dad remarried Donna when I was four. She was my mother in every sense of the word."

Erin's mouth opened. "I had no idea. So your brothers…"

"Are my half-brothers."

"Where is she now?"

He shrugged. "Don't know. She hated the ranch. She met my father one summer when she was staying in Pattinson. She went to the rodeo there and met my dad. They were married too quickly. It was one big adventure to her at first. She grew up in Spokane, and her family had money; and she wasn't used to this kind of life. Eventually, reality set in and she hated it here. It was too quiet, too rural, too backwoodsy. My dad worked long hours…"

"Like you do?"

He paused and then nodded. "Yeah, like I do. Anyway, she left."

"You never heard from her again?"

"No. In some ways, I don't blame her. This place, and this lifestyle, isn't something most people can marry into. You gotta be born into it, and raised in it. If not, most people can't handle it, and eventually leave."

"My mother was mentally ill, depressed, and half the time, stoned out on drugs or scripts. She wasn't exactly the ideal example of motherly love and affection. But she was all I had. And now that Chance has completely deserted me, I'm really alone. All alone and it scares the shit out of me. If I died, who would even care?"

Shaking her head, she sat down. Why did she say that to Jack? He didn't want to hear her problems or phobias. He couldn't understand what it was like to have no home or enduring ties, since for his entire life, he'd had far too many.

"That's not true."

"Yes, it is. There's not one family member. My mom never stayed in one place long enough for there to be family

196

friends. I know you wouldn't be glad if I died, but really, Jack, you'd only feel sorry because you're a decent person, and wouldn't want anyone to die. But as for me, and who I am, there isn't a soul alive who would miss me, grieve for me, or mourn me."

Jack sat down next to her and she looked up at him in surprise before scooting to the left as far as she could. His knees rose up, as the bench was too low for him. Leaning an arm on one knee, he stared out over the river.

"That is unequivocally not true. We might not be your life long friends and family but we care. And you have the chance to build new relationships. Hopefully far better than you had with Chance or your mother. Trust me, all of it gets easier. It just takes time."

She shook her head finally. "Yes. You're right. It's not like you don't know grief, huh?"

Jack nodded, without looking at her, but didn't elaborate.

Finally, she asked, "How did she die?"

Jack's lips were pursed, and he was quiet. The bugs suddenly seemed much louder, and the sun felt hotter on her arms. "She had a rare, genetic heart condition. Before we learned about it, it was too late. She pretty much died out of nowhere. There was little warning, or way of knowing."

"That's terrible. I'm sorry. Were you and she the same age?"

"Yeah."

"Kara mentioned that. She said you'd been together since you were fifteen."

"Kara Fisher? When did you meet her?"

"At Charlie's classroom Tea. She didn't like hearing that I stay here, at the ranch."

He didn't comment for a long moment; then to her surprise, he laughed. "Is that what had you so wigged out after the Tea?"

"Well, yeah. Sure. Part of it. Plus, the fact that I couldn't read what a third grader wrote to me. It wasn't exactly my proudest moment. Anyway, Kara mentioned she was Lily's best friend and kept grilling me about why I was here."

"Kara Fisher was never Lily's best friend. She came on to me at Lily's funeral. That's what a great friend she is."

After the solemnity of their discussion, and the sadness of the day, Erin felt a smile finally starting in her lips. After all she got stressed over, it turned out that Kara wasn't someone's opinion who should matter.

"Oh. I just thought her bitchiness stemmed from her friendship with your wife, not jealousy."

He turned and finally smiled at her fully. Her heart practically stopped. "You know what? She is a bitch. Lily never liked her."

"She said Charlie and her son were best friends."

Jack sighed. "They're good friends, which is the only reason why I tolerate her. Don't, however, let her get to you again."

She allowed a quiet moment to pass before she finally asked, "Were you happy?"

"Happy? With what?"

"With Lily."

His expression changed from affable to the familiar, usual sternness he often looked at her with. "Why would you ask that?"

She shrugged. "I just wondered."

He closed his eyes and leaned his head back as if letting the sun wash over him. Finally, he let out a long breath. "Yeah. I was happy."

"How did you get through it? I mean, when it ended?"

"I had no choice. I had three kids to raise, a roof to provide over everyone's head, and horses to feed."

"Did you eventually get over it? Does the passage of time get you over it?"

He opened his eyes and looked at her. "No. Time doesn't get you over it."

"Then how do you stand it? When you see your sons at their mother's grave, and Charlie doesn't even remember her, while Ben's heart breaks all over again, how do you stand it?"

"Again I have no choice. I have to stand it."

She dropped her shoulders and squeezed her eyes shut. "What if I can't stand it?"

"You already are. You're finding new interests with horses, and developing skills you never had. Things are better then when you got here, so you are already standing it. And the thing is? Just keep putting one foot in front of the other."

She shook her head as the tears burned her eyeballs and she tried to hold them back. "I don't know. You're just so strong, and I'm so useless. You lost so much more than I did, but went on to raise three kids, while I can't even manage to feed, clothe or provide myself shelter. When I see what you've done, and handled, it makes me so ashamed of what I can't do, and can't handle."

"I've had a few more years to get here."

"Bullshit. You always dealt with life face on. And you dealt well."

He shrugged. "I made a lot of mistakes raising my kids, especially after Lily died. You just gotta keep moving, keep trying."

"You've seen how well I do. I was literally abandoned on your door step."

"You were. Again, your brother is a blood-sucking lowlife, whom I wouldn't trust to take care of one of my dogs. So, not totally your fault."

"When Chance first saw me, he told me to use Joey to get what I wanted out of him. I was repelled initially by what my brother was suggesting, but then, isn't that exactly who I am? I knew Joey four days before I slept with him. And only got to stay here because of that. If I hadn't, I wouldn't still be here now. I am exactly what Chance said I was."

"Yeah, then why did you tell me that? Why did you warn me Chance was likely to steal from me? I don't know everything about you, Erin, but I do know whatever motivates you isn't sleazy or evil like whatever is festering inside your brother. And if you really want to know the truth, what I saw your brother do to you with that snake was why you were invited by me to stay, not because of Joey."

"What do you mean?"

He shrugged and stretched his legs before him. "I mean, I clearly saw that your brother meant you harm of some kind or another. I also knew you had no one else, and no place to go. It didn't take me long to figure that out. So I decided you could stay. Even before Chance pulled that stunt. Didn't you wonder why I didn't fire him? I hated him. I detested the work he did and never trusted him getting near any of my horses. Why did you think I let him stay?"

"Because of Joey."

"No. It was because I knew you had nowhere else to go."

She snapped her mouth shut and felt the deep heat of a blush that started in her chest and swiftly rose up her neck and into her face.

"You risked letting me stay. I could have easily turned out to be like Chance."

His gaze brushed over her face. "No. You couldn't. I knew that much."

"You always trust your judgment despite the obvious proof otherwise?"

"Yeah, I do, and I've never been wrong yet." Then he

shook his head and gave her a small grin. "That's a lie. I was wrong about you. When you first came I was convinced you were like Chance. About that was wrong."

She shook her head at his cockiness. And confidence in himself. She'd never felt sure of anything in her life, or any thought she'd ever had.

"Your brothers don't like me."

"My sons do."

She was closer to him. Physically, their bodies moved closer, as if drawn together. His face was turned towards hers, looking down. She froze. What did the look in his eyes mean? What were the strange emotions roiling in her gut? And why was her attention pinned on his mouth?

She swallowed and felt like her heart just climbed up her throat and lodged into her tonsils. "I should go."

It was a stupid thing to say, yet again. She had nowhere to go and nothing to do. Jack knew that. Of all the people in the entire world, Jack most certainly knew that about her.

He finally stood up. "I was thinking you're ready to try riding outside the arena. Want to take a walk down the road?"

She let air fill her lungs as the strange tension left. "You mean on horseback?"

He chuckled. "Of course, on horseback. What better way to hurry this day over? You up for it?"

She hesitated, then nodded. She might have been a loser in every other aspect of her life, but she could learn to ride a horse. And happily spend the worst day of her life with Jack, instead of all alone and feeling depressed.

CHAPTER 18

*J*ack and his brothers were busy over the next few weeks. They planted all the fields and spent hours of their days moving sprinklers and keeping the alfalfa damp. The crop would help offset feed costs when winter came. As the days lingered longer, the work to do also increased. They started before sunrise, and worked long into the twilight. Jack was busy as always with his sons, his brothers, the ranch business, and horse training. Most nights, he fell into his bed, asleep before he managed to even cover himself.

Once in a while, he wished for a woman. For Lily. For sex. Luckily, however, he was too busy to spend a lot of time wanting what he couldn't easily have. River's End was a small place. He sure as hell wasn't sleeping with someone's sister or daughter from around there. And since he wasn't interested in a relationship of any sort, he mostly took care of such urges when he was out of town. Plus, he didn't want his sons to ever find out what he was up to or with whom. He frequently left the ranch overnight to take one of his horses to market, or return a trained horse to its home or a buyer.

He met up with people from all around the west coast, seeking to buy one of his horses or asking him to train their horses.

It previously wasn't as tough to deal with however. Frequently, he could go months without sex. But now, there was Erin. Right there on the ranch, not five hundred feet from the house, every single day. He saw her often enough, since he continued to teach her to ride, and other times when she wandered around the beach and barns. For a city girl, she spent hours on end out and about. Looking, walking, sitting, talking to the horses, and figuring out weekly chores she could do, as well as taking the initiative to do them.

She was downright helpful and always tried extremely hard to do anything he said. She strove to remember all the instructions he gave her, with an earnestness and sincerity that made him turn away rather than let her see his amused smile.

Regularly seeing her out and about on the ranch, he now had an attractive, adult female in his constant sight. It wasn't like he wanted to see Erin. It was just hard not to notice her subtle cleavage whenever she bent over to scoop hay into a stall, or her firm, little ass in jeans as she stretched to get her leg over a horse. It wasn't like he wanted Erin Poletti; he was sure of that. He wanted a woman, but having Erin there always reminded him what he lacked, and soon became a bigger distraction than he counted on. Not since Lily first died did he miss having someone in his bed every night so much.

But she slept with his brother. Not only that, but he saw her with his little brother, all dewy and fresh in the morning at the beach. Beyond her tryst with Joey, she was completely wrong for him. He had a fifteen, almost sixteen-year-old son who was as close to Erin's age as he was. There was something very strange about that.

Besides, they were so different, it wasn't even possible to imagine them together.

Joey didn't like having her there, and was barely civil to her the few times he was forced into her proximity. She made a huge effort to stay away from the house, and out of their way. He'd give her that. He didn't see her like he formerly had, except after he volunteered and asked her to learn to ride. But that was part of who he was. He loved to teach people to ride. Erin wasn't special just because he did so for her.

His brothers were often in the same position as he was. There weren't a lot of women to have discreet sex with. Shane and Joey weren't very discreet. But Jack had a teenage son to worry about, and Ian was as private as Jack. In fact, Jack rarely knew the girls his brothers were sleeping with. Other than, of course, Joey. He knew Joey had a woman from up the river coming over. Unlike Erin, this woman was very vocal, loud, and not the least bit shy of the other three men and two boys who lived there. He often wondered how Erin felt about it. She never said.

Joey expressed on many occasions that he wanted Erin to leave. Jack finally told Joey to get over it, since there was nowhere for her to go. She was staying.

Jack was okay with his decision. He didn't mind her staying there, or living there, and soon grew used to her presence in the barn, the corrals, or watching him train. She often sat up on one of the fences and just observed him. She only spoke to him if he came over to her. She never disturbed or interrupted him, so it was easy to let her stay. Soon it became so normal it stopped being odd.

ERIN'S FEET HURT. Finishing the car's order, she stretched her arm far out the window of her booth to take the five-dollar bill the man held purposely out of reach so she'd have to lean for it and grab it. Of course, that was part of earning his tip, giving him a closer look at her tits. She grabbed the money, and smiled, as if she enjoyed it, then slid back into the booth and shut the window. Turning towards the other window, where another truck waited, she put a smile on her face as she opened the sliding glass.

"Hi, what can I…"

She quit talking mid-sentence when she realized it was Jack, in his idling truck. He looked into her eyes as his gaze wandered down over her. She'd been getting ogled for months and barely registered it anymore. Now, suddenly, with Jack looking at her, she felt the twinge of a blush flooding her face. His gaze met hers and his jaw clenched. He suddenly reached over, putting his truck into gear, and squealed out of the drive-through without a word to her. She stared after his truck in shock.

Holy shit! She never expected Jack to come to her stand. Shane had come through often enough, and Ian once or twice. She had even served some of Ben's friends. Ben had the good grace to not look at her, and stared at her face with a smile that seemed to apologize for coming there.

She never expected Jack to come through. She sighed as she shut the window and finished her shift. Finally, she was done. She redressed in shorts, a t-shirt and sandals. The weather had been above seventy all week.

Once back at the ranch, she pulled in towards her trailer. It was two-thirty. Charlie and Ben weren't home from school yet, and everyone else's truck was gone, except Jack's.

She quickly ran inside to change her clothes. Putting her jeans and boots on, she hastily started towards the barn.

Jack hadn't opened up the main doors. Usually he did

whenever he worked in there. When they were shut, the barn was dark and gloomy. She walked inside, finding Jack in the back. He had saddles spread out before him and was rubbing one of them with a rag. Whatever he was putting on them had a strong odor that singed her nose as she got closer.

He didn't look up as she approached from where he sat on a stool before one of workbenches. He had to know she was there. The place was silent, but for the horses' occasional hoof "clomps" and the soft nickering amongst them.

"Jack?" she finally said to his back. He stiffened, but rubbed harder at the leather. He didn't look at her. She waited, but he refused to acknowledge her.

"Look if this is about earlier…"

He slammed the saddle down. "You don't even think it's a big deal, do you?"

She frowned. "What? Working the coffee stand? It's not my first choice, but it's something I can do."

"Quit. You're not working there anymore, not like that."

Her mouth opened. Was he out of his mind? The fumes from the oil must have been affecting his judgment. "What are you talking about? I can't quit. It's my job. You have no say as to where I work. Besides, why now? Why is this such a big deal now?"

He stood up and whipped around on his heel. "Because I didn't know you were working there half-naked. I thought you were merely serving coffee."

He didn't know? All this time and no one ever mentioned she worked at the *Bikini Babes Barista*? Everyone else knew she worked there. "Your brothers didn't tell you?"

"No one told me."

"Even Ben?"

His jaw clenched. Okay, that wasn't the thing to say. She didn't get it. Why was he so angry? "What are you so pissed off about?"

"You shouldn't work in a place like that. All it does is re-enforce every negative stereotype you think about yourself. And it encourages others to think it too."

"I thought you knew. I mean it wasn't a secret I could ever expect to keep. And besides, I don't get why you're so upset about what I'm doing. If I don't mind, why the hell should you?"

"Why? Because you live on my ranch. Everyone already knows about you and Joey. But Joey's moved on. And now they think it's me. They think I let you stay here for me. So do you really think your working half-naked in a smutty coffee stand helps to squelch that rumor? What you do reflects on me, on my name, and on this ranch. And anything I do reflects on my two sons. That's what this has to do with. And having to explain this to you finally does suggest perhaps you actually are stupid."

Her mouth came open; first, from the shock of his crude-ness, and second, that he'd go so far as to call her stupid. She stepped back as if he'd physically hit her.

"It's just a swimsuit."

"Yeah, right. Just a swimsuit."

"If you're so against it, why did you come there?"

He paused. She stumped him. He scowled harder at her.

"You were there to look at the woman in the bikini, weren't you? Because I recall perfectly you telling me you never drink those drinks. So what? You can go there to look, but me working there makes me somehow bad? You're being, oh big surprise, a chauvinistic asshole!"

He didn't answer her. Silence settled over the darkened barn as her angry words hung between them. She regretted them the minute they left her mouth. She closed her eyes and took a breath. "I have no skills, Jack. I can't read. Where do you think I can find work? The local library? Maybe the law firm in town would employ me. When I told you I have nothing and no choices, this is just one of them."

He shook his head in obvious disgust, then turned his back on her, leaning his arms on the workbench and staring at it.

"See? The negative ways you feel about yourself? This makes it worse."

"This is something I can do that allows me to make money. To head towards independence and taking care of myself again. It is the best thing I can do to find a way to believe in myself again."

She stepped closer to him. Guilt gnawed at her stomach. He hated her now. He thought she was cheap, slutty and easy. He'd seen her first with Joey, and now this. And he thought she was stupid. Which, of course she was, but to date, she somehow thought maybe he didn't really think that of her.

"I'm sorry. I didn't know you'd get this upset at me. I didn't even know I was hiding it from you. I assumed Shane told you the first day he dropped me off there."

Jack didn't answer her and didn't move. She felt tears burning her eyes. She couldn't take Jack hating her. "I'll quit. I will. I just need time to find something else, you know because…"

"Because you're stupid?" he filled in for her. He turned his head to the side so he could see her and she nodded in the affirmative.

He let out a long sigh and she started to turn, stopping suddenly when his hand grabbed her wrist. Shocked, she looked down to where his long fingers encircled her wrist, then up into his eyes. He turned towards her. "You're not stupid, Erin. I shouldn't have said that. I don't think that at all. I was mad. I'm an asshole. But you are not."

She shook her head. Who cares? She was and she knew it, just as long as Jack wasn't mad at her. "It's okay."

"No. It's not. It's not okay you so blithely, or so easily think anyone can call you stupid."

"You didn't. Not really."

"It's not okay that job does nothing but reinforce that idea to you, and other people. It's not okay no one ever taught you the basic skills to survive in life."

She didn't know what to say or what he wanted from her. He looked at her and there was heat in his eyes, his anger very obvious. She didn't know what he wanted her to do about the job.

He pulled her forward as his other hand came to her waist. She froze in his arms. *She was in Jack's arms.* She didn't get it. It couldn't be real or happening. Jack couldn't mean to do this. Then he shifted her closer to him, and the heat of his body burned through her clothes and seemed to radiate into her. Lowering his head, that quickly, his lips met hers.

He kissed her and she didn't know what to do. Both of his hands moved to her waist. Then his tongue licked her lips. Her insides liquefied at his soft, gentle touch. *It was incredible.* She opened her mouth to him, as his tongue felt hot and wet. Her tongue met his, and their lips moved and danced, making her blood boil like it would explode from her. Jack was kissing her. The shock and thrill of it left her weak-kneed.

Then he shifted, placing his leg between hers as he moved her, and lifted her up against him. She could feel him getting hard and warm as he cradled her against his belly. His hands moved restlessly on her back until they found the hemline of her shirt. His hands felt so warm against her bare back and she sighed at the touch. He suddenly pulled her with him, turning her as he guided her somewhere. She was too focused on his mouth over hers to care where or what they were doing. She'd never felt a kiss so long, or deep, or so intimate.

A wall hit her back. The barn wall and he lifted her up. Her legs were now supported by the leg he thrust between hers. What was happening? Where was this coming from? They weren't like this. They were careful to not even brush hands when they switched lead ropes back and forth. How could Jack's hands now be on her? Or Jack's mouth be on hers?

His hand came to her stomach, so warm and soft, she groaned. He gently pushed up, his fingertips brushing over the lace of her bra and the tight beads of her nipples. At his touch, her insides seemed to twist around. The sudden fire that ignited wherever he touched ran lower and much hotter inside her.

He suddenly lifted his mouth off hers, and dropped down, pushing her shirt and bra out of the way and placing his mouth on her. She nearly screamed at the sudden wet, hot sensations. His lips circled her puckered, tight nipple, as his tongue licked over it, first one and then the other. His hands ran down her stomach, into her jeans and beneath her underwear. She nearly quit breathing as her breath hitched and her vision went fuzzy. His hand pushed the seam of her underwear aside as he touched her. Inside her. She ran her hands in the silky strands of his red hair as she felt the pressure of his fingers. It was incredible; so quick and hard, she felt the spirals of delightful sensations starting and soon couldn't hold herself up.

He suddenly straightened, pulling his mouth back to hers as she nearly collapsed against the wall and onto his hand. Her hands circled up around his neck and she held on. She couldn't stand it. She felt the pressure, and saw the colors swirling behind her closed eyes. He watched her face and she could feel his gaze on her, but could not open her eyes. She would not open her eyes.

He was thick and hot against her and his hand moved to the top of her jeans, where he started to undo them.

"Dad? Are you out here?"

They both froze in unison. Erin's eyes flew open as she looked up at Jack. He was leaning close to her, and her arms were around his neck. She could see the start of whiskers on his cheeks, and the faint color of his eyes in the murky light. Jack suddenly whipped his hands off her and took his fist, slamming it into the wall, high above her head. "Fuck me," he muttered, as he unclasped her arms from around his neck, and stepped back, breathing hard. She pulled her shirt and bra back into place.

Jack's scouring gaze raked over her. Then he turned and walked out of the barn to go to his older son who nearly walked in on his father screwing her against the barn wall. Erin almost fell onto the hay-strewn floor, she was so mortified. With herself. And with Jack. Especially, since Ben or anyone else could have caught them.

What just happened? Why would Jack do that? Kiss her? Touch her? And why did she let him? She wrapped her arms around herself as she scrambled to her feet. Tiptoeing towards the back of the barn, she planned to get out and sneak back to her trailer and hide while she figured out how she could ever, ever, ever again in her lifetime, be in the same room as Jack Rydell.

CHAPTER 19

*J*ack glanced around the barn, but she was long gone. He didn't know whether to be glad or not. Ben was beside him, chatting away about a girl from school. He couldn't have repeated a word his son said to him if his life depended on it.

What just happened? He didn't know. One moment, he was about to kick Erin off his ranch, and the next, he was kissing her. And nearly having sex with her in his barn. Right about the same time his elder son always got home from school. Jack ran a hand through his hair. What came over him?

He had no clue or foresight that he would do that. He never contemplated kissing Erin, let alone, doing what he'd done. He was mad at her, sure; and shocked at seeing the job where she worked. At last, all the wayward comments he kept hearing from various men in the valley made sense to him.

And what did he do about it? He nearly made all their innuendos a fact. He felt his stomach pinching. This wasn't like other situations. He had to face Erin, and couldn't merely ignore her, or not call her since she freaking lived on his ranch.

He wasn't sure exactly how he could ever face her again, which was an odd sensation for him to have. It wasn't like he usually got shy about sex or whom he had it with. But never before had he had a sexual encounter with his little brother's former girlfriend. He felt ashamed, which shook him up. When was the last time he'd done anything but the right thing? The honorable thing? It had been a while, and he wasn't glad to see he still hadn't outgrown some of his urges and reckless behavior.

It wasn't long before Charlie came home and he, too, joined them out in the arena with the horses. He was talking a mile a minute and excited about the end of the school year project they all planned to do. He wanted to collect horse manure and start a compost pile with food scraps, from which he could show the before and after results of his efforts. Jack had a tough time not chuckling; only eight-year-old boys could find horse crap interesting enough to turn into a class project.

"Hey Dad, is it okay if I asked Ms. Gray to dinner tonight?"

Jack stopped before the horse he was saddling. "You invited your teacher to dinner? Tonight?"

"Actually, I asked her last Monday. I forgot to tell you. She said yes though."

Jack stared at Charlie. "Your teacher is coming to dinner tonight? Are you kidding me, Charlie?"

"No. Isn't that okay? She's really nice. I think you'll like her."

"I know she's nice, but why would you invite her to dinner and not tell me?"

He avoided Jack's gaze. Jack wasn't sure what Charlie's intent was all about. He exhaled a sigh as he glanced at his watch, and saw it was four-thirty.

"We'd better put the horses away and get to the house. Lynnie will at least have it clean, but we'd better wash up and see about dinner. And next time, ask me first. And don't forget to tell me."

Jack rubbed a hand to his temple. He already had a headache from his previous encounter with Erin and the resulting aftermath he didn't want to deal with. Now this? Charlie setting up a dinner with his teacher? Was there something going on at school that he didn't know about? He looked at all of Charlie's work, and talked to Charlie daily about his school day. Could he be missing something important?

Erin, of course, would not be out to ride horses today. Of that, Jack had no doubt. Between the way he yelled at her and then... what? Made up with her? Nearly tried to have sex with her? He was so ashamed, he couldn't even contemplate where to go next.

Charlie followed him towards the house, talking again about Ms. Gray's fun way of teaching them their math facts, and how she always planned parties for every student's birthday.

He met Allison Gray at Charlie's parent-teacher conference. She was a pretty woman in her mid-twenties with red hair, like him. She had a fun, warm, nurturing air about her. Jack stopped at the bottom of the porch steps and frowned. Why exactly did Charlie invite his teacher for dinner?

Charlie ran inside to his room to change. Jack took his boots off and walked inside. Kailynn was finishing up. She had a stew simmering on the stove and the entire house smelled of spices and warm bread from the bread maker. She had cooked something that resembled a meal one might serve to company.

"Did Charlie mention to you that he invited his teacher to dinner?"

Kailynn turned at Jack's voice and nodded. "He asked me to make your favorite stew. He didn't ask permission first?"

"About twenty minutes ago."

Kailynn smiled. "I wonder what he's up to?"

Jack grumbled, "Got me."

Ian came through the door then and glanced at Kailynn with a hello. She smiled and turned back towards the laundry room to get her things to leave. "It's all cooked and prepared; it should stay warm until you're ready to serve it.

"Thanks, Lynnie, I don't know what we'd do without you."

She ducked her head at the compliment, then slid past him without another word. Ian looked after her, then back to Jack before stomping towards the closet and returning with a coat. "I'm going to town for a drink."

Jack watched Ian leave. Who knew what was eating him? Not like Ian would ever say. And Jack had his own drama to deal with. He headed off into his room to shower and change before Charlie's teacher showed up. He really wished Charlie hadn't sprung this on him, and that the day would end soon.

When he finished showering, he threw on some dark slacks and a tan, button-up shirt. He came out of his room twenty minutes later and stopped dead in his tracks when he found Erin standing in the middle of the living room. His mouth opened in shock. This was not how he planned to face her. Not now. Not after today. Not in front of his sons. He muttered a curse as she raised her head and her eyes met his.

~

ERIN GLANCED up when she heard Jack and rubbed her hands on her jeans to dry out the sweat on her palms. She felt like she might throw up from nerves. She'd never been so anxious to face someone before. But what choice did she have? She stared at Jack when she heard him across the room and gulped in shock. He looked so... different. And good. He wore dark slacks, with his shirt tucked in that showed off his long, strong build and made his red hair seem darker. He always looked tough, strong, and handsome, but dressed this way, he was devastating. He got dressed up for a teacher? She didn't get it.

His eyes met hers for a second before he looked away. Or did she look away first? She wasn't sure, but now found herself staring at the couch to the left of her. Charlie bounced over to his dad.

"I asked Erin to dinner. That's okay too, isn't it?"

She glanced at Jack's face because she knew his eyes would be focused on his son, and not her. Jack's face showed displeasure, and no doubt, the next question he wanted to ask Charlie was why did Charlie ask Erin to dinner? Especially tonight, of all nights?

Erin wondered the same question. He finally looked over his shoulder at her. She fidgeted under his vacant stare. She came there in only worn jeans and a sweatshirt. Nothing to mistake her as the slutty siren Jack liked to portray her as; but not nearly dressy enough next to him now.

She didn't know what to say when Charlie came knocking at her trailer and begged her to come to dinner with his teacher. She knew Jack would be there, of course, but what possible reason could she give Charlie for not attending? She was too busy? Everyone knew she wasn't. So there she stood.

Jack straightened to his full height, towering over Charlie

and her. His hands, long and firm, gripped the edge of one of the chairs. She had to look away as a heat wave swelled in her stomach when she pictured those hands. How could she now face Jack? The only thing to make a bad situation worse would be to have Joey join them.

Charlie trotted off to start setting the table. Ben came down from upstairs and helped Charlie. Erin stood there, feeling useless, with her hands stuck into the pocket of her hoodie.

She finally walked forward, but stared down at the floor and not up at Jack. "Charlie cornered me. I couldn't say no."

Jack was, no doubt, looking down at her because she felt the energy radiating off him. He was quiet before she finally raised her eyes to his and thought he looked as grim as she felt. She jerked her eyes away as a flush covered her skin.

"We need to talk."

She nodded. She knew that. Oh, did she know how they needed to talk. She didn't know how she could, however. There was no way her tongue could work properly anywhere near Jack, and possibly, not ever again.

Hearing a knock on the door, Erin nearly whimpered with relief. Jack answered it. She made an effort to avoid staring at the way his shirt stretched over his back and narrowed down to where he tucked it into his pants. He wore his clothes quite well.

Into the room came Allison. Erin closed her eyes in frustration. Jack looked out of the ordinary tonight, which must have been in honor of Ms. Gray. Why shouldn't he want to look nice and mannerly before the lovely, respectful lady who taught his son third grade?

Allison came in and Jack gallantly took her lightweight suede jacket to hang it on the coat tree. Clad in pretty, tan slacks and a soft, short-sleeved sweater, which looked utterly appropriate and was of obvious fine quality, her outfit barely hinting at the good figure she had.

Allison noticed her and smiled. "Erin, I didn't know you were joining us. How nice to see you again."

Erin stared at her with a suspicious expression as she tried to judge Allison's sincerity.

She glanced over at Charlie as he ran towards his teacher, taking her hand and guiding her inside to show her around. Erin watched for a while. It didn't take long to figure out what Charlie was up to: setting his father up with his teacher. Erin was a hundred percent convinced of that as she watched them. Charlie sat his dad directly across from Allison, and he sat by his teacher. He chatted the entire meal. Erin sat in a chair that prevented her from staring directly at Jack. She put Ben between them and tried to shrink inside her seat. How often did it occur for Ian, Shane and Joey to all be out of the home at once? Not often. But of course, tonight it would be so. So why did Charlie ask her to dinner too?

Erin barely ate. Her stomach churned in knots as she listened to the conversation that was cheerful, friendly and warm all around her. There was no way to ignore Allison, she was so affable and lively. Being well read, she could talk about anything from the horses to her classroom to current events, and she possessed an ease with herself and her conversation that Erin had never experienced.

Erin poked at her food before taking her plate to the sink and cleaning up when she could no longer stand to sit there. It was a liberty she'd never taken before. She felt Allison's eyes on her. Allison couldn't figure out where Erin fit into the dynamics of the Rydell household.

Jack came up behind her. She could feel the heat coming off him as he stood there before he set his plate to the right of her elbow. He didn't touch her, but stayed directly behind her, and she could feel his arm reaching around her. She froze, letting the water run, while the kids talked, but it all felt far away, almost like she just entered a tunnel.

"You don't need to do those."

His voice was low, and felt warm on her neck when he spoke. Shivers broke out over her skin. She licked her lips. "I don't mind."

He finally stepped back, walking to the side of her where he started the coffee maker. She only breathed after he turned back to Allison.

Jack was chuckling at something Charlie said, and then Erin heard the sweet tone of Allison's voice as she told a funny story about a kid she used to teach. Erin scrubbed furiously at the pot, banging around in the kitchen and putting things away before filling the dishwasher. She didn't dare let Allison know she wasn't fully at ease in the Rydells' house, and refused to ask where any dishware and glasses went. She simply stuck them wherever she chose. Why should Allison know that she spent almost less time than Allison did inside there? After being intimate with one brother, and starting up with another, she was no more asked to sit at their table than they would ask a stray cat.

Well, that wasn't entirely true. Jack had asked her to come to dinner on more than one occasion. It was her own doubts that kept from accepting. But still, the fact remained she wasn't often inside the house with them.

She was annoyed when she finished the dishes and had nothing to do. It meant she had to return her focus to them again. On Jack. Or on Charlie's adoring gaze at the woman he, no doubt, was picturing as his next mother. Erin slid into the chair beside Ben. Jack was watching her. She hated the blush that warmed her cheeks and the awkwardness she felt.

Eventually, Charlie lost interest and got onto the floor to play with his Matchbox cars. Someone mentioned something, although Erin wasn't following the conversation with any great interest. Whoever it was said that Allison did volunteer work at the local library, tutoring adults two nights a week. *Great.* Not only was she a teacher to young, impressionable kids, she volunteered her time too. Erin nearly rolled her eyes at the goody-two-shoes Charlie had selected, and probably made a wise choice as his father's date.

"Well, why couldn't you tutor Erin?"

Erin's head jerked up as she crashed-landed back into the moment after hearing Ben's statement. He sat up straighter and suddenly grew animated as Allison waited to respond. "You could teach Erin to read, couldn't you? If you teach other adults?"

Erin's mouth dropped open and she felt all eyes turning towards her. She met the big, blue, caring eyes of Allison. "I could certainly try. In the literacy center I work with, it's centered around readers where English is their second language. Which isn't the case for you, but I'd be willing to try and figure out the best way to teach you."

She looked down. How dare they? "I don't think so, Ms. Gray."

The table went silent and Erin dared not look up until she heard Jack's voice.

"Why not? Why couldn't you?"

She jerked her face up. Jack was impatiently staring at her. "Because I can't learn. I already told you that. I was in all the reading services and interventions. They all tried, clear through early high school. I could barely stumble through a paragraph, and that was only if I had some context to what I was trying to read. It just never worked."

"Are you dyslexic?"

That wasn't mentioned to her as a cause. If it were true, why wouldn't one of the many schools she attended have tested her? No one ever did. No one even suggested it. Erin glared at Allison. "I doubt I'm dyslexic. I just can't read."

Silence followed her outburst. Ben looked at her strangely, wondering why wouldn't she want to learn? How could they understand what it was like to be as stupid as she was? She *couldn't* learn. Many truly kind, caring, intelligent teachers, had already tried and never succeeded. She didn't see letters backwards, or upside-down, but neither could she seem to grasp the simple concept required to read accurately, consistently and with any kind of fluency.

Allison tilted her head, her eyes shining with sympathy. "You might not have known. This state hasn't historically tested for dyslexia. Only now, are school districts starting to identify it, in the lower elementary grades, but they usually only test to see if a child matches certain dyslexia markers. The next step would be to use a scientifically proven *dyslexia* reading program. These include programs that are highly direct, systematic, explicit, multisensory, and with repetition to mastery. They must be explicit, and structured, in phonemic and phonics awareness, sound and symbol correlation, and include phonics-based spelling instruction that follows a scope and sequence. It isn't often, as of now, that this type of dyslexia reading remediation is used effectively in any public or private school district. The most likely place effective intervention occurs is with a private tutor specializing in the right type of reading program. Anyone with dyslexia can learn to read and spell, it's a myth that they can't. But it *must* be the right kind of program."

Heat rose up her throat and face. There was an irrational fear, anxiety and embarrassment that filled her when speaking about her formative years and reading. Crossing her arms over her chest she said with a huff, "Or sometimes, people are just stupid, Ms. Gray."

Jack's voice interrupted her. "You're not stupid. Give me one good reason why you couldn't at least try?"

She looked up and found him staring directly at her with his brow furrowed. He couldn't understand what it was like to try in earnest to do something and it wouldn't work. It didn't matter how many "readers" she was given by well-meaning reading specialists; *she could not* decode them to read. She could not memorize all the sight words she was expected to know. She didn't understand the different sounds in the words, and how her peers seemed to just "know" what each printed words said.

To then sit in grade after grade, and understand the spoken word, perhaps better than others in the classroom, but the moment print was involved, she could no longer function on her own. She'd guess at the words and most of her guesses were wrong.

And wrong.

And wrong.

How often could one be wrong and not come to the truly obvious conclusion? There was something wrong with them.

No one ever offered another explanation to her.

That maybe Allison just had, felt too hard to believe.

There was nothing Jack couldn't do. Whatever he attempted to do, he merely invested some effort in, and voila. It was done. Like raising two kids alone, or taking care of his family's business and making it thrive while he looked after his younger brothers. He could do anything or be anything he set out to be. He was strong, confident, and smart. He knew he could handle anything he encountered because he already handled it all. He could never understand what it was like being her. Being considered weak. And stupid. Or the joke of the classroom.

Allison spoke before Erin could answer. She looked uneasily at Jack, then said to Erin, "I apologize, if I made you feel uncomfortable. Charlie actually suggested I talk to you. He had a lot of questions about reading and wanted to know if I could teach kids younger than he, why couldn't I teach you? I really thought it was you asking through Charlie."

Erin glanced over to where Charlie played so sweetly on the floor. His lips moved as he made car "vrooming" sounds. He asked his teacher to help her? That's the reason he invited her to dinner tonight?

"Charlie really asked you about teaching me?"

Allison nodded. "Yes. He did. I would be more than willing to approach it, if and when you are ever willing. One-on-one tutoring will be very different then the classroom situation. I won't make you feel stupid. It won't be like when you were in school. I can't imagine it was easy for you."

"I didn't graduate."

"Neither did many of the adults I currently work with. You'd be surprised how many there are. You aren't alone. Look, this is a lot of pressure. I really thought that Charlie's request originally came from you. I definitely see now, however, that it didn't. But that doesn't change my willingness to help you. So I'll leave you my number, and please call me, Erin, if you decide later that you'd like my help."

"I don't have any money," Erin replied finally. It was her last excuse for why she couldn't possibly accept the woman's offer.

"I don't need your money. I would do it for free, pro bono."

Erin crossed her arms over her chest. "Why? Why would you do it for free?"

She smiled. "For one, because it's the decent thing to do. But also, it's part of the volunteer work I do. Most people who can't read don't have good paying jobs, therefore they don't have access to finding help out there. A vicious cycle, if you will. So you see, you really aren't alone."

She wasn't? Allison's words started a crack in the wall she kept around herself to shelter her from the ridicule of a literate world. The world of mothers, fathers, brothers and sisters who cared about you. She felt ridiculous tears building up in her eyes and gulped back the tightening in her throat. She stared down at her shoes in order to avoid crying in front of Allison. And Jack.

She finally muttered, "I'll think about it."

~

JACK STOOD silent for a moment next to Allison's car. "Sorry, about this. Honestly, Charlie didn't tell me he did this until an hour before you showed up, and nothing about Erin being involved."

She grinned. "I only came because I thought he was trying to set us up and I thought we should have a conversation about that. To find he was trying so in earnest to help Erin, well, you're a lucky man, Jack Rydell."

He smiled back. "Yeah. He's a great kid. But what about Erin? Why wouldn't she learn to read? Why is she so sure she can't do it?"

Allison ran a hand through her hair. "Best guess? This is without once working with her or even discussing her circumstances, I'd guess she actually has dyslexia. It's the most common cause of reading and spelling problems. It can have a severe effect on learning. It can include slow processing and recall, trouble with memorization, and an often, severe to even profound weakness in reading and spelling."

He blew out a breath. "I had no idea."

"Neither does she."

"What can I do? How do I get her to take you up on your

help? Which is so kind of you by the way. That isn't lost on me."

She shook her head. "Don't. I like doing it. There is a particularly high illiteracy rate for adults in this area due to so many for whom English is a second language. But you'd be surprised at the number of adults who are. And what can you do? Make her feel safe. Secure. Convince her she can do it. She's so obviously not ready. I can tell you nothing will work until she feels safe to try it again."

"But why wouldn't she jump at your offer?"

Allison shrugged. "Studies show dyslexia for children is as shameful as molestation. Consider that, Jack. Consider the shame she feels. She's isn't looking for compliments and for us to reassure her when she says she's stupid. She is stating her learned experience. Confirmed by the very real fact she can't read or spell. It's her truth. She believes it with a faith you or I can't talk out of her."

He blew out a breath. "Holy crap. This is… a lot."

She nodded. "It is. Show her she's smart and confident in other ways. Maybe, with time, it will convince her to risk trying it again. She tried to do something for *years* that her peers seemed able to just "do". The anxiety and stress that causes a child, then youth, isn't something that can be wiped away with one or two conversations."

"We've been working with the horses. She blossoms with them. She's grown more confident and surer of herself in the short time we've done it."

"Then keep doing it. But it has to be her realization she can do it, not everyone else's."

He opened her car door for her. "Thank you. This has been the most enlightening conversation of my life. I can't thank you enough."

"Good luck, Jack. I hope it works. She is a really lovely person."

Jack's face scrunched up. Damn. Allison was right. Erin was a sweet, kind, shy person so wrapped in her own shame. And he had missed that all. He cleared his throat. "She's not my girlfriend or anything. She's just... my friend."

He had a damn long way to prove that. To let her see that.

Allison touched his hand as she slid past him and into her car. "That's really good. You should be a good friend to her. If anyone in the world could use a friend it's Erin Poletti."

～

JACK CAME BACK in from telling Allison Gray goodbye. The silence grew thick after Jack shut the door. Ben went to his bedroom to do homework, and Jack's gaze was on her before he glanced at Charlie.

"Charlie, we need to talk."

She looked up in surprise and started to rise and leave. Jack shook his head. To Charlie, he said, "You asked Ms. Gray here to help Erin, didn't you?"

Charlie stood up and smiled sheepishly at her and then at his dad. "Yeah. Ms. Gray's so nice, I figured Erin might like her."

"So you asked Erin to dinner?"

He shrugged. "It seems kind of silly for her to eat out there all alone anyways. I mean, she lives here, doesn't she? Plus, I thought Ms. Gray could help her."

Jack put a hand on Charlie's shoulder. "I approve of the thoughts you had. I like knowing you thought to help Erin, but you have to ask people first. You can't just spring it onto adults. Do you understand?"

Charlie nodded and looked at Erin apologetically. "I was just trying to help."

Her heart flipped and she stepped closer to Charlie. "Thank you. For thinking of me."

He looked up at her, and his eyes grew big and eager. "So you will let Ms. Gray help you? You're going to learn to read?"

What could she say? How could she snatch away the look of hope and excitement on Charlie's face? But they didn't understand why she simply *couldn't* do it. She would prove that to them all soon enough. She nodded finally to get them off her back. "Yes, I'll try it, Charlie."

He suddenly came forward and flung his arms around her middle. His head came up to her shoulders and she was almost knocked over by the force of his unexpected embrace. She caught her footing. Charlie was hugging *her*. Her heart did a back flip for the motherless little boy. She could not look at Jack. Somehow, she knew she was not the woman whom he wanted his son hugging.

Charlie suddenly let her go and turned to his dad. "I won't do it again, Dad, but see? It worked out. I'm going to go get ready for bed now."

He skipped off. She was all alone with Jack who turned finally, and looked down at her. The silence between them was uncomfortably thick. He walked to the door where she watched him wearily take his brown jacket off the rack and put it on. "I'll walk you back to the trailer."

She glanced up. *No.* No, she would not walk back to her trailer in the dark with Jack. She felt ill as it was. Or did he intend to come in? She could earn her keep by doing him? Now that she wasn't with Joey? The very idea of Jack thinking that made her want to cry. She didn't want him to think that. But what else could he think?

She followed behind him when he opened the door and stepped out without another glance at her. It was pleasantly cool, as the days were getting warmer now, and the nights became much more refreshing with the cooler air.

He didn't say a word, but jammed his hands into the front

pockets of his pants. He was in step with her as they walked across the dusty driveway. Crickets chirped like a choir all around them and the night stars were clear, shining forever around them.

Finally, they reached the door of her trailer. She wanted nothing more than to escape behind it and never face Jack again.

Jack stood in front of the door handle so she couldn't get to it without touching him. He ran his hand through his hair, tousling it. "So…"

Her heart leapt at his voice. She could not discuss anything with him. She was about to speak when the sudden flash and roar of truck came behind her. She looked back to see Joey pulling up to a screeching stop, the radio blaring before he finally turned his truck off. He wasn't alone. A woman scooted out after him. They linked arms and started towards the house without another glance backwards.

She pressed her lips together. She had slept with Joey, but now couldn't care less whom he'd gone into the house with. And yet… with Jack what she briefly did with him set her heart on fire and rocked her world upside down. Her biggest enigma was why her reaction to Jack was so strong. She'd done a lot more with guys she knew far less than she did Jack, and no one ever made her feel like he did.

"Does it bother you?"

Jack's voice came behind her, sounding deep and quiet. The night was dark around them and eerily still after Joey's dramatic entrance home.

"Joey? No. I wish it did."

"Why?"

She closed her eyes, keeping her back to Jack. How could she explain why she wanted sex to mean more to her? Or why she didn't want to be the woman she was? The woman who slept with his brother.

"Because then you wouldn't think it was okay to treat me the same way."

"Yeah? And how do I treat you?"

She blinked at the sudden tears welling in her eyes, unwilling to turn around. She kept them tightly shut. How could she tell him he treated her like she was someone much better than she really was? Someone who was worth something. In the darkness, she whispered, "I thought you disliked and distrusted me. I thought you tolerated me here because I was more or less trapped. I didn't think…"

He stepped closer behind her. "You didn't think what?"

His arm come around her, and his big hand rested on her stomach. She could feel the warmth of his fingertips and closed her eyes. "I just don't understand."

His other arm came around as he enveloped her. She finally leaned back into him, breathing in his scent. The sense of safety she felt, of being held and protected in his arms, made her almost think she was truly cared about.

His deep voice interrupted her. "Ben could have caught us today. I've never done what I did today. Not with anyone. Especially, not with my son due home from school so soon. The thing was, I temporarily forgot."

She didn't know what to say. Was he blaming her? What did he mean?

"You forgot what?"

"I forgot where I was. I forgot everything. Everything, but you."

"Why did you kiss me?"

She had to know, and had to hear him say it. He had to tell her that she was physically there and he was horny, so why not hit on her? She needed to hear Jack would treat her as every other man she'd ever been with.

"Because it's all I think about when you're around me. It takes all my will power and effort not to. Because I've been alone a long time; and now here you are every day of my life."

"Joey found me quite convenient too."

She waited for him to lash back at her. "Joey wasn't really with you, was he? Not the real Erin, anyway. The one I've met out in the barn and working with the horses."

She paused. Holding her breath.

"Joey was never with the woman I was with in the barn, was he?"

How did he know? Her heart rate increased. Tears she'd been fighting all night finally slipped over her lower eyelids and she shook her head.

Jack turned her around. His finger came to her chin and he raised her face up to his view.

"Why don't you know you deserve better?"

"Better? As in you? You want to sleep with me too, don't you? You don't even pretend to like me."

"I don't have to pretend. But you also live with me. I'm responsible for you in a way I shouldn't have done what I did."

She wanted to jerk her arms off him, but he anticipated that and held her arms tighter. "I don't need to be another of your responsibilities. I'm not a child."

"Of course not. It's the power dynamics of it all. Plus Joey is my brother. I can't believe I…"

"Well you did. Or at least you tried. And we only stopped because of Ben, not because you suddenly remembered all the reasons *why not.*"

"Don't, Erin. Please. The last thing I want is to hurt you. And you damn well know that about me. Or at least I hope you do. It wasn't like that. And there is no way you can convince me otherwise."

"All you see when you look at me is that I had sex Joey, and wear a bikini to work."

He stared at her and shook his head. "I'm tired, Erin. Tired of this thing between us that can't happen. Tired of trying to understand what I'm supposed to do about you. All I know is my relationship with my fifteen-year-old son would have soured for a long while if he walked into the barn just a few seconds sooner. I also know my little brother has the rights to you, that I never should have taken."

Her cheeks reddened at his flat rejection of her. And at her own gall. How could she act that way with Jack, of all men? She knew not to be that way around him. That's why she liked being with him, because he didn't want her to be like that.

"I'll leave."

He shook his head with a long, weary sigh. "No. You won't. This is where you live and we all have to accept that. You have nowhere else to go. And I'm sick of pretending you're just visiting. You live here. Charlie's right, it's ridiculous for you to eat out here alone. It's ridiculous you feel like you have to pussyfoot around, intimidated of me and everyone else here. From now on, you eat inside with us. You can come and go from the house as you like. You don't have to keep living like this. And your job isn't any of my business. I should never have reacted the way I did. I had no right, and I'm sorry. So let's forget the barn ever happened. The only thing I will ask of you is to give some serious thought to what Charlie tried to do for you tonight."

She didn't know what to say. What was Jack doing? "I don't understand."

Jack let her go and shrugged. "I realized when Allison was here, you're more awkward in the house than any guest. And it's because of how I've treated you. That makes me the stupid one. You belong here. And it's about time we all started acting like it. Ben and Charlie are the only ones who treat you like you live here, and I finally realized I should take a page out of my own sons' books. You're so worried about what's coming at you next, you can't even begin to relax. Or contemplate learning to read. So it's done. You live here. We all have to accept it. You have a home now here. The trailer is yours. No more scathing innuendos from any of us. You can ride the horses or walk to the beach anytime you want. You don't have to ask my permission anymore. For anything."

"I don't understand."

"Yeah, you do. We've been treating you like shit. Like an intrusive stranger. Like Chance's bad sister. And that's what makes you act out. It's over. You don't owe me anything. You don't owe any of us anything. Next time Joey mouths off or gets rude to you, tell him off. Next time, Shane says something offhand or impolite, nail his ass. And the next time you feel pressured by me, just say no. Tell me to fuck off because I don't like how you dress for your job. Your spot here at the ranch is safe. This is your home, Erin."

Her head spun since she had expected Jack to blame her for what happened earlier. Or want her to come in and finish what she started. She never dreamed Jack would do that. Give her the trailer. He was giving her freedom. The freedom to live her own life.

Could he really mean she was at home? She'd never been at home in all her life. Never. Not once did anyone try to make her feel at home.

She swallowed and shook her head. "Do you mean that?"

He smiled. A smile that left her knees shaking and her heart racing. "I mean it. No more shit from us, Erin. You earned your place here, and it's about damn time you started living it."

She nodded, her tears nearly choking her. How she got to this point, she'd never understand, but certainly would take it. Freedom. A life. A home. No more bad Erin.

"So are we good? We'll just forget it. And you can say you live here now?"

She nodded her head, too confused and choked up to reply. Eventually, she smiled. She fully intended to show Jack how much his gift to her today meant. And she'd prove that she was worthy of it.

CHAPTER 20

*E*verything changed after that night. Erin didn't understand why Jack did what he did, or why his sudden, unconditional acceptance of her seemed to make the entire valley more receptive to her. Suddenly, Ian, Shane and even Joey started being nicer to her. They quit avoiding her and started socializing with her. Suddenly, she was routinely inside the house. She realized how much the Rydells revered Jack's opinion. When Jack didn't like her, no one else did; and when Jack turned lukewarm towards her, so did everyone else. But once Jack had fully embraced and accepted her, she was unanimously accepted.

She kept her job at the coffee stand. A week later, she stopped dead in her tracks when she turned from an order to find Jack parked at the opposite window. He wore sunglasses and his customary cowboy hat. She couldn't make out his expression, and hesitated, anticipating his irrational wrath becoming directed at her. But instead, he just smiled at her, and his eyes made a conscious effort to stay focused above her chin as he ordered a cup of black coffee. He paid and touched the brim of his hat with a hand before smiling at her again, and leaving. She stared after his truck, which glinted in the hot, powerful sun. What was that?

It was Jack's total acceptance, she realized as she served the next man in his dusty pickup. The smile that curled her lips had nothing to do with the leering, bearded man, but rather, at the changes Jack's reception of her brought into her life.

As May faded into June, River's End grew alive with the explosion of lush, green leaves that filled in all the gaps in the landscape. Erin had never experienced having sunshine every day and it did wonders for her moods. The days started to get hot, and already several were past eighty degrees. She was told regularly that she'd soon hate the incessant heat and sunshine when July and August brought endless dust, no rain, and scorching days on end of ninety degrees and above temperatures.

The river became a swollen, muddy mess for a month as the snowmelt filled it with a dangerously swift, rushing mass of brown water mixed with logs, boulders, and sticks. She had to move further up on her beach to sit because her favorite spots were now submerged beneath the spring melt. She spent every afternoon there. Already clad in shorts, she managed to get a tan for the first time in her life.

She lay on the beach for hours, sometimes letting the sun's rays soak into her, heating her up, and warming her skin along with her brain. She was... relaxed. She didn't know what to do about that. She had a place to live, where she could stay on without fear of eviction. She had security for the first time in her life and that changed everything for her.

She thought about Jack. Every single day, she thought about everything Jack had done for her. He managed to give her a new life. He gave her a sense of freedom and the chance for a life she never dared to imagine. However, all she could think about was that day in the barn; and the taste of his mouth with his strong body all around her, and his hand inside her. When she thought about Jack, she felt very different from how she ever had before with men and sex.

Usually after having sex with anyone, even Joey, she never thought about it again. She didn't think about how it felt, or why she did it. She simply forgot about it, buried it, and moved on with her life. But with Jack, she thought about it all the time. She thought about how it felt, how she felt, and could feel him still. It was a new experience to her and she didn't know what it meant. His presence, whenever he was near her, set her skin on fire and made her feel safe. She couldn't explain that because for so long, he was the source of all her anxiety. She saw him as a threat and a vehicle for homelessness. But he nevertheless made her feel safe and protected. It was dangerous for her to feel that for a man who would never take another step towards her.

Erin sighed, sitting up off the sand after her thoughts, once again, traveled to that day in the barn. She wished, as she did so often, she'd taken a minute longer that first day she came on the ranch and just looked at Jack. If she had really looked at Jack, deeply into his eyes, she was sure she would have never, ever looked at Joey again. She was sure she'd get the hot, flushing awareness she now felt each and every time she even glimpsed Jack. If only she'd been smart enough to take a second look that first day.

It wasn't the right thing to do, or the decent thing to do, and now she saw Jack as the most decent, upstanding man she'd ever known.

She often came to dinner now and each evening had a decent meal to eat. She started to gain weight that was much needed and made her look and feel better. Her skin seemed to glow and radiate a healthy color instead of the sickly pallor of before.

She started showing up earlier in the evenings because she knew Jack would still be out working, and hung out with Charlie, or Ben, and sometimes, even Kailynn.

Erin liked Kailynn. She decided that one evening when she was drawing with Charlie and Kailynn was finishing up before getting ready to leave. Kailynn was quiet, and thorough, seeming to avoid even looking at Erin. She barely answered anything Erin said to her, but despite all that, Erin still liked Kailynn.

Erin wanted to make friends with Kailynn because she wanted a woman in her life, someone to talk to, and relate with. She wasn't sure how to make that happen, though, since Kailynn seemed to disapprove of her.

She figured at some point, if she got into Kailynn's way often enough, she'd finally get Kailynn to acknowledge her.

Erin also hoped by being around Jack more frequently, and inside his house, she could finally grow immune to his charm. It always worked for her in the past. After she was with any guy long enough, he lost all his appeal and attraction, which she once harbored towards him. The problem with Jack was, the more time she spent near him, watching him, and listening to him with those around him, she only grew more interested, more attracted, and even more reticent around him. She couldn't understand her strange reaction to him.

Kailynn was cutting up vegetables and Erin had been talking to Charlie. Erin got up and came closer to Kailynn. "Do you need any help?"

Kailynn glanced up and her gray eyes had a strange hue to them, an almost a whitish cast. They were incredibly beautiful. Usually, however, Kailynn kept her eyes downcast and focused on whatever she was doing with her hands. "No."

Erin picked up a carrot and took a bite from it, not missing the frown Kailynn gave her. "I would like to help."

"They pay me to do this. I don't need your help."

Erin shrugged. "Well, I owe them for letting me live here. I could help cook since you usually try to leave about now, I could take over for you sometimes."

"Can you cook?"

"Well, no. But I could learn."

Kailynn lifted her eyes, piercing Erin with their laser-like glow. "You can't read a recipe."

Erin flinched and set the carrot down. "And here you act so nice to the Rydells. I know I can't read. I thought people learned to cook by 'know-how.'"

"Yeah, if you have any 'know-how.'"

"What's your problem with me?"

"No problem, Erin. I just have work to do."

"Is it Joey? Because we're nothing now."

"I don't care who you're having sex with."

"I'm not. Having sex with anyone, that is. So what? You hate me because I'm not a virgin?"

Kailynn turned as she mixed up dough in a bowl, which she spread over the vegetables and chicken she had in a pan. Erin guessed she had some kind of potpie concoction going on. "I don't have any opinion on you."

"So you're just bitchy in general?"

Kailynn hesitated, but finally, looked Erin in the eye. "No one else thinks I'm a bitch."

"Well, I'm thinking it right now."

Kailynn tapped a finger on the counter. "Can you make a pie crust?"

"No."

"Then can you slice apples?"

"Yeah. I can slice apples."

"Good," Kailynn said as she handed Erin a knife and pushed a bowl of apples towards her. "Start peeling and then cut them into slices."

Erin looked at Kailynn and didn't react. Her face was a mask of disinterest. Erin smiled at her. Kailynn finally lifted the corners of her mouth as she turned and stuck the potpie into the warm oven.

"So how long have worked here?"

Kailynn took a long while before she talked to Erin. It took days to get the barest information out of her. Erin eventually learned Kailynn was twenty-two years old and lived with her father and two older brothers who were also good friends with Ian and Shane. Kailynn eventually showed Erin how to make spaghetti, tacos, Jack's favorite beef stew, several chicken casseroles, and various homemade pies. Most of what she taught Erin were things she could reproduce without a cookbook. One asset Erin possessed was a faultless memory.

Erin liked the food prep and the aromas of the finished products as she set them on the table. She liked the few moments she and Kailynn could chat.

Erin soon came to the house seeking Kailynn's company much more than that of the men. Kailynn always left as they sat down to eat, and Erin always felt sorry to see her leave. She was quiet during the first few meals she shared with the Rydells. In no time, however, she was being talked to, and asked questions so she began to open up more towards them. She always sat at the far end, and opposite side of the table to Jack in her attempts to avoid him. That was back-asswards because it put her next to Joey, whom she didn't give a damn about being near or not. She had nothing to say to him, and had no residual tenderness towards him either.

Joey ignored her as much as she did him. He even brought his new date home with no skin off Erin's nose.

One day in June, Joey announced with little warning and no apparent concern at the impact of his news that he was leaving for the summer. His brothers all stopped eating and stared at him in utter shock. No one knew what he had in mind. Erin did, however. She remembered hearing his doubts about working on the ranch because he didn't know anything else, and had never known any other place. She just didn't know what his latest plan entailed.

"I joined the Army."

Jack stared at him for a full thirty seconds before setting his fork down with a pronounced "clink!" Then he laughed. "You don't just up and join the Army, Joe."

"Well, I did. I can't spend my life hanging around here, shoveling shit."

Jack stared at Joey, and Joey stared back, his anger palpable. Jack suddenly stood up and left the room, with everyone staring open-mouthed after him. Joey let out a breath and hunched his shoulders, not quite as sure about standing up to Jack as he originally tried to portray.

No one spoke after that. Joey got up and followed Jack to the porch.

Erin stared after them, absorbing the silence from the rest of the family deeply in her gut. She wondered if they blamed her. She also was impressed by the depths to which these men loved each other, though usually unspoken. They had lived together rather successfully well into their adult lives, something most siblings could never do without killing each other. But the Rydell brothers made it work. And now one of them was leaving.

JACK SAT DOWN ON A CHAIR, looking out over the land, now lit in pretty, soft hues beneath the setting summer sun. It seemed to linger this time of year for hours. He grabbed a case of beer and now drank it liberally in place of dinner. Joey eventually came out, leaning against the porch railing.

"It's not about you. I don't want to be a rebel or anything. I just need to do something more, something that I can't do here. I don't have the grades for college, and that's not for me either. I don't know what else to do. I've been drifting for three years. I'll keep drifting if I don't leave, and suddenly, I'll be forty years old, and living with you still, and working the ranch. I need to find my own way."

"And if you die?"

Joey scoffed. "That's what has you so upset? Not me leaving... but you think I'll die? Kind of getting ahead of yourself, aren't you? I haven't even taken the training yet. Come on, it's not that likely."

"Yeah, well there's a definite possibility in that job description, now isn't there?"

"I accept that risk."

"You know shit about death. You know shit about what it's like to bury someone you love."

"I won't die."

"You don't know that, Joe."

"Look, I guess it's harder for you because of Lily and all, but I'm not Lily. I'm just, making my own way in life."

Jack looked past Joey, towards the strange orange light now glowing over the black line of mountains. He closed his eyes as the familiar pain shot into his gut. *Lily.* How it hurt to think about her still. Even after several years to get used to it, he wasn't.

"You're not just my brother, Joey," he finally said quietly. "You're more like my son. I took over being your parent when you were five years old. You don't know what that's like."

"I know it. I do. But I can't live your life, and for the life of me, I can't figure out who I am. Shane is the mechanic. Ian knows the horses and farming; and you're the damn horse whisperer. I'm just the pretty, younger brother, right? Even you think that. You made that pretty clear when Erin showed up. You think that about me, and you can't deny it. The thing is: I can't deny that it's who I am right now. But I need more than that."

"Is it because of Erin?"

Joey glanced at him and Jack focused on the horses grazing out in the pastures to the right of him. "No. It has nothing to do with her. If it did, what would you do, Jack? Kick her out?"

"I would choose you," he said simply. "You know that."

Joey nodded. "It's never been Erin. She's your problem, not mine."

Jack raised the beer and let the cool liquid slide down his throat. "Why did you do it? Why didn't you talk to me first?"

"Because you would have talked me out of it. You'd have used my previous bad judgment, like with Chance and Erin, to convince me I didn't know what I wanted, or what I was doing."

Jack was about to argue, but he realized Joey was right. That's exactly what he would have done. "I guess there's nothing else to say about it, is there?"

"No, there really isn't."

"It won't be the same around here without you."

"I'll be back. This will always be my home."

Jack stretched his legs out. "Yeah, we'll always be here. When do you leave then?"

"Two weeks."

"Do you need anything?"

Joey smiled. "No. Just… thanks, for asking. For accepting my decision. For, hell, for, you know, everything."

Jack nodded at the brother he raised as his son. The gut-wrenching pain of watching Joey leave, and thinking about Joey getting in harm's way filled him. But Joey was a grown man, and he had to find his own way. He was right; he'd been floundering and drifting for a while now. This life, this ranch, fit Jack, and not all the brothers quite as well as it did him.

Jack watched Joey go inside, and stared back out at the land. The anchor that tied him, the albatross that hung around his neck.

He never had the chance or choice to find his own way in life. He was twenty years old, with a wife and baby, when his parents died. That quickly, five-year-old Joey became his other kid, along with Shane and Ian, older, true, but now totally his responsibility. He had no skills beyond working with horses. There was never any question about what he intended to do with his life. He would naturally take over for his dad. He and Lily moved into the house his parents built, and that was where he planned to stay for the rest of his life. It was where he and Lily planned to raise their family.

He sometimes wondered what it would have been like to have any kind of freedom or choice in the matter. But… he still would have ended up right there. Doing what he already did. He was a rancher, and the only place he had any real skills or knowledge was with his horses.

Darkness settled around him and he kept drinking the beer. The empty bottles grew to nearly seven, lined up at his feet.

"Jack?"

He turned when he heard her voice. Erin was standing to his left, and the yard light shimmered on her dark as night hair. Her face was in shadows. Wearing jeans and a sweatshirt, she looked about as young as Ben standing there. Only she wasn't. His hand gripped the glass bottle tighter at the images of her that had taken up residence in his head. "You need something?"

"Are you all right?"

Was he all right? No. He hadn't been okay in years. Not

since his wife died and he had to raise three boys alone, two of whom needed his help accepting the death of their mother. All the while, he had a business to run and money to make for a family name that extended further back than a century. No pressure there. Except there was. All of it was like a pressure cooker he could never escape. He felt his neck tightening now, just by thinking of Joey leaving, and what could happen to him. Just another thing to stress over.

And now Erin. He couldn't get her out of his head, or his gut. He hated that and almost hated her for it sometimes. He knew she'd be trouble since the first time he ever laid eyes on her. Little did he realize the kind of trouble she'd become to *him*. The kind that set his body on fire, all the while he pictured her naked *with his brother*.

She walked closer and stood where Joey had been, leaning her small butt against the porch railing. She seemed to glow against the darkening twilight.

"Leave me alone. I'm no fit company."

She stared at him, tapping her fingers on the wood post next to her. He found it annoying.

"He'll be back, he just needs to know that the world out there isn't any better than here. He'll discover that, and come straight back home."

Jack glared up at her. "Really? Did he tell you that in one of your post-coital moments?"

The skin around her small mouth tightened into a frown, and her jaw moved back and forth. "Why do you do that? You can be the kindest man sometimes, and at others, the cruelest."

No one ever accused him of being cruel before; although no one ever accused him of being all that kind either.

"Well, isn't it true? Isn't that how you know my little brother?"

She turned her face, then her whole body to stare off into

the darkening yard. "Yes. We were down on the beach, right after I arrived here. I told him this place was beautiful, and he said it was, but he wouldn't know any differently because he'd never been away from it. I just think he needs some time to find himself, away from here, away from you, even, but I feel sure he will be back, and when he does return, it'll be for good."

"You think he needs to get away from me?"

"You cast a long shadow here, and you know it."

"I know my brother doesn't like you living here."

She tipped her head and he heard her sigh. "That again? I thought you said..."

He sighed in his own right, and stood up, gulping the rest of the now warm beer. He swayed on his feet and was starting to get drunk. "I said you have a home here. I just didn't expect it to keep being so damn hard."

She didn't pursue the conversation or ask him why. She knew exactly what he was talking about. "Joey just needs some space."

He hated that she knew Joey so well. As well as she could possibly know him. He hated not being able to control his reaction to her, and wanting her more than any woman he'd met in the last five years.

He leaned his elbows onto the railing near her. "Space, huh? I wonder what that's like? To choose what you want, and where you get to be. Or how you get to be."

"It doesn't matter if you were allowed the same space; you'd have ended up right here, being who you are, and doing what you do. The family was lucky you were the oldest, because no one else could have fulfilled the roles that needed filling. You wouldn't have left, even if you could have."

"How the hell do you know that?"

She shrugged. "Because I've never met anyone who was

so where he was supposed to be and doing what he was supposed to be doing. I've never spent one day feeling as fulfilled as you do on each of your days. So yeah, you've had a lot of responsibility for a long time, but then again, we both know you were built for it. Joey wasn't. At least, not yet."

Erin was thoughtful, sentimental, and sweet. Sweeter than anyone he'd met in years. So many years, her softness and tender emotions called to him far more than the alcohol he swallowed, or the sex he got whenever he was out of town.

The problem was: she was with his brother. She was as close in age to his son as she was to him, and the least appropriate woman he knew to even contemplate having a role in his life that could be construed as anything close to motherly for his sons. She was completely inappropriate for him, and perhaps, that was why he so wanted her. He'd always been appropriate for his entire life. He never got to sow his wild oats or explore anything that wasn't for his greater good or that of his family. He never got to run off and see the world because he wasn't ready to grow up yet.

"Couldn't he have found a safer way to get out of here?"

Erin looked up at him and finally smiled. "I don't think he thinks of it like that. At twenty, you're immortal, and nothing can happen to you; the danger is never real. You surely remember that."

He held her gaze and stood up straighter. He finally whispered his tone nearly guttural, "Why Joey? Why did you choose Joey?"

She didn't look away or pretend to be clueless about what he was asking. She licked her lips and whispered, "Because I didn't know any better."

They were quiet. The crickets made a loud background of constant noise and darkness surrounded the ranch. A soft breeze pushed some stray strands of hair towards her shoulders. He looked away to avoid getting the urge to run his hands into her thick, tangled, mass of shiny black hair.

"I heard what you said to Joey."

"About what?"

"About burying someone you love. I'm sorry. I was ready to go home when I heard you two."

"So you listened."

"Yes."

"So you heard me say I'd side with Joey if he demanded it?"

She smiled. "That's exactly what I'd expect from you. It's one of the things I most admire; you're loyal to a fault. I wish I had anyone who was that loyal to me, especially my own brother. Actually, I was wondering more about Lily."

His armor fell back over his heart. *No.* He didn't talk about Lily. He didn't grieve for Lily with anyone. Not even his own sons. But... her big green eyes were searching his face with care and curiosity. She wanted to know. She wanted to know him. And damn, if he didn't want her to know him.

"How old were you and she when she died?"

His jaw tightened. His stomach twisted. He hated discussing Lily. Finally he said, his tone abrupt, "Twenty-nine. Why are you asking this?"

"Context. I want to understand what you went through."

He looked out into the night. "I knew her my entire life. We went on our first date when we were fifteen years old. We got married when we were just nineteen, and purposely tried to have Ben, starting on our honeymoon. She was the only woman I'll ever love."

Erin's gaze was on his face and he could feel her looking at him, evaluating him, processing what he just told her in case she had any delusions otherwise. "It's like you lived a whole lifetime before you were thirty. And I haven't even started my life."

"That's because you're a chicken, Erin."

Her eyes widened when he turned and fully looked at her. "What was that for?"

"For not calling Allison. You won't even try. And the only reason I can see is because you're too scared to fail."

"You don't understand what it's like."

"No. I don't. But I do understand that life is unfair, and it often sucks, but when you can change things, you have to do it. You don't give up just because you're scared."

"You don't know the first thing about being weak, inept, or unimportant, now do you? You've always been in charge of your life, and had this ranch as your backup. You've never been known as the stupid one in the room. You've never doubted yourself. It's not a choice for me to make. It's just a fact for me. Yeah, I'm scared. I'm scared every day of my life. Every day I used to wake up, wondering what's going to happen to me. Will I eat today? Or have a place to sleep tonight? So, you're damn right, I'm scared. I'm always scared and alone, and sometimes, it seems like it will never change."

He was quiet, but finally said, "It has changed for you. You have a place to sleep every night, that's guaranteed. You also have enough to eat too. No one will hurt you on my ranch, and no one will make you leave either. Why won't you believe that?"

"Because no one has ever lasted. There was no father, no friends, my brother was Chance and my mother," her voice cracked. "Even my mother is gone. So it's hard to believe it when it's never been my reality."

Tears welled in her eyes and she used the back of her hand to wipe them.

"Erin?"

She held a hand up. "Forget it. I know what you were trying to say. I know I should call Allison. I just… can't."

"Look, I'm sorry. I shouldn't have said that. Sometimes, I'm not real sensitive. Lily was always telling me that."

She snorted, then looked at up at him. "She wasn't wrong."

He smiled. "You know you didn't deserve it, right? The things done to you. The fact that no one stayed and especially that they didn't find supports for you that helped you with learning."

She shrugged. "You'd think so, huh? That I would know it wasn't my fault. Thing is, most times I don't agree with you."

"Well, you should."

"Is that you being sensitive?" She asked tilting her head.

Grinning he shrugged. "Lily said sometimes I had my good moments."

Lily. She knew little of the woman who Jack had loved.

"It's not often you willingly mention her."

"No."

"You never want to talk about her."

"You never want to talk about why you can't read. And that's a hell of a lot more relevant to now, than my dead wife."

She didn't answer, but gripped the edge of the railing until her knuckles turned white. "Okay, fine. I guess, I don't talk about it."

"Would you?" he finally asked, his tone far gentler. "I'd like to understand it. It would really help me to understand this about you."

She swallowed and shifted her gaze out to the darkened land. "I tried to learn. I really did. My mom yanked me out of school every few months, so I was so far behind, there never seemed to be a chance to get caught up. Everyone knew it and ridiculed me for it. When I quit going, no one noticed.

And when I started getting into trouble, still, no one noticed. It wasn't like it is for Ben. There was no one like you to see that I went to school, did my homework, and came home each day. No one cared if I needed any help. No one gave a crap. So I pretended I didn't either. Mom read and signed anything I ever needed. That was it. I worked and partied and slept around, there was no reason for me not to. And never once did she or anyone else tell me to do anything differently. I managed to stay away from the pills and alcohol, but that was the only really smart thing I've ever done. When Mom died, Brian did what he did. So I left. I came here."

Jack didn't like hearing it. Not any of it. Imaging the young, vulnerable, teenager that Erin must have been to be left so alone and abandoned. She was lucky something worse didn't happen to her. Having a teenage son of his own, Jack couldn't imagine not doing what was best for him.

"How did Chance fit into all this?"

"He was around when I was little. But from the time I was a teen on, Chance was usually gone. He came back once in a while; but he'd always screw up and take off again."

Jack felt a fierce stabbing in his heart that nearly doubled him over. *No more.* No more would Erin be left alone and vulnerable, unwanted, and unable to read, and essentially helpless. He would see to it no harm ever came to her again. No matter what.

"Allison seemed to think you could actually be dyslexic and not realize it. There all kinds of different ways it shows itself. She said…"

She nodded and dropped her head. "I don't know. But what if I can't learn?"

He stepped forward, putting his hand to her chin as he raised her eyes to his. "Even if you can't learn to read, you're tough, smart and you figure things out. Everything you've done here was new to you, and you've learned it all. No, you've mastered it all. You're a survivor. That's why I know you can do it. But if you can't, so what? What will it cost? Nothing. Who will it hurt? No one. I won't ridicule you. No one here would ever do that to you. I will never let anyone again hurt you over this. Do you understand me? No one will ever hurt you again."

Her gaze wavered before she shut her eyelids. Sighing, she said, "That's hard to imagine."

"Imagine it. Believe it. Believe in me."

She nodded as her eyes filled with tears. "I do. I believe in you. I promise I'll think about it."

He let her go. "That's all I'm asking of you. Just try. I don't like how vulnerable it makes you."

"I've never had anyone care about it's affect on my life before."

He sighed. "You really need to find new people to hang out with."

A laugh escaped her lips. "You know, I think you might be right."

He finally smiled. How could he not smile at her? He relished seeing her rare smiles when the worry vanished, and her eyes lit up.

CHAPTER 21

*T*he two weeks leading up to Joey's departure were busy, fast and inevitable. Jack watched his little brother, the man he raised, leave the ranch on a beautiful morning, pulling away in his truck to begin his new life. The morning Joey left, Jack's stomach had him nearly buckled over in pain. Eventually, it faded when he realized Joey was finally and truly gone. The odd quiet that fell over the ranch seemed as thick as it was when Lily died.

Jack kept busy primarily to avoid the pain. The boys were out of school for the summer, so the ranch became busier than ever with their constant chatter and friends over. They hung out more with Jack, and spent more time in the barns. Erin, too, was out more whenever they were around and they continued to insist upon her riding around the arena. He tried to ignore how he felt whenever he saw them together, and how happy Charlie appeared with her. How different Erin was with the boys than the way she was with him or his brothers. She had concerns that neither he nor his brothers ever even considered. She was softer, kinder, and more attentive towards the children than any of the men thought to be.

He hired a new foreman and a ranch hand, and each occupied the two trailers near Erin's. He didn't like their close proximity, and decided it was time to move Erin's trailer to a better spot. The parking lot was no place for Erin to live. The roughnecked ranch hands he expected to live in the trailers didn't mind the parking lot vistas of where they were parked. But Erin deserved better. She deserved to live in a house. But he couldn't do that and he knew it. The only empty room there belonged to Joey, so there was no way he could move Erin in. He settled by disconnecting her trailer from the water, electricity and dump station, and hooking it up to his truck. He moved it to a new spot, across the front yard and closer towards the river. He'd already run new power, water and a dump line out there; and doubted she had a clue about what he spent those several days doing. He also leveled out the site and built a deck for her. Once the trailer was set up, she could look out over the river on one side, and into the horse pastures and the main house on the other side. Her deck gave her more privacy, and offered beatific views whenever she left or entered the trailer. He did it all while she was at work just to surprise her.

When she pulled in, he jogged over to her truck and indicated for her to roll down her window. When he pointed to her new home, her jaw dropped and she eyed him curiously.

"What did you do?"

"Not much. You need a better spot if you're staying here permanently. The place where you were was only temporary. We pull the trailers out of the storage shop each spring for the ranch hands to use. We never intended for anyone to live there permanently, however. We'll have to get it covered before winter too, since the snow loads around here would cave the roof in. If you're staying, that is."

She finally smiled. "I'm staying as long as I'm welcome."

"Well, this way it'll be more pleasant for you."

He watched her park her truck, and walk around the side of her trailer, where she discovered her new deck. It was nothing really, just a fourteen-by-fourteen square. She, however, was so overwhelmed by the move, the view, and the deck, he almost felt embarrassed for her. Why didn't she think she deserved more than just a dumpy, old trailer parked beside a small deck? How could this small change warrant her tears? Or her unending, effusive gratitude? It was hard for him not to feel humbled by her. He was astonished at how little it took to make Erin happy. While he always had a place to live and call home, this trailer was it for her.

It was several days after the relocation of her trailer when the new ranch hands started. AJ was a tall, muscular cowboy, who seemed to know as much about horses and their proper care as Jack. Jack could only hope this one might stick. He raised his pay and promised even more, as well as a decent place to live, if AJ chose to stay on. The other was a young, kid, named Pedro, who said he was eighteen, but Jack was skeptical. Still, it was the kid's business. He was only there for the summer to help with the alfalfa crop, which was already sprouting as high as Jack's ankles. Every day, Jack went out to the alfalfa fields to relocate the sprinklers. June moved into July, and on the Fourth of July, they had their first day of the temperature exceeding a hundred degrees. It was hot. Even to Jack.

That evening, with the temperatures still hovering in the eighties, they drove into Pattinson and watched the fireworks. It was a twenty-minute display of colorful rockets exploding over the Columbia River. Erin was as thrilled by it as Charlie. Jack started to notice things like that about her. Everything they did, things that were normal, everyday stuff to him, his brothers, and his boys, seemed to delight, intrigue, interest, and even thrill Erin. It didn't take much. Things as simple as sharing dinner visibly elated her. She gave him an appreciation for his life, his family, their home, hell, even the damn sunrise, that was like nothing he ever had before. Sure, he felt fortunate before, but not with the same deep sense of appreciation and gratitude that Erin seemed to find for everything.

Erin's skin started to tan and she put on a little weight. She seemed to glow the longer she was there. She ate real food, and soon started to trust him more, finally feeling like she was home. She looked better and healthier immediately and it did wonders for her. It changed her, making her more beautiful than she'd ever been. It was a startling trans-formation.

It was different, however, without Joey. Jack missed him. Joey was the loudest of the brothers, and the most full of bullshit and crap, which Jack missed dearly. The table seemed too quiet, too mundane, and sometimes, too serious. Joey never let things get serious for long.

It was also different because he suddenly didn't see Joey anymore when he looked at Erin, or even imagine him with Erin anymore. The longer Joey was gone, the hazier Jack's memory was of their brief affair. But it remained something, which he could not let go of or forget. There was no way for him to ignore it, although, he invariably tried to.

Grumpy and annoyed at himself, and his fascination for a woman who would always be the wrong one, despite staying forever in his sights, pissed him off in general. He was pissed at her and at Joey for circumstances he never asked to be involved in and couldn't change. By August, he wasn't in the best of moods.

"Jack, I think you ought to take this trip instead of me."

Jack glanced up when Ian walked in and sat on a

sawhorse near him. Jack was cleaning out the hooves of Cleo, one of their personal horses.

"Why's that?"

"You haven't been away in a while. I think it might do you good."

Jack frowned. "What are you getting at?"

"Just that maybe you could use, you know, some time away. A short escape."

"A short escape from what?"

"From Erin," Ian said after a long moment before frowning at Jack. "You're edgy as hell around here, and it's time you fixed that."

Jack paused as he considered Ian. Was his brother suggesting he needed to get laid to be in a better mood?

"It has been awhile... since, you know, you left town."

Jack went back to the hooves. Maybe Ian was right. Maybe that *was* his problem. He nodded. "Fine. I'll leave tomorrow. You're in charge of the boys."

Ian agreed and left. Jack wondered what more Ian thought about Erin, since he had very little to say about her addition to the ranch.

ERIN LOVED HER NEW LOCATION. She spent hours outside on her deck. She bought a cheap patio chair and often enjoyed the views of the river and mountains and pine trees. She let the sun warm her, tan her, and relax her. She could look out towards rural nature, or watch the horses behind her; and farther off, she could see the main house. With mostly grass around her now, the constant clouds of driveway dust were over. Washing the trailer windows, she was shocked to see how clear they became, like she just put on new glasses.

She was happy and content for the first time she could ever remember.

Until one morning she noticed Jack and Ian out and about early loading up their six-stall horse trailer to Jack's big truck. As it idled, the exhaust dispersed into the air. Jack threw a duffel bag into his truck and walked around towards Ian. He spotted Erin as she rounded the trailer.

"Are you going somewhere?"

"Oregon. Got a horse to look at."

"Oh." She didn't like the sound of that. *Jack was leaving?* He was always there. She might not see or talk to him for days on end, but she always knew he was there nevertheless. He was there if she ever needed anything. How could she endure his absence if she needed him? "How long will you be gone?"

"Why?" he asked while absently, rifling through the gear stowed in the back of his truck. He seemed to be barely listening to her. "You need something?"

"Uh… No. I can take care of it." Her toilet was leaking fresh water around the base. Seemed like something it should not be doing.

He walked towards the small tack area of the horse trailer before his head popped back out and he looked at her around the door. "What is it? I can tell by your nervous fidgeting that something is up. I don't have a lot of time, so out with it."

Warmth flooded her face and she kicked the dirt near her feet, which was so dry, puffs of it swirled around her ankles. "My uh, trailer seems to be having a problem."

"What kind of problem?"

"The uh… well, the toilet."

He shut the door on the horse trailer. "All right; let's take a look."

His tone was easy and mild. "Aren't you leaving right now?"

"Don't you need a place to go?"

Her facial skin felt instantly sunburned. She could *not* discuss this subject with Jack. "What are you going to do?"

He raised an eyebrow at her and replied quizzically, "Fix it. Not a big deal. Trailers can be a pain sometimes. Come on."

She was miserable and well beyond embarrassed as she trailed behind Jack. He entered her trailer, opened her bathroom door and looked at it. She stayed outside, wanting to die rather than think about what he was looking at, and worse, what he was thinking. He came out and walked past her, heading outside to where the hose from the trailer tanks hooked into a pipe in the ground. She had only a vague idea of how it all worked.

"A fitting broke. I'll be right back."

She didn't look up when he said that. She had no idea what he meant, but damn if she would ask. He walked towards Shane's shop, where they kept all their tools. He was back only minutes later with some tools piled in a bucket. He went inside and she could hear him thumping around. She refused to go in the trailer, or even look up at him when he finally emerged, apparently satisfied with his success. She crossed her arms over her chest and glared out, red-faced, over the valley, suddenly hating the trailer.

He finally reappeared with a casual, "If it happens again, just tell Ian. Or even Ben. They know how to take care of it."

He spoke as if it were no big deal. When she didn't answer, he finally nudged her toe with his boot. "Erin?"

She narrowed her gaze onto a tree she spotted across the river. "How could you not tell me you were leaving?"

His expression went from amused to surprised. "Like I said it just came up. Why? You going to miss me?"

Yes, desperately. Instead she said, "Well, what if something goes wrong again? Or I need something fixed?"

"Then ask Ian or even Ben. They can handle most anything that comes up on these trailers."

She buried her face into her arms.

"Look, I've got to get on the road. I'll see you in a few days."

She didn't like hearing that either. She finally looked at him as he started down the steps of the deck. He had her attention now. "How many days?"

He shrugged. "Don't know. A week, maybe two. It's a long drive. And I got more than one stop. I'm delivering that two-year-old mare I've been working with to its new owner, and looking at a couple of others to see about training."

"How come you never mentioned this before?"

"I didn't know I had to. Besides, I thought Ian was going, and at the last minute, he asked me to go. Anyway, like I said, if anything happens, just tell Ian."

With that, he waved and started towards Shane's shop, whistling as he swung the bucket by his side. *He was whistling.* At ease. He was acting happy to be leaving. She glared after him. Why was he so happy about leaving? Because he got away from her? How could he leave her there as if it were nothing? She sat down in a huff, and let her anger roil around in her gut to counteract the unease of Jack leaving. How dare he just leave her like that?

It was a full two weeks and a day before Jack finally pulled into his own driveway. The horse trailer was empty. The horse he specifically left to see about was still too wild to even load into the horse trailer. He might return for it in a few weeks if the group in charge of its care could get close enough to slip a rope over its neck.

It was mid-afternoon by the time he reached the ranch.

259

The day was very hot outside. He glanced at the dash of his truck, which said it was over a hundred degrees. The air conditioning was on high, but he fully expected the furnace-like air that would engulf him when he got out. He pulled a U-turn in the driveway and backed the trailer up until it was under the lean-to of the storage shop. Once in place, he unhooked the hitch before unloading his gear into the barn. Beads of sweat rolled off his face and arms. He finally got back into the truck, and pulled it forward before parking next to Ian's truck. It was Saturday afternoon and seemed like everyone was home.

He got out, and started up the porch steps, eager to return and see his boys, and… well, maybe he was even glad to see Erin. So what? He'd gotten used to her presence over the last few weeks. He stopped dead when something blue caught his eye and, curious, walked down the porch, turning the corner to the far side of the house.

There, smack dab in the middle of his alfalfa field, was a big, blue, above-ground, round pool. It was hideous. It stood off the ground about five feet, with a white ladder that hooked over the end nearest to him. And there, in the middle of the pool, was Erin, floating in an inner tube with her legs trailing along and the water up to her shins. Her butt hung down and her arms rested on the sides. Her head was back with a pair of sunglasses stuck on top of it. She wore a bikini. That same damned, flowered, yellow-and-pink bikini she wore to work. Now she was wearing it in the middle of his alfalfa field.

He stalked over, but she didn't seem to know he was there. She floated along as if worry free and without a care in the world. Bees buzzed in the wildflowers, and the heat seemed to shimmer off the land, nearly blinding him.

She was sound asleep.

"What the hell is this piece of shit?"

Her eyes popped open and she almost fell right into the water. She looked at him, disoriented, for a moment and finally caught the edge of the pool with her hand before she could steady herself. With his eyes firmly on her face, he tried to ignore the visible strain and pull of her bare thighs as she tried to reposition the inner tube. She had gorgeous legs, small, slim and tan, with well-shaped knees and slender thighs that blossomed into a small, trim ass.

"Jack! You're back."

"Yeah, I'm back." He mimicked her exclamation with a grumpy tone. He nodded at the monstrosity in his field. "Now what the hell is this? And why is it in the middle of my alfalfa field?"

"It's a swimming pool."

"I can damn well see that. What is it doing here? How did it get here, for that matter?"

"Oh... well, Ian and Ben helped me. Shane couldn't because he took off a few days ago on his motorcycle. I'm sure Ian knows where he was going and why."

"Who bought the pool?"

She squirmed around in the inner tube, her legs slipping and making squealing sounds on the plastic. A crease marred her forehead. "Uh, well, I guess you did."

"I sure as shit didn't buy a blow up pool and put it in the middle of my horses' alfalfa fields."

"Well, it was the only flat spot we could find," she said, her voice sounding as if that was a perfectly reasonable excuse.

"You used *my money* to buy this? How?"

"No. Not your money per se. It was more like the ranch money. You know, for ranch improvements."

He shut his eyes and counted backwards from ten. "You took petty cash for this?"

She shook her head vigorously. "No, I didn't," she said

with a hearty shake of her head. "I would never do that… but, well, Ben did."

"Ben stole money from me?"

"It wasn't like that. It was a hundred degrees or more each day you were gone."

"And we have a nice, cold river located right down there."

"Well, yeah, but we can't spend all day there. This helps a lot and Charlie just loves it. It was his idea. I simply, you know, helped him pick out the best one."

He sucked in a breath and slowly exhaled. "Let me get this straight: you drove my younger son into town, to buy this monstrosity of a pool with money you had my older son steal from the ranch funds, and then you had them set it up here?"

Her gaze seemed suddenly weary as she swallowed and nodded, "Well, yes. I suppose so. But it wasn't like that. Certainly not as sinister as you're making it sound."

There was a sudden ruckus behind him and Jack turned to find Charlie running across the porch before launching himself into Jack's arms in a happy hug. Ben, too, came forward with a hug, and Ian stood at the edge, smiling, until he saw Jack's face.

Jack glowered back at Erin. Charlie jumped around, appearing very excited. "Isn't it great, Dad? We use it every single day."

"It's in the middle of my alfalfa field."

"You surely won't miss this little bit," Erin muttered.

He glared at Erin. "And what do you know of how much feed I need for the horses? You know exactly shit about my business. And you had no right to put this… this piece of crap here or spend my money on it."

Charlie's face fell and Ben took a step back. Erin slid off the inner tube to stand up. The water came up to her collarbone. She walked towards the ladder.

"You're overreacting."

"How did you get it all set up?"

She looked towards Ian, who glanced at Jack before he smiled and shrugged. "You helped them?" Jack asked incredulously.

"Sure. They asked me. And it seemed harmless enough. It *has* been hot."

He opened his mouth to speak and looked at Erin, and then at Ian. They shared a smile. Since when did these two get so chummy? As far as he knew, they never once talked to one another. Now they were... what? BFFs?

Suddenly walking over to the ladder, Jack climbed up on it, and leaned down to grab Erin by her waist. He pulled her up and threw her over his shoulder. Her wet body dripped, soaking his denim shirt as she twisted, squirmed and screamed. He put a hand on her ass to hold her there.

"Jack Rydell! Put me down this second. What is wrong with you? What the hell are you doing?"

"Doing? I'm just showing you where we swim on my ranch," he said as he started walking across the field. He went down the driveway and towards the path to the beach. His kids stared, open-mouthed, as they trailed behind, but at a distance. No doubt, they were just as unsure of what the hell to do. Meanwhile, Erin screamed and kicked her legs the entire journey to the river's edge. He had to loop an arm around her shins to hold her still. She weighed no more than a sack of feed, so it wasn't hard for him to carry her, although she was slippery as an eel.

He quickly strode towards the river, now in full summer, which made it lower and warmer. It looked beautiful in the sunlight shimmering around it and the mountains, all hazy and purple, above it. He strode up towards Rydell Rock and she started shrieking louder.

"Ian! Stop him!" She yelled loudly behind him. By then, he

had quickly picked his way up the rocky trail, right to the top of the large rock that jutted a good twenty feet above the river. He couldn't chance looking back with Erin screaming and fighting him. He carefully climbed to the top without losing his balance or his hold of her. She twisted and fought as hard as a caterpillar caught in a spider web. He was surprised at her strength, once she figured out what he intended to do.

At the top, he stood on the edge of the rock. Below him was a deep, clear, slow-moving pool of water. It glowed with dappled sunlight on the sandy bottom. It was perfectly safe. She'd be fine.

"Don't you dare! *Don't you dare!* I swear I'll get you back. I will. If you do this, I'll make you regret it every day for the rest of your life."

"Yeah? How's that?" he asked, suddenly visibly amused by her while his anger seemed to instantly diminish. Her ass was firm and tight under his hand as she struggled. Her breasts bumped against his back and she pounded her fists into his lower back, from where she hung with her hair dangling nearly to the ground.

She didn't answer him, but yelled towards the beach again. He glanced back. Ian, Ben and Charlie just stood there, shading their eyes as they watched them.

"Do something! One of you. Please help me!"

He grinned as a fresh batch of anger seemed to consume her. The more she fought his unrelenting grip, the more she merely ground herself closer to him. He suddenly popped her up, so she was upright in his arms, and then smiled before letting his arms out and throwing her off the rock.

CHAPTER 22

The water surrounded her body, breaking her fall and leaving her buoyant. She had her nose plugged and kicked towards the surface, anger rushing through her bloodstream, and propelling her forward. How dare he? How dare Jack Rydell storm back home, then carry her down to the river just to throw her off a cliff? She could have hit her head on one of the rocks! She could have broken a bone by hitting the sandy bottom. Or drowned. She could have freaking died. She finally surfaced, coughing and sputtering.

Looking above, she saw where Jack stood, silhouetted against the eye-searing blue of the afternoon sky. His eyes were shaded as he stared down at her. He looked big and hulking against the sky, like the king of the river, watching over her. His hands were on his hips, with his elbows out, and he was laughing. At her. Again. She glowered at him, but doubted he could see her expression. She would never, ever forgive him. Never. Ever. He could crawl over broken glass and cut his hands and knees to shreds, and she wouldn't feel any pity for him. She wouldn't even offer him a Band-Aid.

Kicking her legs towards the base of the rock she'd just

been thrown off, the river circled around her, creating a mini cove-like effect. Once she set her feet down, the surrounding rock blocked her off from the beach as well as Jack above her.

She was stuck. She couldn't swim up the river because the current was too swift and deep. She had no shoes on, so she couldn't climb up the steep ledge either. Jack yelled over towards the beach that she was fine. *Fine?* Fine to be stuck in a rushing river with no way out? Yeah, sure; she was peachy.

She glanced up when tiny pebbles slid past her hands where she clung to the edge of the rock. Jack's silhouette came above her again. He was climbing down the deep V of the rocks that provided the only access to where she was stuck.

"What the hell is the matter with you? You could have killed me. I don't know who you think you are, but you had no right to do that to me!" She started yelling at him before he took another step.

He paused on the rock, leaning back. "You keep yelling and I'm turning back, Ms. Poletti. And by no means did I almost kill you."

"What if I couldn't swim?"

"Seeing as how this started over a pool you put in my alfalfa field, I took a wild guess that wasn't the case."

"You're a lowdown asshole! You had no right to manhandle me just because you happen to be bigger than me. I…"

She stopped mid-sentence with her mouth hanging open, when she saw him turn and start to climb back up. "Hey. Where are you going?" she called after him.

"Better stop or I'll leave you down there."

She frowned. How dare he order her to stop after what *he'd* just done to *her*. But she was bobbing in deep water, with no shoes, no floaties, no life jacket and therefore, no means of safely getting across the river and back home.

Snapping her mouth shut, she quit looking up and instead, glared down into the river, watching the sunlight sway as it outlined the sandy river bottom with golden spider webs. It was so clear and pretty, the sight almost made her ache.

Finally, Jack's feet dropped down to the rocks next to her. His boots splashed at the water edges where he was forced to stand in three inches of water. She hoped his socks were wet and soggy. Besides it was a hundred and seven degrees today, who else but Jack would have on jeans and leather cowboys boots? Even Ian wore shorts and flip-flops as he spent most of the afternoon with her and the boys at the river.

"Out. I have work to get back to."

She glared up at him as she treaded water. She didn't want to pull herself out with Jack right there, which was ridiculous. He, along with everyone else within fifty miles, had, at some point, seen her working a coffee machine in her bikini. But now, here, in this small, tight spot, soaking wet, she didn't want to be on display for him. He stood there, his hands on his hips, frowning, as he waited for her to exit the water.

"You're still an asshole, Jack," she said as she scrambled up the rocky incline and stood right next to him. They were on a three-foot wide flat rock, which was the only stable spot to stand. She was way too aware of her wet body next to Jack's fully clothed, dry body. She refused to look up at him. The air was so hot, her skin could have had steam evaporating off it.

"And you shouldn't spend my money on such crap."

"It isn't crap. Charlie loves it. He swims until nine o'clock at night in it."

"He does that down here too."

"It's his summer too. He can't always be getting back to work. He wanted it."

"Yeah. I know. He's asked for it the last three summers. The thing is: there's a perfectly good river less than a five-minute walk away with our own beach and swimming hole. There is no reason to put some oversized wading pool in the middle of a working ranch. And if you knew anything at all about parenting, you'd understand that I can't grant every single desire or wish my kids ask for. Charlie wanted to light his own fireworks on the Fourth of July; think I should have let him do that too?"

She glared at her pink-painted toenails as the sun-laced water lapped over them. "No," she said with grudging annoyance. "You still didn't have to throw me off a cliff. Why would you do that?"

"Because." He grinned and shrugged. "I've wanted to do it too many times ever since you first drove up my driveway. You don't even know how much."

She took her foot back and kicked his shin. All she managed to do, however, was hurt her toes. His boots were that high. She swore as she hopped into the water and fell backwards; then screamed in pain as the rocks hit her butt.

Jack's hands came under armpits and he lifted her effortlessly out of the water. "You are one giant pain in my ass."

Then he shuffled her around, and told her to get on his back, climbing up the rock as easily as he walked up his driveway. She shut her eyes, afraid to fall back onto the sharp rocks. They would scrape her skin if she fell. Finally, she felt his body shifting and saw they were on level ground. She opened her eyes and looked around. They were on top of the rock. The river rushed towards them, clashing into the rock and then turning nearly horizontally to keep flowing downstream. Mountains lined the view and the sky glowed in a blinding, bright blue. It was breathtaking to see in the dazzling sun. Then she felt the hot rocks beneath her bare feet, which might have been a hundred and seventeen degrees. Jack glanced at her feet when she made a whimpering noise.

"Oh, yeah, that's gonna be hot," he said and once again, flipped her up and over his shoulder, starting down towards the beach where the others waited. This time, she was silent even though she wanted to pummel his back. Her ass was heads up for Ian and the rest of the world to see. The tips of her hair dragged over the rocks and sand. She looked like a cavewomen being hauled around by the Neanderthal asshole, Jack Rydell. He finally flipped her over and her bare feet hit the hot, dry sand.

She straightened her back with as much dignity as she could muster in the situation. She had been manhandled, humiliated, and now stood soaking wet with all four males looking at her.

She turned on Ian. "You are the biggest, wimpiest, asshole I've ever met besides Jack. You and Ben. You're big enough. You could have taken him. That pool was partly your doing too. Both of you insisted. But when the lord of the ranch over here comes home, you two cower like little pansy-asses. I hope to no one ever needs actual help when you two are the only ones around, because you'll probably throw them under the bus like you did to me."

"I didn't know what Jack was doing!"

"He had me draped over his shoulder like a throw rug. You could have done something."

Ben glanced at his dad. "I did get the compressor to blow the top ring on the pool up."

"I helped fill it with water," Charlie added.

"And all of you put your asses in it too!" She was so mad, she felt like she could breathe fire on all of them. She didn't deserve the blame, or to be manhandled simply because she was the only girl, and therefore, smaller than the rest of them. She reached down, and before Jack could figure out what she intended to do, picked up a fistful of dry, fine, white sand. She stood up and threw it directly into his face. Straight into his eyes and mouth.

He jerked back in surprise and put his fists in his eyes, rubbing them as he spit sand from his mouth. She grabbed more and threw it at him. She could only hit his neck and back as he was bent over, rubbing it off his face. She was about to do it a third time when he grabbed her wrists with both of his hands. He was breathing hard and glared at her with his eyes narrowing.

"You shouldn't have done that."

"Oh yeah. Why not? You gonna drown me this time? The only reason you get to do anything to me is because you're bigger than I am. Congratulations, Jack. You can pick on someone half your size. Why don't you throw Charlie next? After all, he's the one who put water in the pool."

Jack nodded and glanced behind her. The boys looked weary and were unusually quiet. Even Ian was apprehensive. She put her shoulders back; in for a penny, in for the pound.

He let her go and she was so surprised, she almost fell backwards again.

"You're right. It wasn't just you."

Jack lifted his shirt over his head, suddenly shirtless and only two feet away from her. His jeans were secured by a brown belt and a shiny belt buckle, which he quickly undid and pulled loose from his pants. He began kicking off his boots and her mouth came open when she saw his bare chest in front of her. It was covered in fine, auburn-colored hair, with a spray of freckles that spattered over his chest and dipped into the wrinkled crunch of a nearly perfect six-pack of abs. He was ripped. She should have already known that from the endless physical work he did around the ranch. But

Jack didn't wear particularly tight shirts to advertise his muscle tone. His arms had muscles, but nothing like his chest. She was so stunned by his suddenly naked chest, she forgot to figure out what he was doing. Only when he picked her up, and again, walked into the water, throwing her over his head, did she remember; he was getting revenge on her.

She came up for air, just in time to see him throwing his older son in and chasing after his younger who was, by then, giggling and shrieking happily as he danced around the beach. Jack caught Charlie, who giggled and pleaded, while Jack, much gentler now, threw his son into the river. Then, just as quickly, Jack was in the water and swimming towards Charlie. He was there when Charlie came up, grabbing him and dragging him towards shallower water. All the while, Charlie laughed and screamed with delight.

Ben went after his dad, trying to push over his father, but he was no match for Jack. Erin was sure of it. Ben was only a few inches shorter than Jack, but his skinny frame was half the width and half the body weight. Still, Jack fell into the water, going under. He came back up, grinning, with water dripping from his hair, now turning nearly brown from being wet. He shook his head, running his hands through it. The sun glittered off the beads of water, spiking his hair; and all the while, he kept grinning, wet, and naked from the waist up as the water rushed over him. Jack looked ten years younger, and ten years hotter. She stared, stunned by how different he suddenly seemed. How much more fun he became as he splashed and frolicked with his two sons. She remembered thinking she couldn't picture Jack ever swimming here at his own beach. Let alone, frolicking. Yet, here he was. His strong arms easily cut the water, as he time and again, threw Charlie in and retrieved him, all the while, laughing and grinning. Ben also tried to outdo Jack in swimming against the current. Ian wondered off after watching them for a while.

Jack didn't forget about Erin. He threw her in a few more times, despite her protests, her screams, and her pleading. He threw her in, held her down, and even tickled her underwater until she felt like she swallowed half the river.

Eventually, the boys started to tire and she did too. Her weary muscles shook from the strain of trying to fight Jack off. He simply held her out and let her struggle. She was no match for him. She finally followed Charlie out and they fell onto the sand, wet and worn out. The sand stuck to them instantly. It was hot on their wet skin and felt wonderful as it warmed her up. It wasn't long before Jack and Ben came out and joined them.

Ben and Charlie were starting to play back and forth, and decided to run up and jump into the pool, leaving her alone with Jack. The once loud, playful noises of kids and fun suddenly stopped. Jack sat near her, leaning back on his elbows, his wet torso gleaming under the sun. She tried not to look. But he was right there. Right in front of her. He ran a hand through his hair, squeezing water off it, and his arm muscles bunched as he moved. She sat up and wrapped her arms around her legs, resting her chin on her knees. Her hair was wet and heavy down her back.

It suddenly felt different. The air seemed strained and weird. She wasn't sure why, or what might have caused the change, but it was like Jack could hear the sudden acceleration of her heart beating. She couldn't think of anything to say.

Why did Jack seem so relaxed, lying in the sun, and drying in the warm air? Ian mentioned at one point that Jack needed the time away. It was the only time he didn't have to worry so much about what he did or how it reflected on the boys. It took her a few days to figure out what Ian meant. Jack was off somewhere getting laid where his kids couldn't find out about it. And ever since learning that, she obsessively imagined what kind of woman Jack would choose to have sex with.

"Your trip was good?" she finally asked when she could no longer take the awkward silence.

He glanced over his tanned, rounded shoulder at her. "Disappointing. But fine."

"Disappointing?"

"The horse I went there to get wasn't ready to travel."

She let out a breath. "Oh… just the horse was disappointing?"

"Yeah, what else would be?"

"Ian said you go out of town when you want to get laid. Is that why you seem a bit more relaxed? Even taking one afternoon off to play with your kids?" Okay, she wanted to now simply bite her tongue off. She blurted it out, but never, ever meant to approach Jack about his sex life. She shut her eyes in abject horror.

Silence followed her comment. She smacked a hand to her face. How could she have said that out loud? His voice was quiet and stern. "I play with my kids, Erin. I'm not always working. And why in the hell were you and Ian talking about me getting laid?"

"Okay, he didn't say that exactly. But I got the picture."

"What picture?"

"What you do when you go out of town."

Jack deliberately sat up. "Where should I do it? With the three single women who live in town? The only ones Lily and I didn't go to school with?" He dropped his voice and added, "Or should I do that with you?"

She stared out at the water and watched a group of inner tubers floating by, all waving and calling hello to Jack. He waved back, but his entire focus was on her. They watched the group round the corner.

"Well? You haven't answered me."

She wouldn't answer him either. He chuckled as he stood up. "You're really not as bad-ass as you pretend. You're so red, you look like a boiled lobster."

"I don't pretend I'm bad-ass."

"Yeah, well, you're not when it comes to me. And I didn't get laid, if it makes you any happier to know."

She shot a glance up at him, but the sun blinded her and she couldn't tell what he was thinking. She slowly rose to her feet. Sand clung everywhere to her, in places she really wished it wouldn't. Since she had no shoes or towel, she waited for Jack to go first with his jeans wet and clinging to him. He stuck his boots on his bare feet and muttered how bad that felt.

As she tiptoed over the hot sand behind him, she asked, "So does the pool get to stay?"

He stopped so abruptly, she ran into his back. "That's what you're most concerned with, isn't it? The damn pool?"

"Well? Can it?"

"You don't give me much choice, now do you? Now that Charlie loves it."

She heard the tone and sensed he knew it was she who loved it too. "It gets really hot here in the afternoons."

"If you were so hot, why didn't you just order air conditioning for the trailer?"

"I can't afford that."

He shrugged. "I'll order you some."

She didn't get why some things with Jack were such a big deal, and others were not. The pool was far cheaper than getting air conditioning, yet the pool was the problem?

She went directly back to the pool, where Charlie and Ben were already swimming happily. It was sun-warmed, warmer than the river, but still very refreshing. She floated forever, staring up above her at the deep, blue, endless sky, and scorching, white sunlight. *This was what a summer was supposed to be like.* It was all she could think of lately as she watched Charlie and Ben playing on the beach, or in the river, or floating down the river with their friends. She loved to watch them frolic and cavort, just being young in the sun. She'd never had a summer like that. And never frolicked anywhere.

Her only concern during Jack's brief absence was how much time Ben was spending with that Marcy Fielding girl. She didn't like how they often ambled up the beach for long periods of time and then disappeared. She intended to talk to Jack about it. There was no doubt in her mind Ben would try and sleep with Marcy. They were too young, and shouldn't be doing such things.

She didn't want Ben doing that. Not like she did when she was his age. She knew it was twisted, considering her past, and that she was not even close to being Ben's guardian. She barely allowed Ben to be alone during the past weeks, and made sure to always follow them as they went up the beach or into the house. During Jack's absence, she strangely got way more comfortable in the Rydell household. It seemed odd, but she was more at ease getting to know Shane, Ian, Ben and Charlie without Jack being there. She was able to move about the house easier, and didn't always have to keep her eyes and ears open while worrying where Jack was and what he'd think of whatever she was doing. She'd spent many evenings watching TV with the brothers, and hanging out with Charlie on the porch playing board games, while, of course, keeping an eye on Ben. She'd also taken to wandering into the cool air of the house whenever she needed a refresher. No one cared. They just said hello, and quickly went back to whatever they were doing.

She realized this should all be good. She was becoming accepted, and grew more comfortable as part of the Rydell household. But it wasn't a good thing. It meant she put way too much stock into what Jack thought about her and whatever she did. It put her on edge, and her heart on high alert. But it mostly scared the shit out of her. No one ever made her feel that way. No one ever had that kind of power over her. No one's opinion ever mattered to her like Jack Rydell's.

With a sinking heart, she realized that his absence proved that to her. She missed him way too much, and found it intolerably lonely there without him. She felt freer, however, and more comfortable to wander around the house and yard. Even enough to buy a pool and set it up.

Jack was busy the rest of the afternoon unpacking his stuff, checking on the horses, and doing the hundred or so other mysterious things that he did daily. Meanwhile, she floated in the pool, looking up at the sky and trying not to feel so tingly and aware. Foremost on her mind was to avoid watching Jack.

Towards evening, she suddenly felt Jack's eyes on her from the porch. She lifted her head up and found him staring at her. The air was still nearly eighty degrees as a deep twilight turned the land to shadows and the mountains into purple smudges.

She nearly fell off her inner tube when she realized what Jack was wearing. *Shorts.* He stood there in navy blue swim trunks that skimmed his knees. She nearly choked on the water, never expecting to see Jack in shorts. His legs were toned, hairy, and not as tan as the rest of him. But he wore them well.

She stood in the pool and noticed the bag next to him. "Are you coming in?"

"No. We're going to swim in a real place, not that plastic tub."

"We?"

"You and me. Come on." He held out a blue towel for her. She quickly got out and grabbed it, drying off. Her hands and feet had long ago turned to ugly, wrinkled prunes.

"The river? Now? It's almost dark."

"Never been night swimming, huh? It's fun."

She stared at his back in a white t-shirt. Why? And why was he acting so companionable towards her? "Are you going to try and kill me again?" she called after him, struggling to get her sandals on. She hopped after him with her towel wrapped around her.

"I didn't try to kill you. I threw you in the river. It was meant in fun."

She finally caught up to him and glanced at the house, which was dark.

"Where is everyone? Doesn't Charlie want to come?"

"Ian went to the bar and dropped Ben and Charlie off at different friends' houses. There's no one here."

She frowned. It wasn't often that the ranch was empty. "So what? I'm your last resort?"

"Something like that."

She quit talking as they walked to the sandy beach. Once there, she stared at the water, now turned an inky color with the tangerine sky reflecting off its surface. It was beautiful, haunting, and totally different from its previous summer glory.

Jack laid out a towel and sat on it. Then opened the bag next to him. He brought out food and beer. Shocked, she came closer. "You wanted to have a picnic?"

"You haven't gotten out of the water in nearly four hours. I've never seen anyone swim like you do. Must be a relief to wear the bikini to work."

She glared at him. "I never got to swim like this as a kid. It was never this hot except for maybe five days a year, if we

277

were lucky, and there was no place for us to swim, but the indoor community pool."

"So hence, I get a new pool?"

She finally smiled as she sat down next to him, cross-legged, with the towel over her lap. She grabbed the cold beer he handed her and the deli sandwich. They ate in silence, watching the sun setting over the river, while the slight breeze stirred the cottonwood leaves behind them. It was so pleasant after the heat of the day, she sighed happily out loud. The beer was nice and warmed her insides as the sandwich and potato chips filled her up. She was more touched at Jack doing this than anything else she could think of.

"So how did you and Ian suddenly get so chummy?"

She glanced up. Was there an acidic tone to his voice? She scrunched her face and tilted her head. "Are you actually checking to see if I was coming on to your other brother while you were gone?"

He stared, waiting for her to answer. She was so offended, she didn't know whether to hit him or get up and leave. "As it happens, when you're not around, they talk to me. I don't understand it. That's it. Shane and Ian are much nicer to me when you're not around. You figure that one out."

"Huh. Interesting."

"No. Not interesting. Annoying. I was also spending a lot of time at the house because of the heat as well as Ben."

"Ben? Why Ben?"

"I hate to tell you this, but he and Marcy are spending way too much time together. Do you have any idea how hard it is to prevent them from being alone together?"

He tipped his face towards her. "And you were trying?"

"Of course. He's way too young to start having sex."

Jack smiled. She didn't know why. He dug his bare toe

into the sand as he took a long drink of beer. "Lil and I were only sixteen."

"Well, I was thirteen the first time. I started doing it regularly by the age of sixteen. That's no age to be having sex. He's just a little kid. He should not even be thinking about it. He's not like the jerks I knew as a kid."

"Thirteen?"

She looked up at his face. The smirk was gone. "Seventh grade. It's how I survived."

"That's not right."

"Well, there was no one like you in my life to tell me differently. You need to talk to Ben. Warn him. Threaten him. Maybe even ground him."

Jack laughed, his teeth flashing, and his eyes twinkled at her. "I can't ground a fifteen-year-old boy for what he might do. That's a sure way for him to sneak out to do it. I'm not so sure there's anything I can do to dissuade him, if he intends to do it."

She didn't like that. "You have to try. You can't just roll over and play dead about this. It's too important."

"It's really important to you, isn't it?"

She nodded. "I think Ben deserves better. He needs to be older so he can understand how important it is, and enjoy it. Maybe even be in love first. It should be when he's good and ready."

"And that's where Ben will disagree with you, he thinks he's ready now."

She glared at him. "You're his father."

He nodded. "I'm well aware of that. Don't you think I'd hog-tie him to his bed if I could? It just doesn't work like that."

She shoved her foot into the loose sand before flinging it. "I just hate to see him look back and regret this. It's too important. Marcy reminds me of misbehaved, bad me when I was growing up. I don't think she's who Ben should be with."

His hand came to her shoulder and she looked up, confused, when he said softly, "You're not bad, Erin."

"I'm not good either. If Ben ran into my equivalent, I'd have already slept with him, and dumped him long ago. Look what I did with your brother."

"I remember."

"Well, don't forget it," she said, not liking the gentle timbre to his voice.

Silence followed and she dug her feet deeper into the beach. Her toes hit the wet sand underneath. She dug deeper still.

"Let's swim."

She glanced up with a scowl at Jack. "Now? It's dark."

"Almost, but the water's still warm from today. Trust me," he said, his cocky smile beaming on his face. She wanted to stop talking about herself and reminding Jack of who she really was, so she agreed without further argument.

She followed Jack to the water's dark edge. A rim of white light hung over the hills across the river, leaving the trees and hills in darkened outlines. He was right; the water was warm. It was nice. She followed Jack in. The water felt refreshing and pleasant in the warm air. The air and water were about the same temperature. And it was fun to dunk and paddle around in the dark water as the night engulfed them and twilight started to fade. After half an hour, she started to finally grow chilled.

She headed towards shore, only to bump into Jack. He stood on the sandy bottom, his shoulders raised above the water as he swayed with the current swirling around him. She froze when his hands clenched around her upper arms, catching her and pulling her back towards his body. Her stomach tightened in uncertainty at his touch, and the soft way his fingertips brushed over her skin. She felt his body so close behind her, she was unable to move. What if he was just mocking her? What if she suddenly turned towards him and he rejected her? Or made fun of her? Or... well... what could Jack possibly be doing?

His hands came to her waist and her bare stomach. He lifted her, turning her towards him as he dropped her along the front of his body. Their wet bodies slid together and she groaned at the sensations. She was surprised sparks didn't shoot off them and sizzle in the water. He was aroused. She could feel him against her middle with the water supporting her weight. Finally, his mouth came down on hers. Warm, wet, and soft at first. She sighed at the pleasure, and the ease of it. How right it felt. He held her there, kissing her for long moments as the chirping crickets grew louder around her, and the light totally faded.

Then suddenly, his hot tongue hastily entered her mouth. He moved his hands until they were at the back of her swimsuit. He undid it and threw it towards the shore in seconds. His hand came around to her wet breast. Her nipples were hard and small already from the cold water. The sensation of his warm, rough hands on her cold, wet nipples had her nearly screaming with the sheer ecstasy it sent towards her center.

He moved, then walked, easily carrying her towards the shore. He took her to the big beach towel, where they ate their dinners previously. Setting her there, his hands took off her swimsuit bottom. And that quick, that unexpectedly, she was naked. With Jack.

The sand felt soft and lumpy against her back. Jack lay down beside her, putting an arm under her head, and leaning in before he started kissing her again. His hands roamed everywhere, touching her, caressing her, igniting her. His hands were very large, with deep calluses that should have scratched her, but instead, only incited her more feverishly.

And he could kiss. His mouth was warm as he moved his lips over hers, complete and thorough without ever over-powering or gagging her.

When he ran his tongue over her lips, and started kissing down her neck, she thought she might melt from the sensual pleasure. His hands caressed her breasts, rubbing over her nipples, until his mouth finally took over. He licked and kissed her, using his teeth with the perfect amount of pressure. She felt it all spiraling deeper into her womb.

She grabbed his head, her fingers digging into the silky strands of glossy red hair. She had to think and stop this. *They could not do this.* They could not have sex. She knew that more than anything else. This was Jack. He didn't want to have sex with her. He'd hate her tomorrow. He'd kick her out. He'd… well, he had the authority to ruin her life. And the potential to break her heart.

She gasped out, "Joey."

He paused and lifted his head. "What did you say?"

"We can't do this. I slept with Joey. Right over there. You…You can't mean to do this."

He dropped his head, with his face nuzzling her stomach, and groaned. "Yeah, I know where it happened."

"Then what… *what are you doing?*"

"I'm going to do this better than my brother did. I'm going to make you scream until you never again remember my brother's name," he said, his voice guttural.

Her mouth fell open in shock. She never expected *that.* Not from the stern, somber, always in control Jack Rydell.

His hands moved again and his face was close to her. She shut her eyes as he kissed her in soft, butterfly-like kisses. She couldn't do this. The thought flashed through her mind, but the swirling behind her eyelids clashed with it. He kissed her between her legs until he touched his tongue inside her. She nearly sat up in shock at the sensations. She couldn't handle it. It was too much, too good, and she was too quick. She came in a blinding scream as she shut her eyes and felt the pulsing aftershocks all the way down to her toes and right through her fingertips. She lay back down, breathing hard, the dark silence filling her after totally letting go.

She heard him move. He was taking off his wet swim trunks. He had a condom. *He planned to do this?* Impossible. No way. Jack never planned to sleep with her. She, who slept with his brother.

"What are you doing?" she finally asked, her voice almost sounding like a croak.

"Getting laid," he said with a boyish, fun grin.

That wasn't right. The thought passed over her brain, and it wasn't what she wanted with Jack. However, after he raised her legs around him, and pushed himself into her, she forgot what to think. He was so good. It was the last thought she had as he moved inside her, against her, over her, and his hand raised her ass and positioned her just the way he wanted. And he was right. It was hot and quick and earth-shattering. She never experienced such sharp, white-hot pulsations from orgasms that were so fast, so furious and so close together.

CHAPTER 23

*J*ack lay down next to her, and as it turned out, he could damn well sleep anywhere, even on a lumpy, sandy beach. It had been a long drive home, made even longer by watching Erin in the pool all afternoon. He tried to convince himself there was nothing there for him. For them. She slept with Joey, and she lived there, with the family. That was no set-up for any kind of relationship, especially with his kids there too. No way.

Except: he did it anyway. She was hotter than he ever fantasized.

Waking up to a face full of sand that exploded over him, entering his mouth and nearly choking him, his eyes automatically snapped opened. Big mistake. He rubbed at them to wipe out the fine, dry sand granules. His eyes were stinging and it was dark around him. It took him a moment to understand what happened. Erin was sitting next to him, her knees pulled up to her chest and a towel wrapped around her, hiding all of her, as she glared at him.

He rolled over and sat up. "What the hell did you do that for?"

"You just went to sleep."

He stared and spat out the sand on his tongue. Then he got up and went to the river to rinse his mouth out as he flushed his stinging eyes. Finally, the pain subsided. Only then, now fully awake, did he turn towards Erin who still sat huddled, her eyes focused straight down towards her toes.

He was naked still, but he didn't care. He stomped forward and sat down next to her. "You want to tell me why you just threw sand in my face?"

She shook her head and wouldn't look at him. He finally noticed the tears. "Have you been crying?" His tone came out more annoyed than he meant to sound. Why was she crying? He was sure he hadn't hurt her. She'd been a lot louder and lustier than he. What was her problem then?

"I want to go back to my trailer now."

Her voice was quiet, almost tragic sounding. He had no idea what the hell was going on with her. Or why exactly she was so upset.

"Fine. Let's go," he said, standing up before grabbing his t-shirt and pulling it over his head. He threw his wet clothes into the bag and wrapped a dry towel around him before jamming his feet into black flip-flops. Erin stood there, wrapped up tightly, her hair half dry and hanging to her waist.

He went first as it was pitch black now on the trail. He kept his eyes wide open and his ears perked up, listening for rattlers. He should have remembered to bring a flashlight. He stopped when he heard Erin whimper.

"What now?"

"I-I heard something. Right there."

He turned and looked to where she pointed. *A rock*. "It's nothing."

He kept walking and she stayed close. He walked faster, his anger growing with each step. Who was she to act like that? He was the one who broke his own code. He never intended to sleep with a woman whom one of his brothers had first. It wasn't something he was proud of, so who was she to act so miffed? Or so offended? He didn't even pretend to get it.

They reached her trailer and she threw her swimsuit onto the deck. She slipped past him, making it obvious she wasn't going to speak to him again. He grabbed her hand and forced her to turn towards him.

"What exactly are you so pissed off about?"

"You told me you were getting laid and then fell sound asleep."

"Yeah? Okay. So? It was a long trip today, and the extreme heat would've zapped anyone."

"*You got laid and fell asleep*, just like you intentionally planned. I'm glad I could help you out with that."

Jack started to answer when he noticed headlights at the top of the driveway turning in with an arc of light that swept over the darkened ranch. Then, rather oddly, the lights on the vehicle went out, as did the engine, and the car gently rolled towards the house, parking very near to where Erin's trailer once sat. Jack tensed up. Was it Chance? Or a random burglar? Who the hell else would approach the ranch so silently and stealthily?

Erin jerked her arm from his hand, and nodded towards the car. "Like father, like son, huh?"

"What?"

She rolled her eyes. "It's Ben and Marcy. Trying to find a quiet spot to park."

Jack closed his eyes. "Well, shit." He glanced down at himself, and decided that wearing a t-shirt and a damp beach towel wasn't exactly how he wanted to confront his son, but what other choice did he have? As Erin so succinctly pointed out, he was Ben's father, and it was time he acted like it, despite however unpopular any confrontation with Ben might become.

He turned and left Erin. No doubt, she wasn't finished with whatever got her so pissed off. He wanted to turn and make a beeline for his bed and stay there, away from Erin, and now his young son who so obviously was making out in the front seat of the truck he borrowed. He almost felt hypocritical, however, when he remembered parking near that very spot and making out with Ben's mother at the very same age. His chest tightened.

He didn't look in the windows, but rather, thumped his fist on the roof of the cab. He waited the few moments for the kids inside to fumble around, until finally, Ben's head popped out.

"You have five minutes to get your ass into the house."

"Yessir," Ben said, not meeting Jack's eyes. For once, he didn't argue or grumble. Ben's eyes were on him as Jack turned and left the car with his towel flapping behind him ridiculously. He stomped into the house. Yeah, great way to appear real fierce.

He threw on a clean t-shirt and black sweats once he got inside before steeling himself for an avenue of fatherhood he never really thought he'd encounter. He wished like hell that Ben's mother were here to tell him what to do. Should he be understanding? And quiet? Or yell? And maybe even ground him? What the hell do you do with your hormonal teenage son? Without ending up looking like a total hypocrite? Being a father was so different from being the teenager who could only think about having sex. Only now could Jack realize all the things that could have gone so wrong for Lily and him, as he instantly saw what might go wrong for Ben and Marcy.

He looked up from the table when Erin walked in. She wore a t-shirt and flannel pajamas pants, and her hair was dry now, falling down to her waist while the curls spiraled around her head. He'd never seen her without the signature headband she always wore. Her hair was crazy beautiful, and extraordinary, really.

"Can we get into this later?" he asked, feeling tired just thinking about everything he'd done wrong. The first mistake was having ever touched her. He ran a hand over his face. "Ben will be right in."

"He saw me."

"He saw me wearing a frickin' beach towel. I'm sure he's figured out what I must've been doing at midnight, walking around the ranch that way."

She looked away as he sighed and ran a hand through his hair. *Shit.* This night that started out so great was ending in painful embarrassment for all involved.

Ben and Marcy walked in. They both hung their heads, refusing to meet Jack's gaze. He waited until they sat down.

"First of all, where is your brother, Ben?"

"He decided to stay the night at the Collivers' house. They called you, but you didn't answer. They got a hold of Ian and he said it was okay. Check your messages, Dad."

The snide tone was there. *Yeah, Ben knew why he didn't answer his phone.*

"And so you decided... what? To pick up Marcy and sneak her back here?"

Ben shrugged.

"Second, you're not supposed to be driving alone yet. What the hell were you thinking? If you'd gotten pulled over, you'd have lost your permit, and probably wouldn't drive for another year. As it is, you have to wait until December."

Ben's head shot up. He was due to turn sixteen in three short weeks. "You can't do that."

Jack grunted. "I sure as shit can. You broke numerous rules here tonight, the least of which we've yet to discuss."

Ben stood up, his youthful age making his skinny arms

quiver. "You mean, like what you and Erin were doing? I saw you. You were wearing a towel. *A towel.* I'm not stupid. I know what that means."

Jack nodded. There was no use denying the obvious. "Yeah, well, the difference is I'm an adult, and Erin is an adult, so it's not the same thing."

"How isn't it the same thing?"

"Because I'm not a stupid kid who's sneaking around with a young woman and about to make the biggest mistake of both of their lives." He walked forward and slammed a fistful of condoms down. "Do you have any of these?"

Ben's cheeks turned a shade of red Jack had never seen a person turn. Ben didn't answer so Jack took that as a no. "Damn it. Have you two already had unprotected sex?"

Ben finally shook his head no and Erin suddenly stepped forward. "Jack, perhaps I should take Marcy home?"

Marcy's head jerked up as relief washed over her face. Jack nodded yes, urging them to go. If Marcy's parents were different, and actually cared, he would have promptly told them what their daughter was up to.

When the girls left, Jack and his son endured a terrible silence. Jack took a breath and sat down across from Ben. "Look, I'm sorry I lost my temper, but you've got to understand how serious your actions tonight were. You stole a truck, you can't legally drive, and you involved Marcy in that, then you nearly had unprotected sex. You can't do that. You know about safe sex and pregnancy. Do you really think I want to help you raise a kid right now? Or stand around worrying while you get tested for some terrible, often incurable, disease?"

Ben's face fell. He never considered any of that in his hormone-driven rush to have sex. "I don't want to talk about it."

Jack laughed harshly. "Yeah, until you can talk about it,

you shouldn't be doing it. Take these," Jack said, pushing the condoms his way. "I can't stop you. If you really think you're ready to do that, I'm sure you'll find a way. But I have to tell you, as your father, it's a huge mistake. You're too young. It's much more than you think, and you need to be more than you are now for your partner. I know you might think you love Marcy, but you're really young."

Ben shook his head. "I don't love Marcy. I kind of like her. I like Dottie Carmichael; she's in the class below me. But she won't, you know, do that kind of stuff."

Jack sat back, his anger finally fading. "You already know then that it isn't right. You're my son, and I know I taught you that much. Just because Marcy might, doesn't mean you should. And Ben, sex is usually a lot more complicated than the act of it."

"I know," Ben said after a while, his cheeks still blushing. Jack sat back, rather surprised to find Ben listening to him. He had previously avoided talking about the subject because he thought Ben wouldn't even hear him out. Instead, Erin's warning rang clearly in his head: he was Ben's father, and he had to at least try to guide him.

Ben continued, "I thought I could get some experience. 'Cause, you know, a lotta guys I know have already done it. I thought I should too."

Jack finally found a reason to smile. "My ass, those boys you hang out with have ever had sex. I've seen every pimply-faced, brace-toothed, skinny, pathetic lot of them, and if they say they're having sex, that's all they're doing: just saying so. I promise you, when you're old enough, and in love, it will become a totally different experience, and so much better than sneaking around in a car with a girl you don't even like."

"You mean different than you sneaking around with Erin? She was Joey's girlfriend. How could you do that?"

Jack had carefully kept his sex life away from home and

his sons for the last five years. And now here they were, at the critical point where Ben finally needed Jack to set a good example, and yet he did just as Ben tried to do. He snuck off to have sex; right on their ranch land with a woman he had no business having sexual relations with.

As he considered what to say, Erin walked back inside. Jack glanced at her, and then at his son.

"No one was awake at Marcy's house. She walked right in through the front door. No one at her house even cares that their fourteen-year-old daughter was out past midnight, do they?"

Ben squirmed. "No. Her dad doesn't pay much attention to her."

Erin nodded. "I told her she deserved better, and was much too young, and that you were just using her to have sex. You should be ashamed of yourself. I only hope she listened to me."

Jack almost spoke up in defense of Ben, but Ben looked truly contrite at hearing Erin's words. Erin wasn't finished. "You don't get it, Ben, what it's like for a girl like her. I was just like her. No one cared what I did. She's hoping by having sex with you, perhaps you'll care about her. I don't think for a second you will, because I also know you have a girl named Dottie who calls and texts you frequently. Decide now what kind of man you'll be."

Ben shifted uncomfortably and Jack did too. Her words were spoken with a level of anger and passion that went far beyond her outrage on behalf of Marcy and Dottie.

Ben stared at his hands. "I thought she wanted to."

"She just wants you to like her. She'll go as far as it takes just to make that happen."

"You mean no girl my age really wants to have sex?"

Erin shrugged. "No. There are girls who want to, and are

ready. But you at least owe her the truth of the situation and that you like someone else."

Ben's eyebrows dropped. "You mean like you and Joey? Is that how it was between you two?"

Erin's eyes met Ben's. Then she looked at Jack. Silence hung between them for a long moment. When she answered, her voice was strong and sure. "That's what it's always been like for me. But that isn't your uncle's fault. And I'm not Marcy. I'm an adult. I knew better."

Ben glanced at Jack. "Then is that what it's like with my dad too?"

Jack tensed and looked up at Erin, but she didn't look his way. She held Ben's gaze. He had to give her credit; she was made of steel. She didn't flinch, or look away, or tell Ben that it wasn't any of his business.

"No. That's not what it's like with your dad."

Ben wouldn't look at Jack. "Then what is it like? Aren't you two sneaking around?"

Erin shook her head. "No. We don't sneak around. We were friends. Until tonight. I'm sorry you found out like this, and I'm sorry if it makes you uncomfortable. But your dad is a good man. Someone you should strive all your life to be just like. He always treats women with respect, whether they deserve it or not. And he doesn't use them."

Ben looked at his hands again. "I didn't mean to use Marcy."

Erin's tone softened. "I know you didn't. But you need to understand what you're doing. I hope you don't do it now, or try to copy your stupid friends. Believe me, very few of them are having all the sex they claim to be having."

Jack was too shocked, uncomfortable, and bewildered to have a clue what to say next. His most recent lover and son were discussing his sex life. It had him blushing and twitching in his chair uneasily. Yet unbelievably, it seemed

Erin's honesty, as well as showing Ben the other side of the coin, managed to accomplish much more than Jack's mere threats.

"So... are you guys like a couple now?"

Jack felt like two hands were being wrapped around his throat and twisting as Ben first looked at him with big eyes before Erin turned hers on him. Her face was far angrier than the expression she showed Ben.

"Well, we're more than friends now. Does that bother you?"

Ben shrugged. "I kind of wondered if you, you know, liked her or something. You always act weird around her. But I've often wondered what you do about sex. You act like it isn't a factor or has any significance in your life."

"You're my son. It never felt right to address *my* sex life with you."

"I'm not Charlie's age. I'm not a kid anymore. When will you see that? You did the same thing to Joey. Why do you think he had to leave here?"

Jack felt the constricting hands choking him again. "I think Joey left because he needed to see more than just ranch life. And you're barely sixteen. In two more years, we can easily discuss you being an adult, okay?"

Ben finally nodded. "Okay, Dad."

"But you're still not getting your license until December; and you get to pay the fee now, along with your own insurance."

"Ahh, Dad. But..."

"You disobeyed several rules. Not feeling so grown up now, are you? Be an adult and accept responsibility for your actions."

Ben shut his mouth. "Okay. I'll work on earning the money."

Ben got up and left the room with his shoulders slumped,

leaving behind the silent living room where Erin now glared at Jack.

Erin stood up. "I lied to your son for you. You owe me for that. But it was worth it if it teaches him to care about his potential sex partners."

She turned to leave, her hair whipping around behind her. He had to stand and reach out to catch her before she could fling open the front door. They both froze when they saw the headlights in the driveway.

"Ian's home," Jack said with a long sigh. *There was no end to it. No privacy or private life.* He always had someone right there, in his space, watching him, judging him, and deciding his life for him. He couldn't even figure out what was happening between Erin and him without his damn son picturing his father buck naked on the beach. "Come to my room. We need to talk."

She stiffened when he took her hand, but finally turned and started down the hallway. Jack had the original primary bedroom of the house. It was the same room his parents once shared, along with his wife and him until she died. Lily died in that very room. It was behind the stairs on the first floor of the house.

Erin followed, and he tried to brace himself for whatever happened next.

CHAPTER 24

$\mathcal{E}$rin preferred to be anywhere else, but there, in Jack's house, and in Jack's room. Tomorrow, the entire Rydell household would know what occurred between Jack and her. The only difference between now and when she used to sleep in there with Joey was that now she gave a shit what they all thought about her. However, with Jack, everything was far different than it had ever been. The sex was different, and the way she felt was different, and the urge to keep it all private was different.

Jack's large bedroom was dominated by a king-sized bed with a pastel blue quilt atop it. Two lamps and matching nightstands stood like sentries on each side, with a long dresser on the opposite wall. There were pictures of horses and his kids framed on the dresser.

She walked forward and spotted a freestanding jewelry box. Lily's also. Atop it, on a lace doily, was their wedding picture. Erin stared at the eight by ten of a young Jack and his bride. She had no expectations about Lily, who was quite tall, only inches below Jack's mouth. She had auburn-colored hair, which was long and curled beneath her veil pinned over it. She wore a long-sleeved, traditional wedding dress and appeared to have wide shoulders, and a sturdy build. Lily was more handsome than traditionally beautiful. She looked like she was built to ride any horse on the ranch.

Jack appeared to be Ben's age. He looked so young, it squeezed her heart to see his shining face next to his young bride. He didn't even look like he shaved yet. Moving to the left, Erin saw more snapshots in a multi-picture frame that held a dozen of them. There was one of Jack, Lily, Ben and Charlie posing before a Christmas tree. *Jack's family.* Her heart contracted.

He already did all of this. And had all of this. He'd been married, and had two sons, one of whom was almost closer to her own age than Jack was. The hard reality deflated her illusions and dropped into her gut. Jack was simply getting laid by her.

Sitting down on his bed, a weariness overcame her and made her heart feel like it suddenly morphed into a block of heavy concrete inside her chest. She stared down at her feet and clutched her hands together. The loneliness that so often gripped her in private suddenly climbed up her chest and lodged like a knot in her throat.

Jack stood in the center of the room with his arms crossed over his chest. "This is going to be awkward no matter what because everyone knows about Joey. And it won't be long before they know what happened with us."

What happened with us. As in the past. As in a one-time event. An event that she didn't see coming, and now that it did, she wished it would mean everything. Tears burned the back of her eyeballs, but she *could not* cry. Not now. He could never see how vulnerable she felt with him, or how he broke her heart, or how pathetic she was. She didn't lie and really was like fourteen-year-old Marcy Fielding. She just wanted Jack to like her too.

"Yeah, it was great. Better than Joey. No one will be surprised. No big deal, it's me, and they already know how I am."

He frowned. "That is not at all what I meant. You are putting words in my mouth that I don't think and nor would I say."

"Why?" she asked suddenly, her eyes meeting his with a scathing expression. "Why did you do this? Why did you have to do this with me? You had no right."

"No right to what? You wanted to, I didn't imagine all of it."

"I might have wanted to, but I never intended to actually do it. I finally fit in here. I finally lived down my episode with Joey. And now, here I am, sleeping with one of the ranch owners."

"That's not what happened."

She stood up and crossed the room, staring out the dark window and the stars shining overhead. "I thought you'd never let that happen. And if it ever did, I guess I thought it would mean..."

She quit talking before she said more than she should have and really let Jack know how much power he possessed over her. Instead, she said, "I thought it would mean more than just you getting laid and falling asleep."

He stood there, staring at his own feet. Finally, he stepped towards her. "It did mean more than that. I get it. I screwed up. I've wanted you and only you since about the first moment after I laid eyes on you. I watched my little brother strike your fancy, and tried to ignore it, and resist it, and be mad at you about it; but no matter what I did, there it was. I didn't just get laid with you. Believe me, I wanted to get laid by someone while I was gone. The thing was: I didn't want anyone else but you, so I didn't even look."

She turned around slowly. "A lot of men have had sex

with me. They all like my hair. And how small I am. They don't care whether or not I'm independent and can't even read. They never once showed me how to do anything. What you want with me now is something I gave your brother, as well as a lot of other men. I'm not interested in giving that to you. I don't want to have meaningless, casual sex with you."

"I never said it was meaningless."

"*You fell asleep.* I asked what you were doing, and you said, 'getting laid,' and then you fell asleep without another word to me. That's meaningless sex."

He stepped in front of her and frowned. "In my defense, I was exhausted today. I didn't plan to do this, not really. Not like you think. I never intended to sleep with you as much as you never intended to let me. So... it happened. I don't know what I said. I was there, inside you, looking at you, so can you cut me a little slack for not being at my most articulate? For months, I just lay awake here, imagining what you were doing upstairs with my brother. Then, you're with me, and you know what? I wasn't thinking straight. But it was never meaningless."

"Then what was it?"

Jack let out a long, weary sigh as he ran his fingers through his hair. "I haven't been with anyone longer than a one-night stand since Lily died. And there was never anyone before Lily. I don't date. There was never anyone I wanted to date. And suddenly, here you are. Living here. Every day. And all I can think about is you. All day, all night. And not just to have sex. I've had enough sex to know the difference. I really don't have a clue what it all means."

"You shouldn't have started this."

"Then you should have stopped me."

She looked away. "I didn't want to stop you."

"Part of the problem is that I have two kids who live with me. It's not as easy as it is for a single man. I have my boys to account for. As you already witnessed. That's why I never brought it home before."

"What are you getting at?"

"I wanted to do this. I wouldn't ask you out on date because of Joey, and because you live here, and because of how awkward all this makes everyone else who lives with us feel. So I did this. So I had no choice. Here we are."

Her eyes shot up to his. "Meaning... you wanted this?"

"Do I want you? Yeah."

"I got that part the first time. What else is *this*?"

He looked down over her. His eyes became more serious and his tone, quiet. "This? As in, you're not sneaking out of here in the middle of the night because I'm done with you."

She tilted her head down. "You mean like Joey and me."

"I mean we are nothing like you and Joey."

Her head snapped back and he put a hand out towards her. She bit her lip and stared at his outstretched hand. Finally, she put her hand into his and stared at their linked fingers. Her heart paused and her breath stopped. *It was more than sex.* She kept her head down so he didn't see the tears welling in her eyes. He couldn't understand the relief, the joy, the amazing sensation that she felt upon hearing that he wanted her near him. With him. And for more than just sex.

"What do we do now?"

He smiled. "Try having it on a bed?"

Her heart skipped a beat when she saw the boyish grin and sparkle in his eyes. How often had she seen Jack so carefree, open, and youthful? Never. She'd never seen Jack that way.

His smiled dimmed.

"What's wrong?" she asked, going on alert.

"I think I gave my son all my condoms."

She hesitated, then said, "Joey has boxes of them in his nightstand. I'm sure they're still there."

She stared at the hooked rug under their feet rather than looking into his once happy face. *Joey.* Once again, he would always come between them.

Jack finally cleared his throat. "Well, at least I can count on my brother for that."

Turning, he left the room and unbelievably to her, seemed intent on borrowing some condoms from his little brother. He was back in minutes with a box in his hand. "Seems you were right. He must have an entire case stored in there."

She looked at his bed, then at him. "Should I go home?"

"Now?"

"No. After. I mean Charlie and Ben; you know the issues it could cause."

He nodded. "I know the issues. They were the reasons I was so sure I wouldn't do this. But no. No more walk of shame, Erin, not in the middle of the night."

"It could be awkward."

"It already is," he said, but smiled as he came towards her. He looked into her eyes and brushed a hand into her hair. "I missed you."

Her heart leapt into her throat. She'd never heard Jack use that tone. It was gentle, soft, sweet. And best of all, he meant it. He had missed her. And it couldn't just be sex, because they never had sex before, so he couldn't have missed that. He had to have missed *her.*

She didn't know what she was supposed to do. She felt strange, and yet, she wanted to be there, no matter how odd she felt.

He took her into his arms, and pulled her closer to him. His mouth came down on hers and he kissed her with a tenderness no man ever showed her before. Her heart picked up speed, and she greedily accepted the kiss, not for the heat of it, but because it felt like he was caressing her soul, and not just her body. They fell back into the bed, and eventually, she forgot to think, or worry, or dread what the light of day might bring for them.

ERIN BLINKED her eyes when she rolled over and shaft of sunlight pierced through the closed curtains. She popped open an eye and looked up at the white light seeping through the window. Sitting up, she pulled the bedsheet with her. She was alone and let out a sigh. Was it relief? Or disappointment? She wasn't sure. It all seemed doable in the shadows of night when she contemplated them being together in front of everyone, despite having been together with Joey first. But now? How did she proceed? She already discussed it with Ben. Now Ian? And Charlie?

She shook her head to clear the fog, fingering through her hair. It felt like a ratty mess. She'd gone swimming and let it dry uncombed. The grit of sand told her she needed a brush, as well as a shower and that she should have gone home last night.

She got up and slipped her pajama bottoms on with her sweatshirt. Wishing she had jeans and a t-shirt, and didn't look like she spent the night doing what they all would, no doubt, guess she'd been doing, she glanced at the mirror over the dresser and winced. Her hair was worse than she feared. It was a jumble of curls and snarls that tangled down her back. Her eyes were smudged with sleep rings, and her face looked pale. She took a deep breath for courage, then stepped out of the bedroom.

The bedroom opened into an alcove at the back, off the kitchen, where the entire household awaited her. She stopped, frozen like a deer in the headlights before backing up a step into the closed bedroom door. Jack was at the counter, pouring coffee into a blue mug. Ian was sitting at the table with Ben. And Shane. Where did Shane come from? Shane was standing up with his back to the kitchen, dressed in full leather, and his long hair in a skinny ponytail. He was talking to Jack.

They all turned towards her as she stepped out, never expecting to greet so many of them. And they were all staring at her as if they'd never seen her before. Even Jack. His face was neutral and there wasn't even a trace or a hint of the man she'd been with last night. The man who flirted, teased, and been kind to her, been honest and open while they had sex. Instead, it was Jack being Jack again. He seemed expressionless when he looked at her, although his eyebrows rose. He lifted the coffee to his mouth and took a sip before cradling it in his hands, and leaning his butt against the counter.

She straightened her back. *Damn him.* He always did that to her. He chickened out and pretended she was the problem. He refused to take responsibility for desiring her. Or liking her. He seemed to forget those things whenever anyone else became involved. She stepped out of the alcove and into the kitchen, but avoided meeting any of their accusing eyes.

Shane grunted. "Well, didn't see that coming. Seems I missed something."

Would Jack stand up for her? And tell Shane to shut up? No. Jack merely took another sip of coffee, and leaned towards the basket behind him before pulling out a donut, which he then bit into.

"Hi Erin." Charlie's warm greeting delivered Erin from her shame. He was smiling at her and she smiled back. If he found it odd that she emerged from his father's bedroom at nine in the morning, he didn't say.

"Hey Erin," Ben said, his gaze glued onto the table, as was hers. Ben, no doubt, felt as awkward conversing with her as she felt talking about his dad with him.

"Hey Ben," she said, her tone quiet. He finally raised his eyes to hers and a small smile turned his lips up before his cheeks went all pink. So did hers, but she managed the same strained smile.

Ian was sitting between the boys and there was no ignoring his scowl. He didn't like it one bit. Ian suddenly stood up, his chair scraping across the hardwood floor. It was as if the chair substituted for the words Ian wanted to say.

"I have to get to work. See you out there, Jack."

Minutes passed in uncomfortable silence. She hated Jack. Right then, she hated him far more than she ever hated Joey. At least, Joey never promised her one thing and acted like another. With Joey, she knew right where she stood from the get-go, and she never expected to be treated any differently. He didn't flatter her with the illusion that she was anything more than a casual affair. She went to the front door and jammed her feet into the flip-flops she wore over there last night. She had to pass Shane who was still staring at her.

"I'll walk you out," Jack said finally, from behind her.

She turned her head. "Don't even bother."

She was outside in a second and leaned her head back into the front door as tears filled her eyes. She straightened up to rush down the steps when she ran smack dab into someone. She looked up and realized it was Joey before staring at him, open-mouthed. Holy shit, where did Joey come from? When did Joey come home?

"Erin?"

"Joey." She brushed away her tears to hide them and smiled at him in a fake, bright smile. "Wh-when did you get here?"

"About five minutes ago," he said as his eyes beheld her gnarled hair, before dropping down over her outfit and the pajamas he'd seen before often enough.

"Who now? Shane?"

She knew by his tone and the unashamed curiosity in his eyes. He didn't even have to fully ask.

"Not Shane. Me."

They both turned when Jack's voice filled the silence between them. Joey stared at Jack, then down at Erin again before his face contorted into rage. "You've got to be shitting me. You said she was nothing but a parasite. Now what? I leave town and you start doing her? After all that crap you gave me? And this is what you do the minute my back is turned?"

Erin wanted to sink into the ground. She'd often felt ill at ease in her life, but never like this.

"It's not like that. Come inside, we'll talk."

He glared at Jack. "Of all the crap I've ever put up with from you. You always thought you were so much better than me. But look at you. Nice. Class act. I'm off, getting my ass kicked; and you're getting your rocks off with my leftovers."

Jack moved so fast, no one could have anticipated him. He had Joey instantly in his grasp. Briskly hauling Joey off his feet, he pulled back a fist before slamming it into Joey's face. Joey grunted in surprise, as well as pain. Jack threw Joey back and Joey stumbled, but soon caught his balance. He turned on Jack, launching himself in an effort to tackle Jack off his feet. Erin screamed as Jack sidestepped his brother, then grabbed Joey and threw him to the ground before falling on top of him. They rolled over, their fists pummeling each other as the sickening "thuds!" of fist to flesh filled the pauses between grunts. Jack was much bigger, but Joey had newly toned, larger muscles, owing to his recent training. Erin screamed and yelled for them to stop when she saw blood.

The front door opened at her screams and out came Shane, followed by both of Jack's sons. They stopped dead, in shock, staring at their father as he swung a fist into their uncle's face.

Ian came running from the barn and Shane ran towards them too. They managed to both grasp a brother and tried to pull them apart. Jack and Joey were at each other, using everything they had, with almost superhuman strength as they tried to shake off Ian and Shane.

Finally, Shane and Ian won the struggle and managed to pull them apart. Instantly, as loud and violent as the front yard just became, everything turned deathly silent. All four brothers stared at each other, while Joey and Jack doubled over and were breathing hard. Blood was smeared over both of their faces and knuckles.

Erin had never seen a fight like that before. Any violence always scared her senseless. It made her think of her mother's bad boyfriends, and of hiding in the closet to avoid them. She wanted to hide now and couldn't believe what was happening all because of her. She had ripped two brothers apart. Two brothers, who were more like a father and son, were torn to shreds. Tears of shock and terror rolled over her face. As well as Charlie's. With a loud hiccup, he ran off the porch, down the steps, and headed towards the beach as fast as his eight-year-old legs could carry him.

Ben looked like he was about to follow, but stared at his father, and then at his uncle.

"What the hell is wrong with you?" Ian yelled. Ian, the one who never yelled, and never raised his voice or even his eyes, it seemed. Ian glared at Jack and his voice was loud and upset.

She felt the eyes glaring into her. Shane glanced her way, but Jack didn't. He jerked his shoulders from Ian's grasp and rubbed his shirt on his bloody lip.

"He can't shut his mouth. He thinks he can say whatever he chooses."

Joey snarled at Jack. "It's about her. Was it worth it? Was she worth it?"

Jack's chest muscles flexed, and his shoulders tensed.

Shane grabbed his arm. "Shut up, Joe. What the hell were you doing, Jack?"

"Erin. He's doing Erin now and didn't like me having her first," Joey taunted.

Ben winced. She should have left, or hidden, anything to not get further involved. But she caused this and had to take responsibility for it.

Especially with Jack's fifteen-year-old son, now nearly in tears and glaring with sudden awareness at his father. He seemed to realize in that moment, that his father wasn't whom he thought he was.

CHAPTER 25

*J*ack rubbed a hand over his opposite fist. *Damn!* His knuckles hurt. He wondered if he sprained it. He tasted the metallic, iron taste of blood on his lips. The fury that engulfed him only a moment before receded to the edge of his brain. He was back in reality, in the moment, and nearly groaned out loud as it hit him harshly. *What was he doing?* He just tried to kick the shit out of his little brother. And now, all three of his brothers stood in the yard, looking with complete amazement at him. He never lost his cool or his temper before. And for what? Like this? Making Joey bleed? He nearly groaned out loud for what he'd done. The sight of Charlie running down the road in fear finally sank into Jack's remorseful brain.

Then Erin stepped between them, looking stricken, and worse, afraid. He scared her. He scared Charlie. He even scared Ben. He jerked his arm from Shane, now back in control of himself.

"Shut up. Your big mouth started all this."

"No. She started this."

Jack rubbed the bottom of his shirt to his lip and shook

his head. "She didn't start this. We started this. We had a lot of shit between us for years that we should have resolved long ago."

Joey shook his head and tugged his arms from Ian. Ian released him, but kept an eye on Jack, as if ready to spring.

"So you were what? Resolving things with my ex-fuck-buddy?"

"Stop, Joey," Erin suddenly ordered as she whipped around. Then she had the sense to do what Jack should have done, and what he normally would have done had he been his normal, responsible self. She told Ben to go inside and wait, as he didn't need to hear any of this. Then she turned to Jack, not Joey.

"You should be ashamed of yourself. You've scared both of your sons. You didn't have to do that. You shouldn't have reacted that way. I don't know what you're doing with me, but you shouldn't have reacted that way about it."

"He wanted you from the first time he saw you. Only you didn't see him. Not at all. You wanted me. And big brother, Jack, couldn't handle it. I had to leave for him to get noticed. No wonder he wants to beat the shit out of me."

"Shut up. It wasn't like that. Any of it. Including you and me. Why are you being like this?" Erin persisted.

He glared at her. "Because you took over my house, my ranch, and now, my brother? Fuck off, Erin. That's all I want. For you to fuck off."

Erin's entire body shuddered as if Joey just shoved her. She never expected such a brutal attack.

Joey looked over Erin's head. "You told me before I left that you'd pick me over her to leave the ranch. I told you it didn't matter. But you know what? It does matter. Pick, Jack. Me or Erin. Who belongs here? Where does your loyalty really lie?"

Erin looked up at him and shook her head. Jack didn't

know what to say. He never expected Joey to say that. Or react like that. Why would Joey give him an ultimatum? It was stupid. Asinine. And Jack would be a damn fool to take the bait.

"You came home. You were surprised by what's been going on between Erin and me. Thing is, so were we. You shouldn't have said that about her. Not to me. And yeah, I shouldn't have attacked you, but damn it, Joe. You can't say things like that. I'm not choosing anything. Now, you're just being an asshole."

"What did she do to you?"

Erin was fading and wouldn't look at him. Joey shamed her. Jack shamed her, although he didn't mean to. He was an asshole this morning. When she came out, he had no clue of how to deal with her in front of his brothers and sons.

But the hell of it was: he *was* old enough, and mature enough, and had been around enough to know what he should have said and done. He knew better than that. Erin deserved better, and he not only told her that, but promised her she'd get it. And what did he do? Nothing. He felt a strange calm suddenly overtaking him. As if the sunlight unexpectedly pierced through his chest, into his heart, his soul, and his guts.

The endless thoughts of her. The endless turmoil over the fact she'd been with his brother. If he merely liked her as a friend, or only wanted to have sex, it wouldn't have bothered him. It was all so much deeper than that. His feelings were raw and rough and inarticulate. They were also real. So real they made his heart ache and grow. He'd done this, he'd made a move on her because he wanted to be with her. More than he cared about anything from either of their pasts.

He was falling in love with her.

The knowledge nearly made his knees buckle from under him.

She stood there, her head hanging, her hair a mess, and her face stricken. He did it all wrong. From the first time he saw her, she got through to him, through the years of grief and numbness that Lily's death condemned him to. He didn't deserve her, however, after how poorly he treated her.

His brothers were all waiting for him to answer and fix what he'd broken today. For him to say *something*.

He smiled and they looked at him even more oddly. Feet were shuffling. Erin raised her head towards Joey and Ian before she glanced at him.

"She made me fall in love with her," he said finally after a long silence, while his eyes stayed firmly on her face. Her eyes rounded, her brow wrinkled, and her lashes blinked in confusion.

No one spoke. He'd never said anything like that in front of anyone. Even about Lily, his own wife. But Lily never needed him to proclaim anything.

"So you see, I can't let you stand there and repeat any of the filth you've been saying. I shouldn't have attacked you, but you shouldn't have attacked Erin. She didn't do anything to deserve that." He turned his softened gaze to Erin. "I'm sorry, Erin. For doing it like this, and for not saying so sooner. I'm sorry for making you feel like being with Joey was some kind of flaw in you. None of that should have mattered. The flaw was in me. You matter to me. And I was too scared to tell you."

She didn't respond at first, but her mouth was still open and her eyes wide. She shook her head and turned on her heel, running off towards her trailer. He deserved it. He deserved all of her hatred and suspicion. He'd been crappy to her. And that didn't become clear until the moment he heard how his brother spoke to her. Then he lost it. He never realized what he was doing to Erin until he heard Joey doing the same thing.

His brothers stared at him in horror and he stared back. "I need to go check on my sons. Then on Erin. Then, Joe, you and I are having a nice long chat about this. At some point, you'll have to apologize to Erin. And just so we're clear: *don't you ever talk about her like that again.*"

He turned on his heel and followed Ben inside the house. Ben sat down, bracing his elbows on his knees with his head hanging down. He looked down at his knuckles when Jack came in. Jack let out a long, weary sigh. He knew he had created a real shithole. He deserved their disdain. He quickly grabbed a towel and wiped his lip, then washed his hands. He took his shirt off and grabbed a clean one before approaching Ben.

"Remember all that stuff I told you about real men are those who accept responsibility? And not to fight because it makes you less than whoever is bothering you? I meant it. I was wrong just now, to do what I did to Joey. Believe me, I'll be making up for it for a long time. I'm sorry I did that in front of you and Charlie. Can you ever forgive me?"

Ben looked up and his eyes were huge. He glanced at Jack's knuckles. A bruise already appeared across them. "Why was Joey saying that stuff about Erin?"

"It had less to do with Erin and more to do with a power struggle between him and me. But I lost it. I was very wrong. No excuse, but I couldn't listen to him anymore."

Ben nodded. "I'm glad you did. Erin doesn't deserve that. She's… well she's always nice to everyone here. I like her."

Jack felt his chest expanding. His son was going to be a good man. Somehow, he did something right with Ben. His son had kindness, empathy, and integrity. Something he himself hadn't been displaying of late.

"I like her too. The mistake I made is being too scared to tell her. And to face you and your uncles about it."

Ben scrunched up his face. "Why? Why would you be scared of what we thought?"

"Because," Jack paused as he ran a hand into his hair, "I don't really know, Ben. It's been a long time since I felt this way. Since... since your mother. It's hard to admit and let go. I guess I didn't know how to love anyone besides your mother. You know I loved her. Nothing can ever change what your mother was to me."

Ben shook his head. "I know. I mean I think I know. It's just, you're different around Erin."

"Different?"

"Happier. You smile more. I don't think I'd care if you wanted to marry her or something."

Jack grimaced at Ben's declaration. From zero to sixty goes a teenager's brain. He had so much to work out still, starting with begging Erin to forgive his shortsightedness. And marriage? But he appreciated Ben's unsolicited support and permission. Most teenage sons wouldn't be as generous, especially after considering it was like replacing their mother.

He put a hand to Ben's shoulder and squeezed. "Thanks, Ben. Look, Charlie ran off and I really need to check on him now."

Ben nodded as Jack left the house. His brothers also dispersed. Erin's trailer door was shut and so were her blinds. Jack itched to go to her, but Charlie needed him first. That was something Erin would have to get used to and let be, if she intended to date him. Right now, it seemed a big *if*.

He found Charlie huddled up on a rock, and knelt down beside him. He skipped the words and just pulled Charlie's into his arms. Charlie stayed in a tight ball, but eventually, relaxed his body.

"I scared you, huh, bud?"

Charlie's head nodded up and down on his arm. "I'm

sorry, Charlie, for doing that. And especially in front of you. It was wrong, okay? Even adults do things they aren't supposed to."

"You hit Joey. You made him bleed."

"I did. I did do that. It was a fight. Not just me beating up Joey. He fought back."

"Doesn't make it any better, Dad."

He sighed. Score one for his son. Of course, Charlie was right.

"No, it doesn't. Look, Joey and I were fighting about some adult stuff. About stuff we let go too far and get too heated. It wasn't right. It was…"

"About *her*. I hate her! I want her to leave and never come back here. You never hit Uncle Joey before she came."

He cringed. Of course, Charlie would blame it on Erin. Almost as simplistically as Joey blamed it on her.

"Erin didn't do anything. Joey and I did."

"She did that stuff with Joey. That stuff you said only happens when people love each other. Like you and Mommy."

He did say that. He had the big sex talk with Charlie at the start of the school year after Charlie heard a very enlightening, but very wrong discussion of sex in the schoolyard. Jack explained that sex occurred between two people who loved each other, trying not to make it seem as gross as the initial description he heard of it implied.

"Well, if Erin did, so did Joey. Do you hate Joey too?"

Charlie bit his lip, and it took all Jack's wherewithal to meet his son's gaze as they talked. "No. I don't hate Joey. But you do for that."

"I hated Joey for saying mean things about her. And I should have handled it better, Charlie. I'll never deny that. But your uncle was very wrong about what he said."

"Are you now doing that with her?"

Sex. Shit. How does one answer an eight-year-old son about having sex? By lying? Charlie would see right through that and respect him even less. By admitting it? Really, no one ever explained that when he had kids, he'd be handing condoms to one son while confessing his sex life to the other.

"Yeah. I am. But I love her. I love Erin. And it's something you're going to have to be okay with."

Charlie frowned and shook his head. "I don't want to."

"I know," he said, kissing his son's forehead. Charlie didn't remember Lily, and their family had always been all men for Charlie. He never shared his father with any woman, not even his own mother, so Jack got why he wouldn't want to now. "But that isn't Erin's fault. Try to remember that, okay, bud?"

Charlie nodded and bit his lip before burying his head in the crook of Jack's arm. He heard a noise and looked behind him. Erin was standing off to his left, in the pine trees. She had been listening. He stood up with Charlie's hands looped around his neck. He needed just five minutes with her, but he couldn't yet. Charlie was still too upset.

He gave her a tight smile as he passed her, and Charlie burrowed against him. He hoped she understood.

ERIN WASN'T EXPECTING to run into Jack. Not so soon. He was sitting on the beach with Charlie curled in his lap. They spoke quietly to each other. Jack brushed his lips to Charlie's white, freckled forehead. And that stabbed her heart. He could be the sweetest, kindest, most tender man she'd ever known. She didn't know too many other fathers, but the ones she did know didn't hold, kiss, or comfort their eight-year-old sons. Not the way Jack did. She quietly moved towards the rock beach and finally sat down. She watched the low river going by. The day was already promising heat. She was glad she showered and put on clean shorts and a tank top. Her hair was now combed and pulled back.

She didn't know what to think or feel. Horrified. Shamed. Embarrassed. Unwelcome. And yet, she wanted nothing more than to stay. Jack said he loved her. *To her* and in front of all of them, the men who so dominated her life nowadays.

She heard him before she saw him. She could feel Jack stepping directly behind her. There was a change in the air and her heartbeat increased. He squatted down next to her and his eyes were on her. She kept hers glued to the rocky river bottom. He finally sat, stretching out his legs in front of him. "So I didn't handle that in the best way I could have, huh?"

She turned and he smiled at her, but she frowned. Why was he smiling at her? Now, of all times? He'd just beaten his brother up. Over her. After being a total jerk to her. Jack who was serious almost all the time, decided now not to be? His smile became a long, lazy grin that made her heart swell.

"You beat up Joey."

"I tried to beat up Joey. He surprised me with all the fighting skills he learned while he was gone. I should have anticipated that."

"You scared your children by hitting their uncle."

"I know, I just spent the last hour explaining why they should never act that way, and to listen to what I say, instead of doing as I do. Somehow, I don't think that was quite how it's supposed to be."

"You..."

"I know what I did, Erin," he said, interrupting her, but his tone remained gentle. "I embarrassed you. I hurt you. I shamed you. I know what I did and Joey was the least of it. Joey can fight back. But you can't."

She frowned. That was not what she meant. But

strangely, Jack raised his hand to her cheek. Who was this new Jack? She didn't get him at all.

"You acted like you'd never seen me. You think Joey was rude to me now, but at least, Joey never lied to me. He always told me where we stood; we always were honest with each other. That's something. Something pretty important."

He nodded. "It's the first time I've woken up beside anyone but Lily. I'm sorry, it might happen sometimes. I don't take change very well. I don't adjust very well. I should have explained that. I should have told you a lot of things before I made love to you."

"You mean, had sex with me."

"No. I mean, made love to you. It wasn't an accident. It wasn't something I didn't intend to have happen. I just couldn't admit that to you, and especially to myself. And not for the reasons you think. It wasn't about you and Joey. It was about letting go of Lily."

Erin jerked her head around. She never expected that. *Lily?* It was *his* past that bothered him? Not her past? He had her attention finally.

"Letting go of Lily?"

He nodded. "I never pictured moving on. Not really. I lived with it. The grief. The pain. Missing her. But I never had any interest in finding someone new. I never thought I would. That's why you got so much shit from me at first. I knew what was going on; and I didn't know how to handle it."

Erin let out a long breath. The heat from the rocks seeped through her cotton shorts and warmed her butt. The sun felt hot on her arms and face, as it lit up the river before her. The air stirred softly as if the heavens were also exhaling a long breath. Mostly, however, she felt her heart lifting as she listened to Jack. But at the same time, her stomach sank. Jack didn't mean that. There was no way Jack meant that.

"I know what you're doing, but you have to stop. Of course, you have to be in love with me; how else can you face your boys? I couldn't figure out why you said that. Not until I saw you with Charlie, comforting Charlie, while trying to explain what you'd done. You have to love me to justify what you did with me, in order to face your kids again. That's the kind of man you are, and the kind of father you want to be. You don't bring home sex. You don't subject your kids to watching you with someone besides their mother. So you have to love me in order to justify sleeping with me. Or wanting what Joey had. I can face that. You need to face it too."

Jack's eyes were hot on her face. She stared into the ripples of the river as it gently moved over the rocky bottom, catching sunlight and glistening before it shattered again.

"I wouldn't do that. Not even for my kids."

She stiffened her back.

"I can love you, and there doesn't have to be an excuse for it. Or a reason. I can love you because you make me smile and laugh, when nothing else has for a long time. I can love you because I feel better just thinking of you, let alone, what you do to my heart when you're near me. It's not new. It's not even that big of a surprise. It just is."

She shook her head. *No.* Jack was wrong. She knew Jack better than he knew himself. He could never love her. *She* wasn't whom he wanted or what he needed.

Jack sighed and pulled his knees near his chest before locking his arms around them. "Okay, Erin. Okay, you don't have to believe me yet. I deserve that. I didn't do anything right with you, starting with the day I first saw you beside your car. I probably deserve your reaction for that. Just tell me one thing, how long?"

She shifted her gaze to his. "How long... what?"

"How long will it take you to believe me? If I still tell you I feel this way, in, say, a month, will you believe it?"

She scoffed. A month was nothing. He smiled. "Okay, six months? Then, will you believe me?"

She shook her head. "You won't be saying that in six months."

"But if I do, will you believe me?"

She hesitated and wanted to believe him now, right this second. But she knew better. She didn't actually believe Jack would be pursuing her in six months. So what harm was there in agreeing now? "Okay, fine. In six months, when I prove you wrong, you'll thank me."

He smiled at her. "Will you move into the house with me?"

"No. Never. You'll thank me for that too."

He threw his head back and flashed his teeth in a smile. "So I get to sneak into your trailer? Okay. That might be fun."

She glanced at him. "You intend to keep on doing this?"

He looked deeply into her eyes and didn't blink or flinch. "I intend to do this for the rest of my life."

Had he just swung a brick into her gut? But... his tone was serious, stern, and soft. He seemed to believe it with every ounce of his upstanding heart. She pitied him on the day he realized she was right, and started to feel bad about all this. But she could wait him out.

She glared at him. "I'm not quitting my job either."

He sighed. "I feared you'd probably dig your heels in about that. Okay. I probably deserve it for being a prick to you about a number of things. I'll deal with it. You can work in your damn bikini and I'll work around your damn pool in the middle of my fields. But have you decided if you'll see Allison yet?"

"No. I haven't decided, and if it doesn't work? I'll still be illiterate. You're willing to keep claiming how much you love me if I'm still stupid?"

He stared at her a moment longer, then got to his feet, towering over her. "I want you to see Allison because I worry about you. Not because I care how it reflects on me. I accept you as you are today. I like you. And most of all, I love you. So I get this is a lot to take in. I have two sons, and there's a lot of responsibility that comes with me. I get you need to adjust to that. But when you do, will you let me know?"

"Let you know?" she repeated. *Could Jack mean any of this?*

"Yeah, let me know. I think you love me. I think you wouldn't be acting the way you do if you didn't. I can live with that. I can give you all the time you need. Just let me know when it's enough."

She frowned, and glared at him. "What do you think will happen with us? I'll somehow step in and what? Become something to Charlie? Or to Ben? Have you met me? I'm the worst person for you to share your life with."

He shook his head and smiled as if he knew some secret she didn't. "I think I was a jerk to let you think that. It simply protected me from admitting what I was so scared to admit. I'm gun-shy, Erin. I lost a wife once, and it's impossible for me to think of facing something like that again. But I would, for you. Because I love you. I think you love me, and we can make the rest of it work. I think tonight though, we should go to dinner."

"Go to dinner?"

"Yeah. Like going out to dinner. Like a real couple. The couple you'll someday get used to being with me."

Saying that, he turned on his foot and walked away, leaving her staring after him with her mouth open, and her eyebrows lowered in confusion.

CHAPTER 26

*J*ack deserved Erin's denial and rejection of what he knew was true. He'd been in love one other time in his life, and could never mistake the feelings. But he was to blame with how piss poor he treated Erin. He denied her, as well as himself, and blamed it all on what happened with Joey, when really, Joey was nothing to the equation at all. Joey was merely the catalyst for Jack to finally face what he was so afraid to face: being in love again.

Joey was sitting on the bottom step of the porch with two black eyes, and a big lip. He had a bag of frozen peas on one eye. He watched Jack walking up, and appeared weary.

"So, I guess I screwed this up."

Joey stared at him for a long moment before a smile tugged on his cracked lips. "You could have just told me."

"You didn't have to be such a dick to her."

Joey nodded. "I think I was just pissed off. You were so sure Erin was a mistake for me; I guess the blatant hypocrisy didn't sit too well. The thing is: she was right; I was always in your shadow. I wanted you to be proud of me. And you weren't. Not about Chance. Or about Erin."

Jack kicked the dust and glanced at his scuffed toe. "Yeah, well, she was a mistake with you, Joey. I was jealous. I should have told you, and her, hell, even myself, a long time ago. I didn't want you to have sex with her. I didn't want anyone else to either. I wanted to, but more than that, I liked her. I blamed you and her for why I couldn't have her. The thing was: it was purely because of me. Because of Lily and my fear of loving again. Whatever, it was my fault. I shouldn't have hit you."

Joey was quiet and finally smiled up at Jack. "I shouldn't have called her those names. You really love her?"

Jack took Joey's smile as permission to sit down, which he did next to his little brother. "Yeah. She doesn't believe me. She thinks I said it just to look good in front of my kids."

"You deserve that."

Jack chuckled. "I do. I deserve that. I also deserve her skepticism."

Joey smiled. "She'll come around."

"I intend to wait it out. You okay with that?"

Joey nodded. "I'm okay with that. I probably oughta apologize to her too."

"You think?" Jack glanced at his brother. "How are you anyway? How long do you get to be home?"

"I'm good, Jack. I really am. I'm not staying, I'm just visiting temporarily."

Jack rubbed his sore jaw. "Where'd you learn to hit like that?"

Joey smiled as he began to tell Jack everything he'd been up against lately. Jack listened, feeling glad his brother was home, and happy that Joey wanted to go back. Erin returned from the beach and walked up to her deck, and inside her trailer. Jack glanced towards the horses now grazing in the sun-drenched meadow beyond, and the river glinting in the sunlight. His sons later joined them. At first they were quiet, but as soon as they realized Joey and him were okay, they opened up, and smiled and laughed. After that, Ian and Shane came out too.

His wife was buried on the ranch. The wife he adored, cherished, worshipped, and finally buried. He had been sure he would never get over it. But he somehow had. Erin was nothing that he envisioned for his life. She was opposite to everything he might have predicted. But she brought him back to life, and his kids, and his home here. Having been here his entire life, not until Erin showed up, did he ever stop and look around to realize what he had, and who he was. He now felt her presence in every breath he took. She was wrong; it wasn't the ranch that told him exactly where he was supposed to be, it was her. He was there now because of her.

And six months? Nothing. Not when he thought about the shared lifetime ahead of them.

He waited until his brothers drifted off, and Ben went to call a girl in his class, while Charlie ran out to play. He finally began his chores and looked up when he heard the barn door open.

Erin stood there, silhouetted against the afternoon sunlight. She changed into her jeans and cowboy boots. She stared at him, long and solemn, before she finally smiled. It was a smile that twisted his heart and warmed his guts. He smiled back at her, and put his hand out towards her. She stared for a long moment, before suddenly launching herself into his embrace. He caught her, nearly falling over to hold her, as he laughed and his heart lifted.

And only then, did they start to feed the horses, side-by-side, together.

EPILOGUE

"*J*ack, wake up. You have to get up now."

Jack sat up with a curse as his head smacked into the overhanging cabinets. He rubbed his head as he eyed Erin through blurry eyes. He glanced at the clock. It was barely after three in the damn morning. He groaned. "This bed is too damned small. I have a perfectly good one in my house. Now you want me to stumble across the ranch in middle of the night?"

"No, I'm not kidding you. I need to leave and you need to get back to the house."

"I'll get up in a little while."

"Last time you said that you slept through until six and Charlie was already up. Please, Jack. It's important."

He grumbled and sighed as he flipped the covers back and swung his legs around. He put a hand out to grab hers and bring her closer. "Can we please just use my bed? Why do I have to keep sneaking around my own damn house? Or sleep on a bed better suited to a doll."

She rolled her eyes as she patted his cheek. "Plenty of

people sleep in trailers. And yes, we are not going to start parading around the house for Charlie to witness."

Who knew Erin would become the police for propriety. She would only stay in his room if the boys weren't in the house. Or once in a while he convinced her to sneak in late and leave early.

She turned to finish slipping her bikini top on. He eyed her bare, slim back with appreciation. "You want a lifejacket to go over that? That would work, you know. You'd be wearing the swimsuit, be in the bikini theme, but I'd be so much happier."

She frowned at him. "No. We've been through this. I make a lot in tips, it's starting to finally add up."

He hated imagining why she made so much in tips. He *really* wanted her to not work there. Just stay here. There was plenty to do on the ranch at any moment. He wasn't even kidding or making up anything. But she would not quit the job, nor move into the ranch house with him, or even let on they slept together. Though everyone knew they did. Who did she think they were kidding? They stared at each other all goofy-eyed all the time. Any idiot could see they were in love with each other.

He stood up. He had six inches of room. He really wished she'd give up a little of her near obsession with the trailer. She loved it to a degree that was almost insulting. She almost liked it more than him.

But he knew it was about a lot more than that. It was about having something to call her own. Her confidence in him, in her place in his life and on the ranch was precarious at best. She truly believed it was simply going to disappear. He'd sold her the truck and trailer outright by tricking her into give him a dollar, which he then handed over the title to both with a bill of sale. They were hers. She had been insistent she could not take them. But she'd finally relented.

Strangely, there was nothing else he could give her, or provide for her, she'd want more.

He shook his head to wake up. She stepped down into the living room and started her coffee maker. He pushed his legs into his jeans and followed her shirtless. Her eyes strayed to his torso and stayed for longer than a second. She unbelievably blushed when she accidentally caught his gaze. It still made him grin like a fool. After the things they did last night, how could she still blush from simply gazing at him? But she did. She was sweet, and quiet, and finally, here at the ranch she got to simply be who she was.

He stepped forward and grabbed her waist and brought her to him. He nuzzled her neck. "You know what the date is today, don't you?"

"February 28th."

"Yes, and you know what that means?"

She frowned and shook her head. "What?"

"Six months. Today is six months to the day."

She stilled. He hadn't mentioned that August conversation since it happened. He'd simply started dating her and wooing her with a vengeance that he'd previously tried to make her leave. There had been a few fights in between it all. Charlie had been a major stumbling block for them. He was not okay with Erin in Jack's life. Jack had tried to explain to Erin that his son could not determine who he dated, but she'd have none of that. She did everything she could to not upset him. Including, making Jack sleep in her freaking trailer more than his poor back could handle. He now constantly had all kinds of aches from her intolerable bed.

Her breath hitched. She dropped her gaze down below his eye sight. "Yes, I guess it is."

"So, I'm still here. Now, when I tell you I love you, do I get to be believed? Did I prove it yet? Convince you yet? Do my penance?"

She slowly lifted her face to his. "Are you sure?"

Her voice was soft and breathy and *still* she didn't believe he could love her. He touched her chin and cupped her face. "I'm sure. Are you?"

A small smile touched her lips. "Yes. I like being with you."

He lifted up one side of his mouth in a half grin. "Yeah, well I *like* you too. I love you. Can I say it now? Will you finally let me say what it is so freaking obvious between us? Everyone but you knows it."

Her brow tilted down. "I know how I feel."

"Well, how's that?"

She blushed again. "I love you."

He lifted her up and twirled her around. "Will you let us just be together now? For real? No more testing. No more just seeing? Just be the couple we so obviously are."

She finally laughed as he set her back to her feet, grinning like he was Charlie on Christmas morning. He'd paid a lot of penance for his short-sighted, asshole behavior. He didn't deny he deserved it, but he was really ready to move forward. To have a girlfriend. To have a life outside of the trailer with Erin.

She still wouldn't see Allison Gray about reading. It's the other subject they went around and around about. She simply refused. There was no talking her into it. He suspected the more he pressured, the less she'd go. She seemed to take his concern about it that he was embarrassed by her. There was no convincing her that he simply worried about her. Still, he hoped the more secure she became of her place in his life, his heart, his family and this ranch, she'd feel safe enough; free enough, to pursue it. He knew it was all tied up in her twisted image of herself. She thought she was inept and useless and unwanted and nearly unlovable. It would take years to undo the negativity she'd listened to and the neglect she'd always been on the receiving end of.

The thing he knew but was still convincing Erin of was that they had the rest of their lives to figure it out. To find a way to teach her to read. And to get her sure enough of him to trust none of this was ever disappearing from her again.

"Will you move into the house now?"

She shook her head. "It's still too soon. I've only been here a year. It's just not right. So, no."

He sighed. He knew somehow she'd say that. He grinned as he tipped his face into hers. "Then will you at least consider being a few minutes late to work?"

Her breath hitched. "I might consider that..."

ABOUT THE AUTHOR

Leanne Davis has earned a business degree from Western Washington University. She worked for several years in the construction management field before turning full time to writing. She lives in the Seattle area with her husband and two children. When she isn't writing, she and her family enjoy camping trips to destinations all across Washington State, many of which become the settings for her novels.

Made in the USA
Las Vegas, NV
23 February 2024

86168960R00184